Peter Lovesey is the only living author in Britain to have received the two highest honours in crime writing – the Diamond Dagger of the Crime Writers' Association and Grand Master of the Mystery Writers of America. He started with the Sergeant Cribb series set in Victorian London and later progressed to modern times with the award-winning Peter Diamond books set in Bath, his home for almost twenty years.

Now living in Shrewsbury with his wife Jax, whom he met at Reading University, he continues to reach and entertain new readers across the world.

Also by Peter Lovesey

SHOWSTOPPER

Peter Lovesey

SPHERE

SPHERE

First published in Great Britain in 2023 by Sphere

1 3 5 7 9 10 8 6 4 2

Copyright © Peter Lovesey 2023

The moral right of the author has been asserted.

*All characters and events in this publication, other than those
clearly in the public domain, are fictitious and any resemblance
to real persons, living or dead, is purely coincidental.*

A CIP catalogue record for this book is available from the British Library.

Hardback ISBN 978-1-4087-2756-0

Typeset in ITC New Baskerville Std by Palimpsest Book Production Limited,
Falkirk, Stirlingshire
Printed and bound in Great Britain by Clays Ltd, Elcograf S.p.A.

Papers used by Sphere are from well-managed forests
and other responsible sources.

Sphere
An imprint of
Little, Brown Book Group
Carmelite House
50 Victoria Embankment
London
EC4Y 0DZ

An Hachette UK Company
www.hachette.co.uk

www.littlebrown.co.uk

SHOWSTOPPER

In appreciation of Thalia Deanna Proctor (1970–2022)
my lovely editor, mentor and friend at
Sphere for fifteen years

1

The old lady lifted a black velvet bag from her sewing box, loosened the cord and took out a silver Smith and Wesson revolver. With a smile any other old lady would bestow on a new grandchild, she murmured, 'Little beauty.' Then, slick as a gunslinger in the Old West, she twirled the weapon twice around her trigger finger, turned at surprising speed, steadied her grip with her free hand and took aim at her reflection in the dressing-table mirror. Three explosive bursts came not from the gun, but the corner of her mouth. She held the pose for five more seconds.

'And cut. Well done, Daisy.'

'Is that it?' the old lady enquired.

'That's it, darling – and a very good "it", as always.'

'Am I free to go?'

'For you, Daisy, it's a wrap.'

Daisy Summerfield glanced up at the control room and smiled her thanks. Her contribution to another season of the TV crime series *Swift* was over. She handed the gun to one of the young people on the crew, who returned it to the bag and stowed it away. They'd done her a huge favour, fitting in her extra scene when the call sheet said she'd be filming again in the morning. The end of each day was supposed to be for re-shooting small mistakes, known as pick-ups. Her scene was a solo one and she had made sure she needed only one take.

She was well pleased. Instead of spending another night in the hotel, she was going home. Richmond, in Surrey, was more than two hours' drive from the Bottle Yard studios in Bristol. Vicky, the ever-reliable production assistant, would order a car and by the time Daisy had cleaned off the make-up and changed into her own clothes her driver would be waiting.

The gun-twirling trick had taken hours of practice with an imitation weapon they'd given her, a perfect replica of the Smith and Wesson. She had professional pride in getting things right. She hadn't ever handled a firearm before getting the role of Caitlin Swift's ex-gangster mother. The casting director had looked at her slightly arthritic fingers and asked if she was willing to take it on. 'What's the problem?' she had said. 'I'm a professional. I won't let you down.'

The first part of her career had been stage work. Only in her late forties had she started in television with a small part in *Coronation Street* in the days when they still filmed on the back lot at the Granada Studios in Manchester. Experience in Corrie was a badge of honour and she'd scarcely rested since. Never a starring role, but enough speaking parts to make her a familiar face and give her a comfortable lifestyle in a nice house in Surrey stuffed with period furniture. She had a collection of jewellery – the real thing – that helped to make the passing years tolerable.

She was seventy-four now and enjoying her best role ever. Viv Swift wasn't your stock elderly mum. She was larger than life (about 30 pounds larger), hard-drinking, never without a cigarette and with a deplorable past that brought colour to every episode. Arch-criminals walked in and out of her scenes and treated her as their matriarch. Often she was ahead of her delinquent daughter in planning the next heist. And the viewers loved it. She got fan-mail from scores of elderly ladies who believed she really did know how to rob a bank and wished they had the nerve to do the same.

In real life, Daisy was law-abiding and careful of her health. She just hoped she would be fit for the next series. She hadn't told anyone about her heart murmur. She wouldn't have known she had one if Dr Patel hadn't insisted on using his stethoscope. He had said the condition wasn't unusual as one grew more senior and let oneself go a bit (such tact: he was much too refined to use the word 'obese') and some people acquired a murmur in early life, the type of murmur that clinicians called 'innocent', and still lived to a great age. She hoped hers was innocent. However, Dr Patel had asked her to see a consultant in case it wasn't, and she was on a waiting list. With luck she would get her appointment and be declared innocent before the next season and no one from Bottle Yard would know.

The private car looked the same as usual, a shiny black limousine with chilled bottles of water and packets of salted peanuts stored in the arm rest along with a selection of newspapers and glossy magazines, but Daisy didn't recognise the driver, who looked rather like one of the grim-featured men she acted with, powerfully built, with damaged skin across much of his face, as if someone had thrown acid at him. He picked up her holdall and said, 'I'm Gerald, ma'am. Would you like this on the seat beside you or shall I stow it away?'

The mouth moved strangely when he spoke, but the voice was liquid honey.

She looked straight into his eyes, ignoring his poor face. She wasn't an actor for nothing. 'On the seat will do nicely, thank you.' Out of courtesy she started to introduce herself and was stopped.

'I know who you are, ma'am. I've watched the show since it started. I'm quite a fan, in fact – honoured to have you as my passenger. Just to confirm, it's Richmond, isn't it?'

'Yes. Richmond upon Thames. The one in Yorkshire would be a long drive.'

His mouth twitched in what may have been a smile. Down the left side his skin couldn't stretch at all. 'It's quiet on the roads now. I should get you home by midnight.'

She squeezed in, plumped herself into the back seat, emitted a sigh of relief and let him find his way through Bristol's maze of streets. She hardly ever saw much of the city because most of the location scenes were shot in Bath. When they reached the motorway, Gerald spoke again. 'I can make it warmer if you wish, ma'am.'

'Thank you, but it's just right.'

'Would you care for some music?'

'No thank you,' Daisy said. 'I enjoy silence. I'm perfectly happy with no sound at all.' She hoped he got the message. His remark about being a fan had sounded a warning bell. She didn't want two hours of being quizzed about the show.

She need not have worried. The next thing she was aware of was Gerald's silky voice saying, 'Quite busy here for the time of night, ma'am.' She looked out of the window and they were already off the motorway and across the river and heading down Kew Bridge Road. Her concern about him had been unfounded. She must have slept for the best part of two hours.

She straightened up in the seat and drank some water. 'Gerald, did they tell you my address?'

'The Vineyard?'

'That's correct. I must have dozed off.' Now she was so

4

near home, she felt she owed him something in the way of personal chat. After all, he'd said he was a fan. Speaking to the back of his head was easier than looking into the damaged face. 'I tell myself I can cope with the hours they work, but I'm glad of a rest by the end of the day.'

'Aren't we all?' he said.

'It can be as much as ten to twelve hours on set, six days a week, and that doesn't include going to make-up. I'm up at the crack of dawn. But I wouldn't change it for the world. And they treat me wonderfully. They have a word for us actors. They call us the talent, as if no one else has any, but they're all wonderfully gifted people, directors, cameramen, sound engineers, or they wouldn't last ten minutes in the job. Goodness, this is my street. You'll see mine on the left three lampposts away.'

She unzipped her bag and felt for her purse. The company was paying the fare, but she always tipped the drivers herself. Five, at least. Ten for really good service. She took out a ten. 'You're as good as your word. It isn't midnight yet. You can pull into the drive.'

'Beautiful house, if I may be so bold, ma'am.'

'Far too big for me really, but I can't face the upheaval of moving.'

He drew up outside the porch. 'I'll get your bag.'

After he had helped her out, she handed him the ten.

'That isn't necessary, ma'am. The company pays me.'

'And I'm recognising exceptional service. Please accept it, Gerald. I insist.'

He thanked her. 'If I may be so bold, ma'am, I don't think Viv Swift would be as generous as this.'

She laughed. 'Viv Swift would put a gun against your head and steal your car.' She had her house key ready. 'Good night, then.'

'Where would you like the bag?' He had a way of clearing his throat before suggesting anything extra. 'I can carry it upstairs if you wish.'

Heavens, no, she thought. No, no, no. He thinks I'm Viv, ever on the lookout for a stud. 'How kind, but just inside the door will do. I can manage perfectly well now.'

After he'd gone, Daisy closed and bolted the door top and bottom. Ten to one he was safe to be with, but you can never be sure what thoughts are in their heads. She made herself hot chocolate and added a dash of brandy. Her nightcap. Viv would have knocked back a neat vodka. Or three.

The holdall was still by the door where she'd left it. She'd sort the washing in the morning.

She poured herself a glass of cold water and swallowed the aspirin Dr Patel had suggested she took each night. She was about to switch off the downstairs lights when a floorboard creaked upstairs.

Her skin prickled.

Be sensible, she told herself. It's something to do with the central heating, with pipes and loose floorboards. But being sensible wasn't any help because she'd been sensible enough to turn the heating off while she was away. The creak had come from another cause.

Panicky thoughts bombarded her. What if someone had got in and was ransacking her bedroom, thinking she was away in Bristol? She'd seen no evidence of a break-in, but she knew from the TV series that modern burglars had clever ways of forcing doors and windows.

For the next twenty minutes she sat in the kitchen drumming her fingers on the table, too nervous to go upstairs. How stupid is this? she told herself several times over. I can't spend the night down here, a prisoner in my own home. It's almost one in the morning, I'm tired and I need my sleep.

Another ten minutes went by before she thought of a solution. She would think herself into her role as Viv Swift. True, she wouldn't have the make-up, the heels or the fire-engine-red suit with the strong shoulders, but she would summon up the inner strength she possessed when she was in character. Playing Viv was transformative.

She did have one confidence-giver. In the drawer of the kitchen table was the dummy revolver she'd used to practise the gun-spinning. She opened the drawer, gripped the gun and immediately felt stronger. She stood up and gave it a twirl. When the butt came to rest in her palm she was Vivienne Swift. The adrenalin coursed through her veins.

She turned the light off and crossed the hall. Her actions now were confident and deliberate. If you're up there, buddy, prepare to be scared shitless. She was up those stairs faster than she would have thought possible. On the landing she paused to listen.

Nothing.

Gripping the gun with both hands and with her shoulder to the wall, she moved towards her bedroom door. It was partially open. She gave it a kick and said in Viv's ball-breaking voice, 'I know you're there. Face the wall with your hands against it. I'm armed and coming in.'

There was no going back. She stepped inside, gun levelled in the shooter's stance. There was enough light from the streetlamp outside to give a clear view as she swept her aim through a slow arc.

Nobody.

She crossed to the en suite and made quite sure.

Almost a disappointment, she was so hyped up.

She sighed, switched on the light, threw the gun on the

bed and became herself again. Shaking her head at her own idiocy, she pulled the curtains and started thinking about the few things she needed to do before climbing into bed. Her night cream was downstairs in the holdall and so was her toothbrush, but she didn't intend to go down for them. She'd shower and do her teeth in the morning. A quick splash at the hand basin would do for now.

She had a fresh nightie hanging in the wardrobe. She slid the door back and had the worst shock of her life. She was eye to eye with someone in a hideous grinning Guy Fawkes mask.

She drew in a huge, gasping breath and felt a blast of pain across her chest and into her neck and arms, a sensation she knew was the cardiac arrest she dreaded.

For Daisy it was truly a wrap.

2

IS SWIFT JINXED?

The top-rated TV crime series *Swift* has been hit once again by the sudden death of one of its stars. Last Thursday night, Daisy Summerfield, the veteran actor who plays Caitlin Swift's mother Vivienne, suffered a fatal heart attack when she discovered an intruder in her bedroom at Richmond upon Thames. This is the third tragic incident involving a cast member in the past two years. The show's award-winning creator and producer, Mary Wroxeter, died suddenly while series five was being filmed. Dan Burbage, who had the part of the clever Sergeant Monaghan, fell while climbing in Snowdonia in January and suffered brain damage that put a premature end to his acting career.

Dogged by misfortune

The show's producer, Greg Deans, last night dismissed suggestions that the series is jinxed, but admitted that *Swift* has been dogged by misfortune ever since it was launched in 2013. 'Right now we're focusing our thoughts on Daisy,' he said. 'She was a regular in the series since it started and a favourite of our TV audience as well as the cast and crew. We'll miss her dreadfully.' Others connected with the show said what a warm-hearted person Daisy was in real life, totally unlike the tough, hard-drinking character she played. Several also expressed concern about the run of bad luck. 'It seems like a hoodoo,' said one actor who didn't wish to be named. 'Hardly a month goes by without some new setback.' A cameraman who has been a crew member since the start said, 'Personally, I'm being ultra-careful. I can't help wondering whose turn is next.'

Crisis of confidence

Undeniably, the chain of disruptive incidents is troubling. Even before filming of the first series began, the unnamed actor originally chosen to play Swift had a crisis of confidence and had to be replaced. During the filming of the pilot episode, there was a fire in a van containing sound equipment and an engineer was seriously burnt trying to save valuable items. Soon after the series was commissioned six months later, a stunt involving a rooftop chase went badly wrong and two stuntmen ended up in hospital. And a strange event occurred during the shooting of the third season, when Dave Tudor, the assistant producer, went missing on the second day of shooting and has not been seen since.

No Comment from Sabine

Despite all these setbacks, *Swift* was an immediate success with viewers and has remained high in the ratings, as well as picking up a clutch of Emmy awards in its first two seasons. The show's main star, Sabine San Sebastian, who plays Swift, was last night unavailable for comment.

Bath's most senior detective was not impressed. 'What am I supposed to say about this?' Peter Diamond asked.

'Whatever you want,' his partner, Paloma Kean, said, well used to his bluntness. They had eaten supper on trays in front of the TV.

'*Swift*. That's the one set in the West Country, isn't it? I watched one episode and switched over. Policing isn't like that.'

'There isn't much policing in it,' Paloma said. 'Swift is a glamorous villain who comes out on top every time. Rides a Harley-Davidson, plays the field with men friends, breaks into big houses and never gets caught.'

'Like I say, it's divorced from reality.'

'That isn't the point, Pete. What matters isn't the storyline. It's what's going on behind the scenes in real life. Don't you think there's something fishy, all these incidents? I know Ellie Pitcairn, who dresses the show, and she says a lot of people are worried.' Paloma's company was the go-to source of images used by costume designers in the theatre, TV and film industries.

'Actors are a superstitious lot,' Diamond said. 'What's the Shakespeare they won't mention by name?'

'The Scottish play?'

He grinned. 'There you go.'

'These aren't superstitions, matey. People have died.'

'Yes, but they're saying it's down to a jinx. That's my point. They've had more than average bad luck and that's all it is.'

A moment of silence followed, before Paloma said, 'I agree with you in principle.'

'But?'

'What if some evil-minded person is behind this?'

He picked up the newspaper again. 'Old lady discovers

11

burglar in her house and has heart attack. Understandable. Producer dies unexpectedly. Okay, that's unfortunate, but sudden deaths do happen. What else? A small fire, a stunt that went wrong, the climber stupid enough to be up a mountain in January and a guy who went AWOL. Most of these are outside anyone else's control. Over how long – five or six years? The paper must be stuck for news.'

'But would you join their show?'

'No thanks. I get all the drama I want at work – and that's from my team.'

'That's dealt with that, then,' Paloma said. 'I should have known you'd shoot the story to bits. The producer should ask you along to restore everyone's confidence.'

'Reality check by Peter Diamond. For a fat fee and my name on the credits at the end? You're on.'

'On second thoughts, no. You should stay well clear. I know what these luvvies are like. They'd give you merry hell.'

Even so, six weeks later there was a reality check for Diamond when he arrived for work in the crime investigation office at Concorde House, near Bristol, on a Monday morning.

'What's new?' he asked when he walked in.

'You know that TV series, *Swift*,' DCI Keith Halliwell, his long-serving deputy, started to say.

'Before you start on that tired old story, Keith, it's bullshit. There's no jinx. I saw the piece in the paper and it doesn't stand up.'

'One of the crew is missing.'

'Old news. If I remember, he was Dave somebody, the assistant producer.'

'Not him. Someone new. This only just happened. And on our patch.'

12

'Here?' His indifference took a nudge, no more.

'They're filming in Bath. A guy called Jacob Nicol, a rigger, didn't turn up for work and hasn't been in touch since.'

Diamond was back on song. 'Am I supposed to be worried? They're paranoid. They saw the piece in the paper and they're panicking because someone takes a couple of days off work. What's a rigger? It doesn't sound like a key role.'

'They put up scaffolding and lay tracks for the camera. Lighting, hoists, that kind of stuff.'

'Manual work. They can replace him.'

'There's more to the job than that. They need experience.'

'I refuse to get excited about this, Keith. When we find his body riddled with bullets I'll sit up and take notice.'

'Hold on, guv. There's more. One of the crew called at the house and all his property has gone. There are stains that might be blood.'

'This was when?'

'Yesterday.'

'How did we get to hear about this – a 101 call?'

'It came through on the local number. The guy on the switchboard wasn't very experienced. He got the main details, the address and so forth, but didn't ask who the informant was.'

'For pity's sake. Did any of our lot take a look?'

'Paul.'

'Does Paul know the difference between blood and tea stains?'

'I told him to get forensics out there.'

'We'll find out, then.' Shaking his head at the triviality of it all, the big man headed for his office.

13

The chest-high stack of paper on his desk had grown markedly since he had last looked at it. He wasn't troubled. A show of paperwork was his strategy for keeping his boss, Assistant Chief Constable Georgina Dallymore, off his back. If he'd read the stuff online he could have spent countless hours with nothing to show for it. So he made sure everything was printed and stacked where it could be seen.

The old CID – as he still thought of it – worked under the umbrella of a polango (his word for a police quango) called MCIT, the Major Crime Investigation Team, that generated much of the paper in front of him, the combined output of three police authorities. In theory it made for more efficient detective work. In Diamond's experience, bad things were done in the name of efficiency. Police numbers had shrunk. Salaries hadn't improved. Worst of all, the old Manvers Street police station in the centre of Bath had been closed and sold and the men and women who worked there dispersed across the county. His own team had been put out to grass fourteen miles away at Emersons Green. He'd told the powers-that-be – Georgina, to be precise – that closing the old nick was an own goal. The only police presence remaining in the city centre, the hole in the wall at the One-Stop shop, was a joke. Not many Bathonians knew it existed and visitors hadn't a hope in hell of finding it.

Twenty minutes passed.

There was a knock on the door from someone who still held him in awe. Anyone else wouldn't wait to be invited. He shouted, 'Come,' and they did and it was DC Paul Gilbert, the junior of the team, but only junior in the sense that he was the youngest of an ageing bunch of detectives.

'News from the lab, guv. You know I went to the missing rigger's place last night? The stains are definitely blood.'

14

'Right.' He chewed on that for a moment. 'I heard there wasn't much.'

'Four spots.'

'Like from a nosebleed?'

'Possibly.'

'Any disturbance?'

'A rug a bit rucked up, that's all. But they took away a pillowcase that they say has traces of snot and saliva.'

'How does that help?'

Gilbert blinked twice and said with an air of disbelief, 'It's a source of DNA. The rigger slept in the bed, so they can see if there's a match with the DNA in the blood spatter.'

Diamond had the glazed expression of a sleuth who had never fully embraced forensic science. 'While the plodding policemen patiently continue their inquiries. Did you ask the landlord if he heard anything?'

'He doesn't live there. It's a maisonette divided into two flats. The student upstairs heard him come in really late the night before he went missing, like one thirty in the morning. That's the last thing anyone knows.'

'Where is this?'

'Fairfield Park.' Maisonette territory, high on the northern slopes where developers made a mint from cheap housing sixty years ago.

'Signs of a break-in? Doors, windows?'

'Nothing. Apart from the rug, it looked normal inside. Well, normal except that none of his stuff was there. All the cupboards and drawers were empty.'

'He'd done a flit.'

'It seems so. The place wasn't much lived in, as far as I could tell, probably rented only for as long as they're here filming.'

'So unless he tripped over the rug, the chances are whoever

15

gave him his bloody nose will be part of the TV set-up.' Diamond sat back and spread his hands. 'Simple. Assemble the suspects in the drawing room and do a Miss Marple.'

Gilbert took most of Diamond's remarks seriously. This time, he could tell it was meant to be amusing, so he played along. 'Guv, have you ever watched the names scroll by at the end of a film?'

Diamond saw the point of that and grinned. 'You'll need a large drawing room. Where are they filming?'

'Below Pulteney Bridge.'

Young Gilbert – as Diamond still thought of him – had done all the right things. His earnestness screamed out for a leg-pull, but Diamond wasn't without mercy. He could see his young self here, transparently keen to impress.

'If you really want to cut your teeth on this one, better make yourself known to them and see what you can dig up on this rigger.'

Gilbert stared at Diamond as if he'd handed him the key of a Porsche. 'Do you think it's worth following up?'

'You're the IO on this one. Go for it.'

Investigating Officer. You could have fitted the Royal Crescent into Paul Gilbert's grin. 'Right now?'

'If they're filming, it's the perfect opportunity. Make yourself known to whoever is running the show and then dive in. I suggest you start with the remaining riggers if any are left alive.'

Opportunities had to be seized by a keen young DC.

A larger crowd than usual lined the balustrade of Grand Parade looking down at the weir, most of them holding up their phones. This is one of the sights of the city and there are always visitors watching the white water cascade down the shallow steps. Unless the Avon is in spate after heavy

16

rain, the flow under Pulteney Bridge is slow until it gets the shock of the descent. Then the movement gives this spectacular show.

Extra action was on view this summer morning. A woman and a man were down there, ankle-deep, crossing the top step of the crescent-shaped weir, the man clearly in pursuit and holding a gun he wouldn't be able to use with any accuracy while keeping his balance. The chase was being filmed by a cameraman under the trees on the narrow man-made island parallel with the east bank. Others were directing the show from a viewing platform over the sluice gate.

'That's so dangerous,' Gilbert said to no one in particular. He had just arrived on his moped, parked it behind the Abbey and joined the spectators.

'They're okay,' one said. 'They're stunt people.'

'I don't care who they are. I live here and it's a death trap.'

'They'll be strong swimmers. They wouldn't do it if it wasn't safe. This is their second take.'

'If they slip, they get sucked in by the undertow, however well they swim. Most years somebody is drowned here.'

'Russell Crowe didn't drown.'

'Russell Crowe is there?'

'Years ago, when they made *Les Mis*. He jumps off the bridge and commits suicide. Haven't you seen it? That was filmed here. You see him jump and get dragged in.'

'That wasn't here,' Gilbert said. 'It was Paris. The River Seine.'

'That's what you were meant to think.'

A guarded okay from Gilbert. He didn't believe what he was hearing, but he wasn't going to argue the point.

'It was definitely here,' the man's wife said in support.

17

The know-all said, 'Russell Crowe didn't really drown or he couldn't have made *Man of Steel.*'

The wife, who seemed to know more about it, said, 'Anyhow, he didn't do the jump. It was a stuntman. And the bridge he jumps off isn't this one. That was trick photography.'

Gilbert didn't have time to stay arguing about *Les Misérables* and he wasn't liking what he could see of the reckless free show at the weir. He needed to get across the river himself to where the film crew was. He headed up the street past the long line of onlookers and crossed the bridge, thinking that Russell Crowe or his stunt double couldn't have jumped off unless they leapt from a roof. Pulteney Bridge is Bath's bijou version of Florence's Ponte Vecchio, lined either side with shops.

Several sets of steps brought him down to the grassed area under the trees and the place where the Pulteney Cruisers pick up passengers. The TV crew had unloaded their equipment – a lot of it – by the sluice gate that can be lowered to control the flow. A group of them were chatting. He produced his ID and asked who was in charge and was told the director was too busy filming to see anyone, even the police.

Gilbert said he was content to wait. 'I wouldn't want to cause an accident.'

'Is that, like, a joke?' a large man asked. He had snakes tattooed on his arms and muscles that rippled and made them wriggle. The words were spoken in a way that made Gilbert feel there was only one answer and he'd better get it right.

'I'm serious. What they're doing is bloody dangerous.'

'Don't you worry about that. They're stunt people. They do more difficult stuff than running along a weir.'

Gilbert didn't argue the point. He turned to the group

in general, inviting someone else to join in. 'I'm here about the missing rigger. Have you heard from him?'

'Jake?' the big man said before any of the others got a word in. 'He'll be fine. You don't want to believe the papers.'

'So he still hasn't shown?'

'He's a grown-up. If he takes a few days off, that's his lookout.'

'Can you manage without him?'

'What does it look like?'

'Are you in charge?'

'I'm the key grip, if that's what you're asking.'

'What's your name?' One basic thing Gilbert had learned when questioning people was to insist they identified themselves. In a slightly hostile situation it was doubly useful.

'Fergus. Fergus Webster. What's yours?'

'Weren't you listening? I'm DC Gilbert. If you're the senior guy, Fergus, you won't mind telling me what you know about Jake.'

'Sod all, basically.' Fergus turned to the others. 'What do we know about the guy who didn't last two days?'

One of them said, 'You want a description, officer?'

'That would help,' Gilbert said.

'I'd say he was –' long pause – 'average.'

Fergus laughed out loud. Clearly he ruled here. They took their cues from him.

'You can do better than that,' Gilbert said.

A look was exchanged between Fergus and the man who had spoken and Fergus gave a nod.

'Average height,' the man said. 'Average build. Put it this way. He wouldn't stand out in a crowd.'

More of them were grinning.

Gilbert didn't appreciate the joke. 'I'm not here to be messed about. What height is he?'

'Five eight . . . give or take,' the spokesman said.

'Age?'

'Thirty to fifty, I'd say.' This got more belly laughs.

It couldn't go on. In a move that excluded all the others, Gilbert took a step closer and pointed his finger at the man's chest. 'This is a warning. It's an offence to obstruct a police officer.'

The message got home. 'Forty, then. Dark hair and not much of it, thin as a rake, pasty-faced with a tash, and didn't have much to say for himself.'

Unsurprising, when Fergus was around.

Gilbert addressed them all. 'So none of you believe this story about the jinx?'

Fergus took over again. 'It sells papers, don't it?'

'Someone from your lot took it seriously enough to report Jake missing, or I wouldn't be here. Do you know who that was?'

'You're the detective.'

'How many are working on this show?'

'Today?'

'Altogether.'

'The entire production team? That's asking.'

'Fifty?'

'Four times fifty, easy. They're not all with our unit.'

'I think I'll get closer to the action,' Gilbert said.

'You won't.' Fergus crossed his tattooed arms. 'Public can't go no closer than this.'

'I'm not public. I'm police.'

'You could be prime minister for all I care. They don't want no one straying into shot.'

'I'll be careful.'

Now the arms unfolded and made fists. 'You can be careful right where you are.'

A stark challenge to Gilbert's authority. He wasn't going to cave in, but he could see this getting physical and he didn't want to ramp up the aggression with a warning of his own. He was deciding his next move when there was a shout from the riverside.

'Get her out!'

They all heard it – a voice in panic that overrode everything. As one, the riggers made a dash for the steps over the sluice gate. Gilbert went with them.

The island on the other side was narrow, but heavily overgrown. It was difficult at first to see what was going on.

Down on the weir, one of the stunt people had lost her footing and been dragged down the slippery steps. She was the woman standing in for the star, the Caitlin Swift character. Paul Gilbert saw her head surface briefly in the churning foam. The undertow was too powerful. She was sucked down again.

3

Despite his best intentions, Diamond was at it again. Paul Gilbert was such an easy foil. 'Did you dive in and rescue her?'

'Me, guv?'

'You're one of Bath's finest. We don't stand by when a life is in danger.' In truth he'd be horrified if Gilbert risked his life in the weir.

'They had a lifeguard there. It's obligatory.'

'And the lifeguard earned his keep?'

Gilbert nodded.

The conversation got serious again. 'The stuntwoman okay?'

'She didn't look great. They called off the filming.'

'Your chance to question people.'

'I tried, but it was difficult. They were busy packing up and re-scheduling things.'

'How about the riggers? Did you see them as I suggested?'

'They don't seem over-worried about Jake, as they call him. He hasn't been long in the job, so they don't know him well. Most of them have worked together before.'

'He must have some experience.'

'Not with this lot. They don't even know who reported him missing. They say it wasn't one of them.'

'Did you get a description?'

'Of sorts. Forty, thin, pale, dark hair going bald, with a moustache.'

'You need to question someone more senior. Is there a foreman?'

'That's who I spoke to, Fergus Webster, the key grip.' The bit of jargon sprang easily from Gilbert's lips and amused Diamond.

'Are they back tomorrow?'

'That's the plan.'

'Same stuntwoman?'

'It's her job, isn't it, if she's recovered?'

'They should ask the woman who plays Swift to do her own stunt.'

'I don't think it works like that, guv.'

'What's her name – the star?'

'Sabine San Sebastian.'

Diamond's eyebrows gave their verdict on the fancy name. 'And the stuntwoman?'

'Ann Bugg.'

'Probably the moniker she was born with, poor thing. I suppose if she stands in for Sabine she looks like her?'

'A dead ringer. I'm hoping to speak to her today.'

'She's that good-looking?'

Gilbert flushed. 'I mean as investigating officer.'

Diamond fingered his right ear lobe as if to check that it was still there. 'You're assuming there's a traitor on the team?'

'Aren't you, guv? You don't believe in the jinx, do you? Someone may have bopped Jake Nicol.'

'True, but speaking to the stuntwoman isn't the best idea you've had. More than likely, her fall was her own fault and she won't welcome questions about it. We're treading on eggs here. They'll have read what the papers are saying and we don't want to ramp up the paranoia. We were asked to investigate the missing rigger. That's what you do.'

'I was thinking she might have some thoughts on how it happened.'

'This isn't the time. Your best bet is to find out who made the call to our lot. We need to know who it was who went to the flat and what their connection is to Jake Nicol.'

Gilbert's mouth formed a perfect O. The boss was right, as usual. 'You're still happy for me to handle this?'

'Full confidence.' Straight speaking from Diamond this time. The young man deserved his respect. He'd been tested many times over and proved his worth.

Alone in his office, Diamond spent some time thinking about the old saying that misfortunes never come singly. Then he picked up the newspaper and re-read the report about the so-called jinx. He reached for the latest directive from headquarters, turned it over and used the back to make a list of the incidents by date:

> 2013 *Star actor (unnamed) pulls out*
> 2013 *Engineer burnt by fire in sound equipment van*
> 2013 *Stuntmen injured in rooftop chase*
> 2015 *Dave Tudor, assistant producer, missing*
> 2017 *Mary Wroxeter, producer, dies suddenly*
> 2019 *Dan Burbage, actor, climbing accident*
> 2019 *Daisy Summerfield, actor, fatal heart attack*
> 2019 *Jacob Nicol, rigger, missing*

After a moment's reflection, he added one that wasn't in the *Post*:

> 2019 *Ann Bugg, stunt double, near drowning*

24

No, he didn't believe in jinxes. Accidents to stunt people were nothing. Every crime show has action scenes, and some go wrong, like the chase across the weir. Daisy Summerfield's sudden death didn't impress him either. He'd seen her on TV. Old age, excessive weight and working long hours would have got her into the coronary club for sure. As for that idiot who went climbing in January, words failed him. He was more interested in the two who had gone missing. The rigger's absence from work had been reported to the police after someone noticed signs of a disturbance in the flat, but how about the one from four years ago, assistant producer Dave Tudor? Had his non-appearance ever become a police matter? Was Tudor ever registered as a missing person?

In spite of himself, he was getting caught up in this story.

He knew which of the team to ask. The newest addition, DC Jean Sharp, lived up to her name as a researcher. 'Try the missing persons unit first,' he told her, 'and then our own case files. I can't recall anything myself, so I'm wondering if Tudor's disappearance ever got reported to us by his family or anyone else. He may have quit the job without telling anyone, in which case it may not be recorded.'

'The newspaper heard from somewhere, guv,' Jean Sharp pointed out. 'Have we asked the TV company?'

'I want to check the official records first.'

'If he was the assistant producer, he must have been a serious loss for them.'

'I'm not so sure. Job titles in TV can be misleading. Ever heard of "best boy"? It can be a fifty-year-old woman.'

Jean Sharp started working her keyboard and read out what she found. '"The assistant producer's duties are assigned by the producer. An AP may provide editorial and logistical back-up for the producer and liaise with writers and the talent. AP is the next grade up from researcher and is an excellent opportunity for learning how a production functions."' She looked up. 'It sounds lower in the pecking order than I thought. So the loss of Mr Tudor may not have been such a setback.'

'He's still a missing person, however unimportant he was. Report directly to me, Jean. I'm not involving anyone else at this stage. Do you watch *Swift?*'

'I've seen it. I wouldn't say I'm a fan.'

'Me neither.'

He left her to start the check.

4

Everyone was back at the weir for a new day of filming, including the stuntwoman rescued the evening before. Ann Bugg was a true professional, willing to go again and get it right. DC Paul Gilbert also wanted to impress as a pro, back and ready for more, eager to solve the mystery of the missing rigger. He still hadn't discovered who had called the police in the first place. Steering clear of the crew members he'd met before, he headed towards the fleet of TV trucks and vans parked along the river bank. A bunch of technicians chatted, coffees in hand, opposite the food truck.

'Jake who? Never heard of him,' was the first answer. 'Got a picture?'

Gilbert was forced to admit he hadn't. 'I was hoping someone would know him.'

'You'd best speak to the grips.'

'I did and all they could tell me is he's about forty, thin, dark-haired and with a bit of a moustache.'

'Could be almost anyone.'

'They don't seem over concerned. I think he's new to their team.'

'Couldn't hack it, I daresay.'

'I don't think he was inexperienced, or he wouldn't have been hired.'

'The others could have given him the elbow. They're a surly mob.'

Gilbert didn't need telling. 'I went to his lodgings and he hasn't been back there.'

'He won't if he jacked in the job. He'll have left Bath by now.'

The same possibility was in Gilbert's mind. His big opportunity as investigating officer could end with a whimper. 'We don't know who reported he was missing.'

'Housemate, I expect,' the techie said.

'He rented his own flat. I'm thinking someone from here.'

'It could be fuck all to do with work.'

'Right, but I have to start somewhere. On the day he disappeared, were you filming here?'

'No, mate. We only started here Monday. We was at the old airfield off the A46.'

'Charmy Down?' Gilbert knew the long-abandoned site of World War Two fighter operations, a bleak, exposed place north of Bath he had cycled to as a boy and hardly ever visited since. He remembered pillboxes and a ruined control tower.

'Charmy it ain't,' the techie said. 'This is heaven compared to up there. Wind, rain, thick mud. Her ladyship didn't like it one bit.'

'The woman who plays Swift?'

'She had her motorhome up there and refused to come out one day it was blowing a gale. Typical British summer. We all froze to death waiting to see if she changed her mind.'

'And Jake Nicol was there?'

'I told you I don't know the guy.'

'He only lasted a couple of days.'

28

'Can't say I blame him.'

'I'm hoping someone has a photo of him.'

'Try the production office. Like as not, they'll have his mugshot. We're all in their rogues' gallery.'

'Where's that – local?'

'The Colonnades. Second floor.'

He could walk it in five minutes. After the warning about treading on eggs, Gilbert decided he'd better check first with the boss, so he moved to a quiet spot behind the food truck and phoned in.

Diamond told him to stay put. 'Between you and me, Paul, I'm looking into the other guy who went missing, the assistant producer.'

'Dave Tudor? Four years ago, guv?'

'Right, but there could be a connection. Thousands of people go missing each year, I know, but if there's anything fishy in all the misfortunes in this show, the two who disappeared are the ones worth looking at.'

Gilbert made a sound of agreement, as if he'd already reached the same conclusion.

'This is still sensitive stuff,' Diamond said. 'Keep your interest low key. We don't want the luvvies getting alarmed.'

'They'll have read the paper, same as the rest of us, won't they?'

'Yes, and some nervous ones will worry, but the majority will laugh it off as a scare story made up to sell papers. However, if we take this to the next level, I want to be well briefed. That's why I'm looking to you to dig up all you can on Jake Nicol.'

'It's difficult without knowing what he looked like. I was told the production office have a photo.'

'Yup, it's a chicken and egg situation. Bear with me and stay right where you are.'

Another egg metaphor. Gilbert was tempted to point out that you can't make an omelette without breaking eggs, but he didn't.

Jean Sharp's searches had found no listing of Dave Tudor as a missing person, so where had the *Post* got its information? Diamond called his ex-journalist sergeant, Ingeborg Smith, to the office and asked if she still had contacts at the newspaper. She said she would need to find out who was still on the staff.

'I'd like to know where the jinx story comes from,' Diamond told her. 'Sounds like someone with an axe to grind. Some of these incidents go back to 2013. Old news. I was going to say "dead and buried" but in the circumstances . . .'

'You think there's something in it – the jinx stuff?'

'Oh, come on, Inge. Someone has an interest in fanning the flames. It's not all deaths and disappearances. They've scraped the barrel for some of these. I don't blame the paper for running the story, but who's behind it and why?'

'Somebody with a grudge against the show?'

'And a strong imagination.'

'The editor will have checked that everything really happened before they went public.'

'What I'm asking, Inge, is who fed them this.'

'Reveal the source? That's the one thing a journo is unlikely to do.'

An hour later, with the phone to her ear, she looked up at Diamond and shook her head. Like Jean Sharp, she'd got nowhere.

Which was why, not long after, Diamond himself pressed the door-phone button for Swift and Proud Productions in the Colonnades. The voice on the intercom snapped from a bored drawl to full attention when he spoke the word 'police'. 'Come right up. Our suite is on the second floor opposite the stairs.'

A short, smiling, red-bearded man in denim shirt and jeans was waiting inside the door. 'So . . . an inspector calls.'

Diamond summoned up a smile to show he got the reference, but made sure his proper rank was noted when he announced himself. 'And you are . . .?'

'Greg Deans.'

'The producer of *Swift?*'

'The producer of everything here, my dear, including rabbits from hats when needed.'

Diamond didn't smile a second time. He wasn't here for laughs and he didn't appreciate being anyone's dear, least of all a man he'd only just met. He wanted straight answers.

He wasn't going to get them from Greg Deans. 'I'm a disappointment to you, I can see. You expected someone twice my size with a loud suit and a large cigar. Actually our executive producer, Saltus Steven, fits the bill better. The bad news is that Saltus isn't in. The good news is we can use his office.'

The room at the back was spacious enough for five leather armchairs as well as a desk the size of a flat-bed truck with nothing on it except a two-foot-high clay sculpture of Charlie Chaplin. The wall opposite was dominated by a framed montage of photos of a grinning overweight man enjoying the company of princes, prime ministers and film stars.

'Mr Steven?' Diamond asked.

'Glad-handing champion of the world.' Spoken with a touch of envy that Deans glossed over by adding, 'Of course, it's good business to keep in with the great and the good.'

'Leaving you to run the show here?'

'That's the way I like it.' He waved his visitor towards a chair and offered tea, coffee or 'something stronger', which Diamond declined.

'How did *Swift* come about? His doing or yours?'

'Neither. All the credit goes to Mary, who had this job before I did.'

Diamond recalled the name from the press report. 'Mary Wroxeter?'

'She was a one-off. Came up with the concept, found a fantastic scriptwriter and saw it through every stage of development, virtually directing as well as producing. The casting, the music, Mary knew exactly what she wanted. Believe me, it took genius to achieve all that. Sadly, she needed liquid fuel to keep going. Except it didn't keep her going. The vodka killed her.'

'An alcoholic?'

Deans looked down, as if the memory was too painful to put into words. 'We all knew and she seemed to cope with it. The night she died she had some in the pub – we were there with her – and she bought an extra bottle to take home with her. What could any of us say? She was the boss.'

'Was she alone?'

'So I was told. One of the other women drove her home, but didn't go in.'

'Who was that?'

'Her former assistant, Candida. She appeared at the inquest along with several others and the pathologist who revealed the cause of death as alcohol.'

Diamond made a mental note to learn all he could about that inquest. 'You knew her personally?'

'I was one of her assistants, forever trying to keep up. A lot of Mary's best ideas weren't in the script. She liked to improve a scene on the hoof, changing the lighting, shooting from angles no one had considered and axing chunks of dialogue. She'd win over the director with a smile like the sun rising and it was my job to square it with the cameramen and the cast.'

'Tough.'

'It's a miracle I didn't hit the bottle myself.'

'People like that can be a nightmare to work with.'

'But she was always right. After her death, I was asked to take over. Talk about a hard act to follow. I was totally unprepared. Season six with me in charge was rubbish and the critics said so. We only kept going because Mary had laid such good foundations. I was learning as I went and I improved, but they were tough times for me and I don't mind admitting the episodes I produce still aren't the equal of hers.'

'The show is extremely popular.'

'Top of the ratings, thanks be to God – and Mary. She won our audience in the first place. Do you watch it? Don't worry, love, I won't stamp my foot if you don't.'

Put on the spot, Diamond scarcely noticed the endearment. 'We work irregular hours. I can never settle down to a series.'

'Likewise,' Deans said. 'I ought to be looking at other people's shows to check what the opposition is doing. Never do.'

With that pitfall avoided, Diamond got down to business. 'I'm here about one of your crew, Jake Nicol, the rigger who is missing.'

'Have you found him?'

'Not yet. We wouldn't normally get involved, but we were told there was a possibility of violence, some blood at his lodgings, which we've since confirmed.'

'Oh my hat, that's so disturbing.'

'And now I need to know more about his life outside work.'

'You're asking the wrong person, I'm afraid. I hardly know him. He joined the crew only two days before he went absent. New staff sometimes find the work is all too much.'

'You say you hardly know him. Wouldn't you have hired him?'

Deans shook his head. 'The rigging company finds its own people. We use a firm who go by the delightful name of Gripmasters, which turns me all of a quiver when I hear it. They supply the equipment and the staff. We're a bit stretched at this time, with units filming here and in Bristol, so they will have brought him in to make up the numbers.'

'I'll need to speak to them.'

'They're based at Cold Ashton. I can give you the details.'

'So you won't have a picture of him here?'

'*Au contraire, chéri*. Everyone on site is in the system for security reasons.' He took out his phone, tapped, scrolled and found a jpeg of a pale, thin-faced individual with signs of middle age around the eyes, a receding hairline and a Clark Gable moustache that had looked better on Clark Gable. 'Jacob Nicol.'

Success. A first sight of the elusive rigger. 'Could you copy this to my phone?'

'I don't see why not.' Deans was more phone-wise than Diamond and had it done in seconds.

Diamond felt he was on a roll now. 'Would you by any chance have a photo of the other man who went missing some years back, when the third season was being filmed, the assistant producer called Tudor?'

'Dave? I'd almost forgotten he existed until I saw that article in the *Post*.' Deans worked his phone again. 'I've got my doubts. We don't keep everyone online.' He shook his

34

head. 'Sorry, I can't access him. Your best chance is with personnel records in the old-fashioned filing system in the next room. I'll show you.'

'Before you do, I'd like your opinion on the jinx story.'

Deans shrugged. 'Horsefeathers, isn't it?'

'Any thoughts who might have fed the story to the press?'

'Well, it wasn't me and it wasn't a PR stunt by the production company.'

'What do they hope to achieve?'

'The *Post*?'

'Their source.'

'Who knows? There's no shortage of disappointed people in our industry. For everyone who gets to work on *Swift*, there are plenty who don't. But I'm thinking it must be an insider. Not all those incidents were public knowledge before the story broke.'

'You don't seem too troubled.'

'Too late to get fussed now it's all over social media, the ultimate rumour machine. They say any publicity is good publicity. We'll find out. In confidence, my main worry is how our leading lady will take it. Sabine has some weird superstitions, like refusing point-blank to work with anyone called John. We ask any Johns in the crew to call themselves Jack while filming is going on, but you can't ask that of well-known actors. It's a pain for the casting director.'

'Is that why you turned down Mr Depp?'

Deans grinned.

'Has Sabine seen the newspaper?'

'I wouldn't know. If she has, she's probably reading the tea leaves right now to see when it's safe to come back. She's been off for four days. We're filming with her stunt double.'

'Did the show turn her into a star?'

'She already had a profile on stage and screen, but nothing as big as this. Between ourselves, Sabine has become quite the diva. Owns an American motorhome the size of a bus that she takes to shoots so she has somewhere to relax between takes, but that's not enough. Employs the toughest agent in the business who insists we pay her driver as well. What's more, she is booked into the best suite at Homewood during filming.'

Diamond knew about Homewood, a five-star hotel at Freshford in ten acres of beautiful gardens.

Deans was working up quite a sweat about his leading lady. 'You should see her contract. We have to fund a private trainer for her, so that she looks strong enough to perform the stunts she refuses to do for safety reasons. She's fitter than Wonder Woman.'

'Do the superstitions make much difference when you're filming?'

Deans rolled his eyes. 'Don't get me started.'

They returned to the outer office, where a photo of Dave Tudor and a paper file were found. The missing assistant producer looked more like a rigger than the rigger had. Thick tattooed neck, buzz cut and the beginnings of a beard. 'And he just failed to turn up for work, like Jake Nicol?'

'Except we recruited Dave ourselves, so there was more of a hoo-ha.'

'That would have been in Mary Wroxeter's time?'

'She took him on, yes. We all got on all right with Dave. He may look like a bruiser in the picture, but he was a sweetie.'

Allowing for luvvie-speak, Diamond took that to mean he caused no trouble. 'Was he reported as missing?'

'Officially? No.'

'You said there was a hoo-ha.'

'What I mean is that unlike Mr Nicol, Dave was on the company payroll and we felt we had a duty to find him. Correction, we were *desperate* to find him. He was one of us, for pity's sake, but we had no success at all. To this day, no one knows what happened and I'm afraid he's almost forgotten now. The television industry works on short contracts. People come and go all the time.'

'But in a long series like *Swift* there must be some continuity.'

'Of the main talent, yes, unless they fall off the perch like dear old Daisy, bless her, and we're forced to write them out of the series.'

'How will you do that?'

'The writers are already working on it. The next episode starts after the funeral with Caitlin Swift sorting through her mother's old letters and photos remembering what a character she was. We use flashbacks from footage made earlier in the series. It's a kind of tribute.'

'Clever.'

'It's the best we can think of. We did something similar for Dan Burbage. Let's face it, any of us are replaceable and we live with that uncertainty. I expect it's the same in your line of work.'

'I hope not.'

'Ours is a cut-throat business.'

'Even you could be replaced?'

'Even me.' But he smiled as if the prospect was as likely as being hit by debris from outer space. 'If Saltus took against me, I'd be history, my dear, believe me.'

'What would Dave Tudor's duties have been?'

'Legion. An AP can be involved in any and every part of the production from words on the page to what you see on the screen, taking care of all the nuts and bolts issues a producer deals with, booking the studio and locations, distributing scripts and call-sheets, liaising with the crew, the talent, the script editor, costumes, make-up, set design, lighting. Do I need to go on?'

'I'm tired just listening.'

'But it's the ideal way to learn the business. Oh brother, when I got the job, did I learn fast.'

'Was Tudor up to the job?'

'Fully. He was very experienced.'

'Happy in his work?'

'So far as one can tell.'

Diamond glanced at the few details on the file. 'The address here is Kipling Avenue. That's up at Beechen Cliff. Was he local?'

'Now you're asking. I haven't a clue. I expect it was a rented room. Most of us find temporary accommodation if we don't live here.'

'And his personal file would have been kept here, in the Colonnades?'

A shake of the head. 'We're talking four years ago. The production office was more humble in those days. We were on a trading estate at Saltford, midway between Bath and Bristol.'

'Did he ever say anything about his personal life? Family? A partner?'

'If he did, I never heard of it.'

'Can you think of anyone else who might remember him?'

'All these questions.'

'The actors? Miss San Sebastian?'

The name prompted a sudden raspberry from Deans. 'In Sabine's lofty world, production people are only there on sufferance. She barely passes the time of day to *me*, so an AP wouldn't have made any impression whatsoever.'

'Unless their name happened to be John?'

Deans snorted. 'That would have got her attention, for sure.'

'Who else? Any other actors?'

'Daisy, but she died, poor darling. And Dan Burbage, who was the sergeant, had the fall in Snowdonia and doesn't remember his own name.'

'The director?' Diamond wasn't giving up. He felt sure somebody must remember Dave Tudor.

'Directors change with each episode. I rotate them to keep the series fresh.'

'The one who was making the show when Tudor went missing.'

'I don't have a computer memory, ducky. I can't say without looking back through any number of working scripts.'

'Would you do that,' Diamond said through gritted teeth, and it was more of an instruction than a request. All the negativity from Deans was tiresome, bordering on obstructive. 'I'll need a list of everyone Tudor worked with.'

Shaking his head, Deans moved to another filing cabinet. 'Do you have any idea how many episodes we've made? It's a new production team each time.'

'Up to the time he went missing.'

Deans started tugging out bulky scripts and slapping them on top of the cabinet. 'These are busy people. They'll be scattered to the four winds.'

'That's no problem.' Diamond picked one off the stack and saw that the title of the episode and the names of the production team were printed on the front. 'What I'm looking for is here on the top sheet.'

39

'I'll get photocopies made for you. Are we done? Because I'm running late. We're filming at a new location tomorrow and there are a million people I need to see.'

'When I've got these, and the contact details for Gripmasters, that'll do . . . for now.'

5

Paul Gilbert had spent the whole of his life in Bath without ever visiting the village with the uninviting name of Cold Ashton. He'd driven past the sign halfway up the A46 hundreds of times. What he found when he finally made the turn was a street of ancient stone houses along an exposed ridge, some of them rather grand, but no shop, no school and no pub. After riding through on his moped, he decided he hadn't missed anything except the gorgeous view along the length of St Catherine's Valley.

Diamond had told him to visit Gripmasters. A half-mile up the road was a line-up of dark green trucks with the company name on their sides. Almost hidden behind them was a single-storey tin-roofed building that would have fitted better into a trading estate than a village older than the Domesday Book. He parked the moped and went in. The front office was managed by a large woman wearing a tin badge that said *Hard of Hearing Please Speak Up.*

Gilbert did so, twice. The second time, he seemed to be understood. He showed his ID.

'And I'm Mabel,' the woman said. 'The boys call me Able Mabel.'

Don't go there, he told himself. 'I'd like a few words with the manager.'

'I beg your pardon.'

'The manager.'

'That's me, darling,' she said. 'There isn't anyone else.'

Spacing his words, he explained what he needed to know and she looked at her computer screen. 'Jake Nicol is new on our books. The job with *Swift* is the first we've given him. He moved down here from London with good references and the National Rigging Certificate, experience with big companies in film and TV. HGV licence. All we could ask for. When Swift and Proud told us they wanted extra muscle we called him up. No reason to think he wouldn't be reliable.'

'He hasn't called in to say he's ill or anything?'

'I haven't heard a thing.' She grinned at her own remark and pointed to the phone. 'It lights up when a call comes in.'

'He did two days with them,' Gilbert said, 'and then went AWOL.'

'Alcohol?' No question she was seriously deaf.

'Absent without leave.'

'They told me. I tried calling him and got a message saying he couldn't be reached.' She looked at the screen again. 'He's forty-two, unmarried, lodging at Fairfield Park.'

'I know. I've been there.'

She was being as helpful as she could. 'His truck was returned at the end of the day.'

'He drove a truck?'

'One of ours. With the equipment in, scaffolding, track rails and that. My riggers take more stuff than they ever need when they're on location.'

'Charmy Down, in this case?'

'I treat them all the same, my dear. Some of them try it on, but they soon find out I'm a married woman who won't take nonsense from anyone.'

She hadn't heard properly.

'Charmy Down, the old airfield.'

'Airfield? Are you talking about Charmy Down? Is that what you said? You have to speak up with me. Yes, that's where they were filming. They've moved down to Pulteney Weir now.'

'Did you see him the evening he returned the truck?'

'Have a heart, darling. They finish after dark. The grips are always first to arrive and last to leave.'

'How would he have got home to Fairfield Park from here?'

'Say that again, would you?'

He did so.

'There's no need to shout. Just don't mumble. They park their own transport here while they're working. If you look up the far end, you'll see some private cars and motorbikes. His blue Vespa isn't there now.'

He'd learned as much as he was likely to get from Able Mabel. He wrote down a number to call if she got any news of Jake.

On the moped again, not much wiser about the missing rigger, he started back towards Bath on the A46. Charmy Down was only two miles down the road, so it made sense to visit the place where Jake had last been seen alive. As a boy, Gilbert had gone there a few times to fly model aircraft with friends. He'd heard that Beaker people from the Bronze Age had been the first to live here, but the barrows had been levelled in 1940 when the Ministry of War had taken over and constructed a base for the night fighters of 87 Squadron. The old airfield was on a plateau about 600 feet above sea level with a main runway almost a mile long. The RAF had given up the place soon after the war.

He'd visited there only once since his childhood, as a

police officer, to help deal with a rave. The enterprising youth of Bath and Bristol had managed to get a generator up there, a sound system, stages and strobe lighting, not to mention a supply of illegal substances. Complaints about the noise in the small hours of Sunday morning had come in from seven miles away.

Silence reigned now. The exposed landscape made the airfield a desolate and windswept scene. Gilbert wished he'd asked where exactly the TV shoot had taken place.

He dismounted and followed the fence along the south-west side until reaching a grey stone block with an inscription like a memorial. He hadn't heard of much loss of life in action and there were no names on it. The stone turned out to be a recently erected memorial to the airfield and all the units and personnel who had served here. These, he knew, included members of the American Air Force, based here in 1944 before the D-Day invasion. For many years after the war, US veterans would visit to see where they were once stationed.

Until the Americans arrived, this had been a night fighter station. One of the main perils wasn't the Luftwaffe; it was the feature Gilbert had admired from Cold Ashton. St Catherine's Valley was notorious for updraughts that bedev-illed the landing approach for the main runway. So many casualties occurred that the pilots called it Death Valley. Up to twenty aircrew were killed in training battling those air currents. In comparison, the number who died in action against the enemy was seven.

An older relic than the memorial was one of the pillboxes he remembered from his visits here as a boy. He climbed on top for a better view. The runways were grassed over now, hunting territory for flocks of birds. To his left was the control tower, a derelict four-square, two-storey structure with a small viewing tower on the roof. He guessed this might have appealed to the TV director as an image, so he wheeled his moped in that direction.

On the turf ahead was a cross-hatch of recent tyre tracks made by heavy vehicles. Spinning wheels had made ruts of mud that convinced him this was where the TV transport had parked, not right up against the control tower, which would have spoiled the shoot, but 30 yards away.

He gave himself a virtual pat on the back. His deductive skills were coming in useful. You don't get to be the investigating officer without noticing stuff like that.

The tower was in a poor state, with every window smashed and parts of the brickwork gone. Even so, it conjured thoughts of Hawker Hurricanes and Westland Whirlwinds revving up, barrelling along the flare-lit runway and taking off into the night sky to do battle with the Luftwaffe.

His thoughts had a sudden interruption – the sound of barking. What could a dog be doing out here? There wasn't one in sight.

It could only be from inside the control tower. If there was a dog, there might also be an owner. As investigating officer, Gilbert knew where his duty lay.

A disturbing memory from his childhood surfaced. Caught in a narrow alleyway, he had been attacked and bitten by a spaniel that was probably as terrified as he had been.

From the deep pitch of the barking, this animal was no spaniel. It must have heard him coming.

He couldn't shirk it.

The entrance was above ground level, up some steps. The door was long gone. The barking had stopped, as if the dog was listening. It could be lying in wait, ready to leap on him.

Gilbert decided it would be a mistake to creep upstairs. Better to announce his presence. He reached the first step and shouted, 'Anyone there?'

Another outbreak of barking and quite an echo with it.

'All right, all right,' Gilbert said, feeling anything but all right.

The dog hadn't yet appeared at the doorway. Gilbert mounted more of the steps, repeating the same words of reassurance. He was hoping his friendly tone would make an impression.

He crossed the threshold.

And heard growling, a low, vibrating note of menace, definitely from inside the building. Surely any dog guarding its territory would have made an attack already.

Could it be tied up? Or trapped?

He was in the main passageway, getting accustomed to near darkness. On each side were open doorways to rooms whose original purpose he could only guess. The one to his right was empty except for some disconnected wires and cables. Probably the communications officer using a tele-printer would have been housed on this level.

He checked the next.

Empty.

The main control room would have been upstairs for better views of the sky, but he didn't think the sounds had come from above.

The growling had stopped – or had it? He thought he could hear something from a room to his left. He took a step forward, felt his foot strike some piece of rubble. The sound was answered at once by a bark from the room opposite.

No dog would wait so long to check on an intruder. It *had* to be tethered. Gilbert repeated those hollow words,

'It's all right,' stepped across the passageway and looked inside.

The biggest dog he had ever seen hurled itself at him, teeth bared and snarling.

He went rigid with shock.

By a few inches he escaped having his throat torn open.

The dog had reared up to head height, forced to its hind legs by the length of the rope that held it.

From the darkness behind, a voice said, 'Caesar. Sit!'

The other end of the rope was gripped by a man with a white beard of biblical size. It was difficult to see much else. He was on the floor wrapped in a grey blanket.

The dog heard the command and flattened itself to the ground, still growling.

Gilbert managed to find words. 'What are you doing here?'

'I'm entitled to ask the same question,' an educated voice answered, 'allowing that I was here first and didn't send you an invitation. Quiet, Caesar.'

Caesar heard and cut the growling.

'If you want to be friends with us, show him the back of your hand. The back, not the palm. Not the fingers, absolutely not the fingers. When he's caught a whiff of you, he'll calm down.'

Gilbert was doubtful, but it mattered awfully to humour the dog's owner. He extended his right hand to within a yard of what he judged as the limit of the rope.

Panting mightily, but without more barking or growling, Caesar stood again and strained to reach him. Gilbert withdrew his hand and swayed back.

'Steady,' the man said – and he was speaking to Gilbert, not the dog. 'It's not good to show fear. Once he's pressed his wet nose to your skin, he'll be your friend for life. Who are you, anyway?'

'I'm Paul Gilbert.' This wasn't the moment to reveal he was with the police. 'What breed is it?'

'I can't tell you. There's some Great Dane for sure and some Rhodesian ridgeback and I suspect a dash of Pyrenean mountain dog gives him the shaggy look. The united nations in a pooch. I acquired him two years ago from some unfortunate whose wife delivered an ultimatum: dog or divorce. He's interested in you. A few inches closer and we'll have some peace.'

There was such certainty in the instruction that Gilbert believed it. He plucked up the courage to reach out again.

Another urgent reminder. 'Fingers tucked in.'

He made a fist, offered the back of his hand and felt the touch of damp – and not only from the nose. A warm, slobbery lick completed the inspection.

Exactly as promised, the huge dog became docile, returned to its owner and squatted beside him. Crisis over.

'If you're looking for a place to doss down, I suggest you try the officers' rest room upstairs,' the man said. 'Every room is draughty, but that's got the best views.'

'I'm not here to doss down.'

'Why disturb us, in that case?'

'I heard the barking and came in to see if the dog was in trouble.'

'How civil. I'm sure he appreciates your concern.'

'You live here?' Gilbert asked.

'A temporary guest. I don't stay anywhere for long. Tomorrow we'll head down the hill into Aquae Sulis for what's left of the tourist season.'

'Have you been to Bath before?'

'Every summer for at least ten years. I come here for the history, the architecture, the civilised living and, best of all, the coins that drop into my tin mug.'

'You're a traveller?'

'On the whole, I prefer gentleman of the road. I've been called everything from crusty to scrounger. Governments do their best to demonise us because we're a comment on their failed policies. Like the polar bear, I'm one of an endangered species.'

Now that his eyes were getting used to the poor light, Gilbert could see the evidence of what he'd heard: a vintage coach-built pram to his left heaped high with objects useful to a tramp, like a folded groundsheet, frying pan and billycan. Yet the man talked as if this was the Athenaeum Club.

Gilbert asked how long he had been living like this.

'I lose track. I'm a Londoner originally. My business went into liquidation soon after the collapse of Lehman Brothers. We were starved of finance. How long ago was that?'

'I'm not sure,' Gilbert said.

'There you are. You're halfway to throwing off the shackles like me and finding freedom beyond the reach of broadband.'

'No chance.'

'You could become a free spirit. "Over hill, over dale, thorough bush, thorough brier, over park, over pale, thorough flood, thorough fire, I do wander everywhere." *A Midsummer Night's Dream.*'

A tramp quoting Shakespeare. Gilbert was lost for words.

'How are your feet?' the gentleman of the road asked. 'You need healthy feet and a sturdy pair of boots. What are you wearing – trainers? They'll soon get holes.'

'I'm trying to tell you I'm not a traveller,' Gilbert said. 'I'm just visiting the airfield.'

'Out for an afternoon walk?'

'Something like that.'

There was a pause for thought.

'Are you about to tell me I'm trespassing on Air Ministry property?'

'I believe the land is privately owned now.'

'That's all right, then. The owners won't begrudge me resting up for a few days. They must have taken a fat fee from the television people.'

Gilbert's interest quickened. He might have found a witness. 'Were you here while they were filming?'

'I was very accommodating. I waited for them to finish before I moved in. I've stayed here often, you see. I always try for a roof over my head at night, be it an empty house, garden shed or barn. And I leave the place as I found it. Point of honour.'

'Did you watch the TV people at work?'

'Why should I? There are better ways of spending one's time.'

'Such as?'

'Foraging for nature's bounty.'

'Mushrooms?'

'Much more. Nuts, berries, edible plants of many varieties. Wounded pheasants I put out of their misery. Eggs, when I can find them.' He winked. 'The occasional past-its-sell-by from the bins at the back of Tesco.'

Now that he had someone to listen to him, the man wouldn't stop talking. Let it flow, Gilbert decided. Humour him and he may come out with the information I want. 'What does Caesar live on? He wouldn't enjoy that stuff.'

'Don't have any concerns about him. When he's hungry, he puts on his dog-at-death's-door performance, lying flat on the ground with his tongue hanging out and ribs showing and people arrive with tins of dog food. There's a brand called Cesar and they think it's amusing to bring him his own signature product. I could get jealous. I'm getting a permanent stoop from carrying his supplies.'

Gilbert got the interview back on track. 'Did the TV crew leave anything behind?'

'Not even a bottle of water. They cleared up everything and took it away in their vans.'

'Were you watching when they packed up?'

'I observed from a distance. I can't think why you're interested.'

Gilbert decided he'd better front up. 'I'm DC Gilbert, from Bath Police, investigating a missing person, one of the crew from the TV unit. I didn't catch your name.'

'I didn't offer it.'

'Do you mind telling me?'

'It's no secret. Everyone calls me Will.'

'But you have a surname?'

'Legat. I'm William Legat, which gets corrupted to Will Leggit. Groan if you like. You won't be the first. A policeman, you said? I like the police. I like the bed and breakfast you offer wandering men like me, but I doubt whether I can help with your investigation.'

Caesar made a whimpering sound and turned to stare at his owner. Maybe the word 'breakfast' had done it.

'You watched them leave, then?' Gilbert pressed on, increasingly hopeful he'd found someone who could help. 'What time would this have been?'

'Young man, one of the joys of this mode of existence is that I don't carry a timepiece.'

'Late in the day?'

'You don't give up, do you? Of course it was late. They're on a budget. They cram as much as possible into the day so that they don't need to come back tomorrow. They work until the light goes and the poor devils left to do the clearing up are there for an hour or two longer.'

'It was dark?'

'Becoming so. I do remember that the last truck had the headlights on when he drove off.'

'About nine, then,' Gilbert said, more to himself than his informant.

The dog started whimpering, pathetic sounds for an animal his size.

'And now we must deal with more pressing matters,' Will Legat said, and lowered the blanket and reached for a pair of mud-encrusted boots. 'Caesar is asking to go outside. All this excitement.'

'I'll come with you.'

'You won't. We're very fastidious about such things. How would you like it if I followed you into the bathroom?' He pulled on the boots without troubling to lace them.

Caesar was now at liberty, waiting patiently in the doorway, the rope dangling from his collar and across the floor.

Gilbert had tensed, but the dog had other matters in mind.

Legat got upright more easily than Gilbert had expected and at once it became clear he wasn't the decrepit old man he'd seemed sitting down. He looked to be in early middle age, broad in back and shoulders, certainly strong enough to manage a large dog.

'How tall are you?' Gilbert asked.

'Six two in my socks, according to my tailor.' A joke. He was in a black shirt frayed at the cuffs and combat trousers fastened with a macho-looking belt with D-rings from which hung two large bunches of rusty keys, a bottle-opener and a jackknife. 'Oblige me, if you would, by staying here and guarding my things.'

Would anyone want to steal them? Gilbert mused, and kept the thought to himself. He stood aside, uneasy at having surrendered the initiative, but pleased of a few minutes to work out whether there was anything else a competent investigating officer should ask a witness. He heard the leather boots clump along the corridor and down the steps.

Looking about him, he knew what his boss would do to fill the few minutes. Diamond would inspect the contents of the pram and the rucksack in the far corner, making certain Legat was everything he claimed to be.

Gilbert stepped across and felt the weight of the rucksack. Heavy, for sure. He heard the clank of tins when he moved it. But he lacked the ruthlessness of Peter Diamond. Opening it would be an invasion of privacy he couldn't justify to himself. Will Legat wasn't under suspicion. Their exchange of background information was off to a good start. He wanted the man to feel confident with him.

He was about to put the rucksack back when he noticed a black leather pouch on the floor underneath. Several other odd items were scattered in the corner, two six-inch spanners, some lengths of yellow Kevlar tether, a coil of string and a carabiner used by climbers. He opened the pouch. Inside was another mystery, an encased pulley.

The sound of the boots returning was the cue to drop the backpack.

Caesar was first in, sniffing at Gilbert's trainers, but in no way threatening.

'That's better,' Legat said. 'He'll get a proper walk on the airfield later. I would offer you tea, but heating the water takes a while to organise.'

'That's all right.' Gilbert hesitated before saying, 'I happened to notice the heap of spanners and things in the corner. Do they belong to you?'

'Not guilty, officer,' came the answer. 'All kinds of rubbish gets left in places like this. If you can make use of them, fill your pockets and I'll look the other way.'

'They look like a workman's tools.'

'Could be. Could well be.'

'I'm thinking they may have belonged to one of the TV crew.'

'I wouldn't know about that,' Legat said with a show of innocence. 'What's there?'

'Spanners, a heavy-duty pulley that I think is called a snatch block, a carabiner used by climbers. They're things a scaffolder would have with him. The missing man is a rigger. He builds scaffolding.'

'Ah, yes, your missing man,' Legat said. 'You were starting to lose me. Are you thinking these objects belonged to him?'

'I spoke to some of his workmates and saw what they had hanging from their belts.'

'You're making more sense now. If he wanted to quit his job, he'd discard the tools of his trade. They're such a giveaway, aren't they?'

Gilbert was sure some evasion was in play. 'Would you mind showing me the belt you're wearing?'

'This?' Legat hitched his thumbs inside the belt and rattled the keys. 'Why? What's wrong with it?'

'Nothing's wrong. It looks like a rigger's belt.'

'It's holding up my trousers. What else would I have for keys and things? They weigh a bit. I need something to hang them on.'

'How long have you had it?'

'What do you expect me to produce, a sales receipt?' He sounded like a guilty man.

'Would you unfasten it and let me see?'

'See what, my friend? It's obvious what it is.'

'I've got to insist.'

'Why? What's this about?'

'It's about a missing man who may have been a victim of violent crime.'

'No, no, no. That's out of order. You can't accuse me of violence. I'm no angel, but I draw the line at injuring anyone.'

'Then you won't mind handing the belt over for inspection.'

'And if I refuse?'

'I'm entitled by law to use reasonable force to search you.'

'You could try. I can't answer for Caesar if he dislikes what he's seeing.'

A telling point. Gilbert said, a little lamely, 'I can send for reinforcements.'

'You'll look silly when it turns out that the belt is mine.'

'I don't suppose anything you're wearing is owned by you.'

'So? I recycle things other people discard. That's to be applauded, is it not?'

'I'm not suggesting you stole it,' Gilbert said, to strike a more conciliatory note. 'I'd like to get a closer look in case it belonged to the missing man.'

'How can you tell?'

'Well, the heap of items in the corner needs explaining. I'll get them tested for DNA. But the whole point is that they could have been attached to the belt.'

'If you take it away for testing, what am I going to use to hold up my trousers?'

'What did you have before?'

'String.' Before the word was uttered, Legat clapped his

hand to his mouth. It was obvious he'd recently acquired the belt.

Gilbert made a snap decision. 'I'll do a deal with you. You said you were planning to go down to Bath tomorrow. I'll phone my boss and fix some transport for you. You can travel in style. In return, I'll need the belt for forensic testing.'

'Transport for me and my dog?'

'Yes.'

'The pram and all my worldly goods?'

'I'll ask for a van.'

'All right,' Legat said. 'Improve the offer and I'll accept.'

'Improve it? What with?'

'A night in the cells and a fried breakfast.'

6

Diamond had never seen anything like it. You couldn't call it a motorhome. This was a two-storey hotel on wheels, twenty of them at least. It was the size of two furniture vans merged into one. How it had been licensed for use on British roads he had no idea. Pink and silver, with more lights mounted on the front than a Rolling Stones concert stage, it screamed swank.

Currently it was parked on private land at Milroy Court, near Trowbridge, the next *Swift* location.

Beside it, Ingeborg's Ka looked like a toy. Diamond struggled out and stood shaking his head at opulence on such a scale. He'd told Ingeborg he was looking forward to meeting Sabine San Sebastian because she was one of the few people who had been part of the production from the beginning. Now he was less sure.

'How do we let her know we're here?' Ingeborg asked. 'I can't see a doorbell.'

'She'll have spotted us already. Haven't you noticed the security cameras at each end?'

No one greeted them. The door was halfway along the side of the vehicle, a metre or more above ground level, and there were no steps. Diamond reached up to rap with his knuckles and got no response. He took off a shoe and banged with the leather heel.

A window on their right opened and a face with Asian features looked out. She was clearly not Sabine. 'Yes?'

'DS Diamond and Detective Sergeant Smith of Bath Police needing to speak to Miss San Sebastian.'

'Sabine is in gym.'

'Pity about that. Which gym is that, ma'am?'

'Upstairs.'

'Here?' A motorhome with a gym of its own was something else.

'She must finish workout. Legs, calves, abs.'

'We'll come in and wait.'

'You wait outside.' The window closed.

'Bloody cheek,' Diamond said to Ingeborg. But they didn't have much choice. The vehicle was a fortress. 'Greg Deans told me about the workouts. The company pays for a personal trainer for her. They must have money to burn.'

'I don't know if you watch the show, guv,' Ingeborg said. 'It's a very active role. She needs to be in shape.'

'Doesn't do her own stunts, though.'

'I know.'

'What a let-down for her fans,' he said, his mind already made up about this woman. 'I've never seen anything in the credits about stunt doubles.'

'It'll be there in the small print.'

'Very small. She's the star. She states her own terms.' Sensing that his rant had gone far enough, he turned his thoughts to some strategy for the interview. 'Everything I hear about Sabine suggests she's a hard nut to crack. But I was told she's superstitious and we can play on the jinx thing. It needs to be taken seriously, right?'

Ingeborg raised her thumb.

They waited another twenty minutes before the door of the motorhome slid open and a set of steps unfolded from a hidden section underneath. The minder looked out. 'You are police? You have ID?'

Diamond showed his card.

'Sabine say you wait inside while she shower.'

'We can do that.' He mounted the steps.

'Remove shoes.'

When he saw the hand-painted ceramic floor tiles inside, he understood the reason and unlaced. Each tile formed part of a reproduction of an old master painting, a crowded composition of armed Roman soldiers and struggling women against a background of classical architecture.

Ingeborg had slipped off her shoes as well. They were in a lounge area with chairs and an L-shaped sofa.

'You sit.'

They sat and were left to wait.

'What's the picture?' he asked Ingeborg.

She turned to look at the wall behind her. 'I don't see one.'

'The floor.'

'That?' she said with distaste. 'Looks to me like the Rape of the Sabine Women. As décor, would you believe? Like it celebrates her name. Disgusting.'

Now it was Ingeborg who was on a rant, he thought. 'Most of them are clothed.'

'You're missing the point, guv.'

Minutes later, they were joined by Sabine herself. Smelling of expensive floral shower gel, in a black robe and with her hair wrapped in a red towel, she was shorter than the familiar image from TV screens. Even if you never watched the show, you knew the face. It was difficult to get through a day without those intense blue eyes looking out at you from magazine covers and computer pop-ups. The sharp, strong features were photogenic from any angle. She took the chair opposite and flipped the gown aside to display a bronzed leg. 'What can I say? I'm so embarrassed, keeping you waiting. I simply wasn't in a state to speak to anyone when you arrived.'

Disarming or deceiving? Either way, the apology was unexpected.

'That's all right. It's not as if we made an appointment,' Diamond said, a past master at trading charm when needed. He knew he was dealing with a role-play professional. He told her who he was and Ingeborg, too. 'We hope you can help us clear up some storylines from real life that weren't ever scripted for the show.'

'I think I know what you're talking about,' she said after a moment's hesitation. 'As for real life, I'd better warn you I'm nothing like Caitlin Swift. Everyone assumes I'm as cool as she is and of course I'm not. The one-liners are written for me and all the action is staged. I have a stunt double who does the dangerous stuff.'

Unexpected modesty.

A compliment was wanted here. 'The success of the show is down to you. You connect with your audience.'

'That's my job. All I'm saying is don't expect Swift-like answers from me.' She looked and sounded nervous. 'I can't think how I can help you.'

He said, 'May I call you Sabine?'

'Please do. Everyone does.'

'You know more about the show than anyone because you were in it from the start. Several of the other actors have gone. Even the producer has changed. Your experience is going to be helpful, I hope.'

She slid her hands along her forearms and pulled in her shoulders, making herself smaller. 'This is what they're tweeting about the jinx, isn't it?'

'Are they? I don't read that stuff.'

'I do.'

'Jinx, bad luck, whatever. We're here about the things that actually happened rather than what people are saying on social media. We're interested mainly in two people who went missing, an assistant producer called Dave Tudor. And, more recently, Jake Nicol, a rigger.'

'I heard about Nicol absconding, but I couldn't tell you who he is. I don't have anything to do with the grips. They do their job and I do mine. I was told he was only with us a couple of days. But I remember Dave. That's going back several years.'

'Four, at least.'

'The time of Mary Wroxeter, who created the show.' The memory evoked a sigh and a sad smile. 'She was brilliant, fizzing with ideas. Before she came to us, she'd had a huge success with *Robeson and the Welsh*. Did you ever see it?'

'It sounds familiar.'

'The one about Paul Robeson, the great African-American bass-baritone, and his love affair for Wales in the 1930s. She cast Aubrey Jones in the role, a black singer with the Welsh Opera she'd known since her student days. His voice was almost as good as Robeson's, and it was magic. Won all the awards. You should seek it out.'

'I will, now you've told me. But I was asking about Dave Tudor.'

'Right. He was Mary's AP and he needed to be good, because so much was unrehearsed and unscripted. It's more controlled now and, between ourselves, less exciting. Dave was Mary's mainstay, telling us actors the last-minute changes. He had to be tactful because there were times when our lines were taken from us and no actor likes that. Almost every scene was re-shot several times over and that's stressful. Dave managed to stay popular. I don't know anyone who crossed swords with him.'

'You're sure of that?'

'I'm speaking from my own experience.'

'Was he also dealing with the crew?'

'Everyone. Mary wanted the extra mile from them as well. She often worked with long lenses and a single camera to get a more filmic look. Every tinpot director in the business does it now, but when she started with the Robeson series, the technique was new in television, tough for everyone from the focus-puller to the cable-basher.'

The terminology went over Diamond's head, but he didn't stop to ask. 'Were there arguments?'

'More like undercurrents. Nothing was out in the open. Dave kept the peace. He had a really likeable personality. I don't know where he was from.'

'Wales, I expect, going by the name.'

'I'm not so sure. There was the trace of a foreign accent when he spoke, quite sexy, in fact.'

Diamond didn't miss an opening like that. 'Did he make out with anyone?'

This got an embarrassed laugh. 'Now you're asking. Not me, unfortunately. No, I'm giving you the wrong idea. We actors talk the talk, but we're no different from anyone else when it comes to personal relationships. He was nice to us all, and I expect that's as far as it went.'

'He must have felt the pressure of working for Mary.'

'No question, but he didn't let it show.'

'So was it a shock when he went missing?'

'Not immediately. We all assumed he was ill when he didn't call in. After a couple of days, Mary sent someone to check at his flat somewhere up at Beechen Cliff.'

'Kipling Avenue.'

'Yes, and he wasn't there. All the signs were that he'd gone out and not returned. That was when it sank in that he was missing.'

'Were there any theories?'

'The one some people favoured is that he was an illegal immigrant and thought the Home Office were on his trail, but I don't think it was proved. The company is careful who it takes on. There's loads of form-filling.'

'Was he reported as a missing person?'

'To the police? I couldn't tell you. The office may have done something. We were in the middle of filming and far too busy to ask. Things move on quickly in this business. Mary needed a new assistant producer and one of the PAs had to step up and fill in.'

'PAs?'

'Production assistant. It's a dogsbody role, running errands and making coffee. They're learning on the job, getting experience.'

'So who got the job – Greg Deans?'

'Not Greg. He'd only just started at Bottle Yard. Candida Jones, who was far more plugged in. Candida joined as a runner after leaving school, before *Swift* was launched.'

A new name to Diamond. He glanced towards Ingeborg, who showed with a twitch of the shoulders that she hadn't heard of this person either. 'Is she still about?'

'I've no idea,' Sabine said. 'She didn't last long as Mary's assistant. She left a year later to start a family.'

'Leaving the field clear for Greg?'

'He was well up to the job by then. He's a quick learner.'

'He needed to be, because in – what? – a couple more years, Mary Wroxeter died and he took over her job as producer.'

'By then, he was the obvious choice. To be fair, he does

it well and makes it easier for us than Mary ever did, but she was more exciting to work with. Don't get me wrong. Greg is a good administrator – that's his strength and that's terribly important, because he doesn't need to be so creative if he brings in the talent and gives it a chance to flourish.' She was making an effort to be fair to Deans, by contrast with the way Deans had characterised her, making no attempt to hide his dislike.

'And how about you?' Diamond asked. 'Do you feel secure in the show?'

The question seemed to unsettle her. She tugged at the gown and covered her leg. 'What exactly do you mean?'

'This jinx. Is there anything in it?'

'I have people around me I can trust.'

'The young lady who showed us in?'

'Chen? My live-in driver, hairdresser, cook and chiropodist.'

'Doorkeeper, too, as we found out,' Ingeborg said, to lighten the mood.

Sabine summoned up a half-smile. 'She's good at that too. It's great to have fans, but I don't want them calling unexpectedly.'

'Chen – is that her first name?'

'No. She's staff. I don't want her getting too familiar.'

'You said "live-in". I hope she gets out sometimes.'

'Hardly ever. Her choice, not mine. Most of the TV crowd have never seen her.'

'You must have thought about all the bad luck,' Diamond pressed her, not wanting to leave the topic.

'I don't let it get to me,' she said, and it sounded like a lie. 'The paper kept badgering me for a comment and I refused to say a word. They could twist my words, couldn't they? If you have any sort of success, they're queuing up to knock you off your perch. A story like mine feeds people's jealousy. There's always a section who want you to come to grief. It's human nature, isn't it?'

'It gets serious if they do something to make the grief happen,' Diamond said. 'Do you think someone is behind these incidents?'

'I don't see how. Anyway, they'd have to be an insider.'

'With a grudge, perhaps because they felt they were treated unfairly?'

'Even if that were true, why would they want the whole show to suffer? No, I can't believe that. I mean, the accident to Dan was just that – an accident.'

'Some of the other things could have been malicious. The fire.'

'That was right at the start before *Swift* was screened. You can't blame that on success.'

'The elderly actress who played your mother,' Ingeborg put in.

'Daisy? She had a heart attack.'

'Brought on by finding a man in her wardrobe.'

'He was obviously a burglar. As I heard it, she returned home unexpectedly, ahead of schedule. She was supposed to be filming next morning, but they added the scene at the end of the day so she could get away. She was found dead in her bedroom and there was evidence of a break-in. Someone had hidden in the wardrobe and disarranged things. The police found her jewellery box in the garden. Nothing in it, of course.'

'Just a very unfortunate incident, then,' Ingeborg said, 'but how did the burglar know Daisy was supposed to be away filming? It suggests he'd seen the call sheet.'

Sabine shuddered. 'That's a horrible thought. It means . . .' She didn't finish the statement.

Diamond was ready to move on. 'One other thing the paper wrote is that the person originally picked to play the part of Caitlin Swift pulled out unexpectedly.'

Sabine shook her head. 'They drag in everything they can. You can't compare that with the accidents that happened.'

'How did it come about?'

'Do you really need to know?'

'Please.'

Before saying any more, she loosened the towel, shook her damp hair, bunched it again and secured it, as if she needed time to decide how she would tell the story.

'As Mary told it to me, they weren't looking for a name. They were confident that the punchy storyline with a female lead – a gal with crime in mind – would sell the series. They wanted a young actor with experience, but they weren't pitching for a star. She had to have the kind of face people find attractive, obviously, and be physically strong. They cast Trixie Playfair, who had done some bit-parts on *Heartbeat* and other things. I don't suppose you've heard of her.'

Diamond would have shaken his head whatever the truth was.

'I was told she signed the contract and the pilot was written and everyone was happy and then in rehearsal she threw in a bombshell saying she wasn't ready for a major role. Amazing. I thought it was everyone's ambition to star in a TV series, but she panicked, poor woman.'

'And they found you instead?'

'Very quickly. I was on the original shortlist. I'd already auditioned for the part – the same day as Trixie and some others.'

'You met Trixie, then?'

'If you can call it that: taller than me, athletic, fussed with her hair a lot. I wouldn't say we got to know each other. A few words while we sat waiting our turn to read the lines. Auditioning is a necessary evil. You're not going to open up with someone who might beat you to the part.'

'You thought you'd been pipped?'

'Let's face it. I was. Nobody likes rejection.'

'Then what happened?'

'A phone call. Mary and the casting director took me and my agent to lunch. They didn't want the public to know I was only the second choice, but someone leaked it to the *Mirror*. Trixie had reporters badgering her for the inside story, but it didn't make headlines because the show was only a script at that stage. Any sniff of a story now and it's everywhere.'

'Have you spoken to Trixie since?'

She frowned as if the thought hadn't occurred before now. 'Do you think I should have done? That's got me worried. I thought she wanted to put the whole thing behind her.'

'You're probably right.' He'd got as much from the jinx story as he was likely to, so he switched to the most recent event. 'I heard you did some filming at Charmy Down airfield.'

'I did.'

'Where Jake Nicol was last seen.'

Her look changed abruptly. With ice, she said, 'You'd better not be suggesting I had anything to do with him disappearing.' For the first time in the interview they got a glimpse of the imperious Sabine.

'Did I say that?' Diamond said, up for the challenge he'd been expecting from the start.

'I was there like all the others to shoot the scenes in the old control tower.'

'You took the motorhome with you?'

'That's what I use it for, location work.'

'Quite something, driving this monster on our local roads.'

'You'd better ask Chen about that.'

'She parked up there beside the other vehicles?'

'You have to. It's the designated area. They don't want the transport getting in shot. After a couple of wet nights we were in a sea of mud. I insisted they put boards down for me to walk over.'

He'd come to the question that interested him most. 'When did you leave? At the first opportunity, I should think.'

She hesitated, as if she, too, knew how much her answer mattered. 'The first opportunity, as you put it, wasn't until late. I was in all the scenes, right to the end, when the light was going.'

'Then what? Did you change your costume, clean off the make-up?'

'I do that in here. If I remember right, I asked Chen to fix me a drink and a sandwich.'

'While the others were clearing up outside? Did you watch?'

'I wasn't interested in what was going on out there. I remember checking my phone and watching some TV.'

'I'm asking because Jake Nicol must have been out there picking up bits of equipment and loading one of the vans. We believe at some point he may have been attacked.'

She blinked several times. 'Really?'

'If you witnessed anything, it could be important.'

'I already told you I don't know Jake Nicol from Adam.'

'It sounds as if you were one of the last to leave.'

She gave an angry sigh. The arrogance Greg Deans had talked about was all too evident now. 'What are you getting at?'

'Was it dark when you finally drove off?'

'Chen drove off. I was resting. You have no idea how tiring it is to go through a day's filming.'

'We'd better speak to Chen.'

She shrugged. 'Good luck with that. You'll need it.'

The charm of the earlier exchanges had vanished as soon as Nicol had been mentioned. She called Chen to show them out and Diamond took the opportunity to ask the stone-faced minder whether she had witnessed anything on the last evening at Charmy Down.

He got a one-word answer.

He got the same answer to each of his other questions. Chen was as chatty as a Buckingham Palace sentry.

The only 'yes' was when Diamond said, 'Perhaps you'll show us out, then.'

In the Ka, he said to Ingeborg, 'Sabine was a sight more pleasant than Greg Deans led me to expect.'

'She's an actor, guv.'

'You don't think it was genuine?'

'Chen was more sincere than she was.'

'I must be a soft touch.'

She said nothing.

In his head, he replayed the key moments of the interview. 'The charm cooled off after I mentioned Jake Nicol, I admit.'

'She couldn't get rid of us quickly enough.'

Ingeborg's judgements on other women were usually reliable. Sabine couldn't be dismissed as innocent. Two of the classic murder trinity – means and opportunity – weren't difficult to pin on her. The motive was the elusive one. She'd made sure she was fireproof by insisting she had liked Dave Tudor enough to want to go out with him. As for Jake, she didn't know the man, scarcely noticed him. But could she be believed?

He'd asked Inge to drive them back to CID head-quarters at Concorde House and they were heading west on the A420 across the valley of the River Boyd, a prettier route than the motorway. They passed through a village called Wick. 'I came here once with Steph,' he said in a rare moment of nostalgia. 'Wick Gorge is quite a beauty spot.'

'I know it,' Ingeborg said. 'I covered a story about Jane Austen in my days as a hack. She mentioned the gorge in *Northanger Abbey*.'

They drove on.

'Speaking of your journalist knowhow,' he said, 'I was banking on you to unlock one of the big mysteries in this jinx business.'

'The whistle-blower? I haven't given up,' she told him. 'I asked an old friend who subs for the *Post* and she said they don't even know themselves who it is. The story was phoned in anonymously. Someone on their switchboard made a few notes and that was all.'

'Wouldn't they need to know their source before they broke the story?'

'Not really. Most of it was public knowledge, but no one had joined the dots. It was only when they started checking that they realised how much had gone wrong with *Swift*. Some of the incidents had been reported in their own pages.'

'The jinx idea would appeal to any journalist.'

'You're right about that, guv.'

'I thought they were protecting someone. The *Post* don't need to know who the source was, but we do.'

'I don't think they can tell us any more than they have. The stuff they know is all in print.'

'There's something useful they can tell us.'

'What's that?'

'Was the caller a man or a woman?'

7

'Is this your doing?'

'Indirectly, ma'am,' Peter Diamond answered in a contrite tone. He was now at an upstairs window of Concorde House, the police building in Emersons Green. At his shoulder was his boss, Georgina Dallymore, the Assistant Chief Constable, along with most of his team. A strange scene was unfolding in the yard below. A tall, disreputable-looking, white-bearded man had emerged from a small police van. He waited for the driver to open the rear doors. Between them, they unloaded various items, an old-fashioned pram, a bedroll and a rucksack. Then a dog the size of a Shetland pony put its head out, took a long look at the yard, and jumped down.

Georgina gasped and said, 'Oh my sainted aunt!'

Some of the others used more colourful language.

Georgina was outraged. 'Does he think he's coming in with that enormous animal and all his paraphernalia? He looks like a vagrant. We could get infested with fleas and heaven only knows what else. Peter, I hold you responsible for this.'

'We believe he can assist with an ongoing inquiry, ma'am. I didn't know he was bringing everything but the kitchen sink.'

But as they watched, the pram and the other things were reloaded in the van. All except the man and the huge dog.

'Whose doing is this?'

Ratting on colleagues wasn't in Diamond's character. 'The buck stops here, ma'am.'

'Someone must have brought them in.'

On cue, a figure on a moped putt-putted into the yard and stopped beside the van.

'Who's that on the scooter?'

DCI Halliwell, Diamond's deputy, said, 'I don't suppose there was room in the van.'

'Send someone down to stop them entering the building. We're a police office, not a dog pound.'

'I'll handle this myself,' Diamond said, spotting the chance to escape.

'You won't.' Georgina turned to Halliwell. 'You can do it.' Then, to Diamond, 'In my office. Now.'

The barring of Will Legat and Caesar was never going to succeed. They were already inside the entrance hall of Concorde House when Halliwell came running downstairs, an action Caesar interpreted as hostile. The barking, echoing off the tiled floor, must have been heard all over the building. Halliwell came to a cartoon-style skidding stop and Legat leaned back in a tug-of-war effort to keep a grip on the rope lead. Repeated shouts of, 'Sit!' had no effect.

Only when Caesar decided he'd barked enough did Halliwell succeed in being heard. 'We have a no-dog rule here.'

'He's with me,' Legat said as if that answered everything. 'No use telling him to sit. He doesn't like this cold flooring. Have you got a carpet somewhere?'

'Can't you put him back in the van?'

'If I do, I won't answer for the throat of the first man to open the doors.'

At this point, Paul Gilbert arrived, crash helmet in hand.

'This isn't going to work,' Halliwell told him. 'The ACC is on the warpath.'

'Why? The dog? He's not causing any trouble.'

'Before you came in, he was.'

Gilbert couldn't resist offering Caesar the back of his hand for drooling over. 'He's a lamb.'

'He can't stay.'

'It's all right. I'm taking them to Keynsham after this. I've already called and they have a spare cell in the custody suite.'

'Why bring him here, then?'

'I have a tracksuit bottom in my locker. Mr Legat is going to change into it. I'm sending the belt and his trousers to forensics. I think the belt belonged to a rigger and I want it checked for DNA.'

'The missing man?'

'Wouldn't that be terrific? Forensics already checked the bloodstains from his flat at Fairfield, so they'll see if there's a match.'

'What will you use as a changing room?'

'The staff locker room. Step this way, Will.'

'Wouldn't it be better to take the dog outside while this is going on?' Halliwell suggested.

'Would you like to be holding the rope when his master walks away?'

There was no argument. 'Get it done quickly, then.'

Upstairs with Georgina, Diamond was hard pressed to justify the investigation. 'The missing man is just the latest in a long run of serious incidents, deaths and disappearances, ma'am. There may be nothing in it, but anyone in my position has a duty to check.'

She wasn't at all convinced. 'What's in it for you? A chance to meet the glamorous actress who plays Swift?'

'Not at all.' He put a comforting spin on the story to ease Georgina's mind. 'I've got a watching brief, which is why I'm here with you and not down there with the dosser they brought in. CID's involvement is low-key, small scale at this stage. A chance for one of my less experienced men to cut his teeth as investigating officer. I like to share out the duties.'

'Who is he?'

'The tramp?'

'The man on the moped. He appears to be one of ours.'

'Like you, I didn't recognise him under the helmet.'

'Do you expect me to believe you don't know who you sent?'

'I delegated the job, ma'am. As I explained, it's a low-level inquiry.'

'He'd better have a very good reason for bringing that vagrant and his animal into Concorde House.'

'Absolutely. I haven't had a chance to speak to him.' He saw another opening he hadn't planned. 'I'll go down directly and find out.'

Georgina gave a flat no. 'Now that you're here you will tell me precisely and without evasion how we became involved in all this nonsense about a jinx, transparently a story cobbled together to sell newspapers.'

She had him over a barrel. They both knew the real reason. He couldn't resist a puzzle and this was a humdinger, a real challenge. Some of it might be nonsense, as she said, but there was enough mystery in it to stretch his brain.

He took a deep breath.

Unfortunately, the next twenty minutes revealed that Georgina had a different agenda. A deeply troubling one.

*

Down in the staff locker room, Gilbert had positioned himself by the door in case anyone entered unexpectedly and got savaged. Caesar, a study in innocence, was lying on his side taking up most of the floor. Behind, Will Legat had removed the combat trousers and belt. His legs were chalk-white, but beefy, testimony to the many miles they'd covered. They could have been carved by Michelangelo. But a pair of oversized Mickey Mouse boxers spoiled the effect.

'I'll need my keys and things.'

'I can unfasten them,' Gilbert said and asked the question he'd puzzled over all afternoon. 'Why does a homeless man need so many keys?'

'For overnight stays,' came the answer. 'It's so much more considerate to one's benefactor if one doesn't break in.' Legat reached across Caesar's recumbent form to hand over the belt. 'Why are you wearing the rubber gloves?'

'Because we don't want my DNA corrupting the evidence.' With tact, Gilbert added, 'If the belt turns out to have had more than one owner.' He unhitched the keys, jackknife and bottle-opener, dropped the belt into an evidence bag and sealed the top. A despatch rider would get it to the lab within the hour.

'Life never ceases to be interesting,' Legat said. 'One learns something new every day.'

'I'd be glad if you'd get into the tracksuit bottom before anyone else learns something new. This room is unisex.'

Diamond was back in his own office licking his wounds after the bruising encounter with Georgina. He'd been ordered to drop all interest in the jinxed TV company and apply himself to the real business of running an efficient department. She'd told him to get up to speed with the directives from headquarters he'd ignored for months, if not years. He was to make sure everyone on the team was taking up the career opportunities open to them. By this, Georgina meant refresher courses. A modern detective force needed to be conversant with every element of the Police and Criminal Evidence Act; cybercrime; counter-terrorism; powers of search and removal; the giving of evidence; record-keeping; interaction with the public; and equality and diversity. He was to report back by the end of the month with a list of names and the courses they'd booked. His own name was to head the list.

Refresher bloody courses.

Privately he thought the blast from Georgina was sour grapes. She'd attended more refresher courses than she'd had hot dinners and still hadn't been upgraded to Deputy Chief Constable when the job became vacant.

All of that paled beside her final swipe. After softening him up by accusing him of being out of touch with modern policing, she hit him with the killer punch.

'It's time you thought about retirement.'

Retirement?

He'd rather roast in hell than end up watching daytime television. His record as a crime-solver was second to none. He'd given his best years to Bath CID. It wasn't as if he was standing in the way of someone who wanted the job. Keith Halliwell, his deputy, was a sweet guy and a huge support with absolutely no desire to lead the team. Ingeborg Smith was as smart as a whip and would cope, but she hadn't enough experience yet. She hadn't long been made up to sergeant. John Leaman, brainy as he was, had bipolar issues and couldn't relate to colleagues. You could send any of those people on courses until they screamed for mercy and they still wouldn't be ready to take over.

Grinding his teeth, he reached for one of the stacks of paper that formed a wall on his desk.

But his mind wasn't on the job any longer. He was picturing the sad old men in suits who sat on benches watching the world go by.

Paul Gilbert drove the van with Will Legat, the dog and all his belongings to the custody suite at Keynsham.

'What's he in for?' the sergeant-in-charge asked.

Legat was in no doubt what he was in for. 'A shower, a cup of cocoa, a good night's sleep and a hot breakfast, if you please.'

'Vagrancy,' Gilbert said.

'What about the dog?'

Legat said, 'He's more of a vagrant than I am, but I wouldn't advise giving him a cell to himself.'

'He can't go in with you.'

'Why not? How long have you been here? We've always managed before.'

The sergeant looked at Paul Gilbert, who shook his head. 'We don't have our own dog pound.'

'You could take him to the kennels in Redlynch Lane.'

Legat didn't like the suggestion. 'The last time somebody tried keeping Caesar in kennels he leaned against the side, walked free, and two chihuahuas and a French bulldog were never seen again.'

True or not, that seemed to persuade the sergeant. Another sensitive moment came when the guest prisoner was asked to empty his pockets. The jackknife was given a filthy look. 'You can't bring that in.'

'What else can I use to butter my toast in the morning?'

'We'll give you a plastic knife. What are all these keys for?'

'I'm a bit of a ladies' man.'

The sergeant was starting to realise this man had been asked the same questions many times over. The only way to deal with him was to fall in with his plans.

Caesar had the floor of the cell and Legat the bunk. The pram was put in the evidence room.

'What are we supposed to do with him in the morning?' the sergeant asked Gilbert before he left.

'I promised him a good breakfast, if you would, sarge. He'll feed the dog himself.'

'I mean after. You don't want him up before the beak?'

'No, but he'd appreciate a lift in the paddy wagon with the other offenders.'

'He'll need a bloody van to himself.'

'What a good idea,' Gilbert said.

'Are you related to this fuckwit by any chance?'

At the end of the day, when Paloma switched off the TV, she said to Diamond, 'Something on your mind?'

'Why?'

'You've scarcely spoken all evening.'

'Tired, I expect.'

'Wasn't anything I said?'

'God, no.'

'Problems at work?'

'There are always problems at work.'

'That's what you enjoy, isn't it, solving them? I expect a night's sleep will help. I'll get my drink and go on up, then.'

'Sure. I won't be long.' He pottered about, checking that the cat's litter tray was ready and the doors and windows were closed. After a bit, he poured himself a glass of water and went upstairs to visit the bathroom. Paloma used the en suite. She was already in bed reading when he changed into his night things.

'I heard that sigh,' she said after the lights were out. 'I've always envied you because you can shut off when you leave work. Not this time apparently.'

He didn't comment. Usually he didn't mind telling her if he had a problem.

A few minutes later, she said, 'I was thinking.'

'What?'

'How long have you been in that job?'

'Don't go there,' he said. 'Don't go there.'

He said no more and neither did Paloma. In the darkness, tears were rolling down his cheek.

8

Diamond was still in anguish next morning over Georgina's bombshell, but he pumped himself up enough to inform Bath's detective squad about the new regime. 'I'll be circulating a list of the many interesting courses headquarters are running and you can get your applications in. Go in with the right attitude and you can have a ball. Take it from me, every course attended will look good on your CV.'

They were bemused. This wasn't the real Diamond talking. Whatever spin he put on it, it was obvious that he wasn't happy and neither were the team. The mention of CVs was particularly unsettling.

Keith Halliwell had a strong suspicion what was really in play. 'Is this Georgina closing us down?'

Diamond didn't answer. He hadn't told them the clincher. That was personal and still hurt like hell. 'I did the firearms course a couple of years ago. I say it myself, I surprised them all.'

Mental picture of a trigger-happy superintendent loosing off shots at random and terrifying his instructors.

The team couldn't even smile at that.

Halliwell spoke for almost everyone. 'If we were Greater Manchester or London, breaking up the team wouldn't be an option. This is a great place to work, but Bath is so bloody safe. We're riding for a fall here. When the worst thing to happen is a missing rigger, we're really up shit creek.'

'If the crime rate was higher, they'd say we were useless anyway,' Ingeborg said.

'Exactly. We can't win. The way I see it, they can close us down and send us all to places that are undermanned.'

'Dealing with knife crime in Manchester,' Paul Gilbert said, shaking his head and sounding like an old man.

'Which is why I'll be signing up for the cybercrime course,' John Leaman announced.

'We've already got a computer expert,' Halliwell said.

Jean Sharp blushed and said nothing.

Someone needed to lighten the mood and as usual it was Ingeborg. 'You want to wise up on some field of crime that makes you indispensable,' she told Leaman.

'Such as?'

'Bee-rustling.'

Nobody else spoke.

'It's one of the fastest-growing crimes. Bath is full of beekeepers.'

Leaman picked up the list of courses and studied it again. 'I don't see anything on bees.'

'Start it. You're world-class at mugging up a topic. We've all seen how you turn yourself into an expert over a weekend. You can offer this brand new course to headquarters. Call it something catchy like Plan Bee. They'll jump at it. You bring in a couple of beekeepers as guest lecturers. PowerPoint shows. An entomologist.'

'And some bees,' Halliwell said, starting to see where this was going. Leaman was easy prey for a wind-up.

'Field trips,' Ingeborg added. 'A chance for everyone to dress up in the kit and use a smoke-gun.'

'And at the end they all take home a pot of honey,' Gilbert chimed in. 'People will sign up for this in droves.'

Diamond hadn't been listening. He'd been wondering how Paloma would react to having him padding around the house all day in carpet slippers looking for yesterday's crossword puzzle. When she'd invited him to live with her it was on the understanding that they were both busy people who met in the evenings.

His sixth sense told him the team was on a distraction exercise. He needed to get a grip. He summoned up a grim smile. 'Joke over. I've been told to hand in your applications before the end of the month and—'

A sound as unsocial as a fart interrupted him.

'Whose is it?' Ingeborg said. 'Who didn't switch off?'

Red-faced, Paul Gilbert felt in his pocket for his phone and looked at the display. 'It's the lab. I wasn't expecting a call-back so soon. Do you mind, guv?'

Diamond shrugged and Gilbert moved to the back of the room with the phone to his ear.

'This bee-rustling,' Leaman said. 'Is it on the statute book?'

He was definitely hooked.

'It comes under theft,' Halliwell said, 'but you might get a law passed if you get some steam behind this.'

'Smoke,' Ingeborg said.

'Be serious,' Halliwell said. 'It could be called Leaman's law.'

Leaman's eyes gleamed. He googled bee-rustling on his phone. 'Forty thousand bees were stolen in one raid in Anglesey.'

'Didn't I tell you?'

He was scrolling rapidly. 'There are clubs all over this area: Bath, Bristol, Keynsham, Saltford, West Wiltshire.' He had to break off in mid-list.

Gilbert was back, looking as if he'd just met Hamlet's father.

'Tell us,' Diamond said.

'They asked if we knew the rigger's belt is heavily encrusted in blood.'

'Hell's bells!'

'It was stained dark,' Gilbert said, wide-eyed, 'and I thought that was dirt from plenty of use. They're carrying out more tests and this is to let us know that it looks like a serious crime was committed, possibly murder. Someone was almost certainly bleeding profusely.'

'And that wasn't Will Legat,' Ingeborg said. 'He's got questions to answer.'

'What time is it?' Gilbert said. 'He'll be in Bath by now.'

'Where?'

'North Parade Road. The law courts.'

'He wasn't charged with anything, was he?'

'No, but they drove him there and released him.'

'We must pull him in again,' Diamond said. 'He's the prime suspect now, not just a witness. Your gentleman of the road may be no gentleman at all.' The head of CID was no longer in the doldrums. He was elated. This could be the saving of his career. '"Heavily encrusted". That's a lot of blood. They're right, we could well be dealing with murder.'

'Shall we still apply for these courses, guv?' Halliwell asked.

'That's on hold. First, we pick up Legat. You and I can take care of that. We'll need to send his clothing and everything he owns to forensics to be tested for more blood. Did you say he had a knife hanging from the belt?'

'A jackknife.'

'Large?'

'Three to four inches.'

'Is it confiscated?'

Gilbert swallowed hard and blushed. 'He was given it back to butter his toast. At first they gave him a plastic knife, but it broke.'

Diamond squeezed his eyes shut in disbelief. People make stupid mistakes, but the police were supposed to be trained to look out for trickery. 'That knife has got to be tested by the lab. What age is he?'

'Forty-two, he told the custody sergeant. He's got the grey beard, but he's younger than he appears.'

'State of fitness? Strong enough to take on a rigger in a fight?'

'Probably.'

'Jean.'

DC Jean Sharp, the team's online researcher, was so alert she spoke the words in Diamond's mind before he could get them out. 'A full check on Legat's form, court appearances, prison terms, instances of violence.'

'Spot on,' he said. 'Especially any links to the rigger. And, Paul?'

Gilbert, shamefaced, expected a roasting for having missed so much that was obvious. 'Guv?'

'This belt. He's supposed to have found it lying about at the airfield, is he?'

'In the mud where everyone parked.'

'It's a heavy-duty thing, obviously. How does it fasten – a pin buckle?'

'No. A quick-release clip. You press the centre and it opens.'

'Easy to remove.'

'It would be, yes.'

'Might come off in a fight?'

'I see what you're thinking, guv. Quite possibly.'

'Right. You're the man who knows the airfield. It's our probable crime scene. Get a CSI team up to Charmy Down.'

'Do you think the body's up there?'

'We'll find out. Let's see how much Legat is willing to tell us.'

The change in mood was electric. Everyone was fired up again.

Two hours later, Legat had not been found and some of the enthusiasm had ebbed away. Diamond was with Halliwell in front of the Abbey. The two detectives had walked the length of Stall Street and seen nothing of their quarry. They'd radioed a description to all patrolling officers and PCSOs and got no response.

How does a six-foot-two grey-bearded tramp with a pram and an enormous dog manage to disappear in a city heaving with sightseers?

They'd phoned the custody sergeant at Keynsham and he'd confirmed that Legat had been driven to North Parade Road outside the court building and allowed to make his own way into town. They'd asked more people than they could remember. Nobody had been able to help.

'He told Paul he was here for the tourist season,' Halliwell said. 'He turns up every year. Right here where we're standing is where he ought to be. This is where the buskers make their money.'

'He doesn't busk. He gets the dog to lie down looking pathetic and people arrive with tins of dog food. A lot of them give money as well.'

'He must spend it somewhere. We haven't tried the super-markets.'

'Good suggestion.'

The good suggestion came to nothing. All they found outside Waitrose were two saffron-robed Buddhist monks with their alms bowls. They had been there over an hour and seen nothing of Legat or his dog.

'He must have left town,' Diamond said.

Halliwell was doubtful. 'He gave the impression he was here for weeks to come.'

'We're not dealing with a truth-teller, Keith. He charmed young Gilbert into believing him, but that doesn't fool me. He knows the belt was sent to forensics. If he also knows how it came to be covered in blood he's not going to hang about, is he?'

'How would he get out of town?'

'From outside the courthouse, where he was last seen? The obvious way is north on the A36.'

'We put out that all-cars message. Someone would have picked him up by now.'

'He may have taken the canal towpath. No cars there.'

'He'd still be spotted. Plenty of people walk their dogs there. Someone would have noticed a monster the size of Caesar.'

'You depress me, but you're right.'

'Can we scale this up into a full-scale manhunt?'

'Call out the plods?' Diamond shook his head. 'Georgina will come down on me like a ton of bricks. We're supposed to be back in Concorde House applying for courses. We have to soft-pedal, Keith.'

'I can't think what else to suggest.'

'Where does a homeless man make for?'

'Julian House?'

It was worth a try. The charity for the homeless offered medical care, resettlement advice and free meals as well as beds in private pods. Legat evidently knew Bath, so he must have known about Julian House. But was he too proud to go there?

'We can ask if they've seen him.'

The police had once been near neighbours of Julian House, which was tucked away below the Baptist church.

Visiting Manvers Street again was a bittersweet experience for the two detectives. The nick they'd worked in for more than twenty years had been sold to the university, refurbished and converted into a study centre. The Virgil Building, as rebranded, had never been much to look at and there had been complaints about it as a workplace, but compared to Concorde House it was the Ritz. Diamond hadn't said anything to the team, but he'd wondered at the time if he and his team would be sacrificial lambs.

'We're keen to know if you've seen anything today of a fellow called Will Legat.'

The woman in reception at Julian House had been running her sympathetic eyes over their clothes, in particular Diamond's creased suit, shiny in places. Were these two in need of support? At the mention of Legat, her face switched on like the Blackpool lights. 'Will? Is he back?' She made him sound like the first swallow of summer.

'You know him, then?'

'Everyone here knows Will. He turns up every year around this time. He's often in the day centre for a meal when he's in town. Cheers us all up.'

But there was disappointment.

'Has he been in today?'

'Not today and not last night. He never uses the night shelter because he won't be parted from his dog. Our bed spaces are too small, four foot by seven. Is he all right?'

Diamond couldn't suppress a sigh of annoyance. 'He's fine, only we'd like to know where he is. Any idea where we might find him?'

'He's not in trouble, I hope?'

All the sympathy for Legat was irksome. Everyone who met the man fell under some sort of spell. 'He's in a good state of health, if that's what you're asking, ma'am. We saw him yesterday.'

'In town?'

'En route.'

'So, he *is* back?'

'As of this morning, yes.'

'Where was he, then?'

'Charmy Down.'

'In that case, I know where he might be. The Together Project.'

It sounded like a dating agency. Legat looking for romance? Diamond couldn't get his head around that.

'They're wonderful,' the woman said. 'They're all registered vets who provide a free service for homeless people's pets. They do it from the goodness of their hearts.'

Pets made more sense.

'They volunteer to give up several hours a week to make sure the animals, dogs mostly, get the treatment they need. The first thing Will does each year is take Caesar – that's his dog – for his medication, the flea and worm treatment.'

Diamond nodded as if the flea and worm treatment was as familiar as getting out of bed in the morning.

'And of course the annual vaccination,' she added. 'Personally, I wouldn't go anywhere near Caesar with a needle and syringe.'

'Me neither.'

'You can tell how devoted Will must be, toiling up the

hill with the pram and his backpack and all his bits and pieces and Caesar in tow, dragging on the lead. Animals know what's in store, don't they? I wouldn't care to try it.'

'Which hill do you mean? Is that where these vets are?'

'Claverton Down. The cat and dog home. It's a Together Project clinic.'

Diamond knew the place on the Avenue, past the university campus. Whichever route you took, it was a stiff climb.

'I'll phone if you like and see if he's been there,' the woman offered.

'No need. We'd prefer to surprise him.'

Halliwell did the driving in his shiny new Prius and it was all too obvious something was troubling him. 'If we want to bring him in, we'll need extra transport,' he made clear to Diamond. 'I can't possibly fit a man, a pram and that dog into my car.'

Diamond was quick to say, 'Legat can have my seat. I wouldn't wish to sit in a car with them.' He knew full well that they'd need to send for a van. He just enjoyed Halliwell's appalled reaction.

Before reaching the cat and dog home, they were treated to the sight of Legat in a high-visibility jacket moving down Claverton Down Road at such a brisk rate behind the ancient pram that Caesar was trotting to keep up. 'The Julian House lady knew what she was talking about,' Diamond said.

Halliwell pulled over and Caesar tugged on the rope and barked at the car.

'Phone for a van and tell transport division it's a secret mission. They're to keep this strictly to themselves.' He didn't want Georgina finding out.

Halliwell wasted no time getting through.

Diamond lowered the window just enough to speak without being savaged. He had to shout. 'Can't you control him?'

'He's just had his shot,' Legat shouted back. 'He doesn't trust anyone now, least of all me.'

He's not the only one, Diamond thought. He had to bellow to be heard. 'Where are you making for?'

'The centre of town.'

'We'd like to speak to you first. We'll organise a van.'

'I can make my own way, thanks. It's easier downhill than coming up. Calm down, old lad.'

Caesar made a leap for the window and spattered it with froth, trying to force his muzzle through.

'His paws are scratching my paintwork,' Halliwell said, as pained as if his own skin was being scarred.

'It's his teeth that worry me. Look at the size of them.'

They had to wait for Legat to get control of the dog and it wasn't done quickly. When it was finally safe to lower the window a fraction more, Diamond made himself heard and insisted on a formal interview. The message wasn't well received.

'We have other plans,' Legat said.

'I don't want to be forced to arrest you.'

'Then don't.'

Halliwell told Diamond the van was not far off.

Legat said, 'Come, Caesar. We're moving on.'

But Caesar didn't wish to go without leaving his mark on these annoying policemen. He reared up again, claws scraping the window, and the barking began afresh. Minutes later, when the Transit van arrived, he switched his attack to that.

An incredibly brave or idiotically reckless driver got out the other side and unlocked the rear doors and Caesar, seeing what he took to be the guts of the thing, jumped inside. Legat, muttering protests, followed him in and the driver lifted the pram aboard and slammed the door.

The interrogation took place at Keynsham police station, the nearest with interviewing facilities and a custody suite. Caesar, by this time exhausted from his medication and all the excitement, wasn't involved. He remained flat out in the van, snoring.

Before entering the interview room, Diamond called Concorde House and asked Jean Sharp for the results of her research into Legat. She sent her notes electronically and he had a copy printed. Minor misdemeanours right across the home counties and south-west, but no record of violence.

He told Halliwell to say nothing at the start about the blood found on the belt. 'We'll learn a lot from his face when he starts to worry how much we know.'

'I want my solicitor present,' Legat said before they'd sat down.

'This isn't under caution, Will,' Diamond told him. 'It's only a chat, to get a few things straight.'

'I know my rights. I'm refusing to answer questions without legal representation.'

'We'd tell you if you were under arrest.'

'So it's voluntary, is it? I can walk out of here just so that you can nick me and recite your little homily about not needing to say anything unless I want to get shot to pieces later in court. I wasn't born yesterday.'

'We know when you were born from the last time you were pulled in for questioning.' Diamond made a performance of studying the printout. In the short time she'd had, Jean Sharp had assembled enough facts to give some leverage if needed. 'We want to ask you about something more recent, up at Charmy Down. How did you come to be there when the TV people were filming?'

'I told all this to the young constable. The airfield is one of my regular stops on my way down to Bath. Caesar and I limit our daily perambulation to no more than ten miles. I plan my sleeping places and the old control tower is one of them. It's not the royal suite at the Savoy, but it rates pretty high in my book.' Legat was a windbag in love with his own voice. He'd already forgotten about not answering questions.

'But it was already occupied?'

'I saw the trucks and the crane and the enormous motor-home and it was obvious that my canine companion and I needed to find somewhere else to rest our weary heads. That first night we had to make do with a poxy pillbox on the edge of the airfield.'

'Wasn't there anywhere else you could go?'

'There's a lady in Combe Hay who lets me use her barn when I come by, a comfortable stop, but that was too far off. We'd done our walk for the day getting to the airfield, the hound and I, and we were footsore and weary.'

'Did you watch any of the filming?'

'I had better things to do.'

'Like what?'

'Foraging for food.'

'Out there on the airfield?'

'You'd be surprised. Nettles are an excellent source of nutrition. Fat hen, as well.'

'You found chickens up there?'

He rolled his eyes at such ignorance. 'It's a common weed, cooks up like spinach and is far more delicious. Also known as dirty dick.'

'You wouldn't be having me on?'

'I'm not stupid, superintendent, and I doubt whether you are.'

'Were you foraging when you found the belt?'

'Aha, the belt. That's what this is all about, isn't it? Am I going to get it back?'

'You've got some nerve, considering it doesn't belong to you. We noticed it's a quick-release clip, simple to unfasten. Where was it?'

'In the vicinity.'

'The vicinity of what?'

'The control tower where they were filming. I almost tripped over the thing in the dark, obviously discarded where the vehicles had been parked. Everyone had gone by then and I was dog-tired and ready to turn in, so I left it where it was and inspected it again in the morning. I can put this to good use, I thought. Seems a shame to leave it here.'

'You say you almost tripped over it. Did you handle it?'

'When? In the morning?'

'The night before.'

Legat frowned, and yet managed to look more puzzled by the question than evasive. 'Does it matter? I held it in my hands in the morning to fit my keys and things to the D-rings. If you're looking for fingerprints, you'll find mine all over it. Doesn't make me a thief.'

'We'll find out what it makes you,' Diamond said. 'I'm asking about the moment you first came across the thing. You said it was dark at the time. You must have wondered what you'd found. You're a scavenger.'

'Forager . . . please.'

'Did you stoop and make a close inspection?'

'I may have done.'

'When someone says to me "I may have done" it's obvious what they mean. You handled it. Was it damp to the touch?'

He didn't contest the point. 'The whole patch was damp. I just told you this was the parking area where the trucks had left ruts of mud. It rained most nights that week. If you go up there, you'll see it's a quagmire.' He seemed untroubled by the line of inquiry.

'Was anyone else about?'

'I told you. This was after they'd all left.'

'The reason I ask is that there's evidence of a violent incident there. Think carefully, Will. If you were left alone, suspicion falls on you.'

'I can't see why,' he said, keeping his cool. 'A man on his own can't do violence to anyone except himself.'

'Unless he's the last man standing.'

He tilted his head ironically like a smart lawyer in court and smiled. 'What's your evidence for that? I didn't see any casualties. Believe me, Caesar would have found them. He was off the leash all morning sniffing around the site.' He had answers to everything.

Diamond was forced into playing his strong card. 'We heard from forensics. The belt was heavily bloodstained.'

'Really?' Legat did look surprised and quite serious, although whether this was from being found out was not obvious. 'I didn't notice any staining.'

'You didn't get any on your hands?'

'I'm positive I didn't.'

'The tests show the presence of human blood even if it wasn't apparent to you. When fresh it will show up red on a dark leather belt, but it soon dries and turns brown. Someone who wore that belt was badly wounded, if not killed.'

'A troubling thought.' But he had already recovered his poise.

'It's a rigger's belt and a rigger called Jake Nicol has gone missing.'

'I know nothing about that.'

'Did you ever meet Jake Nicol?'

'The name is completely unknown to me.'

Diamond took out his phone and found the photo of Nicol.

Legat took one glance and shook his head. 'A total stranger. And now I've answered your questions I'll retrieve my dog and my property and get on my way.'

'If you're as innocent as you make out, you won't object to a simple DNA test.'

'Why is that necessary?'

'So that we can eliminate you from our inquiries. You said your prints are all over the belt. We may well find other people's DNA and we'll know who else to question.'

'Will this go on to the dossier you have in front of you?'

'We can destroy it once we've ended our investigation.'

'Can or will?'

'You have my word.'

Legat took time to decide whether Diamond's word mattered more than a hill of beans. 'Very well, you may run the test.' He gave a slow grin. 'Consider it a gesture of good Will.'

'Thanks.'

'In return, I need a favour from you, superintendent. While you're here, would you make a reservation for me and my dog for the custody cell we had last night?'

Later, Diamond explained to Halliwell why the questioning of Legat had stopped. They wouldn't achieve anything until the belt and jackknife had been fully tested at the lab. 'We'll need to keep tabs on him. I don't want another manhunt like we had today.'

'Now he knows about the custody suite, our problem will be keeping him away,' Halliwell said. 'What did you think of his story, guv?'

'There's more to come. Quite a bit more. He's no fool.'

9

'I haven't been here for years,' Diamond said. 'It's a god-forsaken place.'

It was rainy with an east wind blowing when they drove to the airfield. The few derelict buildings remaining had the look of ancient ruins. The monolith that had once been a hi-tech control tower remained standing, skeletal and sad. Bath council bulldozers had done their damnedest in 1955 to make Charmy Down inhospitable for squatters and the weather had taken care of the rest. Most of the RAF buildings, the thirteen hangars, the field maintenance shops, the ammunition pens and the Nissen huts, had been levelled, but their footings still scarred the ground. The concrete runways and perimeter track remained if you could make them out under a coating of weed and scrub.

A short distance from the control tower a scene-of-crime unit was at work in thick mud, having taped off an area rutted with tyre tracks. Paul Gilbert had been quick to get them up here.

'To you and me, this looks like a dog's dinner,' Diamond commented to Keith Halliwell as they watched the activity from behind the tape, 'but to a SOCO it's sheer joy, all those tread marks and shoeprints.'

The stooping SOCOs in their overalls looked as joyful as lobsters in the tank at a seafood restaurant.

'What do you expect them to find, guv?'

'A body would be good.'

'I don't see any sign of one. Do you think he buried it? Did he have a spade?'

'I was joking. These lads are professionals. They would have found a recent grave as soon as they looked.' He turned for a wider view of the landscape. 'If it really was murder, he must have disposed of his victim somewhere. What are those mounds the other side of the tower – the old air-raid shelters?'

Two moss-covered concrete domes projected above ground not far off. If, indeed, they were shelters, they would have underground rooms, a simple solution to a murderer's problem. No digging necessary, which surely would have appealed to Will Legat.

'Let's explore.'

They wandered over to inspect one and found the entrance barred by a metal grille, secured and padlocked. No way could Legat have got inside.

Diamond wasn't giving up. 'The pillboxes. He told us he spent a night inside one of them.'

The structures along the perimeter fence had been built as a line of defence against German parachutists. They were inward-facing, with slits for machine guns. Partly submerged, they had resisted the creep of nature for eighty years, stark grey excrescences that stuck up from the hillside.

The nearest was some way across the airfield. The two detectives weren't dressed for a field trek. It had been dry and sunny when they'd left Concorde House. Now the rain was hitting them as if by design. They took the shortest route along the grassed-over main runway and soon their trouser legs were saturated below the knees.

Halliwell kept harping on about the practical difficulties. 'How would he have moved the body this far if the murder took place where we think it did?'

'Must have used the pram. You'd be surprised how well those things were built. Well-sprung, too.'

'There'd be a trail of blood.'

'There wouldn't. A body doesn't keep bleeding after death.'

'Even if he left other traces of some sort, we'll never find them in this big area without a fingertip search.'

'I'm not authorising that while Georgina's breathing down my neck.'

The pillbox they inspected was six-sided and accessible from the rear, with steps down to a shallow underground room. Inside, they found a Y-shaped anti-ricochet wall along the centre and narrow horizontal embrasures where the troops could view the airfield and position their light machine guns.

'But no corpse,' Halliwell said after doing the circuit around the internal wall.

'Don't let that get you down, Keith. There are plenty more of these.'

Halliwell wasn't encouraged. 'Shall we wait for the weather to improve?'

Diamond stared through the slot at the downpour outside. 'Looks like it's set to carry on all day. I don't intend to spend the night here . . . like his nibs. What's that?'

'What?'

'Keep your voice down. There's someone out there.'

'Where?'

He'd spotted a figure wearing a dark windcheater with

the hood up. When hoods came into fashion, crime investigation suffered a setback it still hadn't recovered from.

'Over to the right, just out of sight. He must have gone inside the next pillbox.'

They couldn't tell for sure. The squat buildings were sited so that each was out of the firing line of the next.

'We'll wait for him to make a move.'

'What if he's only a local out for a stroll?'

'No one is local here. It's deserted.'

They waited. If nothing else, they were out of the rain, but their damp clothes clung coldly to their skin.

'I heard something,' Diamond muttered. 'He's on the move again. God, he's right here.'

The hooded man passed so close to the slit they were looking through that all they could see of him were the lower part of the windcheater and the top half of a pair of waterproof trousers. He was rounding the front of their pillbox, about to come in.

The two detectives stood flat to the wall each side.

They heard the scrape of boots on the steps.

The instant he entered, each grabbed an arm. He went rigid and the hood slipped from his head.

'You?'

Their own man, Paul Gilbert.

Explanations were exchanged. On Gilbert's side, he said as investigating officer he'd felt he had a duty come to the site and see how the SOCOs were faring. They'd wanted to get on with their work, so he'd decided to walk the perimeter looking into each pillbox in case the body was hidden there. All he'd found was the skeleton of a sheep along the north side.

'You've been right round?'

'There are two or three more to go, guv.'

Diamond was touched by Gilbert's devotion to the task. Some tact was wanted here. 'You're doing a fine job. And you had the sense to dress for the weather, which is more than we did. We're not taking over. It's still your case, but you can't do everything alone.'

'That's for sure. Is the tramp in custody?'

'We had to let him go, but we're keeping tabs on him. He likes the cells at Keynsham and he'll be back there tonight. We took a DNA sample and sent it to the lab.'

'You don't think he'll do a runner?'

'No, he'll stick around Bath as long as he can. We thought he'd left earlier, but it was a false alarm.'

'Is he playing games with us?'

'You mean is he a killer? I'm not sure. He was in the right place at the right time, but the motive is uncertain. Jean Sharp is looking through his record to see if there's any history between the two men.'

'She'll need to go through the rigger's record as well. All Gripmasters could tell me is that Jake Nicol was new on their books. He came from London with good references and the riggers' certificate, whatever that is.'

Halliwell spoke. 'I doubt whether Will Legat roams as far as London. I got the impression he prefers the open countryside.'

'In his former life he worked in the city,' Gilbert said. 'He told me he had a business of his own that went bust after the collapse of Lehman Brothers. I don't think he was joking.'

'Useful,' Diamond said. 'It joins some dots. I kept wondering about his background.'

'But if we can't find a body, we won't have much of a case. It must be up here somewhere. He didn't have the means to move it far.'

'The pram,' Halliwell reminded him.

'I meant far away from the airfield,' Gilbert said. 'I haven't explored all of it yet, but I've done the obvious places. Can we bring some bobbies up here and carry out a bigger search?'

Diamond thought of Georgina and shook his head. 'Sorry. The way forward is to get tougher with Legat, give him a real grilling and find out if there's any history with Jake Nicol. I don't believe he'd murder a man just to rob him of his belt.'

'I'm with you there, guv. And even if he did, he'd be an idiot to start wearing it straight after, knowing it was blood-stained. He'd hide it somewhere until the fuss died down. Maybe come back for it next year.'

'It's up to you as IO,' Diamond told Gilbert. 'Do you want another go at him tomorrow morning, or would you rather one of us had a try?'

'With me in attendance? Sounds good. He might act differently with you across the desk.'

'And we'll get forensics to test the pram for blood residue.'

The evidence was stacking up. More results came in from the lab late in the afternoon, more than enough to blast holes in Legat's story when he faced a formal interview.

'Where will you do it, guv?' Paul Gilbert asked.

'His residence. He seems to have found one at Keynsham.'

By evening, the seriousness of what he had done caught up with Diamond. Georgina was sure to hear about the van called out to Claverton Down, the scene-of-crime unit at work on the airfield and the tramp and his dog in the custody cell. She'd be livid. He'd ignored her instruction to drop all interest in the jinx story, go into virtual lockdown and get the team applying for refresher courses. If his future as a police officer had looked doubtful then, it was in free fall now.

Paloma was out tonight, giving a talk at the Museum of Costume. Afterwards, the committee members would take her for a drink and supper and she wouldn't get back until late. But it wasn't being alone that got to him. It was the throbbing open wound of impending retirement. Stupidly, he'd behaved as if it wasn't there.

Georgina had not been joking. She didn't do humour. She wanted him out. No doubt she was under instructions from headquarters to let him go, or whatever euphemism they used. She wouldn't have protested that he was her top detective and had been for the whole of her time as Assistant Chief Constable. She wouldn't have trumpeted his successes. She only ever took note of his so-called failings – ignoring the budget, running up expense claims, failure to delegate, poor record-keeping, incompetence with technology, unwillingness to involve her in decision-making and open contempt for modern policing. Only the year before, she had tried to ambush him by setting up an official reprimand from the Chief Constable for running up unauthorised overtime, only for it to collapse around her ears when Diamond had appeared on crutches and wearing a surgical boot, the result of an accident underground sustained in the course of duty.

He felt pressure against his right leg.

Raffles.

He leaned down, curled a hand under the furry chest and lifted his veteran cat up to the seat of the sofa. The arthritic legs couldn't manage the leap these days and Paloma wouldn't welcome scuffed leather from repeated attempts to climb up.

Raffles sniffed the seat, made a slow circle and lowered himself into a resting position, making sure his back pressed against Diamond's thigh, the feline way of showing support. Cats can sense troubled emotion in their owners, Diamond was sure. He needed comforting and his pet, Steph's pet, was making an effort to supply it.

'Thanks, old friend. Retirement wouldn't bother you one bit. You're the master of it.'

Raffles purred – or was it snoring?

10

Next morning they didn't literally visit Legat in the cell. That would have been impractical while his dog was taking up three-quarters of the floor.

'This isn't civilised,' the gentleman of the road complained when he was led into the interview room. 'We've barely finished breakfast. I hope this won't be long. Caesar doesn't take kindly to being left alone.'

Diamond was starting to get the measure of the man. If you weren't careful, he dominated every exchange by force of personality. 'We can get through in no time if you speak the truth. A lot of what you told me yesterday was bollocks.'

'Unkind,' Legat said, unfazed, 'not to say distasteful. What exactly is the problem?'

'The problem, Will, is that we sent the belt and your combat trousers to be forensically tested and they tell a different story to yours. I told you yesterday the belt was heavily bloodstained and you told me you didn't notice any staining.'

'Which is the truth.'

'The latest tests found staining on your trousers as well. The same blood, now verified as that of the missing rigger, Jake Nicol.'

'Whose name, I told you, means nothing to me.'

'We'll come to that. The point is that if some of the

blood ended up on your clothes, it was still damp. You must have been present at the scene when Nicol was attacked. You were selective with the truth.'

Legat said after a pause, 'How is your memory, officer? Do you need to write things down, or is it stored in a cloud? I was told about clouds by someone more conversant than I am with the technology. Personally, I prefer to rely on my own grey matter.'

Diamond took that as a crude attempt to divert him. 'I thought you wanted to keep this brief.'

'Then let me remind you that I found the belt in the dark when I almost tripped over it. I recall your asking me if it was damp to the touch and I didn't deny it. I explained that everything was damp because I was standing in a quagmire.'

'Quagmire or bloodbath?'

'I'm willing to bet my house – or would if I owned one – on my confidence that your forensic testers found more mud on my clothes than blood. What am I supposed to have done – killed the rigger because I took a fancy to his belt?'

'You were carrying a jackknife.'

'The knife. Now I see where you're going with this. Did you test it for blood?'

'We believe you washed it clean.'

'Basic hygiene, isn't it? In my situation, a knife is a much-used tool. I need it to break up cardboard and make bedding, clean mud and other substances off my boots—'

'We get that.'

He was unstoppable. '—split firewood and remove the splinters from my fingers, cut string to the required length, put wounded gamebirds out of their misery and skin them for supper. And when I eat, I prefer not to use my fingers.

I have a fork and I use the knife with it. If you were me, wouldn't you insist on a clean blade at mealtimes?'

Far from being shaken by the questioning, Legat was enjoying the verbal sparring, giving as good as he got. He carried a knife that could be a murder weapon, yet he'd justified himself with sheer oratory, this harangue about the life of a tramp.

As if he sensed he'd softened the opposition, he went on the offensive. 'Was the man attacked with a knife?'

'We don't know for certain,' Diamond was forced to admit.

'You don't know?'

'We haven't found his body. Where is it, Will?'

The voice shrilled in protest. 'How would I know? I haven't seen it.'

'Did you bury him?'

'This is absurd. It's a jackknife, not a garden spade.'

'How long were you alone at the airfield before Detective Constable Gilbert found you? Several days? Ample time to dispose of a body.'

'More than absurd. Slanderous. I think I shall insist on legal aid. I know what you policemen are like, pinning crimes on innocent men.'

Diamond ignored the slur. He didn't want a solicitor getting in on the act so he switched to a less contentious line of questioning. 'Jake Nicol was living in Fairfield. Do you know that part of Bath?'

'I'm not a local. I was brought up in suburban London.'

'But you come here each summer.'

'The parts of town I know are the backs of supermarkets where they dump their unsold products. Millions of tons of good food in this country goes into crushers and ends up as landfill, but first it's dumped in bins and skips behind shops and it can be retrieved if you know how. We travellers

108

call it skipping. The hoboes in America have a more colourful expression: dumpster-diving.'

'We don't need to know this. I'm simply trying to discover if you visit Fairfield.'

'The short answer is no. Can I go now?'

'You had a business in London, you told DC Gilbert. Jake Nicol worked there before he got the job here.'

'"There", as you put it, is a metropolis of nine million residents and countless visitors.'

'Do you go back at all?'

'Not since I quit the place. I'm travelling all the time, but I never head in the London direction. Never will. West country people are far more tolerant towards wayfarers like me.'

'Was Nicol unpleasant to you? Was there an argument?'

'How many times do I have to tell you I had nothing to do with the man? We didn't speak.'

Gilbert chipped in. 'You told me you watched the riggers packing up. Did you see him leave?'

Will Legat pondered the question, drummed his fingertips on the desk and said, 'No comment.'

'What?' Diamond doubted his own hearing. He turned to look at Gilbert, who was equally surprised.

'I said, "No comment."'

'You're not under caution. You can't incriminate yourself, if that's what bothers you.'

He got no reply. The switch to non-cooperation was wholly out of character.

'What's the problem here?' Diamond asked after several more seconds. 'You already admitted you watched them leave before you moved in. Did you witness something you don't wish to speak about?' He realised as he completed the question that he'd laid himself open again.

109

'No comment.'

'This is getting serious, Will. If you know something and refuse to speak about it, you could force me to get more formal. I may need to caution you after all.'

'And we both know how the caution goes: "You have the right to remain silent." Comforting words to a man in this situation.' Legat stifled a yawn. 'Can I go back to the cell, then?'

Diamond was tempted to answer with a 'no comment' of his own. Instead, he pushed his chair back and stood up. 'All right. We'll end it there. I'll call the custody sergeant.'

Legat looked suspicious, as if he hadn't really expected the interview to stop so abruptly.

Outside the building, Gilbert, too, expressed surprise. 'What are you up to now, guv?'

'Couldn't you see it was going nowhere?' Diamond said. 'He's working his ticket. He wants more nights in that cell. We could hold him on a minor charge like being in possession, but that would be playing his game.'

'Do you still think he's our suspect?'

'He's all we've got. The blood on his clothes is serious. We've only got his word that he didn't know Jake Nicol and didn't go anywhere near him.'

'The blood could have come off the belt.'

'Almost certainly. Even if he didn't carry out the killing, he knows how it was done and where the body went.'

'Could more than one person be involved?'

'We won't rule it out.' Even as the words came out, he remembered who was nominally running the case. 'Or, rather, you, as investigating officer, won't want to rule it out. The choice is yours, Paul, but my inclination is to get all the evidence we can, see if the SOCOs find anything and meanwhile question more of the TV people. You may need help. I'm available and so are some of the others.'

'What should we do about Will?'

'Let him stew in uncertainty. He thought he was going to be held and now he isn't. He's your witness, but I suggest you turf him out of the cell and see what his next move is.'

'Let him go?' This clearly wasn't in Gilbert's plans.

'He won't get far with the dog and the pram.'

'Was the knife really clean of blood?'

'No. You can't clean a jackknife with water alone, not enough to pass a forensic test. Bits of muck get lodged inside where the blade folds.'

'So they found some?'

'Blood residue.' He paused. 'Unfortunately . . .' He left Gilbert to complete the line.

'. . . it wasn't human?'

'Left over from one of his meals.'

11

Before they left Keynsham police station, Gilbert checked his phone and found a text from Ingeborg asking him to tell the boss to call her urgently. When told, Diamond said, 'Why didn't she text *me*?' Like most of us, he had a large blind spot about his own faults.

Gilbert had the good sense to shake his head as if he had never noticed that Diamond treated his phone as if it was a used tissue he was keeping in his pocket until he passed the next litterbin.

He took the alien object out and stared at it. The urgency from Inge, he guessed with a sinking heart, was because Georgina was on the attack with all guns blazing.

A small amount of battery strength remained. 'Is that you, Inge?'

'Guv, where are you – still at Keynsham?'

'What's the fuss about?'

Her answer wasn't what he expected. 'Remember when we interviewed Sabine and you asked about the actor who was originally cast as Swift?'

'Trixie Playfair?'

'I've managed to trace her and she's not at all keen to talk to us, which makes me think she's got something to hide. If I pin her down, would you like to be in on the action?'

She made it sound like an assault, but he knew what she meant and he trusted Ingeborg's judgement. If Trixie was being evasive, all the more reason to see her – and sucks to Georgina. 'Where is she, then?'

'Not far from where you are. You *did* say you're still at Keynsham?'

'I didn't, but I am.'

'Trixie is now a drama teacher in a private school for girls called Chimneys in Compton Dando. That's only two miles south of where you are. I can meet you there in half an hour.'

'Have you made an appointment?'

'I sent a text and she doesn't want to see us, which is why I suggest we turn up unannounced.'

'Good thinking.'

Leaving Gilbert to eject Will Legat from custody and get him back on the road, he walked off to find his car.

No need to ask how Chimneys got its name. They were visible against the sky from a long way off, ornamented red-brick pillars three metres high in clusters of three capped with clay pots. The eighteenth-century mansion had been in use as a private school since the 1980s, a venture that had prospered because an extension twice the size had been added at the back in more recent times. How such an ugly thing had met the building regulations was a mystery.

Ingeborg's yellow Ka was already on the drive. She got out. 'How would you like to play this, guv?'

'The office first. I can't march into a girls' school unannounced.' He didn't mind marching into most places, but there were limits.

'Before we go in,' Ingeborg said, 'there's something I should tell you.'

'I should be wearing a suit and tie?' For the first time in years, he was wearing casual clothes for work, or what he took to be casual: open-neck shirt, sports jacket, corduroy trousers and brown brogues. His thinking was that a new image might persuade Georgina he could move with the times. Just his luck that he was now about to visit an upmarket girls' school.

She smiled. 'Not at all. You're fine.' She hesitated. 'Has Paloma seen the new ensemble?'

'Not yet. It's not actually new. I've had it in the wardrobe for a while. Paloma will suggest I buy a whole new outfit.'

'She's usually right. She knows about clothes.'

'Historic clothes.'

She bit back the comment she could have made. 'I was about to say I called my contact at the *Post* and asked about the mysterious caller.'

He was still thinking about Georgina.

She said, 'You wanted to know if the voice was male or female.'

'Got you. Any luck with it?'

'She checked with the switchboard and phoned back this morning. Definitely a woman.'

'Good work, Inge. That narrows it down.'

The school secretary, a friendly middle-aged woman dressed in a Take That T-shirt and jeans and wearing a nametag that said *Sheelagh*, seemed untroubled when Diamond explained that they were police officers needing assistance about an ongoing inquiry. In fact, her eyes glinted with what looked like relish when Miss Playfair was named. She studied her computer screen. 'She's finishing off a year-twelve session in the drama studio. Does she know you're coming?'

'We texted her.'

The glint became a gleam. 'If you step out, you'll catch her before she goes to lunch. The studio is at the far end of the annexe. As far as you can along the corridor and you'll see it in front of you.'

'Did you get the impression I did?' Diamond asked Ingeborg as they made their way past a row of classroom doors.

'That Trixie isn't the flavour of the month?'

'You did.'

The drama studio was circular and glass-sided, giving a view of the music and movement session for about fifteen senior girls in black leotards led by a woman in a white spandex suit. A red headband kept the sweat from her eyes and allowed her blonde ponytail to swing freely. She would have made a striking Caitlin Swift.

'Seems confident,' Diamond said.

'Teachers need to be.'

'Difficult to square with what we've heard about her.'

'She's in charge here,' Ingeborg said. 'Altogether different from a TV studio where she's being directed.'

But Diamond was already asking himself whether Trixie's reason for quitting *Swift* had been something other than the TV equivalent of stage fright.

'Are we going in?' Ingeborg asked.

He looked through the glass again at all those leggy schoolgirls. 'Better wait.'

She smiled faintly and didn't comment.

Only after the session ended and the last girl had disappeared through a door on the left did they enter.

Trixie must have heard the door open, yet she didn't turn her head. She hadn't lost her dramatic timing. She removed the headband and freed the hair. It fell lightly against her neck and shoulders as if it had just been brushed. 'Yes?'

'I sent a text earlier,' Ingeborg said. 'DI Smith and DS Diamond of Bath Police.'

Trixie still chose not to look at them. As if reading from an autocue, she said, 'Didn't you get my reply? It's not convenient. I'm about to shower. You have no right to be here.'

'We checked in at the office and were sent here,' Diamond said to the back of her head. 'You're not in trouble, Miss Playfair. We're looking into events connected with the TV company that makes *Swift*. You auditioned for the part and got it.'

'That's over and done with,' she said. 'Years ago. I didn't go through with it.'

'And we need to know why,' Ingeborg said. 'I don't know if you've seen the article in the *Post*.'

'Nothing to do with me.'

'But you're in it.'

'I don't think so.'

'They don't print your name, but the jinx is supposed to have started with the actor originally cast as Swift having to be replaced. Unless we're mistaken, that's you.'

Finally, she turned her head. 'Piss off, will you?'

Diamond blinked. Sane people don't speak to the police like that.

The hostility contrasted with Sabine's eagerness to please when she had been interviewed. Sabine with the fearsome reputation had disarmed them with charm. Trixie, supposedly a victim of nerves, was a spitting cobra.

'Was there pressure from anyone else for you to pull out?'

'Was I fired? No.'

'I don't mean that. I'm talking about heavy persuasion.'

She shook her head. 'I made my own decision.'

'You walked away from a part most actors would give an arm and a leg to get?'

'So?'

'You must have known the damage you were doing your reputation. No casting director would want to use you in a main role after that.'

'You don't have to tell me. I knew what I was doing. I didn't just quit the show, I finished with professional acting.'

'Why?'

She gave a sigh that was more impatient than regretful. 'You're going to push and push, aren't you?'

'I have to. We heard you had a crisis of confidence.'

'There's no more to be said, then.'

'It's true, is it?'

'Broadly.'

Sensing an opening, he said, 'But not the whole truth?'

She was silent for a tense interval before saying, 'I don't speak about it because most people aren't capable of understanding.'

He waited through another period of non-communication.

Finally, she said, 'It wasn't stage fright. I can't tell you how many times I've been told about brave souls like Stephen Fry and Michael Gambon who battled through stage fright. Even Laurence Olivier. But I wasn't facing an audience. I was rehearsing in a TV studio, for Christ's sake, in front of a camera, a director and a crew and I couldn't hack it. Is that what you want to hear me say?'

'All we want, Trixie, is the truth of what happened.'

'And I'm giving it to you. Until you've experienced it, you can't know the terror I felt. It came from nowhere, like a computer crashing. One day I was in command, the next I was shot to pieces.'

'A stress attack?'

'Call it what you like. It felt like an out-of-body experience. I watched myself trying to be the character I was playing and I knew I couldn't do it. Heard myself speaking the lines and that's fatal. I was never going to make it. To succeed as an actor, you have to become whoever you're trying to play. If you don't believe, you're screwed.'

Ingeborg said, 'You were gutsy to admit it.'

'It was screamingly obvious.'

'But not to everyone else. Who did you tell?'

'My agent, obviously.'

'Who is that?'

'Moore and Moore Talent.' She glared at them, daring them to laugh.

They didn't.

'It's a company. Several different people did their best to get me back on track, but no amount of persuasion was going to work.'

'Were they sympathetic?' Diamond said.

'No.' She immediately corrected herself. 'At first they were and then, when they realised I wasn't going to budge, it was more like pull yourself together, woman, because we all stand to lose a fortune.'

'Unhelpful.'

'Nothing was going to help.'

'So the agents informed the TV people?'

'They did and had a lot of trouble convincing them. I went in to see the producer later.' She paused. 'She was lovely. Very understanding.'

'Mary Wroxeter?'

She nodded, her expression softening at the mention of the name.

'Had you given Mary any hint of your decision?'

'She'd been there when I flipped. She understood how devastating it was. She had amazing empathy.'

'Did she try and talk you round?'

'When I went to see her? No. She knew it was over. She listened and believed. At the end, she hugged me.'

For all the aggro she'd shown, her account had come across as genuine. The decision to quit had been her own. Even at this distance in time, Diamond could feel her humiliation. And although he'd never met Mary Wroxeter, he could picture her giving comfort. 'Did you have to return a lot of money?'

'A settlement was agreed.'

'I expect the lawyers came out the winners.'

'Tell me about it!'

'No regrets?'

'I'd be stupid if I didn't wonder sometimes how things might have turned out. None of us knew the show would win awards and run for years. Now can I get my shower?'

'Sabine, the actor who replaced you—' Ingeborg started to say.

'I don't give a toss about Sabine.' But the eyes said otherwise. The name was a needle plunged into her flesh.

'We've spoken to her,' Diamond said to wind her up, quick to pick up on the reaction. 'We found her easy to get on with. She's in a good place, one of the highest earners on TV. She can name her terms. Have you met her since you left?'

'Why would I? I don't need favours from her.'

'I expect you watch the show.'

'Hardly ever. I soon got tired of it. When Mary died, all the originality died with her.'

'Do you keep up with any of the others?'

She flared up again. 'What's this about? Are you trying

to suggest I had something to do with all the jinx stuff?'

Diamond was there to ask questions, not answer them. 'Did you make friends with any of the cast or crew?'

'I wasn't there long enough to know anyone properly. And now I really do have to go. I've got another class in under an hour and I won't get a lunchbreak.'

Before they left he insisted on calling at the office again. Sheelagh, the school secretary with the enquiring mind, greeted them like old friends. 'You found her? How did it go?'

'We got all we needed,' he told her, which wasn't quite true. In his job, you never got all you needed. 'How does madam fit in here?' A mischievous question that made Ingeborg look away in embarrassment.

'She doesn't even try. She's got her own private hideaway in that gorgeous studio. Nice if you can get it. Did you see her changing room?'

'We weren't invited in. We spoke in the dance area.'

'Typical. Hardly anyone has seen inside. She's got it all on tap. Coffee-maker, fridge, washing machine, TV and sofa-bed, would you believe? It wouldn't surprise me if there's booze as well.'

'So, Sheelagh, what does she get up to?'

'That's anyone's guess.'

'Are there men on the staff?'

'Not enough.' She laughed. 'No, I'm joking. To be fair, I don't think there's anything like that. She lives with a guy we've seen a couple of times when he came to pick her up because the weather was really bad and she couldn't cycle home. They seem to hit it off. But she doesn't mix with the rest of us and people can easily take that personally.'

'Is she popular with the students?'

120

'They don't mind her. She puts in the work with them. Did you get what you came for?'

'You asked me that already.' He wasn't interested in fuelling the school gossip machine. He was ready to leave.

12

He would have preferred taking the ride back to Concorde House as Ingeborg's passenger and hearing her thoughts, but that would have left his own car standing on the Chimneys drive. Life was never tidy for Peter Diamond.

Most of the team were at their desks when he arrived, so he presided over a 'catch-up session', as he called it, insisting they came from behind their screens and sat in a circle at the far end of the room like kids in school. So be it. Nothing was more annoying than fingers working phones and keyboards while he wanted attention. 'Between us, we've covered quite a bit of the so-called jinx story. What's your verdict? Does it stack up?'

They were slow to respond. He suspected some were distracted by his new look. They'd have to learn to live with it.

'Too soon to say,' John Leaman said eventually. He was uncomfortable with unproved opinions.

'John's right,' Ingeborg said. 'None of us have got the full picture.'

Diamond had been thinking about the full picture more than he was ready to admit. 'For me, it comes down to this: it makes a good newspaper story if you believe in bad luck, and even if you don't, other people's troubles make interesting reading. Many, if not most, of the incidents seem to have been accidents or acts of God. Stuff happens, as that American statesman famously said about the Iraq war.'

'He was talking about the looting of the museum in Baghdad, not the war,' Leaman said.

'Doesn't matter, John. The phrase stuck.'

'And papers always print the bad news,' Keith Halliwell said. 'Good news stories don't interest people.'

'Which is why a jinx makes good reading,' Diamond said. 'This morning Inge and I met the woman originally chosen for the plum part of Caitlin Swift, the one who took fright and pulled out. I'm satisfied she wasn't under orders from anyone else. She insists she acted alone. Her quitting was a setback for the show, so it ticks the jinx box, but I don't think we need to dig deeper. She's given up TV work now.'

'Is she bitter about it?' Keith Halliwell asked.

'Bitter with herself, but she doesn't blame anyone on the show. Am I right, Inge?'

Ingeborg said, 'That's how I saw it, guv.'

'She was treated kindly by the producer, Mary Wroxeter, and there was some kind of settlement. They filled the gap with another actor they'd auditioned before who happened to be Sabine San Sebastian. The show became a hit and Trixie Playfair was soon forgotten.'

'No actor wants that,' Halliwell said.

'I just told you she stopped being an actor. She's a school-teacher now. It's a new way of life.' Concern crept up Diamond's spine as he spoke the words. He'd soon be out of a job himself.

Halliwell didn't want to leave it. 'She must have hated what happened.'

'Of course. It was a personal failure, but she's put that

behind her, as you do. I don't see her wanting to make trouble for the show.'

'I'm only saying she almost certainly carries the scars. You can never tell how big a hurt it is.' Halliwell carried scars of his own that no one but Diamond knew about.

'True, Keith, but it happened years ago. The *Post* must have been hard-pressed to dust that off and use it.' Before Halliwell could say more, Diamond continued without pause, 'The next thing to go wrong was the fire in the van while they were filming the pilot episode. It could well have been started deliberately. Some expensive sound equipment was lost and one of the engineers got burnt trying to rescue items.'

'Arson?' John Leaman said.

'Arson can't be ruled out.'

'Fire investigators usually discover how fires start.'

'Yes, and the insurance company produced a report that I've seen. The seat of the fire was literally a seat in the van – the passenger seat. There's a lot of waiting about at a TV shoot and several sound engineers used the cab between takes. They all denied smoking, but a cigarette butt was given as the likeliest cause.'

'Accidental, then,' Leaman said, more for his own satisfaction than anyone else's.

'What did the insurers say?' Paul Gilbert asked.

'They agreed it wasn't deliberate.'

'Did they pay up?'

'They found a clause in the policy obliging the company to take reasonable precautions. Allowing people to smoke in the front seats was held to be unreasonable. After months of arguing, some kind of payment was made, but it didn't cover the legal costs, let alone the costs of the fire. Was this the jinx? You can just about argue that it was.'

'The guy who was burnt,' Gilbert said. 'Was he one of the smokers?'

'I've no idea.'

'If he thought he caused the fire, he may have risked his life to keep the damage to a minimum.'

'Speculation,' Ingeborg said.

'It's all speculation until we nail someone.'

Diamond knew the tensions in the team and didn't want anyone feeling inhibited from speaking, but the fire investigation had been thorough and he couldn't see any value in probing more. He moved on. 'Next up, two stuntmen were injured during the first season. They were in a rooftop chase and they both fell and broke limbs. I haven't looked into this one, but I suspect it was a genuine accident.'

Paul Gilbert felt his voice needed to be heard. He was still the IO. '*Swift* is a high-action show and there are going to be accidents to stunt people. This was serious, so I guess it got reported in the media, but I doubt if it was down to sabotage.'

Leaman said, 'You can't say. None of us can say.' He could always be relied on to expose loose reasoning.

'Which is why I'd like you to follow up on it, John,' Diamond said. 'It shouldn't be difficult to trace the two guys. If there was the slightest suggestion of dodgy goings-on, they'll know.'

Leaman had walked into that.

'So we come to season three, and incident number four in the *Post* article, a mystery we can't ignore because it's still unsolved. The disappearance of Dave Tudor. He was an experienced assistant producer, Mary Wroxeter's main support. He didn't show up for work one day and there was no phone call, text, nothing. He's not been seen since.'

'What do we know about him?' Halliwell asked. 'Was he really up to the job?'

'I heard from more than one source that he was a key man doing a tough job and doing it well. Mary often made last-minute changes that Tudor had to sell to the cast and crew. Don't ask me how, but he managed to stay popular. Even Sabine speaks well of him. The current producer, Greg Deans, said he doubted if Sabine even noticed him, but she remembered quite a lot. In fact, she's the only one who came up with a theory. She said he had a bit of a foreign accent and her suggestion was that he didn't have a work permit and someone threatened to blow his cover.'

'With a name like Dave Tudor?' Halliwell said. 'Come on.'

'So he upped and left, just like that?' Gilbert said. 'What do you think, guv?'

'I think he's dead.'

No one said anything for a few seconds.

'Is there something you haven't told us?'

'No. The way I see it, Tudor was obviously a bright guy doing a good job, really valuable to Mary. If there was a problem in his personal life, she'd have gone out of her way to support him. He'd have known this. There was no reason to quit.'

'He may have got a better offer. Maybe he's using another name and working for a rival company.'

'That's unlikely. TV is a small world. He'd have been recognised as soon as he set foot in another studio.'

'Where was he living when he disappeared?'

'Kipling Avenue, at Beechen Cliff. His possessions were still there, as if he meant to come back.'

'I don't get it. Why would anyone want to get rid of him if he was such a useful guy to have around?'

'That's the big question, Keith.'

'What was his life outside TV?'

'There wasn't any to speak of. He lived alone, used the local shops for his everyday needs, had the occasional pint in the local pub, but didn't socialise. He had a healthy bank balance and there were no unusual payments.'

'Who got the job after he left?'

'One of the other assistants, Candida Jones. She was the obvious replacement, with more experience than anyone else.'

Halliwell widened his eyes. 'If we're looking for a suspect . . .'

'You mean Candida killed him to get the job?' Diamond wasn't impressed. 'She wasn't wedded to her career. She left after a year to start a family.'

'Because she wasn't much good?' Halliwell said.

Ingeborg pounced. 'Do you mind? You wouldn't talk like that about a man.'

'Because when a man starts a family, he stays in the job.'

'If you want to argue that working women shouldn't be allowed maternity leave, you're a hundred years behind the times.'

'I said no such thing.'

'We all heard you. And now you're saying the reason she left was she wasn't much good.'

Diamond raised a calming hand. 'Okay, people. I started this hare when I said she wasn't wedded to the job. I was out of order. I had no grounds for saying so. I'm sorry. Can we get back to Dave Tudor? I got the impression he was a hard act to follow. Does that make more sense?'

'Barely,' Ingeborg said. 'It's another cliché.' She was really nettled by the sexist remarks. 'Is Candida still about?'

'The company probably keeps track, but memories

seem to have faded. Greg Deans remembered her because he used to work with her. He was the other production assistant.'

'Did he think she was incompetent?'

'He said nothing of the sort. Can we leave it, Inge?'

'Could Deans be in the frame?'

'As Tudor's killer? I can't see why. He was new in the job when the guy went missing. They barely knew each other and he was too inexperienced to have designs on Tudor's job. His turn as producer came later after Candida retired.'

'He had a quick rise to the top,' Ingeborg said. 'From rookie production assistant to boss of the entire show in how many years?'

'Three to four. He's certainly a smart operator, the obvious person to take charge after Mary died. I heard he can't match her for ideas, so he makes up for that by efficiency. But a murderer? He had a vested interest in success for the show and still does.'

Gilbert said, 'He steadied the ship after Candida left, a couple of years as Mary's assistant without anything going wrong.'

'It was no cakewalk,' Diamond said. 'He will have seen the signs she was drinking heavily. I haven't said this before, but we need to look at Mary's death and if there was anything iffy about it.'

He'd thrown a fizzing firecracker into the discussion. Startled looks and frowns were exchanged. Nothing like this had been suggested in the newspaper. If true, it had huge implications.

'We were told it was down to the alcohol,' Ingeborg said, trying to stay composed. 'She was far too popular and brilliant for anyone to want her dead.'

'It still has to be checked. In particular her final hours,

where she was and who was with her.' He turned to Jean Sharp. 'Would you take that on?' He knew the right person to ask to get every detail that was known.

'Of course, guv.'

'The coroner's office will have a file on the inquest.'

'Leave it with me.'

The suspicion that something was wrong about the sudden death of the brilliant woman everyone on the show was supposed to idolise had been germinating in Diamond's brain for days. They all owed their employment to her. She was one of those gifted people who turn an idea into an opportunity for a mass of others. Nobody had suggested the over-drinking that killed her was anything else but her own fatal flaw. You had to be a massive sceptic to throw doubt on the conclusion.

He was spreading the workload. Paul Gilbert was already covering Jake Nicol's disappearance; Diamond himself was investigating Dave Tudor; now John Leaman would probe the accident to the stuntmen, and Jean Sharp would look for anything unexplained about Mary Wroxeter's death. Daisy Summerfield's cardiac arrest had happened in Richmond and was being dealt with by the Met. He would remember to call them for an update.

'What's happening with the tramp?' Leaman asked.

'He wasn't charged with anything. He's free to wander the streets.'

'Is he in the clear?'

'I wouldn't say that. He wasn't entirely open with us and we're keeping an eye on him. He'll stay in Bath for some time now he's here.'

'How can we be sure of that? If the rigger is dead, as we believe he is, Will Legat is the main suspect, isn't he? Blood on his clothes. Possession of a weapon. He was found wearing the belt. Men have been sent down for life for less than that.'

'Agreed, John, but we're looking at two possible murders and maybe even a third.'

'Who is to say Legat wasn't around at the time Dave Tudor disappeared? He seems to visit here each summer.'

'True. But what did he do with the bodies?'

13

'My office immediately,' Georgina Dallymore said in a voice of doom. She had finally caught up with Diamond, collared him as he came out of the CID office and steered him upstairs.

She closed the door and said, 'Look at this.'

'I can see straight away, ma'am.'

But this wasn't the full frontal attack he'd expected.

That day's *Bristol Post* had been pushed in front of him, with the headline shouting the story:

POLICE PROBE SWIFT JINX

The jinx that is said to have plagued the TV series *Swift* – revealed exclusively last week by the *Bristol Post* – is now the subject of a police inquiry headed by Supt. Peter Diamond, Bath's top detective. As recently as June this year, veteran actress Daisy Summerfield, who played Viv Swift, Caitlin's gangster mother, suffered a fatal heart attack when she discovered a burglar in her bedroom. And now yet another setback has happened: Jacob Nicol, one of the rigging crew, has gone missing. These are the latest in a series of misfortunes going back to 2013, when *Swift* first came to our screens. They include the sudden death of Mary

Wroxeter, who devised and produced the award-winning show; a climbing accident in Snowdonia that caused permanent brain damage to Dan Burbage, known to viewers as Sergeant Monaghan; a fire in a sound engineers' van; stunts that went badly wrong and crew members disappearing. We understand that Supt. Diamond and his team take the jinx seriously enough to have interviewed key people in the show, including Sabine San Sebastian, who plays Caitlin Swift, and Greg Deans, the producer.

The disappearance of crew member Jake Nicol happened while he was on location at Charmy Down, the Second World War airfield, where a scene was being filmed earlier this week. He didn't return to his lodging and there is concern for his well-being. Scene-of-crime investigators have been examining the site and the ruined RAF buildings have been searched. 'We're worried that something terrible has happened to Jake,' a source told the *Post*. 'All these incidents can't be dismissed as bad luck. The police seem to think the jinx may turn out to be some malicious person with a grudge against the show.'

While reading, his mind was in overdrive. He'd fully expected Georgina to hit him with the measures he'd taken in open defiance of her instruction. Somehow, all that was dwarfed by this newspaper story. She was so wound up that she hadn't even noticed his fashion statement.

'So the horse has bolted,' he said. There was an opportunity here.

Georgina frowned. 'Meaning what?'

'Meaning we can't deny we took an interest in the jinx. The truth is out. Our reputation is on a knife edge.'

Ingeborg would have shouted, 'Clichés!' by now, but each one was making an impact on Georgina.

'I don't know how you have the nerve to talk to me about our reputation. You've put a stain on it forever, getting us caught up in this nonsense in the first place. I ordered you in no uncertain terms to have no more to do with it.'

'And how right you were, ma'am.'

For this, he got a sharp, suspicious look. Georgina was too wily to ask what he meant, so he pressed on. 'I called a team meeting and told them to book themselves on refresher courses, just as you said. We agreed to turn our backs on *Swift* and its problems.'

'It says here that you're heading a police inquiry.'

'Fake news, ma'am. There was only ever a detective constable keeping tabs on it. I'll call the editor directly and tell him his story is untrue. We're not interested in the wretched jinx.'

She shook her head with such force that her cheeks carried on quivering after she stopped. 'You can't say that. They'll accuse us of failing in our duties. They'll use it to attack us. This is a public relations disaster.'

'In that case, I won't call the editor.'

Georgina was in two minds. 'People reading the paper will expect us to investigate now.'

He nodded. 'Got to agree. And it's all over social media,' he said as if he constantly checked his phone.

'What do you suggest, then?'

'You'll find a way through, ma'am. You always do.'

This rare declaration of confidence caught Georgina off guard. It was double-edged, a challenge as well as a compliment.

She blinked several times and reddened. A strained silence followed while she faced this mountainous dilemma.

Finally she sighed and spread her hands, forced to put survival first. 'The only way out is to do what I least wanted, make a U-turn and put all our efforts into finding what's behind this so-called jinx.'

'Clever,' Diamond said as if the thought hadn't crossed his mind. 'So clever. A full-on investigation?'

'Regrettably.'

'No expense spared?'

'I didn't say that.'

'But I will need a budget for this.'

She snatched up the newspaper and tossed it at him. 'Get on with it, damn you.'

The team was jubilant, so full of it that they made Diamond nervous.

'Where shall we have the major incident room?' Leaman asked.

'Er – here will do.'

'Shall we give it a name?' Halliwell asked.

'Give what?'

'The operation, now it's out in the open. Operation Jinx?'

'The jinx is non-existent.'

Gilbert joined in. 'Showstopper?'

'I don't care for labels.'

Halliwell wouldn't let it rest. 'But you said Georgina wants the public to know we're doing something. Shouldn't we be setting the agenda, generating our own publicity?'

Ingeborg raised her hand and waved. 'I'm happy to be press officer, if that's what we want. Personally, I think "Showstopper" is great.'

By common consent, Operation Showstopper was launched.

With Ingeborg preparing a press release and Leaman

shifting furniture in the room across the corridor, Diamond was freed to do what he thought of as mending fences. He could see tell-tale lines of concern on Paul Gilbert's face. The young man was going to need reassurance that he still had a role to play. He took him to one side. 'You're firmly in charge of the Jake Nicol end of the inquiry. Have you notified the UK missing persons unit?'

'I saw to that, guv, and stressed there was real concern about his well-being.'

'That's for sure. Do you actually believe he's alive?'

Gilbert shook his head. 'You and I think the same way on this. But I haven't the first idea where the body is.'

'Did you complete your search of the airfield buildings?'

Gilbert nodded. 'It's a big area, but I'm satisfied I didn't miss anything.'

'Let's go over what we know. Nicol was last seen at the airfield when they packed up, right? Being a rigger, he was one of the last to leave.'

'And all the trucks were returned to Gripmasters at the end of the day, so it looks as if he was still alive at that stage – but the bloodstained belt was found in the mud where the trucks were parked.'

'What if he was killed there and the killer drove his truck to the depot?'

Gilbert gave a low whistle. 'That's smart, guv. He could carry the body in the back. Then, when he gets to Cold Ashton it's already dark and he's the only one in the car park so he transfers it to his own vehicle and drives off. He could dispose of it anywhere he wants.'

This scenario was already in Diamond's mind and had been for days. 'It's a possibility.'

'And if that's what happened,' Gilbert said in some excitement, 'the tramp isn't the killer. He can't be, because he doesn't have wheels – except the wheels of the pram, and he wouldn't get far with that.' His mind galloped on. 'It also eliminates Sabine. She doesn't drive.

'Mind you,' he went on – he was on a roll now, 'there's another possibility. She's a strong, fit woman. Has to be, to play the part. If she was the killer, she could have hoisted the body into the motorhome. Have you thought of that?'

Diamond smiled to himself and let the remark pass. 'It crossed my mind when I interviewed her. But there's a problem with it.'

'Oh?'

'She has a live-in driver called Chen. "Driver, hairdresser, cook and chiropodist", in her own words. Chen is extremely loyal and protective, but I'm doubtful whether Sabine would share a secret like that with her or anyone else.'

Having poured out all his thoughts, Gilbert was at a loss. He scratched his head.

Diamond prompted him. 'So what's next? Is there any more from the scene-of-crime lot?'

'Nothing helpful. The blood on the belt was the big discovery – and the fact that it matched Nicol's DNA. They were asked to check the interiors of every one of the trucks used for the Charmy Down shoot and there was no more blood evidence. It doesn't mean the body wasn't moved from there. The killer may have been careful.'

'Have you spoken to the other riggers?'

'They all swear they scarcely knew the guy. I'm still thinking Will Legat knows more than he told us. You asked Jean Sharp to look into his background and see if there was any contact in the past with Nicol.'

'Has she found anything?'

'No.'

'She's thorough.'

'I know. She said it didn't mean there wasn't some overlap. Just that it wasn't there in the written records.'

'Legat is a challenge,' Diamond said. 'He likes the sound of his own voice so much that if we let him witter on, there is a good chance he would tell us everything we want to know. That sudden switch to "no comment" when you and I questioned him at Keynsham came as a shock.'

'I can't remember what triggered the first "no comment".'

'It was when I reminded him he'd told us he'd watched the riggers loading the lorries at the end of the day. I asked if he'd seen Jake Nicol leave and he shut up like a clam.'

Gilbert was frowning. 'He didn't need to. His story was that he'd never met Nicol. If that's true, he had no way of knowing which one he was.'

A telling point. The DC was shaping up as a canny detective. 'Exactly. I'm wondering if he was on the point of saying something else and stopped himself just in time.'

'Like "I saw Jake Nicol drive off" – which would have been the giveaway. Was it a trick question, guv?'

Diamond said in all honesty, 'I can't pretend it was. I was treating him as a witness, trying to find out whether there were threats or violence.'

'But he saw it as a trap.'

'Apparently. And what does that tell us?'

'Either he lied about not knowing the guy, or he saw something he doesn't want to tell us, or' – Gilbert took in a sharp breath – 'he wasn't just a witness, but the killer.'

'That pretty well sums it up. And I need to look at him as the possible killer of Dave Tudor.'

'Should we pull him in again?'

'We must get more background on them both, but if you want another go at him, don't let me stop you.'

'I'll wait,' Gilbert said. 'I'll see what I can get from the other riggers. They're a cagey lot.'

The major incident room across the corridor was taking shape. John Leaman was in his element, making sure computers were active and desks labelled. Diamond noted his own at the far end with the sign *Senior Investigating Officer*. If he'd had delusions of grandeur he would have enjoyed seeing how the other desks were sized by status, from Office Manager (Halliwell) to one no bigger than a card table for the Exhibits Officer (one of the civilian staff).

'Quick work, John,' he told Leaman. 'Quick and faultless.'

Leaman beamed.

'Did you find time to check on the accident with the stuntmen?'

The sort of question you don't ask an obsessive compulsive. 'Didn't you see my written report? I put a copy in your in-tray. I know you don't always read emails.'

'I have a backlog of paperwork to get through,' Diamond admitted. 'Can you sum it up in words?'

'Now? I haven't got my notes.'

'The gist will do.'

The struggle in Leaman's brain was apparent in his troubled features. He liked to please and he was intensely loyal. 'Well, I can try.'

'Thanks. Appreciated.'

'I spoke to the man who coordinates stunts and he told me neither of the pair works on *Swift* now. They were doing a rooftop chase above the Roman Baths with the woman who doubles for the main actor. She landed safely, but the stuntmen got in a tangle with each other and fell about forty feet.'

Diamond winced, imagining it. He was squeamish about injuries of any sort.

'Luckily they fell in the water.'

'Ah.'

'Unluckily—'

'Don't tell me.'

'Unluckily one fell on top of the other and broke his own collarbone and three of his mate's ribs.'

Diamond's indrawn breath sounded like a burst from a blowtorch. 'Nasty.'

'But no one else was involved. It was their own fault.'

'You're sure?'

'It happened in full view of everyone. It's on film, in fact.'

'So can we cross them off the jinx list?'

'That's what I recommended in my report.' Leaman gave one of his penetrating stares. 'Will you still want to read it, guv?'

'I can't wait.'

'I can print a copy now if you want.'

'Don't bother. I know where to find it. You did well, John. I knew I could rely on you.'

He returned to the office, where Jean Sharp was waiting to speak to him. Another earnest and dedicated team member. 'You asked me to look into the circumstances of Mary Wroxeter's death, guv.'

'Have you got anywhere?'

'I'm not ready to report back in full.'

Why were his best researchers so touchy? he asked himself. 'That's all right. Was there anything dodgy?'

'It's too soon to say for sure.'

'But . . .?'

'According to the death certificate, she died of sudden

arrhythmic cardiac arrest and chronic alcohol abuse. I contacted the doctor who performed the post-mortem and he looked at his notes and said she must have been on a real bender because the BAC was right at the top of the scale.'

'You're losing me, Jean.'

'Blood alcohol concentration. They measure the number of grams of alcohol in each millilitre of blood. A chronic alcoholic can appear quite sober at a high BAC, but anything over two hundred fifty is dangerous and may lead to coma. Hers was above four hundred.'

'Phew! But you said cardiac arrest. I thought liver disease was the killer for alcoholics.'

'He told me that's a widespread belief, but recent research has shown that if you drink to excess, the heart is more vulnerable than the liver. In cases of sudden death, cardiovascular disease is the real killer. It's often misattributed to other causes.'

'I wonder what she was drinking.'

'She liked vodka. It was revealed at the inquest that her bin was filled with empties.'

'You've read the coroner's report?'

'Yes. A couple of witnesses spoke about her addiction.'

'Do you recall who they were?'

'One was Candida Jones, her former assistant, who knew her best. She said she'd never seen Mary incapable in working time, but if you caught a whiff of her breath, the sweet smell of alcohol was always there.'

'After work – was that when she did the heavy drinking?'

'People knew it wasn't wise to call her in the evenings.'

'So sad,' he said. 'A brilliant brain. Was any evidence given about the hours leading up to her death?'

'They'd had a long day filming at Bottle Yard studios and

finally got the scene done to Mary's satisfaction, so Mary and some of the actors and crew celebrated at a nearby pub, the Shield and Dagger.'

'And Candida – was she there?'

'She was.'

'She turned up at the pub that evening, to meet with old friends, I suppose. Mary had about four vodkas and appeared to be well in control of herself. In fact, she organised a taxi for one of the actors who was definitely slurring her words.'

'What time did they finish?'

'It wasn't late. Before nine.'

'She must have done the heavy drinking at home. Where did she live?'

'A house in Whitchurch village, not far from the studios.'

'Where's that in relation to the pub?'

'The Shield and Dagger is her local, only ten minutes away.'

'You've done well, finding all this. What else do you hope to discover?'

Jean Sharp looked a little embarrassed by the question. As the newest member of the team, had she exceeded her duties? 'I just wanted to know why on that particular night she drank so much. We know she was alcoholic. Everyone knew, but she was managing it quite well. She must have been, to make all the decisions she had to.'

'It's the nature of the condition,' Diamond said. 'They're not really in control. They drink so much of the stuff that their body adjusts and they appear to cope, but there's a tipping point.'

'But why that night?'

'We need to ask someone who was there.'

'The main witness at the inquest was Candida.'

His thoughts were racing ahead. 'Do we know if Mary went home alone?'

'Candida drove her. It wasn't far, but it was a kindness.'

'We'd better find Candida – unless you're ahead of me.'

She was.

'That's a bit of a problem, guv. The TV people seem to think she's still living in the area, but I haven't traced her through electoral registers or anything else I can think of.'

'Maybe she doesn't vote.'

'I tried hospital records because she left the job to start a family and she may have gone into the RUH to have the baby, but they won't divulge patient details. Day nurseries: same result.'

'Rightly so. You're up against the Data Protection Act.'

'She hasn't done anything unlawful as far as we know, so we can't claim we need the information as part of a criminal investigation.'

'Stymied.' He scratched his head. If Jean Sharp couldn't root out the information, was that the end of the matter? He'd come to rely on this young officer as a second-to-none researcher. But it occurred to him that all her discoveries were made using the internet or the phone. She rarely left the office. 'We must explore the grapevine.'

She looked uneasy at the prospect.

'Don't worry,' he said. 'I know who to ask. Ingeborg used to be a journalist. She's trained to know what's going on. If she's finished writing the press release, we'll ask her to put out some feelers. I'm not giving up on this.'

14

'Candida wasn't hiding from us, then,' Diamond said. 'Well done. I was confident you'd track her down.'

Ingeborg shrugged. 'There was nothing clever about it. Some of the Bottle Yard studios crowd meet up at the Shield and Dagger at the end of the day. I joined them last night and got chatting.'

'Jean will be pleased. Have you told her?'

'Not yet. I thought you'd want to know first.'

'I'm thinking of taking her with me. Get her out of the madhouse for a bit.'

'She'll enjoy that . . . I think.'

Jean Sharp was overawed when he asked. She'd not been on an assignment with the boss before.

'When I visit a female witness, I make a point of having a woman officer sitting beside me,' Diamond told her. 'Ingeborg usually gets the job, but I thought you'd like to be in on this one. Did you bring your car today?' He knew she often drove an expensive Volvo belonging to her husband.

'Yes, guv.'

'You can be chauffeur as well, then.'

Her eyes registered something close to panic.

'Don't worry. We'll pay for the fuel.'

The cost of petrol wasn't the problem. Diamond was

known on the team to be a nervous passenger. Fortunately it wouldn't be a long trip, just over ten miles, and, as he explained, he liked to be driven well within the speed limit.

'Do you know Saltford Marina?' he asked as they prepared to leave.

'Can't say I do, guv.'

'Me neither. Never heard of it. The car will know where to go, I hope.'

She set the GPS. 'It should do.'

'Then it will be up to you and me to find a narrowboat called *Deck the Halls*. Shouldn't be difficult. The marina isn't huge.' Wanting to appear more relaxed than he felt, he became chatty. '*Deck the Halls*. People choose strange names for boats. My guess is that the first owners were a Mr and Mrs Hall. You can drop your speed a little. We're in no hurry.'

Jean Sharp dealt with her own nerves by saying little and concentrating on her driving, her knuckles white from her grip on the steering wheel. Diamond's chat became a monologue.

'I used to think of Saltford as a boring stretch of the A4, but I've learned more about it over the years and now I know it was where Swift and Proud Productions had their office on some trading estate before they came to Bath. Did you see the road works sign? Temporary traffic lights. They seem to be slowing down. I don't know if Candida has been living in the canal boat ever since. There could be kids. And a partner. It's green. We can move again, but watch out for the idiot coming the other way. I've met them in my time. They think they can sneak through somehow and next thing they hit you head-on.'

Sharp got them to Saltford without screaming at him to

shut up and they parked outside the Riverside Inn right next to the marina. 'Good facilities,' Diamond said, meaning the pub, not the moorings or the marina buildings.

They found the gate, checked at the office and were told *Deck the Halls* had a long-term berth at one end.

The name was in large white letters on the prow of a long red boat. 'And someone is at home,' Diamond said. The door at the front end stood open. 'Better not cause alarm by stepping aboard.' The four windows along the side were at hip level. He tapped on the glass and immediately a toddler came out to the foredeck and looked up at them from under a mass of black curls. A confident kid considering his pants were round his ankles.

'Looks like we interrupted him,' Diamond said.

A voice from inside called out, 'What are you doing, Bart? Get back on your potty.'

Bart didn't seem to have heard. He continued to eye up the visitors.

'Better do as Mummy says,' Diamond tried to advise him.

A young woman of mixed race emerged, said, 'For God's sake,' grabbed the child and hoisted him inside. She reappeared a moment later and said, 'If it's religion or a survey, save your breath. I'm not interested.'

'It's neither, ma'am,' Diamond said. 'May we call you Candida?'

She glared. 'How do you know my name?'

'Our job,' he said. 'Avon and Somerset Police. Can we come aboard and speak in private?'

'I don't have much choice, do I? Mind your heads when you come in.'

The inside seemed poorly lit until their eyes adjusted. A narrow cabin with two swivel armchairs and a TV. Shelving along the sides loaded with books, crockery and soft toys making the best use of the elongated living space. Hooks on the shelves holding cups and mugs.

'Why don't you sit down?'

They trod carefully. The floor was strewn with toys. The end, against the bulkhead, was occupied by the child on his plastic throne, but not for long. As Diamond and Jean Sharp sat down, Bart stood up and said, 'Finished.'

Candida mouthed a swearword and said she needed to deal with him. She carried him and his pot into the cabin behind. She called out, 'Talk among yourselves. This won't take long.'

In a low voice, Diamond asked DC Sharp, 'Would you give up a good job in television for this?'

She said, 'It's hormonal, guv. The biology takes over.'

From nowhere, he felt a stab of grief. His beloved wife, Steph, had used almost the same words half a lifetime ago. She'd suffered miscarriages in her first unhappy marriage. Then she'd married him and got pregnant again, but with the same distressing result. Worse, she'd been informed by the doctors that a hysterectomy was essential. When she'd got over the operation, they'd thought about applying to adopt, but they were both in early middle age by then and it didn't seem fair to the child. He wouldn't have minded taking on a school-age child, but Steph had yearned for a baby to cuddle. The memory still had the power to hurt.

Candida returned carrying a large cushion which she dropped in front of them before sitting on it. 'He's in his cot, but he's not going to like it for long. I'd stick him in a playpen, but there isn't room in this floating matchbox. There isn't room for shit. Correction: there has to be room, as I well know from emptying the chemical loo every morning. What's this about?'

'Do you read the local paper?' Diamond asked her, realising as the words left his mouth that he sounded like a guest at the vicar's tea party.

'What would I want with a paper?'

'The *Bristol Post* ran a couple of articles recently about the *Swift* series.'

'The jinx?'

'So you *have* seen it?'

'I've seen Twitter. Bollocks, isn't it?'

This wasn't shaping up as a tea party of any sort.

'I've got to agree with you, except the jinx may be in human form, someone with a grudge.'

'Why come to me, then? I left three years ago, before most of those things happened.'

'Not all of them. You were there at the start when Trixie Playfair dropped out.'

'Trixie?' she said with a roll of her eyes. 'I'd forgotten about her. That wasn't bad for the show. It was the best thing that could have happened. Sabine took over and made the part her own. She's a star now.'

'Then there was the fire in the engineers' van.'

'Some idiot with a cigarette. No one was ever found out. I expect the guys covered for each other.'

'The accident to the stuntmen.'

'Accidents and stunt-people go hand-in-hand. That's why they employ them, to save the stars from hurting themselves. *Swift* is an action show. You're going to have injuries. Listen, I don't have time to go through all the shit that happened.'

'Let's talk about you, then. You became Mary Wroxeter's assistant producer.'

'I was the obvious choice when Dave Tudor left the show. I was a PA at the time.'

He remembered asking Sabine what the initials stood for and being told it was a dogsbody job.

Candida gave it a far better spin. 'Production assistant, helping the director and the producer in practical ways, like running errands, making notes at meetings and logging tapes. It's a support role, one up from being a runner. There were two of us, Greg and me.'

'Greg Deans?'

'Yes, Greg was the new boy, just appointed, so he couldn't step up. Mary was in a hole.'

'Tudor had gone missing for no apparent reason. Is that the inside story – the true one?'

She frowned. 'What are you getting at?'

'Was there bad blood between him and Mary?'

The suggestion seemed to surprise her. 'I never heard of any. Dave got on fine with everyone. He was Mary's fixer. She would come up with some genius idea and Dave made it happen without causing ructions and bringing the crew out on strike. He was a people person. We only appreciated how good he was after he left.'

Bart's voice piped up from the next cabin, calling for his mummy. She let out a sharp, short-tempered sigh.

'You've no clue as to why Dave Tudor quit?'

'If you find out, I'll be fascinated to know the reason. It must have been something in his private life.'

'Which he kept to himself?'

She shot him a hostile look. 'There's no crime in that.'

Diamond let the remark pass, not without noting the force behind it. This young woman had come out fighting. He was used to people being cowed by a visit from the police. He'd come here to get her take on Mary Wroxeter, but it was becoming clear that a bigger prize was here to be won, a secret she was desperate to hide by being defiant.

148

'We spoke to Sabine,' he said. 'She said there was a theory that Tudor was from abroad, living here illegally under another name, and got word that the Home Office was on his case.'

She shook her head. 'That old yarn doesn't fit the facts. I was the one Mary sent to Dave's flat in Kipling Avenue and it was like the *Mary Celeste*, everything lying about as if he'd gone out briefly and expected to return. Anyone moving out for good would have taken his reading glasses with him. His passport, for Christ's sake. No, it doesn't wash with me.'

Bart's shouts were getting more insistent.

'Was he really a foreigner?'

'There was the trace of an accent, but I thought he was Welsh. Tudor is a Welsh name, isn't it? He'd known Mary a long time. He first worked with her on a biopic she made about Paul Robeson and his links to Wales.'

'*Robeson and the Welsh.* Sabine told me about that, but I didn't know Tudor was involved. You said his passport was still at the flat.'

'On a side table with letters, unpaid bills, an A–Z street atlas and some photos.'

'Did you look at it?'

Another fierce glance. 'What kind of snitch do you take me for? I was there to find Dave, not nose into his private life.'

'What happened to his things after he disappeared?'

'No idea. You'd better ask his landlord.'

Bart had started screaming. Candida swore again, got up and went through to see to him.

Diamond asked DC Sharp, 'Did we check with the landlord?'

'He died three years ago, guv. The house was sold and

it's a private dwelling now. If Tudor's personal things had been kept that long, I expect the sellers disposed of them.'

He got up from the chair to look at the shelves opposite. Unlike Candida, he had no conscience about nosing through other people's things. Prying came with the job.

There wasn't much of interest except two unopened letters. She must have collected them from the marina office, where the postman would have delivered them. Both were addressed to a Mr Fergus Webster, presumably her partner, the father of Bart. One was handwritten and the other had the return address printed on the front: *Gripmasters, Hyde's Lane, Cold Ashton, SN14.*

Diamond's brain did a rapid reboot. Fergus Webster's name had come up when Paul Gilbert had reported on his visit to the film shoot at Pulteney Bridge.

'Hey-ho,' he said. 'Something here we didn't know.'

Jean Sharp got up to see. And at that precise moment, Candida returned with the child in her arms.

Diamond still had the letters in his hand.

Sharp had the quick wit to divert attention by stepping towards the mother and child. 'Will he come to me?'

Bart turned his face away in fright and threw his arms around his mother's neck. Candida gave a triumphant smile.

But the real triumph was Sharp's. Diamond had managed to return the letters to the shelf without being noticed. He took up the conversation again. 'It must be a trial bringing up a toddler in a houseboat.'

Candida gave him a withering look and turned to Sharp. 'Is he for real?'

'He's a bright kid,' Diamond carried on, unperturbed. 'He wanted to know why these strangers were talking to his mother.'

'You think so? I call it slave-driving. He never lets up.'

'Is he used to visitors?'

'You're the first I've seen all week. You lose all your friends when you live like this.'

'Don't you get to know the other boat owners?'

'I've got sweet FA in common with them. They don't have young families. They're either senile or students.'

'But you keep up with your television friends, I expect.'

She gave a hollow laugh. 'A card at Christmas if I'm lucky.'

'No more contact than that?'

'It's a closed book since Bart arrived. My life now is all about baby food and soiled nappies.'

He pressed her, leading her gently into a trap. 'So you're cut off completely from all that goes on at Bottle Yard studios?'

'Haven't I made that clear?'

'It will have moved on from when you were employed there. A new regime with different ways of working.'

'You tell *me*. I've no idea.'

'You were part of the Mary Wroxeter era. Was that tough, working for her?'

She was transparently pleased to be offered this escape route. 'It was no picnic, but I found it inspiring. Kept me on my toes. There was always plenty to do. Like I said, I was in at the deep end, but I was chuffed to bits, working so closely with Mary.'

'There was no suggestion that the work was all too much for you?'

She rose to the bait again. 'Who said that? Greg? He never liked me.'

'It's me speculating,' Diamond said. 'Everyone tells me she kept coming up with wonderful ideas that her assistants had the hard job of selling to the people who actually did the filming.'

'I knew that from the start. I didn't mind. I loved every minute of it.'

'But you didn't last long in the job.'

'Over a year.'

'You wanted to start a family. Is that right? It's a bit of a cliché when politicians leave their jobs to say that they want to spend more time with their families. That's why I'm asking.'

'Are you being sarcastic? I wasn't kicked out. Mary wanted me to stay, but I was pregnant and I wanted kids, right?' She parked Bart on the floor without much tenderness and used her foot to shift one of the toys towards him. 'I lost that baby at fifteen weeks, and I was upset and emotional, big time.' Her voice broke up as she remembered. 'I needed counselling. You have no idea what it's like.'

Diamond could have said something from personal experience, but he chose not to.

'I didn't ask for my job back,' she went on. 'I was in no state to work. It took longer than we expected before Bart came along. All I could think about was getting pregnant again.'

'I understand.' The mental pain still kicked in all these years after.

There was a pause. A long one. Neither seemed able to go on.

Jean Sharp cleared her throat and asked Diamond, 'Mind if I ask a couple of questions about Mary Wroxeter, guv?'

He turned to look at her, so caught up in the exchange with Candida that he'd quite forgotten he'd asked Sharp to investigate the producer's death from alcoholism. 'Go ahead.'

She rotated her chair to face Candida. 'Mary drank heavily, didn't she?'

'Not during the day.'

'We heard it was the drink that killed her.'

'That's what they said.'

'Don't you believe it?'

'I drove her back from the pub the evening she died.'

Sharp wasn't going to let that pass by. 'What were you doing there? I thought you'd left the show.'

'I had something important I wanted to tell Mary. I was pregnant again. I knew she would be in the pub with the others, so I joined them. There were some new faces, but most of them remembered me. I didn't drink with them. I was on tonic water. I'm not daft. I just wanted to tell Mary my good news.'

'Who else was there that night?'

'Dan, Daisy, Greg, Sabine and some others I didn't know. It was some kind of wrap, so they were there in numbers.'

'And you say you drove Mary home?'

'Quite early, about nine. I still had my own car in those days. She'd had no more than usual when she was with friends, three or four vodkas. She was pretty well sober. Alcoholics can drink a lot before it shows.'

'She bought a bottle of vodka to take home, didn't she?'

'You know a lot about it.'

'I'm trying to learn as much as I can. Did you go in with her when you got to the house?'

'No. She invited me, but I didn't. I knew it would be a late night if I did. I'd told her my news in the car. She gave me a hug and said how happy she was for me and told me to take care. Then she put her key in the door – straight in the keyhole, no problem – and let herself in. I never saw her again. Next day she was found dead.'

Sharp turned to Diamond and nodded. She had got all she wanted.

He took up the questioning again. 'And you have no curiosity about what goes on now? A closed book, you said?'

Candida swallowed hard.

Casually, he asked the killer question. 'Is Fergus Webster your partner?'

She stared back, ashen-faced.

'And did you and Fergus meet while you were both working on the *Swift* show? He's one of the riggers, isn't he – the key grip? He's still there. One of my team met him only the other day.'

She made a poor attempt to wriggle free. 'It's the twenty-first century. I can live with whoever I want.'

'Fine,' Diamond said. 'But why did you tell me you're cut off completely from all that goes on at Bottle Yard and your only contact is through Christmas cards when you're living with a guy who works on the show and knows everything that happens? You get a daily update over your evening meal.'

'We have more important things to talk about than tittle-tattle from his work.'

'I'm not on about the tittle-tattle. He will have told you the big things that went wrong, like Mary dying and the accident to Dan Burbage.'

'I don't know why you're making such a big deal out of this.'

'You do, Candida. You want us to believe you have no knowledge of what goes on, but you have a line into the show and you follow every twist and turn.'

She was still in denial. 'I haven't been near Bottle Yard since Bart was born and that's the truth. I don't even watch the show on TV.'

'Because it can't compare with the show you and Mary produced. You resent the success it has, still doing well in the ratings.'

'I'm allowed an opinion,' she said. 'It's crap now.'

'So you do watch it.'

154

She looked away at Jean Sharp and slid her eyes upwards as if to ask if her tiresome boss was always like this.

He said, 'I don't blame you for thinking it's gone downhill. Most drama series do when new people take over. Even I know that, and I don't watch anything much. I'm trying to tell what motivates you. You obviously feel strongly. I can imagine how tough it is being stuck in a boat like this for years on end with a small child and remembering the important job you had in television. I can understand you feeling resentful of the people still at work there earning good salaries, Fergus included.'

Her mouth tightened. 'Leave him out of this.'

The look that came with those five words said everything Diamond needed to know. This was not a happy family.

'Ah,' he said. 'I wondered. He has no part in what you did, right? You're getting back at him as well as the show?'

'I said lay off.'

'It's not a crime to talk to the press as long as what you tell them is true. You're the whistle-blower who told the *Post* about the jinx, aren't you?'

She thought about her response for a couple of seconds and said, 'You make me feel like the class sneak.'

It was as good as a yes. He felt the surge of elation that comes with a breakthrough. 'Why did you do it?'

'For devilment.'

The response rang true. He waited for her to expand on it.

'I'm stuck here, day in, day out and that lot are still milking Mary's success two years after she died.'

'You're jealous of them?'

'Wouldn't you be?'

'And it's a way of getting back at Fergus?'

A faint smile.

'You heard about the things that were going wrong and you guessed the local press would run the story? I hope you got paid.'

She shook her head. 'They don't know who I am. I called them on an old mobile we've never used.'

'Suggesting the show is jinxed?'

The smile returned and was wider.

'Did you use the word "jinx"?'

A nod. 'I wanted them to know what I was on about.'

'All they had to do was check your facts and see how they hung together.'

'Right.'

'And did you make a second call saying it was now a police investigation?'

'Yes.'

'You heard that from Fergus?'

'Everyone knows.'

'Everyone who works on the show, I grant you. Has it made you feel better, getting it out to the world?'

She picked her word with care. 'Marginally.'

'Does Fergus know you're the source?'

A gasp. 'God, no. Does he have to?'

He didn't answer that.

Back in Jean Sharp's car, he thanked her for covering for him by getting Candida's attention at a critical moment. 'I would have been caught with the letters in my hand.'

'You'd have thought of something to say, guv.'

'I don't know what.'

She started up and drove out of the car park. 'Anyway, recognising his name on the envelope was a game-changer.'

'Bit of luck, if I'm honest,' he said, not really meaning

it. Privately, he thought his sleuthing had been worthy of Sherlock Holmes.

'You made your luck by getting up to look at the things on the shelf,' she said.

'Nosiness.'

'Professionalism.'

He laughed. 'If ever I need a reference, I know who to ask. And I also want to thank you for chipping in with your questions about Mary Wroxeter. Nicely timed.'

'It seemed like a pause in the questioning.'

'I lost concentration, thrown by something she said.'

Sharp seemed worried about losing concentration herself, unready for this debrief while she was driving.

'What did you think of her answers?' he pressed her.

'They rang true, I thought.'

'You don't think she had any part in Dave Tudor's disappearance?'

She frowned, but whether this was in disbelief or irritation wasn't clear. 'Do you?'

'She's the only person we've met with an obvious motive for doing away with him.'

Sharp's eyes stood out as if she'd seen a charging rhino on the road ahead. 'Killing him, you mean? *Candida?*'

'She has to be a suspect. She took over his job. She gave the impression she was shoehorned into it, but she knew Mary would turn to her if Tudor left. It was a big step-up in her career and she idolised Mary.'

'Now you explain, I can see it.'

'Watch your speed. It's supposed to be thirty along here, not thirty-two.'

Her hands opened and then closed on the steering wheel.

'If she did murder him,' Diamond went on, 'it raises other questions.'

'Like how she did it?'

'That's not so important at this stage.'

'What she did with the body, then?'

'She told us she had a car. She could have driven it to the marina after dark. I was looking before we came away and there are possibilities. You could submerge a body there out of sight under a jetty. Even if it surfaced you wouldn't see it.'

'Is it worth making a search?'

'We'd need more evidence. She may provide it if she thinks we're on her case.'

Sharp drove in silence for a while, but she must have been thinking about what he'd said. 'If you're right, she was incredibly cool under questioning.'

'Yes,' he said. 'When she told us Tudor's flat was like the *Mary Celeste*, she didn't help her own cause. She could easily have said it looked as if he'd packed his things and cleared off.'

'I hadn't thought of that.'

'She's a class act if she's a killer. And if she's that good, she could have murdered Mary as well.'

The steering wobbled.

He tensed. 'Don't do that.'

'Sorry, guv. You keep surprising me.'

'We can pull over if you want.'

'I'll be okay.'

'Didn't the possibility of murder cross your mind when she admitted she was the last person to see Mary alive? She was almost challenging us to put her in the frame.'

'I missed that entirely. Why would she do that?'

'Because someone else was sure to mention it when we interviewed the others. I can see a cyclist up ahead. Give him a wide berth.'

Sharp was tight-lipped until they had passed the cyclist.

'I can't think why she would want to murder Mary. She had nothing but praise for her.'

'The same goes for everyone in the show as far as I can tell. It's our job to question anything that can't be proved. We've only got Candida's word that she didn't go inside the house with Mary.'

'And do what? Encourage Mary to drink herself to death?'

'An alcoholic doesn't need encouragement. We know the blood alcohol count was lethal. What was the phrase the pathologist used?'

'About being on a real bender?'

'Right. Why did she drink so much that particular night? Was Candida egging her on?'

'That's theoretically possible, I suppose.' She used the words grudgingly, out of respect. It was clear that Diamond's latest outrageous theory was way ahead of anything she was willing to believe.

'She'd just told Mary she was pregnant,' he said. 'What's an alcoholic's response going to be – "I'll drink to that"?'

Sharp didn't respond for a while.

They reached the turn at Keynsham before either of them spoke again, and it was Diamond. 'You want to know why she did it?'

'Try me, guv.'

'She's an angry woman, stuck at home. She couldn't hack it when she saw her old boss working happily with other people.'

'That's a new one,' Sharp said without enthusiasm. 'I hadn't thought of that.'

15

Even Peter Diamond would admit that Mary Wroxeter as a murder victim was a speculative theory. Clearly Jean Sharp wasn't persuaded. He didn't mind much. This was work in progress. It might come to nothing, but the possibility had to be explored.

The chilling new scenario was that three people from the show had been murdered. All his experience told him that if this was true, the killings must be linked. In serial murders, the first is the big one. The perpetrator crosses the red line and becomes a killer. When he or she has done the deed once, they feel less constrained about doing it again when new pressures come into play. The motive could be a matter of covering up for the first. Somebody became suspicious or saw something and had to be silenced. Was that how Mary Wroxeter sealed her fate?

In the privacy of his office, he put through a call to one of his pet hates, the sarcastic Bertram Sealy. There was no one else he could ask. All the other forensic pathologists he knew had retired or left the district.

'You?' Sealy said when Diamond announced himself. 'I didn't expect to hear from you. I thought you were one of the ghostbusters now. Do you wear a proton pack?'

Diamond was in no mood to trade insults. 'Can we have a serious conversation? I need information.'

'Sorry, old boy. I'm a scientist. I know nothing about the dark arts.'

'Okay, you've had your fun. You shouldn't believe everything they print in the papers.'

'It was on Instagram. The word is that you're trying to arrest a hoodoo. Is that right? It's not a good way to go. You're going to meet some very strange people.'

'You're not amusing me, Sealy.'

'No, but you crease me up. I never know what you're going to do next, and it's always hilarious. What do you want from me – the address of a good shrink?'

He controlled his anger. Graver issues were at stake than his self-respect. 'I want some professional advice about death from alcoholism – and before you go off on another tangent, it's nothing to do with me personally. Laugh if you want and get it out of your system. This is a case I'm investigating. You must have carried out scores of autopsies on drunks.'

'Hundreds. I had one this week. Liquor is present in a high percentage of unnatural deaths, forty per cent at a guess. I know straight away by the smell.' The man was becoming interested, as Diamond knew he would.

'As obvious as that?'

'It is to an old-stager like me. Some of the younger ones smear wintergreen oil or some such inside their masks to eliminate the odours of the dissecting room. They don't know what they're missing.'

'Are you saying the smell tells you exactly what they drank? Beer, say, or wine?'

'I didn't say that at all. All alcohol is ethanol by the time I get to sniff it, with a distinctly sweet smell. Death is the great leveller. Whatever they imbibed, be it home-made hooch or the finest champagne, it ends up in the blood-stream as ethanol, also known as ethyl alcohol.'

'You can't tell if it was vodka or gin?'

'Are you listening, or do I have to repeat everything? Like anything else we consume, the drink metabolises. The enzyme systems reduce it to its basic form. The liver deals with ninety-five per cent of it, reducing it to water and carbon dioxide. What's left, the remaining five per cent, is excreted through the kidneys and lungs. If the drinker is still alive and tested with a breathalyser, the level of intoxication can be measured that way. If he ends up on my slab, I'll send a blood sample to the lab, but my nose has already told me what I'm dealing with.'

Diamond had started getting lost when enzymes were mentioned, but he'd got the gist of Sealy's explanation and now he made an attempt to sound informed. 'BAC levels.'

'What do you know about them?' Sealy said.

'I know five hundred is about the maximum. The woman I'm interested in had a reading above four hundred.'

'She wouldn't have survived.'

'She didn't.'

'Anything above three hundred is likely to induce a coma. The figure you're talking about is curtains. Asphyxiation generally.'

'This was cardiac arrest.'

Sealy made a sound like the hinges of a church door being opened. 'Sudden cardiac death. Interesting. Strictly speaking, this isn't a heart attack, but the outcome is the same. Prolonged alcoholism weakens the heart function and the ticker doesn't get the oxygen it needs when it pumps. It's more usual in middle-aged men than women. You said this woman was an alcoholic. What age?'

'Late forties.'

'Plausible enough if she'd been poisoning her system for years.'

162

'Can this kind of sudden death be induced by a massive extra intake of alcohol?'

'Binge-drinking?'

'You could call it that. Someone else wants to finish her off and makes sure she drinks more in a short time than she ever has before.'

'Homicide?' No response came from Sealy for several seconds. 'There's no way I could tell at autopsy. Alcohol in a very high dose could well precipitate a rhythm disorder. On the face of it, a sudden cardiac arrest is possible, but you'd have small chance of proving premeditation.'

'What if her usual drink, which was vodka, was doctored with alcohol in a higher concentration?'

'I object to that term, "doctored" – a slur on my profession.'

'Happier with "corrupted"?'

'What are you suggesting the supposed murderer added to the drink – pure ethanol?'

'It's available online for the price of a coffee and biscuits,' Diamond said.

'If it's that cheap, it wouldn't be pure.'

'More than ninety-five per cent alcohol as compared with vodka at about forty.'

'You *are* taking this seriously,' Sealy said. 'My only observation is that I've never come across such a method of despatching a victim. Theoretically, it could be done. Excessive intake such as this would quickly overrun the body's coping mechanism. I could tell from the state of the organs that the deceased was an alcoholic and the blood test would tell me she'd consumed a lethal amount.'

'What would be the result of drinking so much at once?'

'Take your pick of coma and asphyxiation or sudden cardiac arrest.'

'And the pathologist can't tell if it was murder?'

'Of course not. That's your job – and the best of British luck.'

Diamond put down the phone and returned to the incident room. John Leaman was using a marker on the whiteboard on the wall inside the door. To the left was a long list of more than fifty names.

'What are these – our suspects?' Diamond asked him. 'You're depressing me, John.'

'They're the cast and crew from the two episodes being shot when Tudor and Nicol went missing,' Leaman said. 'Quite a lot will be deleted for various reasons and we'll get down to a hard core of people who could have been involved in both disappearances.'

'This is if we have one perpetrator?'

'Isn't that what we're working on?'

'It's my assumption.' He exhaled audibly through soft vibrating lips. 'I didn't expect quite so many. You took them from the lists I collected from the production office?'

Leaman nodded.

'We can scrub some straight away. Daisy Summerfield is dead and Dan Burbage had the climbing accident.'

'I didn't like to remove any of them without your permission, guv.'

Diamond looked for the names that interested him most. Greg Deans was there. Sabine, of course, and her stunt double, Ann Bugg. Candida, near the top of the list. Fergus Webster, the key grip. He borrowed the marker and drew a thick line linking Candida to Fergus. 'These two are an item, I found out today.'

Leaman winced visibly as his pristine list was defaced.

'Unfortunately there are names to add,' Diamond told him. 'Trixie Playfair, the original choice for the plum part.

And Will Legat, the tramp who was stained with Jake Nicol's blood. Do you want to write them in, or shall I?'

'I'll do it if you don't mind.' Leaman's neat, small lettering was tidier than Diamond's.

'You can add one more while you're at it.'

'Who's that?'

'She's known as Chen and she's Sabine's sidekick, except you'd think twice about kicking her. A young woman capable of just about anything.' After the name was written in, Diamond said, 'Do you want to put lines through the ones we just mentioned?'

'I'll probably print a new list.'

'As you wish. Something else we could do with here is a schedule from the studio telling us where everyone is at any given time. It's known as a call sheet. This week they're filming at Milroy Court, out Trowbridge way, and that's where I'm going next, but I don't know who I'll find there.'

He found everyone he needed. When he arrived, they were filming an exterior on the south-facing side of the house and a gathering of cast and crew was there to watch. An ancient wisteria with vines like petrified pythons grew up the side of the building attached to wires screwed into the structure. You could scarcely see the stonework, the plant was so abundant. Window spaces had been cut, but new shoots were already threatening to cover them over. The spring blooms had come and gone. There was a display of another kind.

One of the top windows was standing open and a naked man had climbed out and was clinging to the foliage. He looked young and fit, tanned and tattooed on the arms and legs, making his backside appear even more undressed than it was. A camera on the end of a jib was swinging about, getting close and then pulling back, controlled from the ground by someone who seemed to know what he was doing. Another camera on a dolly was at ground level and quite a collection of people stood nearby, some holding scripts.

Diamond joined a group standing out of shot observing the spectacle. Among them he had spotted one of his own, Paul Gilbert.

'What's going on?'

'Hello, guv. It's the bum shot.'

'I can see that.'

'There's one in each episode, a kind of running joke the audience looks out for – half the audience, anyway. He's supposed to be the handyman. The story goes that he's having it away in bed with the daughter of the house when they are interrupted by Swift, who has come to crack the safe. This poor guy thinks he's been caught in the act by one of the family and takes the only route out he can think of, which is the window. Luckily he's able to hang on to the creepers.'

'He doesn't look as if he can hold on much longer.'

'Tired, I expect. This is the third take of him hugging the tree. They want to get his position right.'

'What happens next?'

'That's what I'm waiting to see.'

A track had been laid across the lawn, suggesting that the action wouldn't end on the wisteria.

'Tell me who the people are.'

'The short one in the cap and white suit is George Spode, the director. The bearded guy beside him with the shades is Greg Deans.'

'The producer. I know him.'

'The bossy one wearing cans is the floor manager. I can't

tell you his name. The woman holding the script is the production assistant, Vicky.'

'Is Fergus there?'

'He's the big fellow standing a bit to the right, near the dolly camera.'

'I want to meet him when this is done.'

The director seemed satisfied with the latest take. He cupped his hands and shouted something to the actor, who now started the tricky descent. Nobody was filming. They simply watched him go through the moves.

'I wouldn't want to try that barefoot,' Diamond said.

'He'd look silly in shoes.'

'He doesn't look clever without them.'

As soon as the young man was on the ground someone handed him a bathrobe while the director conferred with those around him, apparently deciding how the climb down could be improved. Creating an action scene was a painstaking process.

The actor was sent inside the house and appeared naked at the window again. Standing on the sill, he reached for the branches, swung across and trusted them to take his weight. This time he came down in a way that got more approval. But the sequence still hadn't been filmed.

Diamond checked the time. He'd been here almost twenty minutes. The scene would take only a few seconds on screen.

The floor manager called for quiet and they went for a take. It didn't satisfy the director. Without protest, the actor returned inside the house to repeat the whole manoeuvre.

'Action.'

In making the move from the window to the main vine, his foot slipped. Anxious gasps came from the watchers. For a moment he was hanging from outstretched arms. He squirmed, found a footing again and completed the descent.

'Is he a stuntman?' Diamond asked Gilbert.

'I was told he's a jobbing actor brought in for the day. It's only a small part.'

'I wouldn't have said so.'

Gilbert grinned.

The film-makers seemed pleased by the stumble on the wisteria. They replayed it on the camera screen and decided another take wasn't needed.

'Is that it? Can we see Fergus now?'

'You can try, guv. It looks like they're taking a coffee break. Do you want me with you?'

'I do. He knows you already, but he hasn't met me.'

They marched over the turf to where the big rigger was standing beside the track laid for another sequence. He was wearing a belt with tools attached to it like the bloodstained one Will Legat had acquired. One of the team had already fetched him a coffee.

'Watch out, lads,' he announced loudly to those around him. 'It's the stop and search squad.'

Diamond gave Fergus a sight of his ID. 'This won't take long. You know what we're interested in.'

Fergus stabbed a finger in Gilbert's direction. 'I already opened my heart to PC Plod here.'

His cohorts grinned.

'Do you mind?' Diamond said to them. 'I'd like a private conversation with Fergus.'

A tilt of the head from Fergus dismissed the team. He waited for them to move off and then said, 'I told you all I know about the missing grip.'

'This isn't just about Jake Nicol. You go back a long way with this show, don't you? You were crewing with it from the start. I've seen your name on the call sheets. You must remember Dave Tudor, who was the assistant producer.'

'I'm a rigger. I can't tell you jack shit about production people. I'm not on the Bottle Yard staff.'

'Don't piss me about, Fergus. You talked to Tudor on a daily basis when he was with the show.'

'You think so?' He stalled, trying to come up with a smart answer. 'He done all the talking.'

'He was with the show when it was launched and so were you.'

'He done his job and I done mine. I was just one of the lads then. I didn't give orders.'

'You were going out with Candida Jones and she was a production assistant.'

He tensed. 'Who told you that?'

'Never mind. You were closer to the production people than you want us to know. It's no crime. I want straight answers now. What did you make of Tudor?'

The big man's thoughts played across his face. A muscle rippled in his cheek. The mention of Candida had clearly caught him off guard. He couldn't tell how much Diamond knew about the relationship. It made him willing, if not eager, to answer the question less close to home. 'Tudor? He done his job like everyone else. Him and Mary went back a long way.'

'You mean professionally, not personally?'

'There was nothing like that. All I'm saying is he worked with her on other stuff.'

'The Robeson thing? Were you on that as well? Did you work with Mary Wroxeter before *Swift* was made?"

Each detail Diamond disclosed cut into Fergus's defensive façade. The answer was written across his face before he made it with a shrug.

'I was told Mary was forever changing her mind. Must have been a pain for the crewmen like you.'

'Fair comment.'

'And Dave Tudor did his best to smooth the way and stopped you all from downing tools and coming out on strike?'

Fergus tried to grin and it was more of a grimace.

'Or murdering her?'

Now he turned ashen. He wasn't ready for a low punch like that.

'Joke,' Diamond said. 'We all know Mary died from the drink.' He'd noted Fergus's alarmed reaction and it was enough for now. 'Everyone seemed to like Tudor. What do you think happened to him?'

A shrug. 'He moved on, that's all.'

'Really? You make it sound as if he's still alive. He wasn't heard of again. All his experience was in television. If he'd got a job with another company one of you would have picked up the news on the grapevine.'

'You reckon?'

'He didn't pack up and go. His stuff was still in his flat.'

'I wouldn't know about that.'

'Get away. Your girlfriend knows. Candida was sent up to Kipling Avenue to look for him. Or did she volunteer?'

Fergus's eyes made tiny, troubled movements.

'Was she upset when she came back?'

No answer.

Diamond knew when he'd touched a raw nerve. 'You were jealous of Tudor, this charming guy everyone liked. He and Candida were too close for your liking. Was he seeing her outside work?'

He chose not to answer.

'Or is that only what you suspected?'

Fergus clenched his fists and the serpent tattoos rippled. Baiting him was a dangerous game, but Diamond wasn't stopping now.

'When Tudor disappeared from the scene, you wouldn't have shed any tears. The field was clear for you to move in with Candida, or were you two already an item?'

This triggered a response from Fergus. A strong one. 'Are you stitching me up?' He slung his coffee cup aside, swayed back, braced himself and made a grab for Diamond's shirt front.

Before Diamond could react, a hand grasped Fergus's wrist and gripped it. Paul Gilbert had stepped between them. He wasn't allowing his boss to be headbutted. 'Don't even think about it.' He wasn't built on the same scale as the rigger, but he was strong and fiercely loyal. He leaned towards Fergus and the pressure forced the big man to take a step back, a step that defused a dangerous confrontation.

Gilbert had saved both men from an outcome they would have regretted. You don't get away with assaulting a police officer. And this wasn't the time or place to make an arrest.

Fergus seemed to come to his senses. He jerked his arm free of Gilbert's hold and muttered something about his rights.

'What's going on here?'

Greg Deans must have been watching. He'd moved fast across the lawn, leaving the director and his team staring after him.

'Nothing serious,' Diamond told Deans. 'Fergus and me catching up on a few things, that's all.'

'What about? Nobody told us you were coming.' Here, in front of his actors and crew, the short, red-bearded man with the carrying voice was every inch the boss.

Cool as outer space, Diamond produced an answer. 'Didn't your office get the message?'

This piece of hokum disarmed Deans. He frowned and shook his head.

'A communications cock-up, obviously,' Diamond said. 'Your people or mine, who's to say?' Far from shaken by the dust-up with Fergus, he was energised and ready for more. 'Now that you're here, Mr Deans, do you have a few minutes to spare?'

'It's not convenient.'

'You'd better make it convenient, then. You're the senior man here, aren't you?'

Senior as Deans was, he didn't have the authority to stand in the way of a police investigation. 'Keep it short, then. We're on a tight schedule.' He turned to Fergus. 'Get your team ready to start scene seventeen as soon as I join you, please.'

Fergus didn't need more encouragement. A convict on the run wouldn't have moved off any faster.

'About Dave Tudor's disappearance,' Diamond said to Deans. 'When we spoke in your office, I didn't appreciate how new you were to the show at the time he went missing. You couldn't have known him.'

'I didn't know anyone. I'd just started.'

'So you wouldn't have understood what the fuss was about?'

'There wasn't much at first. Candida filled in for him. After a few days Mary got worried and sent Candida to check the flat.' He stopped. 'I'm sure I told you this.'

Diamond shook his head. 'Her name didn't come up when we spoke.'

'That's understandable, pet. No one has seen her for years.'

172

The 'pet' rankled, but blandishments like that were built into the persona Deans had developed to deal with everyone. There was no point in objecting, so Diamond stayed on track. 'You will have seen her the evening before Mary died. She joined you in the Shield and Dagger.'

Deans raised a finger as if his memory was working again. 'You're right. We'd finished filming an entire episode and Candida turned up out of the blue. I don't think I spoke to her apart from a hello darling and a quick peck when she came in. I feel sure I told you about that evening.'

'You did, but we didn't go into who else was there.'

'The usual suspects.' He grinned and added, 'As they say. The Shield is our favourite watering place.'

'Crew as well as actors?'

'Decidedly. There's no discrimination.'

'Fergus?'

'Sure to have been. He likes his drink and Mary was buying. She was always generous.'

'Who else? Sabine?'

'All the cast for sure. Even dear old Daisy Summerfield, bless her. They didn't all stay late. In fact, Mary herself left about nine.'

'Well tanked?'

Deans flapped his hand in dissent. 'I told you before, sweetie. She'd had a few vodkas, that's all, but she bought an extra bottle at the bar and took it with her. I guess she drank it all at home. Solitary drinking. Isn't that the saddest thing?'

'She was definitely alone, then?'

'Not when she left the pub. Candida offered to drive her home – which was only a short walk away – but Candie was on soft drinks and we learned later that she was pregnant and being extra careful.'

'Yes, she told me herself she didn't go inside the house. So if Mary got through that entire bottle, how many shots was that? Twenty? It depends on the size of the glass, I suppose.'

Deans nodded. 'Dylan Thomas's famous last words come to mind: "I've had eighteen straight whiskies. I think that's a record."'

'Did Candida feel responsible for Mary, offering to take her home?'

'Why do you ask?'

'Just a vague theory. She didn't announce her pregnancy in the pub that evening, did she? She told me she shared the good news with Mary in the car.'

'I can understand that. I expect she wanted her old boss to know first. She'd been Mary's AP for over a year after Tudor left, so they were close.'

'That would explain it, then.'

'So,' Deans brought his hands together in front of his chest, 'what's your theory, officer?'

'Doesn't matter.'

'I can guess. You think Mary was so thrilled to hear about the baby that she went home and sank the rest of the vodka in one session. It seems as good an explanation as any, thinking back.'

Diamond gave the slight nod that said his mind had been there already.

Deans sighed and said with genuine pathos in his voice, 'Candie had quit the job when she first got pregnant a couple of years before, but she miscarried not long after, poor love. Conceiving another baby must have made her very excited. She kept it from the rest of us because she wanted to share her feelings with Mary first. We never heard who the father was.'

174

And Diamond wasn't going to break that confidence, even though the father had tried to headbutt him. How interesting that none of the company knew of the relationship. Fergus kept his private life well concealed. Maybe it was about his macho image. It was hard to imagine the hard man sharing baby pictures with his workmates. 'Are you a family man, Greg?'

Deans gave Diamond a sharp look. 'What's that got to do with it?'

'The sympathetic way you talked about the miscarriage made me think you must be in a relationship.'

He looked down at his watch. 'Time's up, I'm afraid.'

'Don't you want me to know?'

'Know what?'

'About your home life.'

Deans gave Diamond a stare that could have cut through granite. 'That's not for debate.'

'I'm not interested in debate. Are you married?'

'You have no right—' he started to say.

'Sorry, but I do. It's my duty to ask questions. You're going to say it's your right to remain silent and you're entitled to do so if you choose, in which case I can get the answer to my question by having you followed, which I'm entitled to do, but I'd find that excessive and so would you.'

He'd seen this obduracy coming. Deans had built a wall around himself. Somewhere behind the theatre-speak, the call sheets, the production schedule and the budget was a real man.

Diamond was determined to break through the wall. 'It was a personal question,' he said, switching to a more reasonable tone. 'Fair play, I'll tell you about my own situation. It's no big deal. I married quite late and sadly it didn't last all that long because my wife was murdered. I lived the life of a widowed man for a long time after and now I've moved in with somebody else.'

In the silence that followed, a series of tiny muscle movements on Deans's features showed he was in two minds. He scratched his beard, pressed his mouth more firmly shut for a few seconds and then gave in to the moral pressure. 'I have a partner, but she has no connection with television, if that's what you're thinking. Natalie is disabled. She's a potter. We first met before I worked in television and before she got this wretched multiple sclerosis. I was a man with a van who did delivery jobs, and she took me on. I drove around the district delivering her products. We became friendly, it got serious and she invited me to live with her. She still works, but we don't know how much longer she can keep going. When I get home, I help her load the kiln and there's no shop talk about *Swift* or anything else I've done in the day. I leave it all behind me. And no, I don't have children.'

'Neither do I,' Diamond said with a sigh so slight it would have passed unnoticed. 'Neither do I.'

16

Unlike Greg Deans, Diamond didn't mind discussing work matters at home. His late wife, Stephanie, had always been willing to listen and chip in with thoughts of her own. More than once she had given him an insight that transformed a case and led to a conviction. His current partner, Paloma, too, brought fresh thinking to his problems. Keeping an open mind was the hardest part of his job. It could be painful to question assumptions he'd already made, but if he was willing to take the pain from anyone, she was the woman closest to his heart.

Paloma enjoyed cooking and had made it her mission to educate Diamond's palette. They didn't often go out for meals. Tonight he'd persuaded her to try the Hudson Steakhouse on London Street. When he'd first come to Bath, the place had been a pub called the Hat and Feather, known to locals as the Hat. Back in its glory days it had been the social hub of the Walcot community, famous for charabanc trips to the seaside, children's parties and lavish wedding receptions, but by Diamond's time it was badly in need of a makeover and he'd shed no tears at the change of use.

Paloma wasn't much of a meat eater, so coming to a steak house was largely an act of altruism. To Diamond's relief she gave a squeak of delight when she saw the menu.

'Tortelloni. And stuffed with the goodies I like most.'

'Specially for you,' he said as if he'd fixed it with the chef. He had no idea what tortelloni was, but he was willing to believe it was delicious as long as he didn't have to eat any. He'd already decided on the twelve-ounce rib eye.

'I expect you know the difference between tortelloni and tortellini,' she said.

He knew he was being teased. 'I thought they were opera singers.'

She solemnly explained and he solemnly listened. 'I'll give you one to sample when it arrives.'

'I can't wait.'

'You need this,' Paloma said when the steak was in front of him. 'If you'll forgive the expression, you were looking jinxed when you left for work this morning.'

Still sensitive about that word, he gave a smile like a reopened wound. 'The day ended better than it started. We made a breakthrough. I discovered who fed the story to the *Bristol Post*.'

'Anyone I've heard of?'

He told her about Candida, the full works.

Paloma took a sympathetic view. 'I can understand why she did it, stuck on that boat with a two-year-old. You feel as if your life has closed down. Talking to the press brought back some of the fun she was missing.'

'No fun for the people she used to work with.'

'Oh, come on, Pete, everyone knows the jinx thing is a load of nonsense.'

'That's what I keep saying. Actually all of it really happened.'

'The incidents, yes. It's the spin the paper gave them.'

'Which came from Candida. She was the one who strung

178

everything together and told the press about the damned jinx.'

'But the substance of the story is true, as you just said. It adds up to a remarkable run of bad luck. It's not as if she made everything up.'

He shook his head. 'It was a calculated act of mischief.'

'I can see it's a sore point, but I do understand why she did it. At least you can cross her off your list of suspects.'

'Really?' He couldn't let that pass.

'Obvious, isn't it? If she'd done anything criminal, she wouldn't have made it public.'

'That's not the way I see it.'

She laughed. 'Typical. Go on then. I'm listening.'

Without seriously interrupting his work on the steak, he did. 'She's firmly in the frame. She profited from Dave Tudor's departure by taking over his plum job as assistant producer. And she was the last to be seen with Mary Wroxeter. She drove Mary home that night.'

'The sainted Mary everyone loved and depended on? Hold on. Are you thinking *she* was murdered?'

'Helped to die, possibly.'

Paloma put down her fork and sat back in her chair. 'You're serious?'

'I'm looking into it.'

'Along with all the other troubles that hit the show?'

He shook his head. 'Only the suspicious ones that could be murder.'

'But if Candida had anything to do with whatever happened, why would she bring it to everyone's attention?'

'The real reason for contacting the newspaper? It's smart. The killings get lumped in with all the other stuff that happened and passed off as more bad luck, the work of the jinx. Tudor went missing and Mary drank too much. They're not viewed as murders.'

Her gaze slipped away from him, taking in the deviousness of such a plan. When their eyes met again, she still seemed unconvinced. 'And the other man who has gone missing – do you think she killed him?'

'Whoever killed the others probably did for Jake Nicol as well.'

'But why? Why would Candida want to kill him? Had she even met him?'

'That's what I need to find out. Jake was a rigger, like Fergus, so there's a link there. Anything more is speculation right now.'

Their debate was interrupted by the waitress asking if their food was acceptable. Paloma said hers was delicious and Diamond made a sign of excellence with his thumb and forefinger.

'One thing is certain,' Paloma said. 'You've got to be grateful to Candida.'

'Why?'

'She's come to the rescue. You told me you were being threatened with retirement, but now the story has broken about you investigating the jinx, everyone is looking to you to find the answer.'

He grinned. 'Cool.'

'You get it now?'

'I do. When you say "everyone", you mean Georgina. She called it a public relations disaster. She thinks her own job is on the line. Suddenly I'm needed. It's Operation Showstopper.' He raised his beer glass. 'To Candida, who saved me from the scrapheap, whatever else she may have done.'

Paloma took a sip of her wine and said, 'Coupled with Georgina, who came to her senses.'

'I can't drink to her. She really spooked me with her talk of retirement. But you're right. I've been given a reprieve.'

They resumed their meal. After some minutes, Paloma said, 'Coming here was a good idea. I'm enjoying this. Did you want to talk about something else?'

'I'm enjoying your take on the case. You've got such a good grasp of it. Who else comes under suspicion?'

'Fergus, of course,' she said at once.

'Tell me why.' He wasn't disagreeing. He was interested to hear her reasons.

'You told me he's been there from the start. I know he isn't employed by the TV company, but he must have known Mary Wroxeter from way back.'

'He did. He worked with her on the Robeson documentary before *Swift* was started. And so did Dave Tudor. Those two have a history.'

'Well, I'm guessing here, but you did ask. Could the motive for Tudor's killing – if indeed he was killed – be a grudge over something that happened years before?'

'That's possible.'

'When did Fergus start his friendship with Candida? Before Tudor went missing?'

He smiled. 'You're so quick. It took me a while to work that out. Neither of them will say much, but it's clear she and Tudor had something going before Fergus started taking an interest in her.'

'The two men were rivals?'

'I'm sure of it.'

'Tudor vanished when?'

'2015.'

'And Mary, who was no fool, may well have got suspicious about what really happened to Tudor. She was working closely with Candida, who she'd appointed as her production assistant. This is starting to make sense. Mary put two and two together and asked Fergus for the truth and so signed her own death warrant.'

'Neat, but I'm not sure Fergus is bright enough to have carried out three killings and covered his tracks.'

'Was he at the Shield and Dagger the evening Mary died?'

'Most of the actors were. I'm less certain about the crew. He could have been.'

'So when Candida offered to drive Mary home, Fergus could have got suspicious about what those two would talk about. If Candida had suspicions about him she might have decided to share them with Mary.'

'But she wanted to tell Mary the good news about the pregnancy. Fergus was the father. He would have known what was on Candida's mind.'

'Not necessarily. Perhaps she hadn't told Fergus at that point. She'd only just got the test result.'

'Surely she'd have phoned him or texted the minute she knew.'

Paloma's answer was a small movement of her shoulders.

He paused his eating. New scenarios were always worth exploring, but this one took some believing. 'I've met them both and there's certainly some friction in the relationship. He doesn't know she spoke to the press about the jinx and she's terrified how he'll react when he finds out. But if he isn't smart enough to figure out that his own partner is the whistle-blower, is he a triple murderer? I've yet to be persuaded.'

'Who else is on your list?'

He smiled. 'How long have you got? Greg Deans, for a start.'

'The producer?'

'A man who ought to be content with running a successful

show, but clearly isn't. He's stuck with a concept that wasn't his own. Everyone knows Mary handled it brilliantly and he'll never come up to her high standards. He can't stand his leading lady or most of the cast and crew, come to that. Whether that's enough to justify murdering them, I couldn't say.'

'Mary's sudden death suited him nicely,' Paloma said.

'Exactly. His rise to the top was meteoric, from production assistant to top banana in under four years, and now he's there, he isn't happy. He may be a good manager, but he's aware of his limitations and so are the people he works with.'

'They see through him?'

'I suspect they always did.'

'Doesn't he have any redeeming features?'

'They're not obvious. There was a moment of insight today when I asked him if he was a family man. He wasn't keen to tell me anything and I had to get heavy with him. Finally he told me he has a disabled wife called Natalie and they never talk shop. She has a pottery studio and he does the heavy work for her when he gets home. He looked and sounded genuine at that moment. The rest of the time he's trying too hard to pass himself off as one of the luvvies.'

'Insecure.'

'I reckon so. At work, he's surrounded by professionals who look to him for a spark of creativity he doesn't possess. I almost feel sorry for the man.'

'Yes,' she said. 'I've never met him, but I'm sometimes in touch with his wardrobe people and he has this reputation of being pleasant and civil without actually letting anyone get up close and personal. What you just told me explains a lot. You did well to get him to open up about his wife. If that was generally known, there might be more sympathy for him. How about the two men who went missing? Were they standing in his way somehow?'

'Not in any obvious sense. He'd only just joined the show when Dave Tudor went missing. The person who benefited was Candida. As for Jake Nicol's disappearance . . .'

'Or death,' Paloma said.

'I'm trying to keep an open mind here. Jake was only a rigger, not even employed by Swift and Proud. I can't think of any way Greg would profit from him being no longer there.'

'Who else is on your list of suspects?'

'You're really into this.'

'Absolutely. It's turning into a whodunit.'

'I hope not. I can't see myself bringing them all together in the last chapter and naming the murderer.'

'What do you want – a car chase and a shoot-out?'

'That wouldn't go down well with my bosses. I expect I'll do it the boring way: an arrest, an interview under caution and a charge.'

'Be predictable, then, but give me another name.'

'You won't have heard of her. Trixie Playfair.'

'Trixie with an "x"?'

He grinned. 'She's not tricksy in the way you're thinking. What you see is what you get. She's the bitter ex-actress originally cast as Caitlin Swift. She quit before it got past the rehearsal stage.'

'Why?'

'She insists it wasn't stage fright, but it seems to have been an extreme form of it. Terror was the word she used. She wasn't in front of an audience at the time, just the director and a few of the crew. She called it an out-of-body experience, watching herself in the studio and knowing she was a flop.'

184

'Poor woman.'

'You're going to feel sympathy for all my suspects, aren't you? Trixie is out of it now, teaching drama in a posh girls' school, claiming to be no longer interested in *Swift*.'

'Don't you believe her?'

'It's clear the anger with herself still burns and she's jealous of Sabine, who took over the role and is now a star performer.'

'I'm not surprised she's bitter. How different life could have been for her.'

'And I must decide if her state of mind is enough to make her a killer. At the beginning, I was doubtful. I remember Keith Halliwell disagreeing with me and I shrugged off his suspicions. Keith has his own hang-ups. I'm more inclined to believe him now. Trixie is a damaged personality.'

'Peter, that isn't the same as murdering someone. Why kill Dave Tudor and Mary? Nice people, both of them, by all accounts.'

'There's the difference between real life and fiction,' he said. 'In a whodunnit, the victims have to get up everyone's nose. The two you just named were heroes. Under questioning Trixie spoke well of Mary, as everyone does. Called her lovely and said she had amazing empathy. The thing is, she lied about other things and she may have been lying about Mary.'

'What other things?'

'Sabine, for one. She claims she doesn't give a toss about her when it's obvious she envies her. She's more jealous than the Mona Lisa's best friend.'

Paloma nearly choked on the tortelloni. 'You come out with some corkers.'

'It's not difficult finding a motive for Trixie. She hates

the show and everyone in it. And she's super-fit, strong enough to murder a man and dispose of a body. Had to be, to get the part of Swift.'

'If that's true, Sabine had better watch out.'

'I don't know about that.' But he realised before the words were out that he *ought* to know. Paloma had touched on a possible flashpoint. He spoke his thoughts aloud. 'Sabine didn't steal the part. She was there from the beginning, when the show was being cast. The two women met at the audition. I was thinking they didn't know each other and there couldn't be any aggro between them.'

'Hadn't you better warn her?'

'About Trixie? No chance.'

'You can just say you believe she's at risk.'

From the look on his face, she could have suggested walking through fire. 'Sabine is a complicated person as it is, deeply superstitious and with a superiority complex, quite the diva, to quote Greg. I don't intend to unsettle her even more.'

'You'll feel terrible if anything happens to her.'

'I'll have to deal with that. This is only a suspicion on our part. God only knows how it will get blown up if I say anything. Sabine isn't the sort to keep calm and carry on. She'll tell her agent we think she's lined up as a serial killer's next victim.'

'Where does she live?'

'In an enormous motorhome built like a fortress. She has a minder and maid-of-all-work called Chen who lives in and drives it for her.'

'And she has an agent looking out for her as well? It sounds as if she's well protected already. Sorry, Peter. On second thoughts, you're right about keeping this to yourself. From what you've told me, she'll be alert to any potential

186

danger.' Paloma leaned back in her chair. 'And I suppose Sabine is also a suspect.'

'Has to be. As the star of the show, she's been there right through. She worked with all the people who came to grief in one way or another – Tudor, Wroxeter, Burbage, Summerfield, Nicol. Her motorhome was parked up at Charmy Down the night Jake Nicol went missing.'

'You've met her, obviously?'

'Interviewed her in the fortress. I expected a tough session, but she was charming. After some of the stuff I'd heard from other people, I was surprised. Not one of my main suspects has a good word to say for Sabine.'

'Except you?'

'Ingeborg was with me.'

'And did Inge find her equally charming?'

He had to think back. 'She wasn't quite so bowled over as I was. She pointed out that she's an actress.'

'Ingeborg saw the effect she had on you.'

'I'm no pushover, Paloma.'

'No?' She smiled.

Challenged, he rested his hands either side of the plate, holding the knife and fork upwards like steel gateposts. 'I'm not easily influenced, you know. Sabine is a serious suspect with the same physical attributes as Trixie.'

Paloma was openly amused by his attempt to get serious. 'You took note of her attributes, then?'

'I'm speaking about her strength and fitness. She's got a mini-gym inside the motorhome. She could take me on in a fight, no problem. And what's more, the motorhome could be used to move a body to some place far away where it could be disposed of.'

'But that would involve her driver.'

'Chen? She's totally loyal.'

'Loyal to the point of being an accomplice? She'd need her help to drag a body on board.'

'True. It's high off the ground. Seriously, she has the means to get away with murder and she can make the opportunity.'

'But what's the motive?'

'For Sabine?'

'She's in a good place here, earning a star's salary, getting treated like royalty. Why would she put that at risk by killing people on the show? It makes no sense.'

'People don't always behave rationally. I almost said "women", but you would have shot me down in flames.'

'And stamped on the wreckage,' she said. 'Fair play, this lady doesn't sound well grounded. Can you think why she might have decided to do away with Dave Tudor?'

'She spoke in glowing terms of him, couldn't recall anyone who clashed with him.' He plucked another phrase from the interview. 'She went so far as to say he was quite sexy.'

'She said that to you?'

'What's wrong with it?'

'It's more like the way one woman speaks to another.'

'Actually, it was his accent she found sexy.'

Paloma's brown eyes locked with his. 'Did she make a play for him and get the elbow? That wouldn't please a diva like her.'

'I hadn't thought of that.'

She gave him the look that said men are not much above the apes in making fine distinctions.

He was thinking back to the conversation in the motor-home. 'I remember asking her if he made out with anybody and her words were "Not me, unfortunately".'

'There you are, then.'

'It was lightly spoken and I took it to be a piece of wit, just something you say in conversation.'

'She doesn't sound like a great wit to me. A few minutes ago you said Candida had something going with Tudor at one time. If he was dating other women on the show and ignoring Sabine, she'd be incensed.'

'I can see that, but wouldn't she focus her anger on Candida?'

'Not at all. Sexy Dave was her target. She's the star and he's supposed to come running when she snaps her fingers. He doesn't and there's wounded pride mixed in with the pull of the hormones. Hell hath no fury *et cetera*. He's a dead man.'

He laughed. 'You've solved it, then. She kills him out of frustration. And now the difficult part. Why kill the others, Mary and Jake?'

Paloma switched her gaze to the chandelier above them. 'Now you're asking.' After a short pause, she had her answer. 'Well, Mary was no fool. She will have summed up Sabine's personality. What if she accused Sabine of killing Dave?'

'Two years after it happened?'

'She'd suspected it for a long time and then something came up like Sabine getting into an argument with Greg – two strong personalities there – and Mary gets annoyed with her and blurts out that if Dave were still alive and in the job as PA she wouldn't have to deal with Greg.'

'That's guesswork.'

'Isn't that how you arrive at the truth, by juggling the facts until you get something that makes sense?'

He grinned. 'Not a method I admit to.'

'Let's settle for this, then: something provoked Mary into speaking out.'

'And that's why Mary had to die? What about Jake? Was

189

his mistake the same as Dave's, being fancied and trying to walk away?'

'Did you speak to Sabine about Jake?'

'I did, and she said she didn't know him from Adam.'

'She would, wouldn't she?'

'I don't know about that. When she told me this, it confirmed what others have told me, that from her lofty height people like riggers are only there on sufferance.'

'That wouldn't stop her from giving him the eye if she fancied him. Was he attractive?'

He took the phone from his pocket and showed her Jake's picture.

'Oooh,' she said, laying it on to tease him. 'Neat moustache.'

'I didn't know you liked them.'

'Douglas Fairbanks Junior.'

'Way before my time.'

'Beast. But you see what I'm driving at? He fails to respond to Sabine's charm and she's humiliated. A common rigger turns her down. She can't bear to have him on set as a reminder. She'd already killed Tudor and made him disappear. She repeated the trick.'

It was a persuasive theory, providing Sabine with a motive, the opportunity and a means of removing the body from the scene, but while listening, Diamond had become increasingly uneasy about Chen's involvement. The minder *had* to be Sabine's accomplice. Is loyalty so blind that it gets led into conspiracy to murder?

He'd been willing to accept the idea until they analysed what Sabine was supposed to have demanded of Chen. Now he was rapidly going cool on it. The short time he'd spent with Chen had shown him she knew exactly where she stood and what her duties were. Anything extra would need to be negotiated. Subordinates don't make good partners in crime.

'After that I need another beer.' He signalled to the waiter.

'Is that a way of telling me to zip up?' Paloma said.

'No, I'm fascinated.'

'Well, there's one more suspect you told me about – the gentleman of the road.'

'Will Legat.'

'Do you want my thoughts on him?'

'I'm on tenterhooks.'

'You said he's been visiting Bath for years at the height of the tourist season.'

'Right. He only has to sit on the street with his enormous dog and people give them money.'

'I've seen them outside the Roman Baths. Have you checked how many of the incidents and accidents over the years happened at times when Will was visiting Bath?'

'Paul Gilbert may have looked at the timing. He's handling the Nicol inquiry for me.'

'It's the first thing I would want to know. Will isn't your average down-and-out, from what you told me. He's eloquent, for one thing.'

'Difficult to stop.'

'And no fool. He had a business of his own in London that was brought down by the global financial crisis, as many others were, right?'

'True.'

'Isn't there some connection with Jake Nicol?'

He shrugged. 'I wouldn't call it that. Nicol also worked in London before joining the show, but as Will pointed out to me, London has a population of nine million.'

'That isn't what I meant. You found Nicol's blood on the belt Will was wearing.'

'Right, I get you now. On the belt and on his clothes. It's the only evidential link we have between any of the suspects and the victims. Normally I'd find blood evidence decisive.'

'But you don't?'

'He had a pretty convincing explanation. He stumbled over the belt when he was crossing the airfield in the dark on his way to doss down in the old control tower. Being a scavenger, he picked it up.'

'And got blood on his clothes, Jake Nicol's blood?'

'That's the worrying bit. If the blood was still moist, the attack must have happened a short time earlier.'

'Does he have an explanation?'

'He claims to have watched the riggers clearing up after the shoot. They're always the last to leave. If he's telling the truth, he may well have witnessed Nicol being attacked. But when I started questioning him about it, he went into "No comment" mode.'

'Why? Is he scared of naming someone?'

'He isn't scared of anything. He could tell how eager I was to find out what he may have witnessed and he saw this as a way of working his ticket. Free overnight accommodation in the cells.'

'Is that worth having?' Paloma asked with surprise.

'It is to Will. His preferred choice would be Julian House, but they can't take Caesar, so he has to look elsewhere. There are usually a couple of empty cells at Keynsham and I had a word with the custody sergeant. It's bed, blankets, breakfast and a shower if he wants. He was there two nights, until I called time.'

'You amaze me. Is this the norm?'

'It's common practice – has been for years – for homeless

192

people to commit minor offences like anti-social behaviour to get a night in the cells. Quite often we don't bother to charge them. Saves us the paperwork. And sometimes they don't bother to commit the offence. They simply turn up and ask if we have a spare cell.'

'And you hoped Will Legat would become cooperative and tell you what he saw?'

'It was worth the try. If I go on hammering away at him in an interview room, he'll put the shutters up forever, stubborn cuss. He's quite prepared to have "no comment" on his gravestone.'

Paloma's eyes sparkled. 'I like it.'

'We also keep tabs on him this way.'

'Did he walk all the way from Keynsham into Bath each morning to do his begging?'

'No chance. He and Caesar got a lift in a police van. He left the pram behind.'

'Giving him a reason to return. This guy has got it made. What I'd like to know is whether he's a key witness or a suspect.'

'Tell me if you find out,' Diamond said. 'On what we know so far, he has to be the prime suspect for Jake Nicol's murder unless his story about finding the belt can be believed. Tying him into the other crimes is more problematic.'

'When Tudor disappeared in 2015, it was late July, the height of the tourist season, when you'd expect Legat to have been here.'

'And Mary's death?'

'August, 2017.'

'So it's likely he was here for all three of these suspicious deaths.'

'That's one thing. Finding a reason why he should want to murder any of them is the challenge.'

. 'Way beyond me, I'm afraid,' Paloma said. 'He doesn't sound like a violent man, but you can never be sure.'

They decided to order coffees rather than a dessert. Even Diamond had his limits after a twelve-ounce steak.

'So you really do have a classic whodunnit to solve,' Paloma said after their plates were taken away. 'Three men and three women. And three bodies, if you're right about Mary Wroxeter.'

'But it's not impossible one of them is still alive and will come back and make a horse's arse of me.'

'Mary won't. You know she's dead.'

'The other two are still missing officially. I've staked a lot on them being dead.'

'You need bodies to back up your theory.'

'That's my biggest headache. How do I find them? My best chance is Nicol, the latest one. All the evidence suggests he was killed on Charmy Down when they finished filming there. The only thing we found was his rigger's belt. We searched all the derelict buildings.'

'Buried, do you think?'

'At the airfield? Doubtful. It's hard to tell how anyone would have had time to do it.'

'Will Legat, who spent the night there,' Paloma said.

'I can't see it. As Legat pointed out to me, he doesn't have a spade.'

'If Nicol was murdered, there are two other theories. Number one: the body was taken away in one of the trucks the riggers use. And two: Sabine's motorhome was parked there until late.'

'You already told me your suspicions about that.'

'It was the last vehicle to leave.'

'Could you get a forensics team to search the motorhome for traces of blood? There must have been some.'

'We'd need a warrant and I haven't got a strong enough case to apply for one.'

'I suppose the same applies to the riggers' trucks? Oh dear. You're really up against it. If one of those trucks was used, the finger points to Fergus, surely?'

'But no one has come up with a motive. Nicol had only been in the job a couple of days, which is why we know so little about him.'

'You don't have much on the other missing man.'

'Dave Tudor? That's because he vanished four years ago. Memories fade.'

Paloma had a suggestion. 'I wonder if Nicol's fate was settled by something as basic as a fight over work duties? He objects to being given all the heavy work just because he's the new man. Fergus can't allow his authority to be challenged.'

He nodded. 'Could be as simple as that.'

'They all carry tools that could be used as weapons, don't they?'

'I heard you,' he said, starting to feel an overload of information. 'Here comes the coffee.'

When it was poured, he added, 'You're so patient with me. This conversation hasn't been most ladies' idea of a nice meal out.'

She laughed. 'Most ladies would consider it a treat to hear a top detective analyse a case in progress.'

'Well, this lady brought some good things to the table.'

'I knew you'd like the tortelloni.'

17

Candida stepped on deck next morning with the idea of calling at the marina office to collect the mail. A fine, clear morning, the sheet of water still as a mirror except for some ducks patterning the surface as they glided closer, making their case for an early feed. She had Bart in her arms. He could walk perfectly well but needed help getting from the narrowboat on to the wooden jetty. Generally it was quiet at this time of day. Not this morning.

On the far side, some men in black were grouped on the plank walkway bordering the perimeter. They were staring down at the water and she recognised one of them, the only one wearing a suit. Overweight and overbearing in the way he stood with arms folded, the detective, Peter Diamond, wasn't directing the action, but he wanted no one to doubt that he was the senior man.

She now saw that two of the others were in wetsuits and holding masks and snorkels and a moment later there was a disturbance in the water in front of them and a diver surfaced. He held up a traffic cone, emptied the water from it and slung it on to a heap of finds on the walkway. There was some amusement that Candida couldn't hear.

She wasn't at all amused. Heart thumping, she set Bart on his feet, held his hand and marched along the jetty past her neighbours' boats towards the end and then around the water's edge to where the unwelcome visitors had set up. She came straight to the point with Diamond. 'You're wasting your time, you know.'

'Morning, Candida, and morning, Bart,' he said as if he had been expecting them. 'You could be right, but it's one of those jobs that has to be done. The underwater search unit are busy people and I'm lucky to get them when I can. The lady in the office knows what's going on.'

'What did you tell her?'

'Don't worry, I was the soul of discretion. Your name wasn't mentioned and neither was Fergus's. I told her we're looking for things of interest that might have been dumped here. A place like this could be irresistible to ne'er-do-wells wanting to get rid of incriminating objects.'

Bart headed for the mud-covered rubbish. Candida dashed after him and scooped him up. 'No, you don't.' He let out yells of protest until distracted by the sight of the man in the water. Peace was restored.

'He must have noticed the little scooter in the heap,' Diamond said. 'It might clean up and be usable. None of this stuff is of any interest to me and you're welcome to help yourself, but I wouldn't let him touch anything yet. The water's not the purest.'

The man making the search pulled the mask over his face and submerged again. He was linked by a safety line to one of the others on the walkway.

'They tell me it's deeper than it looks,' Diamond said. 'There could be a crashed aircraft in here for all I know.'

Candida said nothing.

'It's going to take days. These guys will tell you there's nil visibility. They're groping through the muck at the bottom and stirring it up as they go. It's not a job I'd do myself.'

She didn't even look at him while he was speaking. She was watching the movement of the yellow line in the water.

'I expected them to start on your side where the boats are moored,' Diamond went on. 'All kinds of stuff could be trapped under the jetty or between the boats. But they have their own way of working. They want to check the stretch of open water first.'

Candida shook her head at the folly of it all. Presently she let Bart down and took out her phone. She put it to her ear, turned and walked off, speaking quietly, with Bart close behind.

Diamond had followed them closely along the duckboard walk and when she pocketed the phone he heard him call out, 'Tipping off Fergus?'

On the point of denial, she thought better of it and said over her shoulder, 'This is our home. He has a right to know.'

'No argument with that. Is he on his way?'

'He's filming.'

'Of course he is. The key grip. He'll come as soon as he can. Does he drive? I suppose he has to, in that job. They all drive the trucks from time to time.'

'He has a motorbike,' she called back.

'Useful.'

Inside himself, Diamond was less laidback than he was showing. A motorcycle was something he hadn't factored in. 'Does he ever have the use of the trucks overnight?'

'They belong to Gripmasters,' Candida said without answering the question.

'I don't suppose they'd mind if he borrowed one.'

She turned to glare at him.

'Say if he had a removal job to do, like picking up a piece of second-hand furniture. They wouldn't need to know, would they?'

'We don't need furniture. The boat was furnished when we moved in. We can hardly move as it is.'

'Bart's things, I meant,' he said. 'High-chair, playpen, cot. A baby needs extras you can't cart home on the back of a motorbike.'

'They were delivered,' she said. 'They weren't second-hand. I don't want my child using things someone else has thrown out. And he won't be given that filthy scooter or anything else from the scrapheap.' She'd come as far as the marina office and she went in, leaving Diamond outside to ponder that parting shot. The word 'scrapheap' couldn't have been intended to strike at his insecurity, but it did. It went deep.

He returned to the search party and checked the heap for any new finds. 'Is there any way you can speed this up?' he asked the dive supervisor. 'You've got two others in their wetsuits doing nothing.'

'Are you telling me my job, sir?'

'No, just enquiring. What's your name?'

The man pointed to a name-tag sewn on to his jacket saying *Earnshaw*.

Diamond grinned sheepishly. 'Didn't spot it.'

'It's no picnic down there. Each diver does a shift and then needs a break. If you want more men in the water, you'd better speak to my boss.'

'Have you done missing-person searches before?'

For that dumb question he was rewarded with a cold stare. 'We do more of them than anything else.'

'Do you really need to bring up all this debris?'

'If you want a proper search, yes,' Earnshaw said. 'The body could be covered in clutter.'

'The most recent one won't be. That was a matter of days ago.'

'We were told there may be one from four years back.'

'You're right,' he said. 'There may be.' He sounded a more cordial note. 'Incidentally, when people ask what you're looking for – as they're sure to – I'd be glad if you'd avoid mentioning corpses.'

Another look.

'Obviously I don't need to tell you guys anything. I'll leave you to get on with your work.'

He'd spotted Candida leaving the office, so he took the opportunity to go inside and speak to the woman on duty. He admitted straight away that he was the senior detective who had authorised the search. 'We may be a few days,' he told her. 'These things can't be hurried.'

'What exactly are you hoping to find?'

'If I knew the answer to that, I'd be a happy man. Nothing is exact about this. But it would help me to know whether you've had any strangers coming and going in the last couple of weeks.'

'On the water, you mean?'

'Or by land, driving up in cars or trucks.'

'No one, to my knowledge. And we don't miss much. We're serious about security. The only people I've seen are known to us – the boat owners we meet every day.'

He drove straight to Milroy Court. The schedule told him they were filming interiors there. But on entering the mansion and showing his ID he was asked to wait in the kitchen downstairs because the bedroom where the shoot was under way was a closed set, meaning people not essential to the filming were barred.

He didn't take it personally. He could understand actors wanting some kind of privacy for sex scenes. Apart from that, he'd seen how many people were needed for the sound and lighting, let alone the camera. With all their equipment inside a bedroom they'd be hard pressed to squeeze in the actors.

The kitchen was busy. Fergus and a few of the riggers were grouped by the window. Diamond had noticed before that they didn't mingle. Then he spotted Sabine, or thought he did until she turned round, coffee in hand. She had the same hairstyle and was wearing the black Swift costume. Her resemblance to the star performer was remarkable except for the mouth, which was wider, with fuller lips.

He worked his way through the crush to get face-to-face. 'I was sure you were Sabine,' he said. 'You must be her double. I expect it happens all the time.'

She nodded and made clear with her voice that the mistake was common and annoying. 'Sorry to disappoint you.' She'd probably said the same thing dozens of times before. She started to move on.

'You're Ann, right?'

At the mention of her own name, Ann Bugg gave him a second look.

'Mind if we talk?' he said. 'I don't know anyone else here.'

She reddened and said nothing, so he went on, 'My name's Peter.' Everyone used first names in television, but he still had a duty to make clear why he was here. 'I'm with the police, trying to make sense of that jinx thing.'

He got the caught-in-the-headlights stare he was used to getting whenever he admitted he was a cop, but her reaction was more, unmistakably more. She wasn't merely shocked. She was alarmed. She looked right and left as if hoping someone would come to the rescue. She hadn't even confirmed her name yet.

'I'm not mistaken, am I? You *are* Ann Bugg?'

A nod.

This would be like chiselling granite.

He tried showing he wasn't totally ignorant about what was going on. 'I should have guessed Sabine will be in front of the camera upstairs. Or in her motorhome if she's on a break.' To lighten the mood, he said, 'She won't be drinking her coffee out of a paper cup.'

She didn't rise to that, so he asked, 'Do we help ourselves here?'

'I'm not stopping you,' she said, eyes darting, wanting to be anywhere but here.

He found a cup, spooned in some instant and tried to be affable while the kettle came to the boil. 'One thing I'm learning about TV production is how good the catering is.' He reached for a chocolate chip muffin. 'These are tempting. Want one?'

She shook her head.

'Shall we move into the other room,' he said when he'd poured his coffee. 'I saw people in there as I came past.'

Like a shepherd controlling a wilful sheep, he held both arms out, at risk of spilling his drink, and guided her into a sitting room almost as crowded as the kitchen.

'Are you filming a scene today?' he asked after he'd backed her into a corner.

'Maybe.'

'Dumb question. You wouldn't be here otherwise. You do the stunts, don't you?'

'Sometimes.'

'Is one lined up for later? I'd love to see it.'

'No.'

'Didn't you just say . . .'

'Sometimes they want me for long shots.'

'I heard about you losing your footing at the weir the other day and getting swept over the edge. Nasty moment for you.'

'I've had worse.'

'No injuries?'

'Some bruising, that's all.'

'How did it happen, exactly?'

If he'd hoped for the full account, he didn't get it. 'I slipped.'

'Can't blame the jinx, then?'

She rolled her eyes and didn't answer. He could have been talking to a stroppy teenager, except that she was at least twenty-five.

Am I really too old for this? he asked himself. His self-confidence had taken one knock at the marina and now it was challenged again. Maybe flattery would loosen her tongue. 'You're a true professional. Back next day to film all over again.'

'That's my job.'

'You do all the dangerous stuff, jumping from roof to roof and driving fast cars and most of the viewers think it's Sabine.'

'That's what they're supposed to think. She doesn't take risks and I don't speak lines and that's all there is to it.' The most she'd said so far, only it sounded ominously like an exit line. She edged sideways.

Diamond had once played rugby for the Met. He took a sidestep and barred her way. She had the prospect of getting coffee spilled on her Swift costume.

He said, 'Do tell me more.' But more didn't come, so he laid it on thick again. 'Let's be clear. The reason most people watch the show is down to you. The action. They get a thrill from the stunts.'

'It's all done in the editing,' she said. 'I don't often get in real danger.'

'I'm sure that can't be true. You're far too modest. I wouldn't do your job for love nor money. But I don't look much like Sabine, so I won't get the offer.'

She actually gave a tight little smile at that, encouraging him to say, 'Has anyone asked you about the jinx?'

'It's newspaper talk.'

'Doesn't bother you?'

'I'm not interested.'

'But I am, just in case someone is pulling the strings. Most of it is nonsense, but people going missing have to be taken seriously. Were you in the cast when Dave Tudor went missing?'

She hesitated, as if sensing a trap. 'I've been part of the show since the first series.'

'I should have realised. You would have got the job soon after Sabine got hers. Did you double for her in the past, in other shows?'

She shook her head.

'They were lucky to find someone who looked like her and could do the stunts. Stunt people aren't necessarily stand-ins as well, are they?'

She shrugged. He was getting more of the silent treatment.

'You should get a double fee.'

She made clear with a sigh that this had gone on long enough.

'Do you get on with Sabine?'

'I don't need to.'

He smiled. 'She can be difficult at times, I'm told.'

She looked away. He'd get none of the lowdown from Ann Bugg.

There was movement at the end of the room and several people came in together carrying coffees. He recognised the camera supervisor and two of his team. They must have taken a break from filming. This was confirmed when two actors, male and female, in white dressing gowns, appeared in the doorway. Behind them came Greg Deans with the director, George Spode. They seemed to be looking for a space to occupy and then Deans spotted Diamond and came over.

'Didn't expect to see you again so soon, sunshine. You've found Ann, I see, our all-action lady, and I mean that in the nicest way. You're our secret star, aren't you, gorgeous?' he said, linking a hand inside Ann Bugg's arm and standing as close to her as she would allow. She looked even more uncomfortable now. 'I don't know if this gent has introduced himself. He's a very senior detective, a superintendent, no less.'

'Ann knows who I am,' Diamond said. 'We met in the kitchen.'

'You really should give us advance warning of your visits, old sport. I was upstairs filming.'

'No problem. I'm not here to see you.'

'I should hope not. We covered everything I can think of when you last came.' He turned to Ann. 'Would you mind, darling? The detective may have something confidential to tell me about his investigation.'

Would she mind? She was only too pleased of the chance to escape. She slipped her arm clear of Deans's and made a beeline for the door.

'That's a nervous young lady,' Diamond said. 'Has she ever been in trouble with the police?'

'Not to my knowledge,' Deans said. 'That's not nice, if I may say so. In this business it isn't done to enquire into each other's police records. It's highly unlikely she has one, I would say, knowing Ann as we do. She drinks in moderation and has a modest lifestyle.'

'A saint, in other words.'

Deans laughed. 'She'd better speak for herself.'

'Not to me she won't. Is she difficult to bring out in conversation, or is it me?'

More amusement. 'You, I expect. Ann is as tough as they come. She'll cheerfully run through a burning building or jump out of a moving car, but she doesn't have much to say, I admit. What were you hoping to get from her – if that isn't an indiscreet question?'

'Her thoughts on the newspaper story. She's a professional risk-taker and she's been here from the start, almost. She must remember every one of the incidents listed by the *Post*. Until I saw her just now I hadn't thought of speaking to her. She's easy to overlook.'

'Ah, there speaks a whodunnit expert. Find the most unlikely suspect and that's your perpetrator.'

'I don't read the things,' Diamond said. 'I'm only interested in true crime and then it's generally obvious who did it.'

'Obvious to a top detective, but not the man in the street like me.'

Deans as the man in the street was a stretch of the imagination Diamond couldn't make. 'Did you come over to tell me something?'

'Not especially, but I might as well ask the question everyone wants to know and doesn't dare ask. What else have you learned about the great jinx mystery?'

'Nothing worth passing on. We're working on several lines of inquiry.'

'You definitely believe there's something sinister afoot?'

'Definitely, no. But the Assistant Chief Constable ordered me to investigate and that's what I'm doing.'

'For how long? No offence, but my actors feel uncomfortable rubbing shoulders with you and your officers. They're sensitive creatures, like racehorses, easily unsettled.'

'No need, if they've done nothing wrong.'

Deans laughed. 'Everyone in this room has done something wrong. I've got three penalty points on my driving licence, but it doesn't make me a serial killer.'

'Is that what you think we're dealing with?'

'Quite the opposite, love. I used the expression to show you how events get twisted out of proportion. TV production is a minefield and I treat you as a UID. Do you know what that is?'

'Go on. Tell me.'

'An unexploded incendiary device.'

Diamond had been called some things in his time, and at least this was new. 'I'd say that's out of proportion, too.'

'Maybe it was slightly OTT. I'll put it another way. As executive producer, I have a vested interest in continuity. My job is dealing with the nasties when they occur and making sure the show goes on.'

'Are you calling me a nasty now?'

'Figure of speech, darling. Nothing personal. You know what I'm saying.'

Actually, Diamond felt more comfortable as a nasty than Greg Deans's darling. He couldn't get used to the endearments. 'Is Sabine herself on your call sheet for today?'

'Sabine? She's come and gone. She was first up this morning. All she had to do was open the door and catch the other two in bed – an in-joke you won't understand unless you watch the series.'

'The handyman panics, climbs out of the window and is seen bare-arsed on the wisteria. I was here yesterday.'

'Ha – so you were.'

'I thought today you must have moved on from there.'

'We don't film in sequence, sweetie.'

Sweetie? Diamond tried to let it wash over him. Thank God none of his team were here.

'That's all sorted out in post-production,' Deans explained. 'This bedroom scene is taking far too long.'

'Perhaps the actors are enjoying themselves.'

'No, no. They hate it. Ask any actor. Anyway, the sex is tame stuff, being a family show. The problem is that George the director thought he'd save time and money by using a real bedroom here with a genuine four-poster rather than build a set at the studio, but we have to be so careful with the furnishings. We can't climb on the dressing-table or back the cameraman into the wardrobe for fear of damaging a priceless Chippendale piece. It's taking longer than anyone thought.' He sighed. 'We'll be running late tonight.'

'Like the night Jake Nicol was last seen alive?'

'Here we go again. You're not very subtle, are you?'

'About that evening up at the airfield. What time did you leave?'

'I remember I was late home and got in trouble with Natalie, my partner. She relies on me for her main meal. We finished filming about eight. Everyone left except the grips.'

'By everyone, you mean all the actors and crew?'

'Absolutely. Charmy Down isn't a place you want to spend your evening in.'

'Everyone including you?'

'I called a wrap and left immediately.'

'How about Sabine? She was still there, surely?'

'In a sense, yes. She went straight into her motorhome.'

'I heard it was still parked there when the riggers left.'

'You'd have to ask her. I'd gone.' He gulped the last of his coffee. 'Listen, honey, I must round everyone up and get back upstairs for yet another take of the tumble in the four-poster.'

In the more sobering surroundings of the incident room that afternoon, Diamond updated himself on all that had come in, and there wasn't much. Ingeborg had been in touch with the *Bristol Post* to see if they'd had much feedback from their readers. Several had sent tweets about their own experience with jinxes.

'No use to us, guv,' she said. 'All it tells us is some people are deeply superstitious even in the twenty-first century.'

'Gullible is the word I'd use. Anything else?'

'A comment from a *Swift* fan saying Caitlin Swift must be causing all the trouble and won't get caught because she's always too smart for the police.'

'That's the kind of horseshit shows like this give rise to.'

She raised an eyebrow. 'There are too many shows where the police come out on top. It's a breath of fresh air to have a master-criminal as the star.'

'You watch it, do you? So we have a mole in the murder squad.'

She gave a slight smile. 'I've streamed a few episodes since we started on the case. It's rather well done.'

'Traitor.'

The remark was meant in fun, but Ingeborg wasn't amused. 'Get real, guv. I'm allowed to watch television without being called disloyal.'

He crossed the room to Paul Gilbert's desk. 'What's the latest on the Jake Nicol mystery?'

'Nothing much, guv. I've spent a lot of time checking

209

with rigging companies and I found one in London that once had him on their books.'

'What did you learn?'

'He was reliable and didn't mind late hours. No family.'

'A ladies' man?'

Gilbert's eyes widened. 'No one said so. Why do you ask?'

He wasn't going to reveal that Paloma had put the idea in his head. 'I keep thinking of the tash.'

Obviously a new word to Gilbert. He frowned. 'Tash? The rapper?'

'The Clark Gable moustache.'

Gilbert still looked lost. He hadn't heard of Clark Gable either. The generation gap was a gulf.

'It's two pencil-thin strips above the lips that don't meet in the middle. A miracle of shaving. I've never enquired how it's done. Maybe a barber trimmed it for him. What I'm saying is that if Nicol went to all that trouble, he probably fancied his chances as a stud.'

'And made a play for one of the women? That's a new angle.'

'Sabine was up at the airfield that afternoon and so was her double, Ann Bugg.'

'I can see where this is going. Stunning women, both of them, but strong enough to look after themselves in a fight.'

'Hold on, Paul,' Diamond said. 'I'm not suggesting either of them stabbed him, but if one of the crew witnessed him forcing himself on one of them, he could have seen red and pulled a knife.'

'Wow – that is a possibility. Someone who felt protective. Does either of them have a boyfriend?'

'Don't know. I met Ann Bugg at Milroy Court this morning and got the clear impression she has things to hide. She could hardly wait to get away from me.'

Across the room, Ingeborg winked at Jean Sharp.

Gilbert was gripped. This was his case. 'Do you think she's protecting the killer? Jake got heavy with her and this guy rescued her. She knows who and no way will she shop him.'

'It might explain a few things. Food for thought, that's all.' Already he was going off the idea. He still felt the deaths of Tudor and Nicol were connected – and possibly Mary Wroxeter's as well – and he couldn't see how the earlier murders – if that was what they were – linked up with a killing done in the heat of the moment.

He left Paul mulling over the matter.

Another line of inquiry was on his mind. He checked with John Leaman, who as office manager dealt with the flow of information to the incident room. 'Anything new from the marina?'

'No. Total silence.'

'They'll have a mountain of scrap by now.'

'Do you want me to text them?'

'Better not. They don't like being nagged. The guy in charge will call if they find anything.'

'Like a body?'

'Right now, John, I'd settle for a coat-button if it ends all the mights and maybes.'

18

It was already dark when Greg Deans finished work at Milroy Court. As he had foreseen, the bedroom scene had put the entire schedule out. He should have been firm with George and insisted on filming it in a studio set at Bottle Yard. Directors come in with fancy ideas and you have to indulge them a bit, but this had been unwise. By the end of the day, they were running two hours over. All work outside contracted hours counts as overtime and plays havoc with the budget, not to mention the extra work for the producer.

Greg's car was one of the last on the drive. The de-rig was done and nearly everyone had left. Before starting up, he called his partner, Natalie, hoping her hands would be dry enough to pick up her phone.

He waited for her soft, 'Yes?'

'Still at Trowbridge, I'm afraid, but just about to leave. I'll pick up fish and chips on the way home. I hope your day was better than mine.'

'I got through as much as I wanted,' she told him.

'Nice work, love. You must have enough for a firing.'

'Not until next week. Today's little fellows have to dry properly. How long will you be?'

'Depends if there's a queue in the chippie. Fifty minutes max.' The pottery was a converted farmhouse on the slopes west of Bath. 'Put the oven on in half an hour, would you? The fish and chips will need warming up.'

If he'd been home earlier, he would have cooked. This was their main meal of the day. He never ate much at lunchtime.

He'd first met Natalie before he'd started his career in TV, when he was struggling to find regular work of any kind in Bristol. He'd put a man-with-van card in a newsagent's window. The van part wasn't true at the time. His plan was to hire one if anyone came up with a worthwhile offer. Natalie had seen it and phoned him. She already had her ceramics business and was making it pay, with a wholesale contract supplying souvenir mugs, microwave-safe and with a durable glaze that didn't fade, to various outlets in the area. Her last driver wasn't reliable and she would pay well for someone who would make several trips a week.

Her location was really remote, up a lane hardly anyone else used. She joked that if he could find the place, he would get the job, so he splashed out, hired a van with a sat nav and drove straight there.

That morning in the pottery she'd made him coffee in one of her Royal Crescent mugs and shown him the address list of her clients. He'd agreed to start right away. Even in her work apron splashed with clay, hair tied up and covered with a scarf, she was enchanting, small, pretty and vivacious. It wasn't love at first sight, but there was a physical attraction from the beginning – on both sides. He saw the spark of interest in her eyes and was happy to encourage it. She was fully fit when they met, divorced and living alone, working long hours. The first signs of her MS didn't appear until two years after.

She had her own website that brought in steady sales of the work she really enjoyed, making much larger pieces. He'd spotted a sensational blue vase out in the yard that she'd rejected because of some flaw in the glaze and he knew straight away he must have it for his flat. She'd let him take it for nothing.

They both appreciated the arts and had good conversations about creative people they admired. In addition to the mugs, he'd started delivering what Natalie called her 'specials' to some high achievers in big houses in Bath and Bristol who were paying hundreds for them. One was Saltus Steven, the TV executive. It was Saltus who later invited Greg to work at Bottle Yard studios.

The chippie was not far off, in Church Walk, and regularly won the 'Best in Wiltshire' competition. The Codfather, a name that made people smile, groan, or do both, had been found by the riggers before the first day of shooting and quickly become popular with others in the *Swift* crowd. Tonight Greg wouldn't have been surprised to find one or two already in there. As it happened, three people he didn't know were ahead of him. His turn didn't take long. 'Two plaice in batter, please, and one portion of chips. No salt or vinegar.' They always added their own at home.

Everyone chatted while the frying was going on. The locals already knew about the filming at Milroy Court. They didn't say so, but they were clearly disappointed he wasn't a familiar face. If you're looking for appreciation, it's better to be an actor than the producer.

He was on the road again in ten minutes. There was no fast road if you wanted to avoid the centre of Bath. He had a route along unlit roads and lanes that kept well south, by way of Wellow and Combe Hay. The worst of the evening traffic was over.

His relationship with Natalie had soon become more than a business one. After two weeks, she had invited him for an evening meal and he'd stayed over. The sex was the best he'd experienced. Next day she'd suggested he move into one of the empty rooms in the farmhouse. He didn't hesitate. He was still struggling financially and she didn't ask him to pay rent, and of course there was a saving in petrol. Even better, she continued paying him for delivering the pots. He drove back to Bristol, told his landlord he was leaving, stacked his few worldly possessions into the van, including his lucky blue vase, and made the move.

When Saltus offered him the chance of being a runner at Bottle Yard, he couldn't turn it down. At the beginning, he had tried doing both jobs, making Natalie's deliveries on his day off, but she soon saw it was too much for him, so she suggested hiring a new driver. Greg stayed on as Natalie's live-in lover and that was no hardship. She was amused when he'd started using the 'luvvie' talk of the showbiz crowd. He'd always been responsive to language, quickly picking up accents and new phrases. So Natalie got used to being called 'love of my life' and 'sweetheart' even though they both knew it wasn't quite true. What they had was a friendly relationship with good sex that pleased them both.

Greg worked hard at the TV job and got promoted to assistant producer after Candida left. So his spectacular rise continued.

It was during this purple patch that Natalie had experienced her first symptoms of the multiple sclerosis: blurred vision, dizziness and numbness down one side of her body.

She thought it was some flu virus. Nothing like it occurred again for several months. The onset was slow and there were long periods when she felt normal. She didn't go for tests until nearly a year later, after being unable to move from bed one day. She was devastated when told that the illness was progressive and not curable even though it could be treated. She most feared losing the sensation in her hands and being unable to work as a potter.

Greg helped her through the shock and was a strong support. For a time, there were no lasting symptoms except that her sex drive became less active, which was understandable. She lost some of her confidence, knowing the control of her body could be taken away from her at any time. There is no certainty, no way of knowing how long you have got. Her hands and arms were spared, but in one terrible week she lost the use of both legs. This time it was permanent.

Greg became her carer and morale-booster. He found her a wheelchair-accessible potter's wheel and she managed to continue with the contract jobs, but it was just about impossible to work on the large pieces that were her joy. He researched chairs and found one she could raise a metre higher by the touch of a button, enabling her to get the height she needed. He shopped, cooked, cleaned, helped her to dress and shower and did the heavy work in the pottery, loading and emptying the kiln. Between them, they kept the business going. 'You rescued me from dire straits at the beginning, my love,' he told her, 'and now I can give something back.'

Somewhere beyond the small village of Combe Hay, deep in a valley, the road became a lane and the lane became little more than a farm track before reverting to tarmac again and continuing west. This was where visitors in search of the pottery had their confidence tested. There was no signposting and precious few landmarks. Greg knew it well, and even he had to concentrate hard on a moonless night. He was using his Range Rover. A four-wheel drive was essential for anyone living in an area where you sometimes got snowed in.

He was little more than a mile from home when he spotted a light ahead, white, like a flashlight, moving as if it was being swung as some kind of signal. He slowed and flicked off his main beam so as not to dazzle the person holding it. Closer still, he could make out a figure wearing a yellow reflective jacket, pointing with the left arm and beckoning to him to turn right with the other. If you're a driver and someone in high-visibility gear is diverting traffic, you don't argue.

A gap in the hedgerow was now revealed, an open gate.

Greg put the headlights back on to make the turn off the lane, up a slight hump and into a field, which was grassed.

He swung the Range Rover through a tight circle and halted facing the lane for an easy exit, leaving enough room for another vehicle to drive in, even though it was highly unlikely anyone else would come that way.

He turned off his headlights and waited with only the sidelights still on. Parked there with the engine running, he could smell the fish and chips in their paper wrapper on the passenger seat. All he could see through the windscreen was the open gateway and the hedge on the opposite side.

He partly unwrapped the packet and took out a chip.

When it became obvious no one had followed him into the field to tell him what was happening, he opened the door and stepped out.

He hadn't taken more than two steps when he sensed a movement nearby. The car's sidelights picked up a fast-moving shape. Something or somebody charged at him out of the darkness. Greg barely had time to register he was under attack. Instinctively he turned, swayed backwards and in that split second saw the glint of a knife blade. His back thumped against the Range Rover. Trapped on the bonnet of his own car, he could do nothing to defend himself.

19

Diamond waited until ten next morning before phoning Earnshaw, the dive supervisor. The exchange was more civil than the morning before even if the basic message hadn't changed.

'I didn't come by last evening. Thought you'd be in touch if you found anything useful.'

'Good decision, sir. Don't want to waste your time. I've hired a skip for all the scrap we fished out. We'll charge that to your budget. That's the way it works.'

No point in arguing. The reckoning would come later when Georgina found out the cost.

'You haven't finished?'

'God, no.'

'How much of the marina have you searched?'

'Nearly all the clear water. We'll start looking between the moored boats before the end of today – that is, if the boat owners don't object.'

'You don't need their permission, do you?'

'Their cooperation would be nice.'

'Are they giving you abuse?'

'I wouldn't call it that. By now they all know what we're looking for and some of them aren't comfortable with it. What's more, they don't like press photographers crawling over their homes to get good shots. Have you seen the *Bristol Post* this morning?'

'I can guess,' Diamond said. 'I have better things to do.'

'We're expecting gawpers today.'

'Can't you keep them at a distance?'

'We'll put tapes across and then the residents will complain about a loss of freedom. Can't win. It's okay. We're used to this.'

'I was thinking you're nicely placed to observe what goes on among the people who live on the boats. You know the couple I'm interested in?'

'*Deck the Halls?* Woman with the young kid? You were talking to her when you were here.'

'Right. The man has the day job. Uses a motorbike.'

'I saw him when we arrived this morning. He visited *Daisy Belle* before he left for work.'

'Who's she?' Diamond asked.

There was a tone of disrespect in Earnshaw's answer. 'It's a boat. The narrowboat moored next to them. I got the impression it was locked and not in use. He had a key and let himself in like he owns it.'

'Perhaps he does. Like a second home, extra storage or something.'

'But the wife doesn't go in. She's here all day and she doesn't set foot on board. It's only him. Do you think he's got another woman installed there?'

Diamond laughed. 'Too close to home, I reckon.' But he wrote *Daisy Belle* on the notepad on his desk, with a question mark beside it. 'Mustn't hold you up. I hope you search under the jetty.'

'I'm standing on it now.'

'I'd be happier if you were underneath.'

'I'm directing operations.'

Hope sprang briefly in Diamond's breast. 'So the diver is underneath?'

'Out in the middle. The final strip of open water. What is it with the jetty?'

'It's the place I would stow a corpse if I had one to dispose of – out of sight in case it rises to the surface.'

'We'll see if you're right, but don't hold your breath. It may not be today.'

Diving for bodies in cold, muddy water doesn't bring out the best in people, Diamond decided.

After ending the call, he took out his phone and found the *Bristol Post* website and the headline POLICE DIVERS SEARCH MARINA. Below was a picture of a black-clad figure jumping into the water in full gear with snorkel cylinders strapped to his back.

He closed the page without reading the main text. He knew what it would say and the publicity would do no harm. The public would be reassured that the police were doing something, or seen to be. He might need to convince Georgina of that.

His self-confidence, usually so robust, was being tested by this case. If nothing was recovered from the marina, his suspicion of Fergus and Candida would have to be reassessed. He might even ask himself whether he'd got it hopelessly wrong and there were no bodies anywhere.

He hadn't slept well. His brain had been struggling to process all the information he and the team had gathered. Worryingly, he couldn't remember a piece of conversation he'd believed at the time was significant, or might be.

Bad sleep, memory lapses, loss of confidence. Could Georgina be right about wanting to pension him off?

Perish the thought.

He stepped into the incident room and found Ingeborg

working her keyboard. 'Your memory is better than mine, Inge. Cast your mind back to when we interviewed Sabine. There was a lot to take in and she was more talkative than you or I expected, right?'

'Quite the charmer.'

'I hear the same note in your voice as when you reminded me she's an actor. Her charm passed you by. Enough of that. I've been trying to recall something you said when we were with her.'

'You did most of the talking, guv.'

'Right, but you chipped in when you felt I was in danger of missing a point, as you do.'

'We were on a steep learning curve,' Ingeborg said. 'There was a lot to take in.'

'Plenty. Isn't it annoying when you're trying to hook things out from the back of your brain and can't? Your comment on something Sabine said made an impression on me – not enough of one, it seems.'

'Something *I* said?'

'And I didn't follow it up at the time. I told myself you and I could discuss it later.'

'Can you give me a rough idea what it was about?'

'I have a feeling it was when we spoke about the jinx incidents with her.'

'Let's go through them, then,' she said, spreading her hand to count them off on her fingers. 'Trixie pulling out?'

'Not that.'

'The fire in the sound engineers' van? The injury to the stuntmen?'

'Keep going.'

'Dave Tudor going missing? Mary Wroxeter's death?'

'Not that.' Does she think I'm losing it? he asked himself.

'Dan Burbage?'

'No.'

'Daisy Summerfield?'

His hand went up. 'Something about the old lady. You took over the questioning when Sabine mentioned her. What was it you said?'

'That the way she died was mostly speculation? The break-in was only discovered after she was found dead.'

'Something else. A remark you made.'

'That it was odd the burglar chose that evening to break in?'

'Yes!' A surge of relief. 'I can almost hear your exact words: "How did the burglar know Daisy was supposed to be away filming?"'

'I said that?'

'I'm sure of it.'

'Maybe I was reading too much into it,' Ingeborg said, without fully appreciating the significance. 'I suggested the burglar had seen the call sheet. But there was this last-minute change he couldn't have known about. She came home early after they filmed her scene as an add-on at the end of the day.'

He felt like hugging her. 'This is what I've been struggling to remember and it has to be followed up.' His brain was in overdrive now. 'We'll call the Met and get the latest on their investigation.'

'"We", meaning me?' she said.

'No. I need your brainwork for this, not your research skills. It's a job for Jean Sharp.'

He crossed the room. Jean saw him coming and turned as pale as the whiteboard behind her.

'Relax,' he said. 'I'm not asking you to drive me anywhere. I have an in-house task for you. Daisy Summerfield, the old dear who played Swift's mother in the show. Cardiac arrest believed to have been triggered by finding a burglar in her bedroom. We haven't examined the full facts.'

She was frowning. 'It's not our case, guv.'

'Right. I need an update from Richmond CID. The name of the investigating officer would be a start. Case notes, post-mortem report, anything the coroner is willing to let us have. Maybe no more can be said about a sad occurrence, but it's part of our brief and we should have looked at it before now.'

Confident she'd deliver what he'd asked for, he returned to Ingeborg. 'It's too much to hope they already arrested the burglar.'

'The Met clear-up rate for residential burglary is about five per cent, guv, and that's better than ours.'

Crime statistics were a sore point for Diamond. He was always being reminded by Georgina that Bath lagged behind everyone else. 'But they're investigating and they may even have their suspicions who it was. Burglars have their MO, whether they favour smashing windows or ringing the door-bell and conning their way in.'

'I can't see how this helps,' she said.

'Trust me, it could.'

'I thought we decided her death couldn't have been deliberate.'

'And we may have made a mistake. Your point was a telling one. The burglar broke in believing Daisy was away in Bristol. Her return to Richmond was a last-minute deci-sion that turned out to be fatal.'

'It was a heart attack. They did the post-mortem. It can't have been murder, guv.'

'But it could have killed off the show. Daisy was one of the main players, wasn't she?'

Ingeborg nodded. 'Swift's villainous old mother, tough and unprincipled and hugely popular with the viewers.'

'And in real life she was a normal old lady and the shock of having her home broken into could easily have made her quit. If she didn't, she'd have the thought of another break-in each time she came here for filming. Do you see? Someone wanting to wreck the show tips off his thieving friend in London when the house will be empty.'

'It's a nasty thought, but I don't buy it, guv, the idea that anyone would go to all that trouble to sabotage the show. Anyhow, that hasn't happened. *Swift* is on its seventh season.'

'You really are well up on it.'

She smiled. 'Comes in useful sometimes, doesn't it, having a mole on the team?'

A shout from across the room interrupted them, John Leaman calling them to his workstation.

'What's he on about now?'

Diamond went over.

Leaman rolled his chair back from his screen. 'You must see this, just posted.'

It was a news release headed MISSING TV PRODUCER:

Avon & Somerset Police are appealing for information about a television executive, Greg Deans, who failed to return home yesterday from a film location in Trowbridge, 15 miles away. He was driving a Range Rover Evoque. Contact Bath Police on 0117 998 9112.

'Deans?' Diamond said. 'What the hell?' He grabbed the phone and got through to the control room – and to a sergeant he knew.

'Yes, sir, you might think it's jumping the gun to be issuing a misper appeal so soon, but we were on to this last

225

night. The guy lives with a disabled woman who called 101. He's her carer.'

'You don't have to tell me about these people,' Diamond said. 'I know Greg Deans. His partner is a potter called Natalie.'

'Well, he phoned her about eight twenty from Milroy Court, where he was filming, and told her he was on his way home. He didn't arrive. She was pretty distressed when she phoned the call centre at ten forty-seven.'

'Did someone go to see her?'

'Not last night. Obviously you know they live out in the sticks, a few miles west of Combe Hay. A family liaison officer did her best over the phone to assess the situation. She calmed the poor lady down and promised we'd get someone out in the morning if he was still missing. Social services are with her as we speak.'

'And no news of Deans?'

'Still missing. He told the lady he was bringing home fish and chips from a shop in Trowbridge. Doesn't sound like he was planning to disappear.'

'Do you know the route home he would have taken?'

'That's anyone's guess, except he would have needed to go through Combe Hay. We've put out an all-cars alert and a team is making a search.'

Diamond's frustration showed. 'We should have been informed last night. Didn't you know we have an inquiry under way about this TV company?'

'I wasn't on the shift, sir, but no, I didn't.'

'We have an incident room here at Concorde House. Two other men went missing from this show, one very recently, with evidence of violence.'

'Christ, no. That puts a different spin on it. There's obviously a communications breakdown. We'll keep you in the loop in future.'

'Fuck the future. I'm on the case right now. I have a bad feeling about this.'

Diamond replaced the phone and stood for a moment trying to deal with his anger while processing the news of yet another disappearance. 'Greg Deans now, the top man. We need the full story from his partner.' He turned to face Ingeborg.

She knew the drill. 'Give me three minutes, guv. See you by the car.'

Finding the place was the first challenge. Natalie's website should have helped, but the map gave only a general idea. The terrain was featureless except for narrow intersecting lanes in patches of woodland that masked the view. GPS turned out to be more of a hindrance than a help. As the passenger, Diamond felt he should take over as navigator. As a result, Ingeborg drove into the wrong farm and when Diamond got out of the car he was treated as the enemy by a territorial goose hissing, honking and flapping its wings. When he turned his back, it chased him and pecked his legs.

'I don't think that was the pottery, guv,' Ingeborg said as they drove off.

'If it was, I'm sending someone else.'

Finally they got directions from a hiker who seemed to know what he was talking about. An artistically lettered board told them they'd reached the right place, a cluster of buildings around a stone farmhouse with a tiled roof that must have been a recent replacement. Two cars were already in the yard. Neither was a Range Rover Evoque.

Their knock was answered by a woman in a blue health-care tunic. She put her finger to her lips as soon as Diamond started to explain why they were there. In a death-bed whisper she said, 'I hope this isn't bad news.'

227

He shook his head and lowered his voice as well, 'May we come in?'

'She's already told everything she knows to the policemen who were here earlier. She's been given a sedative.'

'Is she asleep, then?'

'No, but she can't take more of your questioning.'

'We haven't started, ma'am.'

They were shown into a large kitchen with whitewashed walls and a tiled floor, where a small, dark-haired woman in a wheelchair looked anything but sedated. Large, anxious eyes locked with Diamond's. 'What's happened? You can tell me.'

He explained that nothing new had happened. The hunt for Greg was under way and she would have to endure more questions.

She gripped the sides of the chair. 'Ask away – anything you like.'

The nurse clicked her tongue.

Diamond was treading on eggs here. Anything adding to Natalie's distress would risk hysterics. He must give no hint of his suspicions about the fate of the other two missing men.

He started with the probable route home Deans had taken. She said she was sure he would have come by the quickest way possible, even if it meant using minor roads. He worked long hours and he didn't hang about when the day was done.

He promised every yard of the way would be searched and CCTV footage examined if available.

Ingeborg was checking her phone. 'The most direct route would take him through Farleigh Hungerford and Wellow.'

'Are there cameras there?' Diamond asked.

The look he got from his sergeant said it was the dumbest question he'd ever asked.

She turned to Natalie. 'He was driving the Range Rover registered to him, right? We have the number.'

Diamond said, 'I believe he phoned you just before leaving. What time was that?'

'About twenty past eight. He said he would pick up fish and chips from a shop nearby. He expected to be with me in fifty minutes and asked me to warm up the oven. He's so reliable usually. It was still warming up two and a half hours later when I called the emergency number. I think he must have had an accident.'

'There were none reported in that time span, ma'am. Did he sound under strain?'

'He was tired and a bit down. It had been a long day, he said, and he hoped mine had gone better than his.'

'Yes, they had trouble shooting one scene,' Diamond said. 'I was out there on another matter and Greg spoke to me.'

'Really? You were at Milroy Court?' Her eyes widened in surprise. She didn't seem to know the show was under investigation.

'He's the boss, isn't he, the producer? He was treating the extra takes as an annoyance rather than a major setback.'

Ingeborg picked up on Natalie's reaction. 'Doesn't he discuss his work with you?'

A hint of colour came to the pale face. 'Hardly ever. He likes to switch off when he gets home. The household jobs take over. He's my only carer. And there's usually a meal to cook.'

'I understand.' Ingeborg got the interview back on track. 'We have officers checking all the chippies in Trowbridge. With luck they'll have security cameras.'

Diamond added, 'This will give us a time and we'll know he definitely started for home. Is anything bothering him?'

229

'He'd have said if it is. We're very open with each other.' Which sounded like a contradiction. She'd said a moment ago that they didn't discuss his work.

'How long have you been together?'

'We met in 2012, before I got ill, before he started in television. He did deliveries for me. We were attracted to each other and it became . . . physical. I suggested Greg moved in. We keep to separate rooms except when . . .' Her eyes slid sideways and she bit her lip. 'But you don't need to know all this.'

'You're doing well. Has he stopped driving for you now?'

'He stopped soon after he started with Swift and Proud. One of my clients happened to be the executive producer there and he offered Greg a job. Saltus Steven.'

Diamond remembered the photo montage in the executive room in the office in the Colonnades.

'So Greg took on the new job, but stayed on.'

'Yes, and I'm so lucky he did. Since my MS took hold, he's become my mainstay. I couldn't keep going without him. He saw what was needed and went online and found new equipment so I can work from the wheelchair. He does the heavy work, loads and unloads the kiln for me, and I'm still able to throw the pots. I was very traditional and loved my kick wheel, but he talked me into going electric and it's the obvious solution.'

'You're brave.'

'Greg is the hero. I can't manage without him.'

Her dependence on Deans was a tragedy in the making.

'After what you just told us, this will sound churlish, but it's a question we have to ask when someone goes missing. Have you noticed any change in his behaviour towards you?'

She frowned. 'What are you suggesting – that he's left me? That's horrible. No, he wouldn't. He wouldn't.'

'I asked, ma'am, because it's my job. I'm not suggesting anything. You've told me what I need to know.'

The nurse was quick to take this as a cue. She'd been a disapproving presence throughout. She took a step forward and said, 'In that case, you'd better leave now. Natalie needs to rest.'

'Understood,' Diamond said, 'but before we do we'll take a look at Mr Deans's bedroom if we may. Has anyone been up there?'

Natalie said, 'No one. It will be just as he left it yesterday morning. The stairs are through the door behind you. His is at the end of the landing on the left.'

A stair lift was installed but there was ample room for them to use the stairs. A second wheelchair was on the landing.

They found the bedroom and there were no surprises. It was nicely furnished in light oak. Apart from the high ceiling and the fireplace, it had a modern look. The duvet had been turned back on the bed and a pair of boxer shorts lay on the pillow. On the bedside table were a newspaper folded back to show a half-finished crossword, a paperback face down and a remote for the plasma TV on the opposite wall. More books were shelved to one side of the bed. Diamond opened the wardrobe and looked in the chest of drawers. Pants and T-shirts folded.

'What do you think?' Diamond asked.

'He expects to return,' Ingeborg said.

'Agreed. He hasn't taken much with him if he's done a runner.'

'Why would he, with a fantastic job, free lodging and someone who appreciates him?'

'I can only think he's reached a crisis point. It's become all too much – the caring, I mean – and he can't face telling

231

her. It can only get harder. They're not in love. It was only ever an arrangement that suited them both, but it doesn't suit him any more. People who get stressed to breaking point sometimes take off.'

Ingeborg shook her head. 'I can't see Greg cracking up. He's got a top job in television. He won't put that at risk.'

'It's not a rational decision, Inge. What's your theory, then?'

'Well, he hasn't cracked up and he isn't dead. This is just about him and Natalie. He wants out and he doesn't have the guts to tell her face to face. I expect he'll send her a text to say he's leaving the pottery. He plans to return for his things later, when she's over the shock.'

'If you're right, he will have turned up for work this morning.'

'Let's find out.' She took out her phone. 'I wonder if anyone's thought of this.'

'Who are you calling?'

'His office.'

It became immediately clear from Ingeborg's end of the conversation that the staff at Swift and Proud hadn't seen Greg Deans or heard from him.

'But it doesn't mean you're right about the breakdown. They aren't expecting him in,' she told Diamond after ending the call. 'Yesterday was the last day of filming at Milroy Court, and some of the crew start setting up at a new location tomorrow. It's all planned. For most of them it's a day off. He picked his time to leave her, the shit.' Ingeborg at her most scathing. The phone in her hand pinged. 'And now I've got a text from John Leaman.' She brought it up on her screen, stared, frowned and shook her head. 'Time for a rethink, guv. Deans bought fish and chips for two at a shop in Trowbridge called the Codfather.

The owners remember him talking about the show and they may have got him on CCTV.'

'So both of us are wrong. He was on his way here, and he did buy supper for Natalie. Not such a shit after all.'

'What now, then?'

'We step up the search for his car. I'll get an all-units out. This sounds like bad news, Inge.'

20

Greg Deans's Range Rover was found at 4.15 p.m. the same day in a field only two miles from the pottery and under a mile from Combe Hay. Because it was off the road, it hadn't been sighted in earlier searches. It was unlocked and there was staining on the bodywork that looked worryingly like blood. On the passenger seat was a partly opened pack of cold fish and chips.

Diamond arrived forty minutes later with Ingeborg and Keith Halliwell. They had to park in a field opposite to avoid blocking the lane.

The missing vehicle was inside a gate and facing the lane in an area already cordoned with police tape. A tall hedge meant it had been almost hidden from anyone driving by, so the searchers had done well. The uniformed sergeant who had made the find admitted he'd passed the gate twice before taking a closer look. 'When we had enough of us, we divided the lane into sections and got a result.'

'Was it you who put the tape in place?' Diamond asked.

'Yes, sir, and the crime scene guys are on their way.'

'Fingers crossed they can tell us the full story, then. Has anyone phoned his partner at the pottery?'

'No. Should we have done?'

'You did the right thing. I'd rather not break the news

until we know more. Obviously, you approached the car to check what was inside.'

'Me and my mate, sir.'

'Opened the door, did you? I'm not knocking you, just noting that the CSI team will need your prints, fingers and shoes, to eliminate them from any others they find. Don't leave before they get here, got it?'

He was eager to get a closer look, but held himself in check.

A short hiatus before the crime scene experts arrived allowed his jangled emotions to process the fast developing tragedy. His overriding concern was for that poor disabled woman waiting for news. Greg Deans wasn't a man it was easy to like or respect, but he seemed to have treated Natalie with affection. It must have taken major efforts to manage his TV work and care for her as well, never off duty. And she was remarkably brave to have kept the pottery business going this far into her progressive illness.

The CSI van stopped in the lane outside for someone to get out, already in his protective suit. Short and spry, he marched over as if he meant business from the word go. 'Do we have a senior investigating officer?'

'Guilty,' Diamond said and got a sharp look back.

Names were exchanged. The man was Wolfgang, and he spoke his name the English way, with a W. 'Good to see the tape in place, but we will need to extend the cordon another three metres in each direction. First we need an officer at the gate to make sure some idiot doesn't drive into the field and override the tyre marks. Will you arrange that?'

'Consider it done.' Diamond beckoned to one of the uniformed bobbies and issued the instruction.

'I heard there's blood,' Wolfgang said. 'Is there a body?'

'If there is, I need to go to Specsavers.'

No smile. 'In that case another vehicle may have removed it from the scene and there should be tracks.' He cupped his hands to his mouth and shouted at the back of the gatekeeper, 'Careful where you tread, particularly in the muddy area.' And then he raised his voice still more. 'Have any of you people brought forensic suits and overshoes? If you have, put them on, please. If not, we have a supply.'

Scene-of-crime officers were always bossy. Everyone else was a menace in their eyes, liable to corrupt the scene and add to their workload, an opinion probably borne out of experience.

Diamond and his colleagues dragged the polyethylene suits over their clothes and watched the first moves from a safe distance. A photographer in the same approved kit started taking overview pictures of the scene from multiple angles on the safe side of the tape. A discussion was held before the next step, after which Wolfgang strutted over to Diamond's group.

'You probably want a closer look.'

'It would help.'

'Can we agree on the common approach path, then? I propose making it over there where my team are standing, in a straight line to the offside of the vehicle. I need to conduct a fingertip search of the strip of ground before anyone else uses it.'

'Suits me.' You didn't argue with Wolfgang.

Two SOCOs shoulder to shoulder and on hands and knees inched into the sealed-off area. Behind them, a note-taker stood ready to log any finds.

It was no use getting impatient, Diamond knew from long experience at crime scenes. This one was about as fresh as it got. The problem with the disappearances of

Tudor and Nicol had been the delay in getting there. In the case of Tudor it was four years. Nicol's absence was more recent but hadn't been treated as serious for four days until his bloodstained belt was found – four days in which the scene was churned up by vehicles. Shocking as it was, this new incident was an opportunity. A fresh crime scene would surely yield valuable information.

'How long before it gets dark?' Halliwell said. 'Three hours maximum? At this rate we'll all be back tomorrow.'

'Speak for yourself,' Ingeborg said. 'I'm not on duty tomorrow.'

'They may bring in arc lamps and work through the night.'

'Oh heck, I hadn't thought of that.'

'Were you planning an evening out, by any chance?'

Diamond got on the phone to Georgina and asked her to authorise a wider search next morning. The SOCOs had staked out their territory. It was up to the police to go over the rest of the field. If there wasn't a body to be found, there might be other evidence, even a discarded murder weapon.

Georgina had already heard about the find and was eager to know what had happened. Diamond couldn't tell her much. To be fair, she didn't need any convincing of the need for more bobbies. She asked if the press had arrived at the scene and was relieved to be told they hadn't. 'Heaven only knows what they'll make of this, following on from everything else.'

Diamond was summoned to the approach path, now marked and ready for use. Stepping plates had been laid over the turf. After Wolfgang's elaborate preparation, the walk out to the Range Rover would feel like the first steps on the moon.

'Don't touch a thing,' he was warned by the pocket-sized CSI supremo. 'Don't even think about touching anything.'

'I wasn't born yesterday, Wolfgang.'

'You'd be amazed how some senior officers behave.'

'And some, like me, always do as we are told.'

Wolfgang was carrying a holdall that looked like a beach bag. He came to a halt about six feet back from the Range Rover. The driver's door had been left partly open. Someone had wiped a space on the window and left a smear. 'Did your people do this?' He was sounding increasingly like a headmaster.

'They're not my people. They're the patrol officers who got here first. I told them you'll need their prints.'

'Also a statement detailing everything they did. I need to know how much of the scene is compromised.' Wolfgang put his left foot forward as if he was testing the thickness of ice. He produced a ruler from the bag and used it to ease the door fully open without using his latex-gloved hands. Then he handed Diamond a torch and stood back. 'You first.' He had his procedures and he was sticking to them. Protocol decrees that the senior investigating officer is the first to examine the scene.

Diamond stepped up.

The cloud cover meant that at this time of day the torch was needed for inspecting the inside of the car. The beam of light showed him the banal but instructive sight of fish and chips on the passenger seat, the packet partially open as if the victim had got hungry and started eating. Deans had kept his word to Natalie.

The seats and safety belts appeared to be unmarked. He backed away and moved the circle of light along the body-work. There was the dried mud you'd expect from a vehicle splashing through country lanes and there were also marks that overlaid the mud and were darker. They had spattered the side from a different angle.

Blood.

He found a smear that he took to be a bloody handprint that had slid down the slippery surface.

'That's a hand mark by the look of it,' he told Wolfgang. 'Looks to me as if he stepped out and was attacked and fell back against the side. Can you get fingerprints?'

'Hard to say,' Wolfgang told him. 'They're not sharp. The blood itself may be a better identifier. There's a large patch on the ground to your right. He was bleeding heavily. Do you know who he was?'

'The owner of the car is a man called Greg Deans, a TV executive who was reported missing last night. You should be able to get a DNA sample from his home. He lived under a mile from here. If he was badly wounded, I wonder if he tried to get home.'

'He wouldn't have got far, going by the blood loss,' Wolfgang said. 'It's more likely he fell right here and didn't get up. Look at the scuff marks made by his shoes as he slid down. Look at the amount of blood on the turf.'

Diamond moved the torch over the dark patch and didn't need any more convincing.

'Are there specks of blood on the fish and chips?'

Diamond leaned right in for a better view and his head touched something. Wolfgang won't thank me for this, he thought. He supposed he'd nudged the rear-view mirror. He hadn't. When he saw what it was he felt an uprush of excitement. He pulled his head and shoulders out of the car. 'Have I gone to heaven, or is that a dash-board camera?'

The stone-faced SOCO changed places with Diamond. 'You're correct,' he said after some time and without a trace of emotion. 'It's not all that modern, but it seems to be hard-wired. We can play it back and see what's on it if you like.'

'Now?'

'Later. We must test it for residues, like everything else.' He backed out and straightened up. 'Don't build up your hopes. It may not have been activated.'

'Dash cams are powered by the ignition, aren't they?'

'Usually. Even if it was working – which isn't certain – it won't have carried on recording after he switched off. The modern cameras have a motion detector that operates even when the vehicle is parked, but this is very basic. And of course you won't see anything outside the camera's range.'

'Let's not get carried away,' Diamond said, riled by so much downbeat comment.

'What do you mean by that?'

'It could still give us vital evidence.'

Wolfgang remained unmoved. 'Have you finished your inspection?'

'I'd like to know if there's anything on the back seat.'

'Couldn't you see from the front?'

Diamond leaned in again, careful not to touch anything. 'The head restraints are in the way.'

'Don't touch them.'

'I don't intend to. Can you see anything through the back window?'

'Not without wiping it clean,' Wolfgang said. 'It's far too dirty.'

'We could open the rear door and have a look.'

The suggestion was met with a sound like the dregs of a drink sucked through a straw. 'Nothing must be touched. Photography next and then we'll go over the exterior.'

No short cuts, then. Wolfgang went by the rules and another twenty minutes passed before he allowed one of the rear doors to be opened.

Diamond approached the car again.

A carrier bag was on the back seat.

'Is it too much to hope we can see what's inside?' Diamond asked.

Wolfgang eyed him with scorn. 'Haven't you ever done the explosive devices course?'

Leaving Halliwell at the scene, Diamond and Ingeborg removed their forensic suits and drove the short distance to the pottery to break the bad news to Natalie. With them came one of the SOCOs on a different mission: to collect DNA samples from Deans's room. She was still in the full protective whites and holding a handful of evidence bags.

'Better not show yourself at the start,' Diamond said, thinking of the shock she would give dressed like that. 'Sit in the car for a few minutes and we'll come out and get you.'

The no-nonsense nurse came to the door and told them Natalie was in bed and sleeping. 'She stopped struggling against the sedation and now she can rest.'

'She'll be out to the world for some time, then?'

'Until tomorrow, for sure.'

'Best thing,' he said, thinking more of himself than Natalie, if truth were told. Giving bad news was a duty every police officer dreaded. It could wait until the morning. 'Are you staying the night?'

'Yes. I'll be here when she wakes up.'

'Excellent. I'll be back tomorrow myself to speak to Natalie after she's rested.' He'd decided not to say anything to the nurse about what had been found in the field. Natalie needed to hear it first-hand from him. 'But as we're here, we'll take a look around the outbuildings. And a colleague of ours will need access to Mr Deans's room.'

The scale of the pottery business was an eye-opener when they visited the buildings grouped around the yard. One barn was stacked with finished mugs, ready for sale, flat-packs of cardboard boxes and rolls of bubble wrap. Another, where a huge kiln was housed, had more filled racks against the wall. The mugs here had been given the bisque firing and awaited the glaze. And in another, they found the potter's wheel adapted for use by a disabled person. A tray on a bench beside it was filled with freshly made mugs.

'Sad sight.' Diamond spoke his thoughts aloud. 'I doubt whether any of this will get finished. She really depended on Deans.'

When they returned to the field, Wolfgang had decided to close down for the day. His team had completed their immediate work and would be back at nine next morning. Two hapless constables would stand by the entrance all night, as Wolfgang put it, 'to safeguard the integrity of the site'.

'What was in the Sainsbury's bag on the back seat?' Diamond asked.

'More Sainsbury's bags,' Wolfgang told him.

'That was all?'

'We found reddish hairs inside the car and on the grass quite close to the large bloodstain. They could be informative.'

'His own, by the sound of it.' Diamond said.

'I will personally deliver all the samples tonight. We use a lab not far from where I live in Midsomer Norton. I believe in keeping the chain of evidence as short as possible.'

'Your colleague found some hairs on a brush and comb in Greg Deans's room.'

'Excellent. They will serve as the control samples.'

'This may be an impossible question, Wolfgang, but how soon can we expect some results?'

'I will ask the head scientist to treat them as a priority. They know me there. They don't usually keep me waiting.'

'I can believe it.'

'One more thing. We removed the memory card from the dash cam. I'll send the footage later today to your computer – if any of it is worth sending.'

'You're a star. Do you want my contact details?'

Wolfgang smiled at the naivety of the question. 'I have you on my phone already. Look for an email at ten this evening, that is if you work outside normal hours.'

On the way back, he listened to Bristol Radio. There was nothing yet about Greg Deans on the regional news. 'We're ahead of the pack this time,' he said. 'I thought someone was sure to have tipped them off.'

'Isn't that your job?' Ingeborg said.

He smiled. 'All in good time. We may issue a statement tomorrow if we have anything definite for them. Right now I'm not looking for more publicity. Fingers crossed, I'll learn something from the dash cam footage.'

As you would expect from the punctilious Wolfgang, the video arrived in Diamond's inbox shortly before ten the same evening. The covering email was typically chastening. 'This will be meat and drink to you people, no doubt. The limitations of the camera are obvious, as you will discover. The best dash cams have night vision. However, I'm sending the footage for what it's worth.'

Paloma offered the use of her all-singing, all-dancing computer to get a generous-sized image. 'Ready?' she said and clicked on the download.

Up came a driver's view of a main road in daylight with other vehicles ahead.

'Early in the day on his way to work, by the look of it,' Diamond said. 'Can we fast-forward?' He was leaving Paloma to manage the technology.

'Should be able to,' she said. Figures along the bottom of the screen displayed the time and date as well as the car's speed. 'What time of day are we looking for?'

'He phoned home at eight twenty and said he was leaving Trowbridge, so if we can pick it up round about then, we'll get to the action, I hope.'

The images after dark were more grainy than the earlier ones, but once the car's headlights had been switched on, the picture quality wasn't bad.

'It's a weird experience watching this,' Paloma said. 'Like I'm in the car and driving it.'

'I know. I feel the same. Have to keep reminding myself it's Greg at the wheel.'

'That's even more spooky, being driven by a dead man. Shall I let it run now? Shout if you want to rewind.'

'Will do. Those are the gates of Milroy Court coming up. He's turning left and he's on his way home. The street lighting helps.'

Not more than five minutes into the trip, the car pulled over into a space in a row of vehicles lining the kerb.

'This must be the chippy,' Diamond said. 'Damn!'

The screen had suddenly gone blank.

'It's okay, he switched off,' Paloma said. 'He'll be going in to buy his fish and chips. We don't have to wait ten minutes while they're cooking it. The action should jump forward.'

She was right. The picture was live again and they were moving off.

'What time are we showing now? Eight forty-five. He will have put the packet on the passenger seat and is making for home.'

'If this was a film, we'd get an establishing shot of the fish and chips,' Paloma said. 'I'm still not adjusted to this way of seeing things.'

'Mustn't complain,' he said. 'At least we have something. I wouldn't have believed a drive through Trowbridge can be so full of interest. Nothing happens now until he's almost home, but we'd better not fast-forward. I need to know the route he takes.'

'Took,' Paloma said. 'This was yesterday.'

They came to a roundabout. 'Wingfield Road, as I expected. This will take us out to Farleigh Hungerford and across the A36 to Hinton Charterhouse. If you don't mind narrow lanes it's the quick way.'

'It looks all the same without street lights.'

'Well, it is between the villages.'

The headlights switched to full beam and showed the cat's eyes for some distance ahead and little else except the occasional road sign until they crossed the A36, the main artery into Bath, swarming with traffic, and started up an even more narrow country lane.

'This is like watching paint dry,' Paloma said after some minutes. 'I might leave you with the mouse and make the tea.'

'Don't,' he said. 'That was Wellow we came through and we're almost at Combe Hay where the incident happened, or just after.'

'He's driving too fast for my liking.'

Diamond had to agree. 'The width exaggerates the speed,

but I'm uncomfortable with it. He wants to get home now. He can smell those chips.'

The lights picked out a drystone wall and some buildings fronting the lane.

'We must be approaching Combe Hay. Something soon causes him to turn off into the field.'

'Too many turns. I'm losing all sense of direction. Even if you live here you could get lost in the dark.'

Diamond had stopped speaking. This was crunch time. The car was through the village and picking up speed again.

'What's that ahead?'

The headlight had picked out a small patch of bright yellow. Someone in a high-visibility jacket was standing in the lane gesturing to the driver to make a right turn. The speed slowed from forty-five to below twenty. The identity of the figure was impossible to make out. And suddenly the light dimmed from full beam to dipped headlights.

'Why did he do that? So as not to dazzle the guy, I suppose.'

The car slowed as it approached the figure directing them through a gateway and into a field. The dipped lights caught the reflective tape on the jacket and sleeves, but wouldn't show more than a vague impression of the person wearing them.

'Can we stop it and replay that bit in slow motion?'

'Now you're asking,' Paloma said. She succeeded in stopping the video and placing them back about fifty yards.

'Infuriating,' Diamond said when it started up again. 'So indistinct.'

'The image is only as good as the equipment. My computer isn't the problem, but the dash cam can't be all that good. They work on a continuous loop as far as I know. I suppose it degrades as time goes on, like the rest of us.'

'You're talking like Wolfgang now.'

'Oh, thanks.'

She tried showing it frame by frame and that didn't help much.

'He must be masked and hooded,' Diamond said. 'You can just about see the whites of the eyes. There's no lighter area where the face should be. It's hard to see anything except the jacket. Any driver is going to do as ordered by an official-looking figure like that. Let's look at the next sequence.'

So the narrative resumed again. The Range Rover turned right and entered the field, making the picture jig up and down as it moved over the uneven ground. It turned in a full circle and came to a stop at a slightly oblique angle facing the gateway.

'Can we go back?' Diamond asked.

'How far?'

'To when we came through the gate.'

Paloma judged it well.

'As he was turning I thought I saw something metallic in the shadow of the hedge,' Diamond said. 'Could have been a small vehicle.'

'You're too close to the screen to see anything properly,' Paloma said. 'Move your chair back a bit.'

He watched the slow-motion judder of the image. 'There!'

She froze the picture and caught, unmistakably, the sheen of metal.

'Not big enough for a car,' he said. 'I think it could be a motorbike.'

'If it isn't farm machinery,' Paloma said. 'No, I think you're right.'

'If I am, we know how one of them got here. This was a planned ambush. Can the video run on now?'

The journey was over, the Range Rover at a standstill, and for two or three minutes it looked and felt as if the show was at an end. The available light had dimmed even more, bringing a dishwater murk to the pixels that formed the image. Slight luminosity at either side suggested that the car's sidelights had been left on.

'He hasn't switched off the engine,' Diamond said. 'He's uncertain what to do next. At some point soon, he'll step out.'

'We won't see that,' Paloma said. 'It happens this side of the camera.'

'That's so infuriating. Hold on. Something is going on here.'

At the bottom right of the screen a domed shadow bobbed up briefly and went out of shot just as suddenly.

'The top of his head. He's out of the car,' Diamond said. 'This is him wanting to find out why he was taken off the road.'

And now some movement from higher up the screen, indistinct, but not for long. A dark shape emerged from the darkness and came into better focus, becoming recognisable as a human figure. It crept close enough to the car's sidelight for the hooded head, shoulders and upper arms to be apparent. And there was something else – the flash of a blade.

Paloma caught her breath.

A scene of violence was enacted at the lower edge of the camera's range. First, the top of a head, shifting left and off camera, as if Deans had backed or been shoved against the bonnet of the car. Then – with shocking clarity – the second figure close up, knife raised above shoulder height. For a moment the gloved fist gripping the knife took up the whole of the screen, the back of the hand and knuckles sharply defined. Then it thrust downwards.

Again and again.

'Dear God,' Paloma said, 'we're watching the murder.'

21

Diamond reran the sequence repeatedly. Paloma had been sickened by it after one look, so he took over the mouse while she went to the kitchen to make tea. He needed to check each detail. The attack seemed to end after five thrusts. The picture reverted to the view of the field and the hedge caught in an eerie stillness like a freeze frame except that the film was running. After a few seconds more, the footage ended, as if the camera was switched off. The time at the foot of the screen when Deans got out of the car was 9.20 p.m. The assault began fifteen seconds later and ended before the minute was up. The attacker merged with the shadows for much of the action, but was definitely masked, gloved and hooded. The knife was a dagger with a pointed end, purpose-built for stabbing. Hatred lay behind this attack.

The images were still with him when he went to bed. Lying there, not ready for sleep, he tried putting this attack in the context of the wider investigation, the fact that this was a third disappearance linked to the same TV show, but his brain wasn't ready to go into analytical mode. The dark shape moving in for the kill kept butting into his thoughts.

Next day, he had a better perspective. His first duty was to bring his team up to speed. He arrived in the incident room at what for him was a savagely early hour. They watched the dash cam footage on the large screen. The contrast between the frenzied stabbing and the stillness of the scene that followed seemed to stun everyone.

There was a respectful silence.

Eventually, Keith Halliwell said, 'Vicious.'

Paul Gilbert said, 'I've heard of road rage, but that was excessive. Where did he come from?'

John Leaman, working the controls, said, 'Shall I rerun the last part?'

'You'd better,' Ingeborg said. 'It was all so sudden.'

They watched a second time, and a third, from the moment the car's lights picked up the figure in the high-visibility jacket.

'Are there two people involved, the one in the lane and the knifeman,' Halliwell said, 'or is it the same guy?'

'This is something I've been asking myself,' Diamond said. 'There's time to have taken off the jacket, entered the field and launched the attack.'

'You don't see much of the one standing in the lane even when the headlights are on him,' Gilbert said. 'The jacket is clear enough, but the rest of him isn't.'

'What do you expect?' Ingeborg said. 'A name plate hanging from his neck?'

'There's nothing to give an idea of scale. He could be six three or five three, male or female, and the same goes for the one with the knife.'

'Fair point,' Ingeborg said. 'I think Keith is right. It's likely to be one individual. It's not like this was a robbery where two people might work together. It's murder – one person out to kill another. He wouldn't risk having a side-kick.'

'There may be ways of enhancing the image,' Diamond said. 'We'll get it analysed by the IT experts.'

'And they'll take a week and say it's definitely male or female between five three and six three.'

Gilbert was frowning. 'You're saying the killer planned it all, the ambush in the deserted lane, the hi-vis jacket, the car diverted into the field and the surprise attack?'

'Exactly that,' Ingeborg said. 'No one else would want to get involved. What's in it for them? Nothing.'

'How many sets of shoeprints were found?' Gilbert asked.

'I saw two at least,' Diamond said.

'The killer and his victim,' Ingeborg said, as if that settled the matter.

'We've got a very tenacious crime scene investigator on the case. Wolfgang has been there for hours. He may have found more. There's one thing no one has mentioned yet. If only one person was involved, how did he remove the body from the scene?'

This silenced everyone.

'He must have come with a van,' Halliwell said eventually. 'And he'd probably need help to load it inside.'

Ingeborg sighed. 'Back to the drawing board. It was a two-man job after all.'

'Whatever happened, it was well planned,' Gilbert said, 'and it worked.'

'If it was so brilliant,' Ingeborg said, 'why did they leave Deans's car at the scene? If the Range Rover hadn't been found it would be a near-perfect crime.'

'The logistics must have defeated them,' Diamond said. 'But if one drove the van, the other was free to drive the Range Rover.'

'I'm pretty certain one got there on a motorbike. You get a glimpse of it in the film.'

'I saw that,' Gilbert said.

'Leaving the bike there would have been a real giveaway,' Halliwell said in support. 'Did they find tread marks?'

'They did,' Diamond said. 'When the lab results are in, I'm backing Wolfgang to give us enough for a prosecution.'

Ingeborg remained sceptical. 'Tell me something else. Why did the killer remove the body? It was obvious a violent crime had happened with so much blood at the scene.'

'This is the killer's MO,' Halliwell said. 'Think back to Tudor and Nicol. Not one of the bodies has been found. Some people still believe you can't be convicted in the absence of a body. He's got some place he disposes of them.'

'Like Saltford Marina, you mean?' she said with scorn. 'We've had divers out there for three days and all they've found so far is a skip-load of scrap.'

Halliwell said, 'Look on the bright side. This film is a gift from the gods. The one thing he didn't factor in was a camera recording it all.'

'There's a nice irony about someone from a TV show being caught on camera,' Ingeborg said.

Diamond was too fired up to appreciate the remark. 'Keith is right. I can't recall ever having a film of the crime under investigation. And we also have hard evidence: the victim's own car with stains on the bodywork and a pool of blood. Samples were taken to the lab last night. The car will be collected this morning for more forensic testing and there's a search of the field under way.'

'As always, we have to be patient,' Halliwell said.

'We also have CCTV footage of Deans in the shop buying the fish and chips. It's part of the chain of evidence proving he was driving his own car and on his way home with the supper, as he promised Natalie.'

'Did the fish and chips go to the lab as well?' Paul Gilbert asked, and got some smiles he hadn't intended.

'Hoping for a share-out?' Ingeborg said.

Gilbert rolled his eyes. Those two were always feuding.

John Leaman had been mostly silent up to now. With his tunnel vision he could be relied on to make a contribution no one else had considered. 'We should collect DNA samples from everyone involved in the show.'

'Hold on,' Ingeborg said. 'We don't have the killer's DNA yet and even if we get it, there are human rights issues here. It would have to be on a voluntary basis.'

'So we ask them to volunteer and anyone who refuses comes under suspicion.' As always with Leaman, the logic was impeccable and the implementation came second by a long distance.

'Let's not get ahead of ourselves,' Diamond said. 'I don't have long. I must get out to Combe Hay. Has anyone dug up anything new since I was last in?'

Jean Sharp raised a hand as if she was in school.

And Diamond felt uncomfortably like the headmaster. 'Yes, Jean?'

'You asked me to look into Daisy Summerfield's cardiac arrest. I've got some papers for you to look at: the inquest report with various depositions, the post-mortem and so on.'

Daisy Summerfield, the elderly actress who had died at home in Richmond. He retrieved her from the back of his thoughts. 'Have you read them? What was the verdict?'

'Unusual. The jury couldn't decide between misadventure and natural causes.'

'I don't blame them. It was neither.'

'So the coroner provided something I hadn't heard of called a narrative verdict.'

'That's been around a few years now.'

'He stated that the fatal heart attack was almost certainly caused by the shock of finding the burglar.'

'Makes sense. Did the Met send you their case notes?'

'Yes, and there's nothing much we didn't know. The burglar seems to have had almost as big a shock as Daisy did. He left by way of the back door, through the garden, shedding things as he went. The police found a Guy Fawkes mask, a bracelet and the box the old lady's jewels were kept in.'

'He got away with some good stuff, I seem to remember.'

'That seems certain, but Daisy didn't live to say what was missing, so none of it can be traced. The good news is that DNA was recovered from the box lid and the mask.'

'And the bad?'

'It didn't match anything on the national database, not even unidentified DNA. This wasn't a known criminal.'

'Huh.' He couldn't hide his disappointment. He'd been nursing the theory that someone from the TV show had given a tip-off to a professional burglar in London that the house was unoccupied. Even the best professionals leave traces. 'Did you ask them to send the DNA profile for our records?'

'I did. It's in the form of an STR graph.'

'Okay,' he said, doing his best to sound as if he could tell an STR graph from a banana.

'They also sent Daisy's graph for comparison, and you can see the difference at once.'

'Get it all on file and see that Wolfgang has access, in case he has some ideas on this. Is there anything else I should know about, people? In that case, I'll get on the road.' He hesitated and looked around the room.

'Need a lift, guv?' Ingeborg asked, grinning.

The Ka wasn't so roomy or well-padded as Jean Sharp's husband's Volvo, but Diamond valued Ingeborg's experience on a delicate mission like this. 'Straight to the pottery, if you would,' he said. 'I must break the news to Natalie that we fear the worst.'

'Hasn't she heard by now?'

'I don't want her to hear it first from the media.'

'Of course.'

'A shock like this, a sudden bereavement, is overwhelming, I know from experience, and being disabled she's got the added problem of being dependent on him.'

'Poor soul. She's finished. She won't be able to carry on with her business.'

'There's that, but the first hammer blow is emotional. Theirs wasn't a love match, not on his part for sure, and probably not hers either. There's still a bond. She's going to feel so alone.'

'You want me to come in with you?'

'Please. She's met you. She won't get much sisterly support from the nurse I met.'

'Let's see.'

They passed through Combe Hay and started along the single-track lane with passing places they hoped they wouldn't need to use. Driving along a Somerset lane adds tension to any journey. This one took them past the field where the Range Rover had been found. A police officer at the gate waved them past. They couldn't see much of what was going on, but there were two rows of vehicles parked in the field opposite.

'Will they know what they're looking for?'

'The murder weapon if it's there. Traces of blood. Shoeprints. Anything, really. Look out, Inge. There are people up ahead.'

She sighed. She'd driven Diamond enough times to know he was on pins all the way, primed for an accident. There was a bend in the lane, so perhaps he really had spotted something she hadn't. 'People' sounded real enough. She slowed. And saw that he was right.

A woman, a man and a dog coming their way, the woman on a mobility scooter, the man, tall and bearded, striding beside, and the dog running loose.

The dog was huge.

'I know who they are,' Diamond said. 'What in the name of sanity is Natalie doing with that waste of space?'

22

'Put up your window,' Diamond warned Ingeborg.

The dog was bounding towards the car.

Cool under threat, Ingeborg had reversed a short distance and pulled into a passing place. 'We can't ignore them, guv.'

'I don't intend to. I want that dog under control first.'

Caesar reached them, made a leap, landed on the bonnet, was unable to get a grip on the shiny surface, slid off, hit the ground, became more enraged and attacked the side. It became a rerun of the experience in Keith Halliwell's car, the barking and the pawing of the windows, steaming them up and spattering foam and saliva over them.

Inside the car, Diamond said, 'This is an arrestable offence.'

'Tell that to the dog,' Ingeborg said.

As if he'd overheard, Will Legat put two fingers to his mouth and produced a whistle so piercing that they heard it inside with all the windows up. Caesar stopped trying to eat the Ka and its occupants, meekly disengaged, trotted back along the lane and allowed himself to have a rope looped through his collar.

'Useful trick,' Ingeborg said.

'Are you okay?' Diamond asked.

'I'm fine.'

'If your bodywork is damaged, we'll send him the repair bill.'

'Haha. You crease me up, guv.'

'Safe to get out now, I think.'

After a moment more, they emerged and waited for the others to approach, Natalie ahead on her scooter, Legat and the dog at a safe distance behind. The tramp was still in the same shabby clothes he'd worn at the airfield, but he had the air of a man about town.

More barking started and some straining on the leash before Caesar seemed to sense that they were not a serious threat and calmed down.

Diamond's brain was working like a search engine to make the connection between Natalie and Legat. No result came up.

Natalie halted the scooter. She looked pale, but composed, wearing a thick black shawl over a grey trouser suit. 'Do you have some news?' she asked Diamond, eyes wide in expectation.

He wasn't going to answer that. This wasn't the time, nor the place, to discuss the violent attack the dashboard camera had picked up. 'We were on our way to visit you, ma'am. You remember Ingeborg?'

Natalie didn't even give Ingeborg a glance. 'What is it? You can tell me.'

'You must have heard something already, I think, or you wouldn't be out.'

'That's why we're going to the field. It's no distance. As soon as I was awake, I phoned the police in Bath and they told me about the car being found. What could have possessed him, driving off the road when he was so close to home? Why hasn't he called me?'

It was obvious that whoever had spoken to her from Bath Police hadn't revealed the full facts.

'There isn't much to see in the field except policemen making a search, ma'am. The car has been taken away for forensic examination. We're hoping they can give some indications of what happened.'

'I want to see where it was found.'

He understood why. He remembered in vivid detail going to Victoria Park on the worst day of his life all those years ago. Visiting the scene of his own wife's murder had been heartrending, but in a strange way had helped him process his unimaginable loss.

'Where's Greg?' she said. 'That's all I want to know.'

'We're doing all we can to find him.'

'He was definitely on his way here. He phoned me from Trowbridge when he was about to leave.'

'You told me this already. If you remember, I called at the pottery yesterday after we first heard he was missing.'

'So you did,' she said. 'The last two days are a blur. I've lost track of what I said to people.' She fixed her eyes on him. 'There's something you haven't told me.'

'Let's walk to the field together,' he said, realising as he spoke that it was a crass remark to make to someone confined to a wheelchair. Without pause, he went on to say, 'Ingeborg will have to move her car. She can meet us there.'

Legat, unusually for him, had stood at a distance and remained silent apart from a few muttered words controlling the dog. He spoke to Ingeborg. 'You'll need to drive up to the pottery to find a turning point.'

She thanked him and returned to the Ka.

Natalie's scooter was already in motion again. She was on a mission. The two men had to step out sharply to keep

260

her in sight, with Diamond almost at a run to keep up with the big man's strides.

Diamond said to Legat, 'I'm struggling to understand what you're doing here.'

This gentleman of the road had bluffed his way through more situations than the miles he'd tramped through Britain. 'What else would you expect? I couldn't allow poor Natalie to make this sorry pilgrimage on her own. She needs support at this time. And apart from that, it's bloody dangerous driving a scooter up a narrow lane. You never know what nuisances are coming the other way, as we discovered.'

Diamond ignored the slur. 'How is it that you know her?'

'She's one of my guardian angels. Has been for years.'

'What does that mean?'

'I'm always assured of bed and a good breakfast at the pottery. I have a barn to myself – Caesar and myself, I should say. A ground sheet, an inflatable bed and we're in clover. But you know about this. I remember telling you I stay with a kind lady at Combe Hay.'

A faint memory stirred from his first interview. 'I thought you were down in Bath.'

'On the streets? I don't make a practice of sleeping rough. After you inhospitably instructed the Keynsham custody sergeant to give me my marching orders next time I needed a night in the cells, I had to look to other resources.'

'You've been here some days, then? You were here the other night when Greg Deans failed to come home.'

'Do you mind? You make it sound positively culpable. I was in the barn all evening. I first heard he was late when I called at the farmhouse for my evening drink and found Natalie beside herself with worry.'

'You know Greg, obviously?'

'Isn't "knew" the operative word? I can guess why you're here, superintendent. I saw it in your eyes and I think she did, although she doesn't want to face the truth. You'll have to break it to her soon. Have you found the body?'

The gall of the man. Diamond was hard pressed to keep this civil. 'I asked if you know Greg.'

'The precious Greg? A bit. I've seen him here from time to time, but Natalie owns the farmhouse and all the outbuildings, so she's my main point of contact. Greg was an adjunct.'

'A what?'

'Something extra she took on one year when I was away on my travels. I'm surprised he lasted as long as he did.'

'You knew her before he moved in?'

'Years before.'

'I gather you don't get on with him.'

'No reason to. He went his way – into the farmhouse – and I went mine – into the small barn. He was something important in television, but it never washed with me. I judge people as I find them and one shouldn't speak ill of the dead, but I can't say I'm sorry he's gone. He didn't care for me or Caesar. More importantly, I don't think he cared much for Natalie.'

'He helped her run the pottery after she got ill. She told me that herself.'

'Yes, turning into chief cook and bottle-washer must have come as a shock to a high-flier like Greg. Living here and using the pottery as a hotel suited him nicely when she was in good health.' He hesitated, stroking his beard, trying to appear in command of these exchanges, yet keen for more information. 'I asked you a moment ago if you've found the body.'

'Not yet,' Diamond said, 'but there's strong evidence he

was murdered and forensics ought to confirm it soon. I think she'd prefer to be told in her own home.'

'If I may say so, your record at failing to find corpses is second to none, superintendent. Is this the third, or the fourth?'

Diamond wasn't taking that without a riposte. 'I can tell when a major crime has been committed and you'll have questions to answer, my friend.'

Natalie had already reached the gateway to the field and was talking to the policeman on duty.

'Oh my hat. If she tries to drive in she could tip over,' Legat told Diamond with genuine alarm. He was acting like a guardian – or a spouse.

Legat legged it. And Caesar went, too.

Diamond followed at a brisk walk while asking himself how serious this relationship was and what it meant to the investigation. Legat had put himself firmly back in the frame. He'd been present at the scene of Jake Nicol's disappearance and now he'd placed himself suspiciously close to another and with an obvious motive for murder.

In the field, white-clad figures in a long row were progressing slowly towards the other side, a surreal spectacle. Within the cordoned area near the gate, the scene-of-crime team were at work, bent like fruit pickers. A curved spine must be a hazard of the job.

By the time Diamond reached the gateway, Natalie had explained who she was and was being helped over a protective tarpaulin and into the field. She didn't get far, even with Legat pushing the scooter. She was forced to watch the search from behind some *DO NOT ENTER* tape. The sight of so much activity could only increase her suspicion that this was being treated as a murder scene.

Diamond had a new concern. Wolfgang would surely be

one of the stooped figures in polypropylene gear and would spot him and start sounding off about bloodstain patterns, so he took the initiative and called out, 'We're not here to interrupt you, Wolfgang. This lady is the missing man's partner.'

One of them straightened, gave a kind of wave, and continued his work.

Natalie turned to face Diamond. 'Now will you tell me the truth about Greg?'

'Shall we return to the pottery?'

The care nurse had left and Will Legat had clearly taken over her duties. He lifted Natalie off the scooter and into her wheelchair as if handling her was as natural as whistling to Caesar. The effort showed considerable strength. And the way the so-called down-and-out moved about the farmhouse kitchen making coffee and knowing where to find everything showed he was no longer confined to the barn.

'I'll take my coffee through and watch television,' he said in a lordly tone. 'I sense that you folk need privacy. Come, Caesar.'

The dog heaved itself up from the warm spot in front of the Aga and padded out to the living room.

'That's what I call tact,' Diamond said after the door was closed, 'and the man showed some as well.'

'He's a good man,' Natalie said.

'I wouldn't go that far.'

She clicked her tongue. This was off to a bad start. 'Well – what have you been keeping from me?'

Diamond took a seat on the opposite side of the large, square kitchen table, with Ingeborg to his right, closer to Natalie. Keeping his account low-key and unemotional, he told her about the dashboard camera and the violence it had captured.

She listened in silence, shut her eyes when he spoke of the large bloodstain on the ground, but otherwise stayed in control.

'To be totally sure, we must wait for the test results,' Diamond thought it right to add.

'Is this why the woman in the forensic suit went up to Greg's room yesterday?'

'For samples of his DNA. If we get a match, we'll know.'

'Know that Greg is dead, you mean?' She wasn't letting him gloss over the obvious.

'I'm afraid you should prepare yourself for that. Can you think of anyone with a grudge against him?'

'I told you before. He doesn't discuss the people at work. He likes to leave all that behind.'

'Any enemies out here at Combe Hay, then?'

'Sometimes buyers of my work find their way here, but they're friendly. They wouldn't have any reason to harm Greg. They're the only visitors. We don't see anyone else except delivery people.'

'Aren't you forgetting someone? Your friend in the next room doesn't deliver things. He expects to be given them.'

'Will is the exception. He turned up out of the blue a long time ago, before I met Greg. He asked to use one of the outbuildings for an overnight stop. I could tell he was a genuine traveller and not a threat.'

'And he became a regular?'

'If once a year is regular.'

'Is he jealous?'

'Of Greg? I can't think why.' But the colour returned to her cheeks, betraying some duplicity in her answer.

'Isn't it obvious?' he said. 'What must Will Legat have

felt the first time he turned up for his annual visit and found Greg installed here, having moved in permanently with you?'

'That shows how little you know Will.'

'I see a different side of him, ma'am.'

'Negative emotions like jealousy are no good to him. He left them behind when he quit the business world and became independent. He had to be mentally strong. He expects nothing but rejection from anyone. He'll take what's offered, but you can't hurt him. Big changes in our lives call for a rethink, as I well know.'

Sharp observations that rang true. She wasn't naive. She had Legat summed up. His strength of personality fitted him well for the alternative life he had chosen. In that last remark, she was talking about her own situation. She'd adjusted to a crippling illness and now she faced another huge reversal, the loss of the man who had enabled her to continue as a potter.

Diamond found himself thinking about the drastic life changes this woman had endured. Beside them, his own current crisis was small beer. What was an enforced retirement compared to Natalie's problems? He should be drawing strength from her bravery.

Ingeborg must have sensed his thoughts going off track. 'We're looking at a bigger picture, Natalie,' she said. 'What seems to have happened to Greg is similar to what happened to two other men connected to the *Swift* show. Did he ever speak about people going missing?'

'Not to me.'

'I'm sure it must have preyed on his mind. There's been a lot in the press. He could have suspected someone he knew was behind the bad things going on.'

'If you say so.'

'Anything you can think of, however trivial, may help us bring them to justice.'

Natalie shook her head. 'There's nothing. You talk about things preying on Greg's mind, but he doesn't let that happen. He deals with problems when they come along. My illness came as a massive shock to me. Greg didn't agonise over it. He thought of practical solutions like finding the right aids for me, an adjustable chair and the power-driven wheel and loading the kiln himself. He runs the house as well, the cooking, the cleaning, everything.'

'That's true devotion.'

She seemed to play the words over before saying, 'I wouldn't call it that. We had sex for a time that we both enjoyed, but we weren't romantically attached in the way most couples are. This will make me sound a selfish bitch, but the reason I'll miss him is that I can't run the pottery without him.'

A piece of candour so unexpected that Diamond felt the need to chip in again, this time speaking to Ingeborg. 'The help wasn't all one way. Greg owed his career to Natalie. He got the *Swift* job through one of her pottery patrons. Before that, he was delivering the pots for her.'

'And before that?' Ingeborg said.

Another shake of the head from Natalie. 'He doesn't talk about his past.'

'Ever? And you didn't ask?'

'Once or twice and then he said something like it was a closed book. He must have had an unhappy time because he'd talk in his sleep and it was obvious he was really distressed.'

'What did he say?'

She shrugged. 'No idea. It was in his own language.'

Diamond sat forward. 'What do you mean by that? What language?'

267

'He's Romanian.'

'I find that hard to believe.'

'I only found out because he renewed his passport and it arrived in the post addressed to Grigore Dinescu. He dismissed it as unimportant and told me he anglicised the name because he wants to be accepted here without having to go over the story each time he meets someone.'

Diamond was so unprepared for this that he slipped into Natalie's way of speaking about the man as if he was still alive. 'There isn't a hint of anything foreign in his speech. I thought only a Brit could do that over-the-top theatre-speak he does.'

'He got in the way of talking like that within days of starting at Bottle Yard studios. He's a born mimic. Before that, he spoke a kind of estuary English. The contrast made me laugh. Made us both laugh.'

'Have you asked him about his life in Romania?'

'Of course, but each time a certain look comes over his face and I know it's not for discussion. I've learned since – but not from Greg – that people suffered terribly there forty years ago when he was growing up.'

Ingeborg had her phone out. 'Would you spell that Romanian name?'

Inge's efficiency prompted Diamond to find a way through his own scrambled thoughts. After Natalie had spelt the name he said, 'I wonder if the passport is in his room.'

'You're welcome to look, but it won't be,' Natalie said. 'He carries it with him at all times. People who've lived in police states get used to being asked for their ID.'

'We'll check, even so,' he said. The previous room search had been made by the crime scene investigator looking for DNA, not a passport. He asked Ingeborg to see to it.

Left alone with Natalie, he said, 'I think you sensed it was bad news about Greg.'

She said with an air of resignation, 'When two police officers come calling, it isn't to talk about the weather.'

'Is Will going to stay the night?'

'He said he would.' Her voice became warmer. 'I'm so fortunate he was here when this happened. He's a hero, better than the carer.'

'He speaks well of you.'

'It's more than just words. Right now he could be in Bath making money from the tourists instead of looking after me.'

'I think Caesar earns the money.'

'I'm getting to appreciate him, too.'

Diamond's brain was in overdrive, deciding whether Natalie's so-called hero could be Greg Deans's killer. Having walked the lane many times, Legat knew how little used it was, ideal for an ambush. He must have been well aware of the gateway to the field where the car was found. He possessed a hi-vis jacket and a knife. He would have known when Deans was expected home. He had the means of murder and the opportunity.

The motive?

A permanent home. Replace Greg. Simple as that.

When Ingeborg returned from searching the room, she spread her hands in disappointment. 'No passport. Nothing personal in there except his clothes.'

Diamond turned to Natalie. 'Where was Will on the evening Greg didn't come home?'

'Will?' She spoke his name as if it hadn't come up at all in their exchanges, but she was pink-faced again. 'In the barn where he stays.'

'You're sure of that?'

'Most of the time he was. Why don't you ask him yourself? He's in the sitting room.'

'I'm asking you and you can't be certain of his movements, can you?'

'I don't know what you mean. He's been staying here for days. He goes into Bath by day with Caesar, and they sleep here at nights.'

'Yes, but how much do you see of him?'

The blush turned even deeper. 'Quite a bit more now that Greg can't help me.'

'And before the attack?'

'He's in here for breakfast, if that's what you're asking. He likes his cooked breakfast.' She added, as if in an afterthought, 'And he makes himself a mug of cocoa about ten in the evening.'

'Here in the kitchen?'

'Yes. It's a treat, he says. We have fresh milk.'

'So you saw him here the evening Greg didn't return home? Think carefully, Natalie. Your answer is important.' Diamond didn't speak the word 'alibi' but each of them knew it was behind the question. If any of this made sense, Legat was a hard, hard man who didn't think twice about killing people. He'd knifed Jake Nicol to death for nothing more than the belt. That and his bloodstained clothes were being held as evidence. He'd probably done for Dave Tudor for some equally trivial reason. And now Deans. All three had gone missing while he was visiting Bath. He might well have committed other unsolved murders around the country.

Natalie said in a calm, confident tone, 'He was here, yes.'

'At his usual time, about ten?'

'I'm sure of it. I was waiting here with the oven on when he came in and I told him Greg was really late.'

'How did he seem – surprised?'

270

'He was sympathetic. He did his best to calm my nerves. I was already worried.'

'You're sure of the time?'

'I remember looking at the clock and telling him Greg was three-quarters of an hour overdue. I was thinking he would get here by nine fifteen, so I'm sure it was ten o'clock.'

Diamond did some mental arithmetic. The time of the murder on the dashboard camera was 9.20. If Will Legat had been here in the kitchen by 10, straight from a bloody murder, cleaned up and ready for his cocoa, he wasn't merely the coolest of killers. He was the quickest. A professional magician might have managed it. Trickery apart, it couldn't be done – even allowing that the crime scene was only half a mile away.

Natalie had provided the alibi. But was she telling the truth, or covering for Legat?

'Did he stay here, to keep you company?'

'For a while, yes.'

'How long, Natalie?'

'I can't tell you. I was too troubled by then to notice what the time was. He had Caesar to think about, so he went back to the barn.'

'Leaving you alone all night?'

She lowered her eyes and sighed. 'He came back and persuaded me to get some sleep on the sofa in the sitting room. I can't see how this has any bearing on what happened to Greg.'

'He seems to have taken over from Greg. You called him your hero a few minutes ago. I saw the way he lifted you off the mobility scooter.'

She nodded. 'He's been doing everything for me since I was left without Greg's help. Intimate things I don't like to speak about.'

'This is going to sound intrusive—'

She cut him off. 'I know what you're going to ask. Will can stay here as long as he likes. He treats me with absolute kindness and he's a pleasure to be with.'

'You have no concerns about him at all?'

'Haven't I made myself clear? He doesn't do drugs, or get drunk, or steal from people. He chose his way of life. He's a good man. I know it.'

'A gentleman of the road?'

'A gentleman through and through.'

As they moved off in the car, Ingeborg said, 'That was quite some character reference.'

'Sincere?'

'I thought so. I found her persuasive, didn't you?'

'Actually, I did,' Diamond said without sounding pleased about it. 'He's worked his charm on her and I doubt whether he'll be sleeping in the barn much longer – if he hasn't moved in already.'

'That's unworthy of you, guv.'

'What do you mean?'

'Cynical.'

'Realistic, Inge.'

'I saw no sign of him when I was upstairs.'

He laughed. 'Did you look in the other bedrooms? You're no better than I am. She was reasonably honest, wasn't she? I believed most of what she said. I think she'd have told us if they were sharing a bed. None of it sounded rehearsed.'

'Not even when she talked about the evening of the attack?'

'Especially that bit.'

'She said he came in at ten. He'd have needed to be

supercharged to do the murder and get there for his cocoa in just over half an hour.'

'Agreed, she's given him an alibi and it would have been watertight if she'd said she saw him at nine fifteen walking the dog across the yard. She didn't. She gave this elaborate account of him appearing in the kitchen at his usual time and it came over as spontaneous, as if she was picturing it in her mind.'

'You don't think she's lying for him?'

'No. She's on the level. She's making a huge mistake letting him into her life, but the poor woman hasn't much choice. Do we agree on that?'

'You still don't trust him?'

'No, but I trust her and I'm now in two minds about him killing Greg Deans. I'm not forgetting we have his blood-stained clothes from the stabbing at Charmy Down and I'm keeping a mental note that he was present in Bath when Dave Tudor disappeared.'

'Not enough for a prosecution, guv.'

'More's the pity, no. What did you make of Greg being Romanian?'

'Amazing. Who would have thought it? I can't wait to look into his past. What was all the secrecy about? Was he an illegal immigrant?'

'Unlikely if he has a passport,' Diamond said. 'Romania is in the European Union. And having worked here so long, he'll have been given settled status.'

'Why hide it from everyone?'

'I'm willing to believe he wanted to identify with the TV people, and no questions asked, as Natalie told us. Like she said, the past was too painful to speak about. Tough times he wanted to forget. Under that dictator with the unpronounceable name—'

'Ceauşescu.'

'Thanks. The secret police were into every corner of society. People guarded their words. There was suffering, starvation and your neighbours ready to inform on you if you put a foot wrong. Who wouldn't want to put that nightmare behind them?'

'Is it a red herring, then, his nationality?'

'It's one more thing to check on. I don't put it higher than that. However, . . .'

Ingeborg waited. Diamond seemed to be lost in thoughts of his own.

He said, 'I don't like these narrow lanes. Slow down a bit.'

She eased her foot on the pedal. 'I wasn't even doing twenty, guv.'

He picked up his thread again. 'One of the others who went missing had a foreign inflection in his voice.'

'David Tudor. They thought it was his Welsh accent.'

'But someone – Sabine, I believe – told me there was suspicion at one time that Tudor was here illegally. What if he was originally Romanian as well? What if all three missing men came from Romania? What did Greg's room look like?'

'Soulless. You wouldn't think he's lived there for years. It could have been a hotel room.'

'Ready for the next guest.'

She laughed. 'Or resident. Do you think Will Legat is ready to exchange his walking boots for carpet slippers?'

'He can hardly wait.'

'I'm worried for Natalie now.'

'He won't attack her. He's happy to play the part of her carer and have a roof over his head. We can let her enjoy being looked after until he gets on the road again.'

'I hope you're right, guv. Too soon to hope for news from the lab, I suppose? Have you checked your phone lately?'

He pulled it out, pressed and waited.

'Not switched on?' she asked.

'It needs charging. I'm conserving the power for emergencies.'

'Got you.' But she didn't sound impressed.

Nothing from the lab. Instead, he found a voice message from Earnshaw, the dive supervisor, asking him to call back. 'I'm not looking forward to this one,' Diamond said. 'He'll tell me they finished at the marina and found nothing but scrap.'

He was wrong.

The words were heavy with recrimination. 'I've been trying to reach you for the past hour and a half. Early this morning we hooked out an item that may be of interest to you. A large suitcase, strapped and heavy.'

He tensed. 'Where was it?'

'Right where *Deck the Halls* is moored.'

With difficulty, he resisted the impulse to yell, What did I tell you?

Earnshaw added, 'We haven't opened it.'

'Don't,' he said. 'That's a job for forensics and I need to be there. Where is it right now?'

'Here on the jetty. There's something bulky inside.'

23

Ingeborg ignored the police officer trying to wave their car into the field where everyone had parked. She drove on to where the action was – if action is not an exaggeration. The searchers were still spread across the field progressing slowly forward and the CSI team in the taped-off area were scarcely moving at all. Diamond got out and shouted to Wolfgang.

The small figure in his forensic suit was stooping in the cordoned area. He looked round, straightened up and ambled over. Diamond gave him the news of the find in the marina and said, 'Hop aboard our car and we'll take you there.'

'Please – it's not as simple as that. If the suitcase has been under water for any appreciable time, I'm not going to be of much use to you.'

'You're a crime scene investigator. What's the problem?'

'For one thing, we don't know for certain if a crime was committed. And for another the marina isn't necessarily the scene.'

'Oh, come on, Wolfgang. Give me a break. I simply want to see what's inside and I need someone like you to make it official.'

'You're better off getting a forensic pathologist. If there is, indeed, a body, they'll want to see the remains in situ and then move them to wherever they do their autopsies.'

'I'll feel an idiot if I call out a pathologist and the case is full of old saucepans.'

'And you won't feel an idiot with me. Is that what you're saying? You're going to need other people anyway. A photographer for a start and possibly a locksmith. You won't want to force it open.'

'For God's sake. It's got straps round. I don't suppose it's locked.'

'If I was disposing of a body in a suitcase, I'd lock it and I'm sure you would do the same. How can I impress on you that there are no short cuts, superintendent? You must definitely find the right experts to help you. I don't mind being there. I can supply a forensic tent. You're going to have an audience otherwise.'

'All this will take hours to set up.'

'A pathologist usually gets to the scene quite soon. I can't come until later anyway. I'm making casts of tyre treads. What time is it?'

So much had already happened this morning that Diamond was surprised it was only a few minutes after eleven.

'Use the time to get your head around what's happening,' Wolfgang said. 'You don't want to lose your grip.'

Diamond could have felt patronised, but the advice was good. He was in shock. The find in the marina called for a rethink. He'd been ready to pull in Will Legat as soon as his guilt was confirmed by a DNA match. But Legat had no conceivable connection with the marina. It was almost impossible that he would dispose of bodies there. The focus switched to the people who lived there: Fergus and Candida.

Wolfgang raised a hand in farewell. 'Let me know what you arrange.'

Back in the car, Diamond told Ingeborg through gritted teeth, 'Change of plan. This is going to take longer.'

277

He phoned the only pathologist he could think of and that was the sarcastic Bertram Sealy, who had made his life a misery on several previous cases. The earliest Sealy could manage was two o'clock and that, he said, would be as a favour for a regular customer.

'You can't make it any sooner?'

'And ruin my lunch?' Sealy said. 'The suitcase won't walk away.'

'I hope not.'

'I assume the divers are already looking for more evidence. They may bring up another while I'm having my Big Mac.'

The thought of a second suitcase hadn't crossed Diamond's mind. Another one hidden under the jetty was a real possibility. He settled for two o'clock and went back to tell Wolfgang the decision.

Next, he phoned the incident room and updated Keith Halliwell on the morning's developments. 'It's almost certain Candida has seen the suitcase on the jetty by now and alerted Fergus. He'll be on another day's filming. The way he reacts will be worth knowing. Find out where they are and get someone out there ASAP. I suggest Paul. Tell him to take someone with him and observe from a distance.'

'Don't you want to collar Fergus?'

'Not yet. His movements will tell us a lot. And I need back-up at the marina. Who do you have?'

'Leaman and Sharp.'

'You have some civilian staff in the office, right? They can hold the fort. I'll meet you three as soon as you can get here. There's a pub called the Riverside Inn.'

After he'd ended the call, Ingeborg asked, 'Where to, guv?'

'Didn't you hear? We'll grab a pint and some lunch and be ready for them.'

At the marina he went straight to look at the suitcase. Big enough, for sure. It was the kind you see people struggling with at airports. Faded red and part-covered in slime, it stood broadside down on the jetty close to where Candida's narrowboat was moored. Two leather straps held it together, and there were telltale bulges in the fabric.

'Was it heavy to lift out?' he asked Earnshaw.

'It took two men and a winch.'

'And where was it found – right below where we're standing?'

'Near enough. Under the front of the second narrowboat. It had to be dug out from the silt. Been there some time, I'd say.'

He thought of Dave Tudor, missing from four years ago. 'Has anyone been by?'

'A couple of the boat owners and the woman from the office.'

'Any press people?'

'Not yet.'

'The *Deck the Halls* lady?'

'A few minutes ago.'

'Did she say anything?'

'No.'

'Or seem surprised?'

'Not that I noticed.'

'Where is she now – inside?'

'I think so.'

Phoning Fergus with the bad news, no doubt.

Diamond informed Earnshaw that the suitcase would be opened at two, when everyone who needed to be there was present. 'We're going to screen off this part of the jetty. We don't want an audience. Are you continuing the search?'

'Does it look like it?' Earnshaw said. 'I gave them a break after they brought up the booty. They earned it.'

'Get them back in the water as soon as possible. We're dealing with multiple crimes. There could be more suitcases down there. If you need me, I'll be in the pub.'

'Oh yeah – while we do all the bloody work?'

The man was far too lippy for Diamond's liking. He felt more in command now. The dive team couldn't complain they'd been brought here under false pretences. 'Any more of that, Earnshaw, and this is the last job you supervise.'

In the pub, he sat with Ingeborg in a window seat after ordering drinks and food for them both.

'So, another twist,' he said before she did. 'This is turning into an Agatha Christie.'

'You're thinking Fergus is our man now?' she said.

'With the help of Candida. She was the lure in the hi-vis and he was the executioner waiting in the field.'

'An hour ago we were ready to arrest Will for three murders. Does this let him off the hook – or are we dealing with two sets of killers working independently?'

'Spare me that, Inge. No, the MO is basically the same each time: the sudden disappearance of someone connected with the show, a knifing and a method of disposing of the body that we haven't cracked . . . until now.'

'We hope,' she said.

'It was smart, stuffing them into suitcases and sinking them here where the narrowboat is moored.'

She smiled. 'Until you brought in the divers. So you're assuming Candida was an accessory from the start?'

'She must have known what was going on.'

'How do you plan to play this, guv?'

'Largely off the top of my head. Let's see how Fergus reacts. That should tell us a lot. Will he leave work and rush back here, or play cool and deny everything, or go on the run? Paul is shadowing him.'

'Shall I make sure Candida stays put?'

'Good thinking, yes.'

Their lunch was served, a salad sandwich for Ingeborg, a beef and ale pie for him, with a double helping of chips.

He said after a few seconds to appreciate the first bite, 'What you said about being ready to nick Will Legat, I'd rather you didn't mention it to Keith or the others. Not good for morale, knowing the boss almost screwed up.'

'Understood,' she said, looking at the ceiling.

'You don't think I'm losing my touch?'

'Why would I think that, guv? It made sense at the time.'

'Be honest with me. Did you ever believe Will was the killer?'

Ingeborg took time to think about her answer. 'Maybe it's the effect he has on people. I haven't seen as much of him as you have. I know you were suspicious of him from early on. I rather admire him. He makes me smile and it's difficult to picture him as the man who stabbed Greg Deans. My head said he must be a killer, but my heart felt differently.'

From the window, they saw Jean Sharp drive into the forecourt in her husband's Volvo. Keith Halliwell and John Leaman were passengers. He would have stood them drinks, he said when they came in, but he was sure they wouldn't want his pie to get cold. Halliwell was quick to say he needed to update Diamond on Fergus and couldn't get the drinks in either. Jean had done the driving, which left Leaman to stump up for the round. 'Mine is a real ale, John,' Diamond called after him. 'I don't mind which.'

The news of Fergus was that he was at the new film location on the ribbon of steps known as Jacob's Ladder that led up Beechen Cliff to Alexandra Park, one of the best viewpoints in Bath. Nothing was allowed to stop the show, not even the demise of the producer. 'Paul should be there by now,' Halliwell said. 'I'll get him for you.' And before Diamond could take another mouthful, he was handed the phone.

'Paul? Where exactly are you?'

'About halfway up, guv.'

'I can hear you breathing.'

'It's steeper than I thought. Stupidly I didn't start from the top. It was a slog. We had to hurry. But we've found the film unit and they're shooting a chase scene with Swift on the run from the inspector, riding down the steps on her motorbike.'

'Sabine?'

'She's here for the close-ups, and the stunt double, Ann Bugg, is doing the dangerous stuff.'

'Is Fergus there?'

'Busy with another guy putting down rails for a tracking shot. They've got their work cut out. The ground's so uneven.'

'He can't leave?'

'No chance in the next half hour.'

'Where are you – not obvious, I hope?'

'With some people who've gathered to watch. He's not aware who we are, I'm sure. I can take a video if you like.'

'Just keep me informed and don't let him out of sight. He will have heard what's going on here from Candida. The first chance he gets, he'll be off. Are there cars there?'

'It's too steep for that. Sabine is complaining about sitting on the bike even when it isn't moving.'

'Don't get distracted. Follow Fergus if he moves off. And take care. He'll be carrying the knife.'

After the drinks arrived and the pie and chips were eaten, Diamond brought the team up to speed on what to expect at 2 p.m. 'The focus is firmly on Fergus and Candida now. We'll nick them as soon as the suitcase has been opened.'

'There's the child, guv,' Jean Sharp reminded him.

'Yes, I've asked social services to send someone over. If they don't get here in time, would you take care of Bart until they come?'

'No problem.'

'That's a phrase I never use,' he said. 'Problems have a way of rearing up, especially with kids. It's how we deal with them that matters.' He heard his own words echo worryingly in his brain. He was dealing with his own problems by assigning duties. Halliwell was to get aboard the *Daisy Belle*, the boat moored next to *Deck the Halls*, force the lock and find out what was inside. 'Be prepared for horrors, Keith. I have a hunch this is where they store the bodies.'

Some minutes later, general conversation had taken over and Sharp moved to the empty seat beside Diamond. She said she'd been waiting for the right moment to mention something.

'You're okay?' he asked her.

'It's not about me, guv. Are you still suspicious about Mary Wroxeter's death? It doesn't seem to fit in with the three men who went missing.'

'True, but I haven't forgotten her. I'm concentrating on the men because we seem to be making real progress with them.'

She blushed. 'I'm sorry. This isn't a good time.'

How could he help her get over her lack of confidence with him? 'It's as good as any, Jean. I'm listening.'

'Well, you said Candida is in the frame now.'

'I mean it. She's got to be involved.'

'The other day when you and I went to see her, you let me question her about the evening Mary died.'

'And you did a fine job,' he said, seizing on a chance to show appreciation. 'Thanks to you, we now know why Candida offered to drive Mary home after the evening in the pub. She wanted her to be the first to know she was pregnant. Has something else cropped up?'

'Er . . . yes. She told us the truth, but not the whole truth, I think.'

'Oh?'

'I felt there must be a bigger reason why she was so keen to share her news with Mary before she told anyone else.'

'You found it – another reason?'

'I think so. Mary was her mother.'

He slopped ale on the table. 'Candida's mother? How on earth . . .?'

'I got her date of birth from the film office. They keep records even of staff who have left.'

'And . . . ?'

'I ordered a copy of her birth certificate and it came this morning. You have to supply the date and the names of the parents. I took a chance with both and I was right about Mary.'

'That *is* a discovery.' He pressed his fingers against his mouth as another mystery presented itself. 'Who was the father, then? Wait, I think I know. Candida is mixed race. He must be the guy who played Paul Robeson. The Welsh tenor.'

'Aubrey Jones.'

'Aubrey Jones. Candida Jones. What an idiot I am. Why didn't I make the connection?'

'There was no reason to,' she said. 'We weren't asking ourselves who Candida's parents were.'

'So how did you get on to it?'

She lowered her eyes and turned self-conscious again. 'By being nosy, more than anything. I wanted to know why it was that Candida had this loyalty to Mary as long as three years after she'd left the job, so I got thinking.'

'To some tune – that's brilliant, Jean. And now we know, it begs all kinds of questions. Why keep it secret that they were mother and daughter?'

'I guess it could have looked like favouritism while she was working as her production assistant. Other people in the company could complain.'

'And maybe Mary didn't want it known she had a love child. Racism could have played its part as well, remembering the attitudes of thirty years ago.'

'I hadn't thought of that.'

'But she couldn't have been all that ashamed. She gave her a theatrical name. Isn't Candida the title of a play?'

'By George Bernard Shaw.'

'You *have* done your homework. I'm seeing this differently now.' He paused to take it in more fully. 'Surely Candida wouldn't have plotted to kill her own mother.'

'It's not unknown,' Sharp said with a detachment Diamond hadn't seen before. 'We don't know what bad blood there was between them. And we only have Candida's account of what happened the night Mary died.'

'You're ahead of me.'

'I've had longer to get my head around it.'

Diamond was spurred into speaking his thoughts aloud. 'She claimed she didn't go into Mary's house after driving her home, but we can't rely on anything she told us. If she did go in and added pure ethanol to the vodka her mother was drinking, it would have been enough to kill her. It makes your blood run cold.'

He could see he wasn't telling Jean Sharp anything she hadn't been through in her mind already. She was able to speak rationally about the probability that they were dealing with matricide, among other crimes. 'Until she's arrested and questioned, we won't know what happened to make her like that.'

He nodded. 'And the fact that everyone else seemed to regard Mary as angelic would only have ramped up Candida's bitterness.' He heaved a large sigh, confronting the chasm of malice that had just opened up. 'You're right. More will come out, I'm sure. We could go on speculating indefinitely. We'll pull them both in and get the truth of it. This is a huge help, Jean. You've given us enough to crack the case.'

She almost fled from the table, she was so relieved to have got the story off her chest.

Through the window, Diamond saw more vehicles arrive in the car park. Dr Bertram Sealy got out and started pulling on his pale blue forensic suit. The photographer Diamond remembered from the crime scene in the field at Combe Hay had also driven in.

'Drink up, everyone. We're going outside.'

He asked Ingeborg to call Paul Gilbert and find out whether Fergus was still at the shoot on Jacob's Ladder.

'He would have told us, guv.'

'Do it.' The tension was getting to him. 'And keep watch on the narrowboat in case Candida appears.'

On the way to the jetty, Ingeborg offered Diamond her phone. 'It's Paul. Do you want to speak to him yourself?'

'Has he got Fergus in sight? That's all I need to know.'

She nodded.

'Tell him to stick with the jerk whatever happens.'

Wolfgang had already erected a forensic tent not much bigger than the sort boy scouts use. 'It's the width of the jetty,' he explained. 'You can't anchor the sides to air.'

'We won't squeeze three people in there as well as the suitcase,' Diamond said.

'Take it down if you like,' Wolfgang said, 'but if you do, you'll be all over the papers tomorrow.' He jerked his head in the direction of a cluster of press photographers who had set up their tripods on the opposite bank.

'They get everywhere,' Diamond said.

Wolfgang handed Diamond a forensic suit. He put it on without complaining. He wouldn't tell anyone he was more excited than a kid on Christmas morning.

Sealy adjusted his face mask, dipped his head and went inside the tent, followed by the forensic photographer. Diamond had to observe from outside with his head between the tent flaps – an undignified pose destined to be picked by several picture editors for next morning's editions.

The small space already smelt musty.

'So how long has it been out of the water?' Dr Sealy asked, starting to loosen the straps.

'Three to four hours,' Diamond said.

'Prepare for an interesting fragrance, then.'

'Is it locked?'

'That won't stop me. Suitcases are easy to force. I always padlock mine when I go on holiday. No, it isn't locked. Hold your noses.'

Sealy unzipped the case. The clicks of the camera shutter provided a kind of incidental music.

He lifted the lid and the foul smell of rotting flesh filled the tent.

Sealy said, 'Ha.'

The lid was masking Diamond's view. 'I can't see from here.'

Sealy said, 'You won't want to.'

'Why?'

'It's not what you led me to expect. It's organic, I'll give you that. It appears to be dead. But you don't need me. You want a zoologist. What you've got here is a large reptile. I'm no expert, but I would say this is a reticulated python.'

24

Humiliation crushed Peter Diamond. The weight of it was overwhelming. At this low point of his career all the experience of a lifetime's service, the cases he had solved, the killers he had brought to justice over the years, counted for nothing. He'd come here confident of a triumph and was hopelessly, ridiculously wrong.

Dr Sealy had a grin wider than a body bag. The forensic photographer had turned his back and was shaking with mirth. Diamond, in his undignified position, his bonneted head inside the tent and the rest of him outside, bent over as if inviting someone to kick him, was at a loss.

Sealy said, 'Are you going to tell them or shall I?'

He was right. They all had to be told they had been brought here on a fool's errand – Earnshaw, the divers, Wolfgang, Halliwell, Leaman, Ingeborg and Sharp. There was no ducking who had cocked up.

Still in a state of shock, Diamond removed his head from the tent.

A cloud had covered the sun and a cool breeze blew across the marina, creating ripples he could hear lapping the sides of the moored boats.

'Sorry, people,' he said in his stricken voice. 'It's not what I expected. It's a dead snake.'

Earnshaw said, 'Speak up.'

Wolfgang said, 'You can take off the mask now.'

He dragged it below his chin. 'A snake.'

'What sort of snake?'

'A python, we think.'

They had to see for themselves. Diamond was practically pushed off the jetty. Only one person hadn't moved. Keith Halliwell waited on the deck of the *Daisy Belle*, the boat berthed next to *Deck the Halls*. 'You'd better look in here, guv,' Keith said. 'I got a bit ahead of myself and opened up.'

Diamond had prepared himself to think of the second narrowboat as a charnel house, a murderer's store where bodies were locked away prior to disposal in the water. He crossed the walkway and stepped on deck. The padlock was still in place. Halliwell had forced the hasp away from the wood.

He pushed the door open and went in.

The interior was so dimly lit that he had to wait a second or two for his eyes to adjust. He could hear a faint mechanical humming he took to be a fridge motor.

That much was correct. He could now make out a large cabinet freezer with the fridge beside it and shelving opposite. Above him was a double tube of strip lighting.

'There's got to be a switch,' he said.

'Found it,' Halliwell said and flicked it on.

The entire length of the boat was revealed, taken up with huge glass tanks two metres high and twice as long, reinforced with steel. Their slatted covers appeared to work on a roller-glide system. Two stood each side of a narrow aisle. Inside each tank was a jungle in miniature, forked logs and branches projecting upwards from a ground cover of stones, ferns and broad-leaved plants.

'I think it's called a vivarium,' Halliwell said. 'He keeps snakes.'

290

Diamond moved along the row in silence, taking it in. At first he couldn't see anything alive. There was no movement. In the second tank he noticed a mottled brownish green surface that wasn't part of the log that lay across the middle.

A coiled unmoving serpent as thick as a man's thigh.

'Can you tell the difference between a boa constrictor and a python?' Halliwell said. 'I can't, but I reckon he's got both.'

Diamond said nothing.

'Part of his macho lifestyle, I suppose,' Halliwell went on. 'I've never wanted to keep exotic reptiles myself. Are you okay, guv?'

Diamond said, 'Let's get out of here.'

Back on deck, he stood facing the open water and not seeing anything. At least his brain was functioning again, seeking to find some understanding of the bizarre things forced on his consciousness.

After some thought, he said, 'What do they feed on – chicks and mice, isn't it?'

'I've never asked.'

'He'll keep them in the fridge.'

'I expect so. I didn't look inside.'

'In the wild, they can go for weeks without eating and then they want something substantial. Big snakes like those are man-eaters, given a chance.'

'That's an ugly thought, guv.'

'I'm in an ugly mood.'

Halliwell had his phone out and was googling man-eating snakes. 'It's rare, but not unknown. A fully-grown python will crush you and try to swallow you whole. The jaws are flexible and expand. Swallowing the shoulders is the hard part.'

'If the body was butchered into joints of meat, the python wouldn't have any difficulty.'

Halliwell screwed up his face in disgust. 'Is that what Fergus did?'

'At this stage, Keith, your guess is as good as mine. It would account for the people who disappeared and were never seen again.'

'That's gross.'

'Keeping large reptiles in captivity is gross. I don't understand the mentality behind it. I'm going to question Candida again and see how much she knows. I don't think Fergus will be here any time soon.' With more of an agenda, he might recover from the humbling he'd let himself in for. Peeling off the forensic suit was a start.

With Ingeborg at his side, he stepped aboard *Deck the Halls*. 'I won't spare her,' he said. 'I tried being nice cop and it didn't work.'

Candida, too, started on a combative note. At the door, she said, 'If you're here to apologise, forget it.'

'Apologise for what, ma'am?' he said.

'Trashing our reputation, that's what. All of Bath and Bristol knows Fergus and me are the reason for the police divers. I've had reporters on at me day and night. Cameramen all over the boat. Next thing we'll be asked to leave and find another mooring.'

'If you'd been more honest before, none of it would have been necessary,' he told her. 'We're bound to be suspicious when you give us half-truths and lies.'

'Like what?'

'Like the horseshit about Mary Wroxeter. You never once mentioned she was your mother.'

Straight to it. She made a sound like one of the pythons hissing. 'Who told you that?'

'We'd better talk inside. It's time to front up, Candida.'

She turned round and stepped into her main cabin, her shoulders and back rigid with tension. Bart was on the floor chewing on an apple.

Candida faced them and said with fury, 'There's no reason I should tell you or anyone who my parents were.'

'Oh, but there is when Mary's death is under investigation and you were the last person to see her alive.'

'Jesus Christ, you're not accusing me of murdering her?'

'Not yet. I want the truth about that night. You said you drove her home from the pub and told her you were pregnant. Why wait? Your own mother? Why not pick up the phone and tell her as soon as you knew about it?'

'I only knew that afternoon, that's why. I couldn't call Mary while she was filming. I didn't lie to you. I gave her my news in the car.'

'You didn't go in with her? That's hard to believe.'

'It's the truth. I had no more to say to her. I knew she'd want to celebrate the only way she knew how and drinking was one thing I shouldn't do, being pregnant. I left her outside her door and drove straight back here. If you think I encouraged her to drink herself to death, you're nuts.'

'You kept it quiet – the fact that you were her daughter – even after she died.'

'She would have wanted that. The studio took charge and fixed the funeral. They gave her a lovely send-off as I knew they would. I was there as someone who'd worked with her, that's all.'

'No regrets about that?'

She clicked her tongue. 'We were never that close. In all

her life I never called her mum. As a kid I was farmed out to foster parents and packed off to a crap private boarding school. I scarcely ever saw my birth parents. My dad died years ago anyway. The one good thing they gave me was my name. At least, I thought it was until my schoolmates found out it's also the name of a fungal infection and called me Thrush.'

Ingeborg said, 'Mary must have cared. She found you the job at Bottle Yard.'

'Years later. I was on her conscience by then. I left school with nothing to show for all the fees and went through a really bad patch. Hard drugs, sleeping rough, nicking stuff, the lot. She found me a flat and fixed it for me to make a start as a runner on the understanding that we'd tell no one I was her daughter. I loved the job straight away and stayed. End of story.'

'Not quite the end. You met Fergus, got pregnant and moved in here.'

She laughed. A bitter laugh. 'Shit-for-brains, me.'

Diamond asked, 'How much did you know about Fergus?'

'He fancied me. That's all I wanted to know.'

'Did you know he kept snakes?'

'He only had the one when we met, the one that died of old age and had the suitcase for its coffin. I refused to have it in here while it was alive, so he bought the old tub you see next to us and spent far too much doing it up and turning it into a snake house. I can't stand them. I never go in there.'

'You say he fancied you,' Ingeborg said. 'Was it more than that?'

'I told myself it was. I wouldn't have got pregnant twice if I didn't think he loved me. I'm not a total slag. I lost the first one and then Bart was born.'

'And what are your feelings now?'

She flared up again. 'What is this – sex therapy? I don't have to tell you what goes on in my private life.'

Diamond said, 'We're asking because we want to know how deeply you're involved. People are missing, believed dead. You could be aiding and abetting a serial killer.'

'Give me strength,' she said, eyes blazing, each word charged with outrage. 'You think Fergus topped those guys? What for? He may be thick, but he's not that thick.'

'Two nights ago,' he said, 'they finished the filming at Milroy Court. It was late in the day. The de-rigging would have been the last thing to happen and Fergus was in charge so he would have got home late. Do you recall what time it was?'

'This was when?' she said. 'Tuesday? Let me think.' She bent down and took the partially eaten apple from Bart and pushed a sippy cup against his mouth before he could protest. 'God, this is ridiculous. Yes, he was late. I was about to watch *News at Ten* when he got in and wanted to eat. He's always late when they de-rig. They have to load the trucks and return them to Gripmasters up at Cold Ashton. He leaves his motorbike there by day and then rides home.'

'Okay,' Diamond said without sounding okay. She'd reminded him Fergus was a motorcyclist. It complicated the scenario. You can't transport a body on a motorbike. But there had been a bike in the field where Greg Deans was attacked. 'How was his mood? Any different from usual?'

'I didn't notice anything different. He was ready for his Irish stew when he got in, hungry as always.'

'What was he wearing? His motorcycle gear?'

'Black leathers.'

'He took them off, I expect.'

'Slung them over the back of the chair like he always does.'

'Does he have a spare set?'

'Of leathers? Do you have any idea what they cost? You don't get much change out of a grand.'

'The answer is no, I take it. He'll be wearing the same jacket and trousers today at the shoot at Jacob's Ladder.'

'Is that where he is?' she said. 'You know more than I do.'

They didn't get anything else from Candida. The nasty cop approach might have brought out new details, but the value of them was far from apparent.

Everyone had left the jetty by the time they emerged from *Deck the Halls*. The forensic tent was gone and so were the divers and their equipment. All that remained, like a rebuke, was the suitcase containing the dead snake.

'She knew all along what was in the case,' Diamond said. 'She could have told the divers straight away.'

'You can bet she phoned Fergus,' Ingeborg said. 'I expect he told her to play dumb. She has to live with him. She wouldn't defy him. I've always had the feeling he's a bully, if not an out-and-out wife-beater.'

'He certainly played it cool himself, staying well away.'

'What's going to happen to the snake?' she asked.

'Don't know. Doesn't belong to me.'

'We can't let Fergus throw it back in the marina.'

'We'll notify the council. They know what to do. Somerset gets more roadkill than anywhere else in Britain.'

'I don't suppose they get many pythons.'

On the drive back to their base at Concorde House, Ingeborg said, 'Candida has been devious in the past, feeding the jinx story to the paper, but I felt she was telling the truth this time. Her personal story rather moved me, actually.'

'I was touched by it as well,' Diamond admitted. 'Almost stopped me in my tracks.'

'If she was being truthful, she wasn't at Combe Hay herself and she provided an alibi for Fergus. She said he got home before ten the night Greg was stabbed. I can't think of any way he could have done the killing and got back to Saltford. The dash cam showed nine twenty. He'd have needed to hide the body somewhere, clean up, change into his leathers and ride back from Combe Hay in under forty minutes. Theoretically possible for someone like Houdini, but . . . Fergus?' She blew a soft raspberry.

'Like you, I believed her,' Diamond said. 'There was the moment I asked what time he got home and it was clear she had to cast her mind back. She hadn't prepared for the question or she wouldn't have hesitated. I've interviewed enough witnesses in my time to know when an answer is spontaneous and genuine.'

'Two in one day,' Ingeborg said.

'You mean Natalie and Candida?'

'Two honest women.'

'Both can't be. Who do you prefer to believe?'

She drove on for a while without answering. The next comment came from Diamond, complaining about farmers who didn't trim their hedges: an indirect way of suggesting she drove more slowly through the narrow lanes.

When Ingeborg spoke again, it was to say, 'I can think of only one of our suspects who ticks all the boxes: motive, means and opportunity. He's already acting as if he is Greg's replacement, he carries a knife and he was just a short walk from the scene. The killer has to be Will Legat.'

297

25

The king of the incident room, John Leaman, came straight over as soon as Diamond and Ingeborg returned. He was rubbing his hands, a rare display of emotion. 'A batch of test results have come in, guv. The lab beat all records.'

'Thanks to Wolfgang cracking the whip,' Diamond said. 'What have we got?'

'The victim was definitely Greg Deans. The bloody handprint on the car was his and so was the blood on the ground, so much, they say, that he couldn't have lived.'

'We know that. What else?'

'They found no traces of anyone else's blood or DNA.'

'Really? That surprises me.'

'The perpetrator was wearing gloves.'

'Shoeprints?'

'Nothing conclusive. The ground was too squelchy.'

'Squelchy? Is that the term they used?'

'No, it's me summing up. Do you want me to read you the exact words?'

'No need. I can read them myself.'

'They did get a tyre print where the ground wasn't quite so muddy, a good one, and made a cast of it.'

Diamond nodded. 'I saw Wolfgang collecting it.'

'It's a clear tread pattern and the interesting thing is that it's not from a car.'

'A motorbike?'

'Yes – the tyre was a Michelin Pilot. They give a range of probable serial numbers and there's enough wear to identify the bike if we can find it.'

'Could be helpful, very helpful. Go on.'

'That's about it. The fingertip search of the field produced a few items like cigarette butts, but no reason to connect them to the killer.'

'Where were they found? Anywhere near the gate?'

'I didn't ask. I was thinking some farm worker dropped them. The killer wouldn't stand around smoking after the stabbing.'

'Before, John, before. He spent some nervous time waiting for the Range Rover to come up the lane. That's when he would have needed a fag.'

Leaman's embarrassed features displayed most of the colours of a Turner sunset. 'I didn't think of that.'

'It's okay. I don't expect you to cover every angle.'

'I'll call the lab and find out.'

'Before you do, run the dash cam footage for me one more time on the large screen, would you, just the sequence in the field? There's a moment when the car is turning and the camera catches a glimpse of something metallic under the hedge.'

'There isn't much to see. Just a gleam of silver.'

He shouldn't have been irritated by Leaman's remark. After all, the man's pathological attention to detail was often of value. But he was feeling the strain himself. 'You're not telling me anything new, John. I've studied it many times over. I want to see it on a bigger scale, understood?'

An injured look settled on Leaman's features. 'Got you.'

Realising he'd caused unintended hurt, Diamond softened the remark by placing some blame elsewhere. 'I asked our IT people to check it frame by frame and enhance it if they can, but we've heard nothing back yet. I'm thinking it may have been this motorbike.'

Ingeborg tried to assist. 'I can guess where you're going with this, guv. Fergus is a biker. He rides to Combe Hay and parks the bike out of sight in the field, ready to ambush Greg. Candida will have driven there in a van and parked in the field opposite. She was the one who stood in the lane and directed Greg off the road and into the field like a lamb to the slaughter. Am I right?'

'Substantially, yes, but that's only a scenario. Let's not get carried away.'

'Like the corpse?' Halliwell said, making his own attempt to lighten the mood.

'What?'

'Carried away in the van.'

'Haha. Are you ready, John?'

Leaman seemed to have got over his angst. 'Do you want the blinds down?'

'Good idea. Gather round, people. The more eyes we have on this, the better.'

They watched the sequence from the moment Greg's headlights picked out the figure in the hi-vis jacket signalling to him to turn off the lane and into the field. The lights were dipped as the car approached the figure and only switched on again to make the turn. The picture gave the illusion of the field moving left as Greg drove in and turned in a tight circle to bring the car to a position facing the lane. It was difficult to see anything clearly because of the bumping over the rutted surface, creating secondary movement up and down as well as sideways.

'Here's the hedge coming back in view,' Diamond said, 'and this is the bit I'm interested in.'

No more than a flash of brightness against the dark band of the hedge, but almost certainly a reflection from a shiny surface – and gone in a fraction of a second. When the car came to a halt, the definition improved, but the object of all the interest was well out of shot.

'Impossible to tell,' Keith Halliwell said.

Leaman stopped the film and ran it a second time. And a third. He froze the frame, and that didn't help.

Ingeborg said, 'I'm thinking the height may be a clue. It's about the level of a bike. If it was the side of a car, the patch of light would be broader and taller, wouldn't it?'

'You're losing me,' Halliwell said.

Diamond told Leaman to run it again in slow motion.

The picture quality was even less clear.

'I give up.'

Halliwell asked Leaman to let the film run on and show the stabbing. They watched the top of Greg's head close to the dash cam after he'd got out to investigate. They saw the moving shape of his attacker in mid-distance creeping towards the front of the car. Next, Greg's head in silhouette crossed the screen from right to left when he backed against the bonnet. Then the close-up of the fist gripping the knife.

'Stop it there.'

Diamond's voice had fresh urgency.

The image froze.

'For crying out loud, why didn't I see this before? That's the back of his hand.'

'So . . . ?' Halliwell said.

'The killer is left-handed. It's obvious, isn't it? He's facing Greg, so his left side is closer to us.'

Silence.

He could almost hear their brains ticking over.

Halliwell was the first to speak. 'We should all have spotted it when we first saw the film. We were so caught up in the killing that we didn't give a toss how the knife was held.'

'One thing is certain now,' Diamond said. 'The killer can't be Will Legat. I've watched him hold the rope he uses as a lead for the dog. I saw him this morning in the pottery carry his coffee out of the kitchen. He's right-handed. He's got to be innocent.'

'How about Fergus?'

'I'm trying to think whether he's right-handed as well,' Diamond said. 'I haven't seen as much of him as Legat.'

Jean Sharp spoke up for the first time. 'Why don't you call Paul? He's got Fergus under observation.'

Paul Gilbert wasn't high in Diamond's thoughts. His last order to the young DC had been to stick with the man, whatever happened. 'Would you get him for me?'

She got through and handed him the phone. He asked Gilbert where he was.

'Erm, it's a pub, guv. They finished filming and de-rigging some time ago and some of them ended up here. I'm keeping watch on Fergus, like you asked. He's in no hurry to leave.'

'And I know why. He's got some explaining to do when he gets home. Have you had a few drinks yourself?'

'Just the one, a half, as cover.'

'And he's still in sight? Tell me something. When he picks up his drink, does he hold it with his left hand or his right?'

There was a pause.

'His right. He's holding it now.'

'You're sure? He's right-handed?'

'Is that what you're asking? Yes, I've watched him using the mallet when he's laying the track. It's always in his right hand.'

In a voice drained of animation, Diamond said, 'In that case, you can drink up and go home. Your work is done for the day.' A pounding had started in his chest and ears, a sure sign of the hypertension the doctors were always warning him about. He handed the phone back to Jean Sharp and sat on the edge of a desk. When he'd got himself together again, he raised his voice for all to listen. 'Did you hear that? Fergus is in the clear. Our two prime suspects are innocent.' Out of ideas, hunched and inert, a beaten man, he added, 'Where do we go from here? Don't ask. You'd better start a whip-round for my retirement present.'

Back at home the same evening, Paloma said what none of the team had dared say: 'Retirement? No, no no. This isn't like you, beating yourself up.'

'I'm simply facing facts. I've had a long career—'

She didn't allow him to go on. 'With any number of successes.'

'Okay, and this time I got the breakthrough that is every investigating officer's dream: film footage of the crime. But I missed the most obvious thing about the killer.'

'You didn't. You were the only one who spotted it.'

'Eventually.'

'Listen, Peter, it wasn't obvious at all. I saw the film myself and it didn't dawn on me that the person holding the knife was left-handed.'

'That's not surprising. You watched it only once and said you couldn't look any more.'

She traded some straight talk of her own. 'No offence, but I'm not a thick-skinned policeman. Your entire team missed it and they must have watched the film over and over. The knife is raised and all the viewer can think of is the violence to come. We're not looking at the hand.'

'I know what you mean,' he said from the depth of his despair, 'but it isn't just that mistake. Everyone knows I've lost the plot. I called out the dive team and convinced myself they'd find something.'

'You ordered a search. That's what detectives do. It needed to be done.'

'And all it produced was a dead snake. I'm a laughing stock. I had forty officers searching the field for a day and a half and what did they find? A few fag ends that it turns out were nowhere near the crime scene and must have been dropped by some farmworker. When all this gets back to Georgina, as it will, it's curtains for me. I'd rather resign before I'm sacked, so I'm seeing her tomorrow at eight thirty.'

She widened her eyes. 'You've already made the appointment?'

'It will make her day.'

'I wouldn't count on that. She relies on you more than she'll ever admit. She puts the boot in when she can because you sometimes need kicking, but if you do this she'll be in schtuck, to put it mildly. There's another expression about a creek and a paddle that comes to mind.'

'I don't give a toss about Georgina. This is the best thing for the team.'

'They won't think so. I can't understand why you're doing this. I thought you had a breakthrough. Didn't the search party find the tyre print of a motorbike?'

'That was Wolfgang and his CSI team. Another chunk out of Georgina's budget.'

'Have you checked your suspects' motorbikes?'

'Fergus is the only one who rides a bike and he's right-handed. He can't have done the stabbing. Legat goes everywhere on his two legs unless he can bum a lift and he is also right-handed. They were the two who could theoretically have murdered Greg Deans.'

'Only those two out of all the people involved in the show?'

'That was my belief until today when both proved negative.'

After some thought, Paloma said, 'Peter, how's your maths? Don't two negatives make a positive?'

'How does that help?'

She smiled and looked a little embarrassed. Apparently she didn't have an answer. 'Sorry. It popped into my head and I thought you might make something of it. Just because Fergus didn't strike the fatal blows, it doesn't mean he wasn't there. I'd get his tyres checked if I were you. Have you thought about Candida as the killer?'

He frowned. 'Not up to now.'

'From the film you can't see what sex the attacker is. You don't get much idea of their size and you don't see their face. I wouldn't rule Candida out. She may already have murdered her own mother.'

'Mary Wroxeter?'

'Lacing her drink with pure alcohol.'

'Did I tell you that? I've changed my opinion. It was another of my wild theories, impossible to prove. Today I heard Candida's version of that evening's events and what she told me made sense and sounded honest.'

'You like her, don't you?'

'I understand where she's coming from. She didn't have an easy upbringing, but I was reassured about her feelings towards Mary. As an adult, she understood that Mary was a caring mother, in spite of all. When she got pregnant herself, she really wanted to share the news with her before anyone else knew of it. She wanted her approval and she got it. If I'm any judge of character, she didn't cause Mary's death.'

'Did someone else?'

He shook his head. 'The more I've thought about this, the more I'm sure it's a red herring. There's only one murderer in this case and he – or she – works to a pattern, making a cold-blooded decision to kill, using a knife on the victim and going to some trouble to make sure the body isn't discovered. None of this fits Mary's death, which was brought on by an excessive intake of alcohol. As a method of murder, it would be unreliable and unpredictable. I was mistaken even to consider it.'

'No, Peter. It was a sudden death. It was your job to look into it.'

'I should have dismissed it earlier than this and given more time to the real crimes. As it is, I'm at a loss now.'

'Were Fergus and Will your only suspects? Can't you cast the net wider? What about all the others? Could any of them have had a grudge against Deans?'

'Almost everyone in the show. He wasn't a lovable man.'

'Perhaps it wants a rethink. Is it worth having a look at some of the other things this jinx is supposed to have caused, like the elderly actress who died suddenly?'

'Daisy Summerfield.' Daisy wasn't someone he had thought much about after reading the coroner's report of her death. 'It's pretty clear Daisy's heart attack was triggered by discovering a burglar. There was no intent to kill. It's just unfortunate she arrived home when she did.'

'Wasn't there something about the timing?'

'Yes, she got home sooner than expected. They filmed her scene at the end of the day instead of next morning.'

'So if they'd followed the schedule she might still be alive?'

He nodded. 'I had a theory about that as well. Someone from the show tips off a burglar that Daisy is away and the last-minute change screws everything up. I asked the Met for help with that one and they sent us the burglar's prints and DNA.'

'Helpful.'

'Except there's nothing on the national database that matches. They reckon the burglar was a newcomer to the trade. It goes down as an unsolved crime.'

'You're jinxed at every turn.'

'No, I'm not blaming anything except myself. I'm past my sell-by date and everyone knows it. The right thing to do is step aside and let someone else take over.' Having reached the decision, he emptied his head of all thoughts about the investigation and slept for seven hours.

Under the shower next morning a remark from the previous evening's conversation crept back into his brain, lodged there and replayed itself like an annoying bar of music. *Peter, how's your maths? Don't two negatives make a positive?* If he remembered rightly, Paloma had picked up on some phrase he'd used himself about his prime suspects, Will Legat and Fergus Webster, turning out to be negatives. When he'd asked her what she meant she'd shrugged and turned pink as if she realised they were empty words. She couldn't explain how a truth that worked in mathematics and grammar had any relevance to the jinx inquiry. But the remark continued to nag him.

He could think of nothing positive about those two. At the time of the latest crime, Will was at the pottery thinking about cocoa and Fergus was on the road to Saltford hungry for Irish stew. Positive for them, maybe, but not for him.

He got dressed – back to the suit and striped tie – and fed Raffles. Paloma was still sleeping, so he found himself having a one-sided conversation with the cat. 'Nothing negative about you, old friend. You know what you want and you get it: the gourmet ocean delicacies. Then it's rest and relaxation. Well, I'll be joining you soon for the R & R, if not the fish.'

Paloma still hadn't stirred when he left the house.

In the slow-moving morning traffic, he put on the car radio, already tuned to a station that played vintage stuff. The voice was Bing Crosby's from another era, with the Andrews Sisters backing: 'You've got to Ac-Cent-Tchu-Ate the Positive.'

He switched off, but the damage was done. He was back with the catch-phrase he'd been trying to forget.

Halfway along the route to Emersons Green, he had his Eureka moment, the spark of connection that made sense of Paloma's remark. She was right. Two negatives *could* make a positive and they probably had.

For that morning only, the Keynsham Bypass became his road to Damascus. It was a good thing he was so used to driving this route because for the rest of the journey he was virtually on autopilot, thinking through the sequence of crimes that had mystified him for so long. The explanation steadily emerged. Enough was there to remove the confusion, make a credible solution and convince him after all that this wasn't the morning to end his career.

He reached Concorde House with ten minutes to spare. Georgina's PA was in the outer office, but the great lady herself had not yet arrived.

'Would you cancel our appointment? Give her my apologies and say it was a personal matter I wanted to see her about and happily it has been resolved, so I won't need to take up any of her valuable time.'

'She'll be in very shortly,' the PA said. 'You can tell her yourself.'

'I wish I could, but I must rally the troops. We have an unbelievably busy day ahead.'

He was out of there quicker than hell would scorch a feather, praying he didn't meet Georgina on the way up.

In the incident room, the working day hadn't begun. Ingeborg was putting on lipstick and Halliwell and Gilbert were talking about cars.

'Right, team,' Diamond alerted them, his voice charged with urgency. 'We have lift-off. Paul, get Wolfgang on the phone for me.' The squad were instantly aware that something major had occurred. He started assigning duties with all the urgency of Montgomery on the eve of El Alamein. But this time there was a notable change of approach. He was giving nothing away about his as-yet unproved conclusions. Twice bitten, once shy.

By rights he should have stayed here at headquarters directing the operation, but he never let rights get in the way of his activities. He needed to be part of the action, so he asked Halliwell to drive him out to Jacob's Ladder where, according to the call sheet, a new day of filming was already under way. Paul Gilbert came too, already tasked to link up with Wolfgang and make sure the crime scene expert knew what was expected of him.

They drove south of the city through the Edwardian estate known as Poet's Corner, up Shakespeare Avenue and into Alexandra Park, turning left on the perimeter road along an avenue of beeches and limes. Off the tarmac at the Jacob's Ladder corner of the park they spotted the television vehicles and the behemoth that was Sabine San Sebastian's motorhome. Halliwell parked where the crew members had lined up their cars.

Diamond knew from the schedule which way to walk. George Spode, the director, had finished filming Swift's reckless descent of the ribbon of steps and today he was shooting a safer scene, her ride along the footpath at the top of Beechen Cliff – which is no cliff at all in any understanding of the term, but a tree-clad slope with a path along the top that was once a promenade known to Jane Austen. Today it provides the leafy backdrop to the railway station visible from many parts of Bath.

They left the park and stepped out for the part of the hillside once landscaped with beech trees and long since overtaken by nature in the form of brambles and rogue sycamores and ash. The filming was going on at a point where the footpath widened into a glade. This was a helpful time to arrive. The camera wasn't rolling. The director and the camera supervisor were deep in discussion. Sabine, bored by the delay, was seated side-saddle on the stationary Harley-Davidson Sportster motorcycle well known to *Swift* fans.

Diamond turned to Gilbert, 'Pull yourself together, man. You're drooling.'

'It's not the woman, guv. It's the bike.'

'Get closer, then. This is our chance to check the tyres. I'll move Sabine to a safe distance while you do the biz.'

'But Wolfgang isn't here yet.'

'You don't need him. You're the bike man of the team. That's why we brought you.' Without waiting for a response Diamond stepped over to Sabine. 'Between takes, are you? I need a few minutes of your time.'

She said, 'I'm working.'

'So am I, Sabine. So am I.'

'It's not convenient.'

'It's your duty to assist me,' he said as imperiously as if he were the head of television drama. 'I'll square it with George. We can talk in your motorhome if you'd prefer to be questioned in private.'

'You can't stop the shoot.'

'Watch me.' He held up a hand as if he was halting traffic. She slid off the bike. She believed him now. 'All right, let's go under the trees where we won't be overheard. But I might break off any second.'

As they marched across the glade, Diamond said, 'Do you really ride that machine or is it faked?'

'You've got a cheek. I'm doing all the takes this morning. I'd do the stunts as well, given the chance, but they won't let me. I'm too valuable to risk.'

'The bike is one of the props, is it, belonging to the company? Do you ever get to borrow it?'

'What for?'

'Joyriding.'

'I've been known to have a spin,' she said with a smirk. Turning, she spotted Paul Gilbert on his knees beside the motorcycle and her tone changed abruptly. 'What the fuck is he up to?'

'Relax, he's one of mine, checking the make and index numbers of the tyres. There was a bike at the crime scene where Greg Deans was attacked.'

The coquettishness switched off. She was seriously alarmed. 'You don't think I had anything to do with that?'

'Why should I?' Diamond said. 'You got on famously with Greg, didn't you?'

'Are you being sarcastic?'

'No.'

'We had our differences. He was a prick, as everyone knows. We were never on the best of terms, but I had to work with the man.' She was increasingly distracted by what Gilbert was doing. 'What's he up to?'

'I told you. He's admiring the bike, I expect. He rides a moped himself. We all have our dreams.'

'He seems to be signalling to you.'

Diamond looked across to where the young DC was now standing with both thumbs raised. Evidently the tyres were Michelin of a type that matched the cast Wolfgang had taken. 'Is that the only bike used in the filming?'

'No. That one is mine and the stuntwoman uses her own. They're identical, both Harleys.'

And fitted with similar tyres. He'd suspected this. 'Where's the other one?'

'Don't ask me. Talk to the Bugg. She's somewhere around.'

He stared at the cluster of people near the director: the camera crew, the sound men, Fergus with his riggers. He couldn't see Ann Bugg among them. He started walking in that direction.

'Is that it, then?' Sabine called after him. 'Have you finished with me?'

He flapped a hand in confirmation. He had not gone a step more when he heard the rasp and roar of a motorbike starting up. Not Sabine's, which still stood out in the middle on its kickstand. The sound was coming from higher up, where the vans were parked.

Almost immediately, this second bike was in sight and heading their way at speed along the footpath, headlight on, the rider bent low. It reached the open area and seemed to be coming straight for Diamond. Using skills learned on the rugby field, he stepped aside, but the bike veered off the path as well. Bouncing over the uneven turf, it hurtled towards him. Escape would be impossible now if the rider intended to run him down.

That didn't happen. The intent must have been to avoid going near the film crew and take the widest route possible, which happened to be where Sabine and Diamond were.

The bike swerved to avoid them and skidded. The rider put one foot to the ground for balance and sent up more dust and dirt. Diamond felt the whoosh of air and was deafened by the sound of the machine coming lethally close. Then he watched the back wheel kick up a spray of mud and grass as the bike speeded towards the steps of Jacob's Ladder.

His angry but pointless reaction was to shout, 'Maniac.'

The motorbike wove off the grass verge and rejoined the footpath. No question now: the course was set straight for the steepest descent, bumping all the way down the perilous steps to Calton Road and Wellsway.

A mix of exhaust fumes and crushed wild garlic hung in the air.

He turned to Sabine. 'Was that the stuntwoman?'

She nodded. 'She must be mad. We did some filming yesterday on the steps, but that was an easy stretch. It's a death trap.'

Then he heard another explosion of sound and yelled, 'No!'

Paul Gilbert had started Sabine's bike and was in motion, bumping over the turf, getting up speed, set to pursue Ann Bugg down Jacob's Ladder.

Diamond couldn't stop him. His shouting wasn't heard above the engine's roar. Gilbert, dressed in his day clothes and without a helmet, opened up, shot towards the first steps and dropped out of sight.

Sabine said, 'She knows what she's doing. He doesn't. He'll never catch her unless they both fall off.'

Diamond didn't need telling. It was an act of extraordinary bravery and total lunacy. He started shaking.

26

It was a good thing Keith Halliwell had his nerves under control. He reported a grade-one emergency command to stop and arrest a blonde female suspect riding a Harley-Davidson in the Wellsway area without a crash helmet, possibly pursued by a male rider, also on a Harley and helmetless, who was a police officer in plain clothes.

Still in shock, Diamond faced two of the film crew who had rushed over for an explanation. 'I only know what I saw, the same as you,' he told them, 'except I saw it too close for comfort.'

All he would say in answer to other questions was that police patrols had been alerted and he'd share any information he got.

By degrees he pulled himself together enough to act more like the senior professional. His concern about Paul Gilbert may have become less obvious, yet hadn't lessened in the least.

Filming was abandoned for the day and the star of the show had already retired to her mansion on wheels when a short familiar figure in a forensic suit and carrying a large bag hobbled from the direction of the parked vehicles. 'Bit bloody late, Wolfgang,' Diamond said, giving vent to his fractured emotions. 'Both motorbikes have gone.'

'Both?' came the surprised response. 'You didn't tell me there were two.'

'Sabine's and the stunt bike.'

'I understand now.' A heavy sigh confirmed Wolfgang's annoyance with himself. 'But you might have told me.'

'I didn't know for sure when I phoned. I deal in certainties, my friend, not speculation.' This was untrue. A detective gets nowhere without speculating. But Diamond felt better for reminding Wolfgang of a piece of crime scene dogma.

Then he noticed that the man's forensic suit was torn at the shoulder and a flap hung loose above the right knee. There was a grass stain down one leg. 'What happened to you?'

'In point of fact, I wasn't a "bit bloody late",' Wolfgang said. 'I was here fifteen minutes before you and your companions. I saw you arrive. You were in too much of a hurry to notice me, even though I waved. If you check your phone, you'll find a text from me.'

'Saying what?'

'What I'm telling you now. I found a motorcycle parked beside one of the TV vans.'

'That would be the stunt bike.'

'I'll have to take your word for that. A Harley-Davidson Sportster. I decided the right thing to do was check the tyres and they turned out to be Michelin, of the right size and index numbers. I inked the surface of one and made a paper pressing and I knew at once that it was the machine that left the imprint at the crime scene in the field.'

'You knew from memory?'

'The memory of many hours examining the cast and recording the wear marks. There were some new marks, from more recent use, but the wear pattern was essentially all there, visible to the naked eye.'

315

'And . . .?'

'I was so absorbed in my work that I didn't notice someone creep up behind, grab my throat and throw me to the ground. It was like a commando attack and it was a young woman, if you can believe that.'

'Oh, I believe it, Wolfgang.'

'Before I could do anything about it, she got on the bike, started up and rode off in this direction. I've no idea who she was.'

'Ann Bugg, Sabine's stunt double. She panicked when she saw you with the stunt bike she uses – the same bike she rode to Combe Hay the night she attacked Greg Deans.'

'*She* was the masked figure in the dash cam footage? She must be extremely strong.'

'Stunt people are, as a rule.' He didn't add that she was at least as tall as Wolfgang.

'And so violent.'

'She's desperate. I just hope we can catch her before she does more harm.'

Wolfgang shook his head. 'It never occurred to me that the figure on camera was female.'

'She was wearing dark clothing. You said yourself that the camera was pretty basic. I got no sense of scale from it.'

'Fair comment.'

'However,' Diamond said. 'I did eventually notice that the hand holding the knife must have been the left. Our masked figure is left-handed.'

Wolfgang closed his eyes, remembering the images. 'Damn it, that's true and I didn't spot it. So if she hasn't crashed and killed herself and you arrest her, it will be interesting to find out which is her dominant hand.'

A shout from Halliwell took over. He had his phone to

his ear and was striding towards them. 'Guv, there's something coming through. They seem to have found her.'

'Where?'

'Near Radstock on the A367. A patrol car spotted her. She ran out of petrol. The tank must have been almost empty when she started.'

'They were using that bike yesterday.'

'Wait, they're talking about someone else.'

'Give it to me.' Heart thumping, he grabbed the phone in time to hear through the static that a second person had been found with the female and identified himself as a police officer. 'He's alive, thank God!'

The voice was saying that the officer had caught up with the suspect and made an arrest.

'Is he okay?' Diamond asked.

But the communication was one-way. No one answered his question. The voice at the scene added that they needed transport for the bikes and as soon as it arrived they would bring the two people in.

He returned the phone to Halliwell and asked him to drive them back to Concorde House.

'Won't they be taking her to Radstock, guv?'

'Yes, and then to Keynsham for questioning.'

'Don't you want to be there?'

'All in good time. I need to know what Ingeborg and Jean have found out. There's a bigger fish to fry than Ann Bugg.'

Halliwell wanted to know more, but Diamond asked him to be patient. He'd shown his hand and regretted it too many times before.

'Good news and bad,' Ingeborg said when he asked what progress she'd made. The incident room was already up to speed with the events at Beechen Cliff and Radstock and everyone was in awe of Paul Gilbert.

'Give me the good bit first.'

'Well, Jean has been exchanging emails all morning with the Romanian embassy and your theory that the missing men were all from Romania is confirmed. The name David Tudor sounds to me as Welsh as a male voice choir, but Tudor is also common in Romania as a given name and the surname.'

It made sense to Diamond.

'And Jake Nicol?'

'He was born Iacob Niculescu. Like Greg Deans, he anglicised his name.'

'How did you work that out?'

'Jean did, looking at typical Romanian surnames. They're listed on the internet if you persevere. The embassy wouldn't give much away at the start, but when they knew we were trying to trace these men they gave us their birthdates, names of parents, Romanian addresses and so on. They keep good records.'

'That I *can* believe.'

'And so do our lot. We got the passport details of all three, including photos, and everything matches up with the Swift and Proud files in Stall Street.'

His confidence soared. 'Okay, so what's the bad news?'

'More of a hiccup, I hope,' Ingeborg said. 'The embassy sent us photos and the one of Greg doesn't look much like him, even allowing that it was taken a long time ago. It's definitely not his red hair, unless he colours it.'

'Ah,' was all he said, but it was a three-beat 'ah', more triumphant than troubled.

'Some sort of filing error, I expect,' she went on. 'The nice woman at the embassy promised to double-check everything at their end. Jean sent them his passport picture as well as the company mugshot.'

He thanked them both and moved to John Leaman's desk. 'Do you have the printouts I asked for?'

Leaman picked up a large sealed envelope. 'It could all go on your phone if you want, guv.'

'No, thanks. It's cluttered up with bumf from headquarters. I'm hoping someone will show me how to unsubscribe.'

Before leaving, he made a call to Wolfgang. 'This time,' he said, 'I'm confident you won't have a wasted journey.'

He and Halliwell had lunch in Keynsham. He fended off another invitation to open up about his new theory by saying he needed to marshal his thoughts before questioning Ann Bugg. 'She's been living with secrets for a long time and she won't disclose them lightly. She gave me sweet FA the last time we met, so I want to get my questions right.'

Fortified, they checked in at the police station and asked for Ms Bugg to be brought up to the interview room. Difficult to tell what effect the wait would have had on her. She could have used the time to prepare a defence, or the nerves may have taken over, leaving her ready to tell all.

'Come in and take a seat, Ann,' he said affably when she was shown in, pale and watchful, wearing a glittery top and skinny jeans that matched Sabine's. 'Bit of a change from last time we spoke, in the kitchen at Milroy Court. You're under arrest, so we have to do this right. You remember who I am, Detective Superintendent Peter Diamond, and this is Chief Inspector Keith Halliwell.' Halliwell switched on the tape and went through the other formalities.

Diamond took over. 'You're quite a problem for me, Ann. In this country you can't be arrested for resisting arrest unless you assault the officer trying to take you in, which you didn't. So you're here because you stole a valuable motorbike and you can argue that you didn't steal it at all. It's at my discretion whether you're charged with something more serious. I'm looking to you to cooperate.' He didn't tap the side of his nose but he might as well have done. 'Understand?'

She gave the nod he was hoping for. Better still, she reached for the glass of water in front of her . . . with her left hand.

To get her talking, he threw in a simple question. 'How is a stunt person paid – by the year, the week or the day?'

She shrugged. 'By the day usually.'

'I'm not going to ask how much you earn, but I hope it's more than when you started with Swift and Proud. You're a top-class stuntwoman and you're also Sabine's, erm . . . what are the words I'm looking for?'

'Body double.'

'Thanks. You should be getting two fees. I bet they pay you a fraction of what she earns, or what the other actors get.'

'I'm not bothered,' she said. 'It's regular work.'

'No complaints, then?'

'None at all.'

He continued in the same disarming tone, but with words that could have been the opening statement of a prosecution. 'When you burgled Daisy Summerfield's house in June it wasn't because you were jealous of her salary, it was simply that you were short of money. Correct me if I'm wrong.'

He was ready for a passionate denial. Instead, she stared through him, as if the wall behind contained more interest.

She was absorbing the shock of being found out, he decided. 'You say it's regular work, but months can go by between productions and even then you might not be needed much. I expect you pay for insurance and you have an agent who takes a slice of your income. The temptation to get easy money by illegal means must be strong.'

Now he'd started, there was little else he could do but set out the facts as he understood them. 'I don't know a lot about the old lady except she'd been in well-paid TV parts for years and owned some nice pieces of jewellery. The Richmond police quickly decided the burglar couldn't have been a professional. They found fingerprints, a shoe-print and a number of stolen items abandoned in the garden.' He picked up the envelope Leaman had given him. 'The prints and the DNA don't match anything on the database of known offenders. I had them sent here so we can compare them with yours. You won't mind, I'm sure.'

Her face drained of the little colour it had. 'It was the stupidest thing I've ever done.'

'Not wholly stupid,' he said, elated as anyone who has scored the winning goal and not showing it. 'You might have got away with it if Daisy hadn't returned home early. According to the call sheet, she'd have to return next day to film her last scene. Bad luck that they made a late change. Even worse luck that she suffered the cardiac arrest when she saw you.'

'Is that how you got on to me – the call sheet?'

'I thought it likely it was an inside job – "inside" meaning people involved in the show. We could eliminate a lot of them who were working at Bottle Yard when the burglary happened, cameramen, riggers, production staff and so on. Yes, the call sheet was a help to me, not so much for the cast members listed on it, but those who were not – and they included you. The burglar had to be someone with wheels and you had the use of the stunt bike. You could do the hundred-odd miles on the motorway in a couple of hours, easy.'

'More like a hundred and twenty,' she said.

'As much as that? You must have started with a full tank and filled up again at some stage. I'm mentioning this because the mileage was your undoing, wasn't it?'

This time she didn't answer, so he moved on.

'The *Swift* show is all about burglaries and break-ins and you ought to be quite the expert by now, but the real thing is a whole different challenge, as you discovered, especially when Daisy arrived unexpectedly. You hid in the wardrobe, the crime scene people reported. Nasty shock for the old lady, fatal as it turned out. Nasty for you, too. I can only imagine the thoughts that went through your head. Would it go down as murder, or manslaughter, or what?'

The danger of this approach, giving the facts of the case as he understood them but with a sympathetic spin, was that she would become the silent listener and confirm or correct none of it. She hadn't contested anything he'd said except the distance between Bristol and Richmond. He was in two minds whether to invite her to tell the rest of the story herself.

'What's that?' he said suddenly. A buzzing sound had interrupted him.

Halliwell, embarrassed, cleared his throat. 'Your phone, guv.'

He tugged it from his pocket. A call from Ingeborg. 'I'd better take it outside. Call a break, Keith. I shouldn't be long.'

Halliwell checked the time and spoke the words that put the interview on hold.

Left alone with Halliwell, Ann asked, 'Is the tape switched off?'

He confirmed it with a nod, so she said, 'I'm in deep trouble, aren't I?'

'Seems so,' he said.

'Is he an understanding man? If I tell him everything, will it work in my favour?'

Halliwell didn't need to think about that. 'It's always a good thing to cooperate.'

'Up to now it hasn't helped me.' She reached for the glass of water and sipped some. No more was said until Diamond returned and the interview was on record again.

Ann spoke before Diamond started. 'I want to make something clear. I didn't steal the motorcycle. I'm allowed to use it when we aren't filming to practise moves I need to make in the show. They turn a blind eye if I ride it privately sometimes.'

'Understood,' Diamond said, 'but a round trip of two hundred and forty miles was going too far, wasn't it? Literally too far.'

There was no arguing with that.

'Did someone query the mileage or the petrol consumption?'

'Are you listening? What I'm saying is I didn't steal the bike, so you can't hold me here.'

He smiled. 'Nice try, Ann, but if I released you I'd rearrest you immediately for the theft of Daisy's jewellery. Getting back to your trip to Richmond and who found out, you know for a fact it was the producer himself. Greg Deans was known as an efficient organiser with an eye for detail. He looked at that mileage and put two and two together: your two-hundred-and-forty-mile ride and Daisy's burglary. Did he call you to his office, or was it a more private meeting?'

'He came to my flat.'

'Smart move. Difficult for him. He should have reported you to the police, but he didn't. He could have sacked you and he didn't. Where was he going to find another body double who did stunts? You couldn't be replaced. The show had to go on at all costs. Fair summary?'

'I can't tell you what was in his mind.'

'Whatever it was, you kept your job.'

'I wish to God I hadn't.'

At least he was getting responses.

'What did Greg actually say to you?'

'He kept it short. He got me to admit what I'd done. I was bricking it thinking he'd hand me in. He said the whole show could go down the tubes because of my criminal behaviour and he was considering my future.'

'Words only? You got off lightly.'

'I thought so.'

'Did anyone else know?'

'I'm certain he told no one.'

Diamond tried putting himself into Greg's shoes. 'He had enough to deal with already, finding a way to write Daisy out of the show.' He hesitated. 'Was there an element of sex? Was he attracted to you?'

Her face creased in disgust. 'Thank Christ, no.'

'And you didn't warm to him after he let you off?'

She shook her head as if she'd just come out of the shower.

'But he didn't forget what you'd done. He saved it up for later.'

Her look became a caught-in-the-headlights stare. 'You know it all, don't you?'

'He forced you into conspiring with him to fake his death.'

She swallowed hard before her words came in a rush. 'He blackmailed me into doing it. He said he'd protected me from prosecution and if I didn't do what he asked he'd make sure I went to prison. The only reason I agreed is that if it worked I'd be free of him in future. He could never threaten me again because he'd be out of it, dead to the world.'

'He set up the attack in the field with you acting the killer?'

A long sigh before the words tumbled out. 'Like you say, he was an organiser and I do stunts, so he planned the whole thing in one take and fitted the dash cam to his car to record it. He knew all there is to know about staging a stunt like that and making it look real. My part was simple. Well, two parts, first standing in the lane, directing him through the gate, and then as the knifeman. The key thing was I had to stay in shot. He'd laid white tape on the ground to make sure I got my moves right.'

'You wore the high-vis jacket in the lane and then discarded it for the stabbing?'

'He'd told me where to throw it out of the camera's range. Each move was planned and rehearsed like an action scene from the show. He made me practise stabbing a side of lamb, so I knew how to make it realistic, not just waving the knife in the air.'

'But you didn't cut him. How did the blood get there?'

'In a big plastic bottle. He'd been collecting it from his own arm, like he was a blood donor. He smeared some on his hand and the side of the car and the rest was poured on the ground to make you lot think he'd bled to death.'

'This was after the camera was switched off?'

'Yes. And then we collected the things and I gave him a lift on the bike to the railway station.'

'I don't suppose he told you where he was going after that?'

She rolled her eyes upwards at such a stupid question.

'You must have wondered why all this was necessary, why he wanted to stage his own death. Was it discussed?'

'I was too scared to ask. He might have killed me.'

'You're lucky he didn't. When his full story is made public, you'll know how close you came. Did you realise you messed up his masterplan by parking the motorcycle in the wrong place? It's briefly visible on the dash cam footage when he drives into the field. That helped us work out what happened.'

She sighed. 'I'm not much good at real crime, am I? What's going to happen to me now?'

'It will help your case if you tell the truth about what got you into this mess. Why did you need to steal the stuff from Daisy?'

Her eyes slid downwards and she muttered, 'That's another can of worms.'

'Better own up to it, Ann.'

After a long pause while the pain of indecision was written across her face, she said, 'I was doing speed. I'd gone through all the money I had and then some.'

'Are you still on it?'

A hesitant nod. 'I need to get myself up for the stunts.'

'What you need, Ann, is help. I'll give you the address of an addiction clinic. We're going to take a statement from you, a truthful account of it all, what happened in Richmond and how Deans found out and used you. You may be called as a witness later and you'll earn some credit for assisting us.'

'Are you going to keep me here?'

'Not if you cooperate. After you've signed the statement and your prints have been taken, you're free to leave. In due course the Metropolitan Police will want to interview you and they'll get a copy of everything you've told us. It's up to them what action they take over the burglary.'

After she'd been taken out, Diamond asked Halliwell to see to the statement.

'What about Deans?' Halliwell asked. 'He's probably out of the country by now with his beard shaved off and his hair a different colour.'

'Immigration enforcement officers are on the lookout for him at all air and sea ports. Personally, I don't think he'll leave the country. He's safer here, probably in London. He knows the ropes here.'

'Won't he make for Romania?'

'That's the last place on earth he'll go.'

27

Next morning at the debrief of Operation Showstopper, Paul Gilbert had to endure another ordeal.

'You were crazy riding down those steps without a crash helmet,' Diamond said, 'but you're also incredibly brave. You made the arrest and we salute you.'

When everyone started clapping, Gilbert turned crimson and looked ready for a fresh stunt – jumping out of the window.

Ingeborg said, 'Show a moped rider a Harley-Davidson and that's what happens.'

Diamond shifted the spotlight. 'And you, Inge, and you, Jean, earn a gold star each for finding the truth about Greg Deans. Not everyone knows yet, so would one of you like to sum up?'

'Oh.'

Put on the spot, the two women looked at each other. Ingeborg said, 'I'll start, then. After Natalie told us Deans was Romanian, somebody not a million miles from here came up with the idea that all three missing men, Tudor, Nicol and Deans, might be Romanian immigrants. Jean did some digging on the internet and Bingo!'

'Get away,' Halliwell said.

'Check if you don't believe me. So we took up our theory with the embassy, sent them photos from the Swift and

Proud personnel files and they confirmed that Tudor and Nicol had both been born there. Then we got into a long to-and-fro with them because the mugshot we sent of Grigore Dinescu, alias Deans, didn't match the one they had. If he wasn't the same man, who was he? Quite a search went on at the embassy and back in their own country. Someone there believed his face was familiar for some reason, but they couldn't place him. Then Jean had the smart idea of suggesting they checked their criminal records and that's how we learned his true identity.' She looked across at her colleague. 'Come out from behind your screen, Jean.'

The shy member of the team surfaced and cleared her throat.

'Can't hear you,' John Leaman said.

'I didn't speak,' Jean said.

'We're waiting.'

'Well,' she said in her soft, apologetic voice that managed to command everyone's attention, 'the Romanians used biometric recognition software and matched our photo to a known offender called Simion Stoica, who was convicted of three murders in Mangalia, on the Black Sea coast, in the year 2007. He's known as the Knifeman of Mangalia.'

'Greg Deans?' Halliwell piped in disbelief.

Diamond said, 'Can we get the picture on the big screen? It's an amazing resemblance.'

Leaman switched on and Jean transferred the image. The red hair was cropped and the face clean-shaven. Even so, Greg's strong features and calculating brown eyes were unmistakable.

'No doubt about that,' Gilbert said.

'The Romanians are confident, or they wouldn't have told us,' Jean said before launching into the back story.

'Stoica was a graduate in drama and he got a job with a theatre company by fatally stabbing the only other applicant. At the time it was believed his victim was mugged in the street. One of the company became suspicious and he, too, was knifed to death outside his house by someone wearing a ski mask.'

'This man feels no guilt,' Diamond said. 'He thinks nothing of taking a life. Anyone who stands in his way is at risk of getting killed.'

Jean resumed. 'His third victim was a new theatre manager who wanted to make changes Stoica didn't like. This time the police got enough evidence for a conviction. He was given a life sentence, but he escaped from a working party in 2009 and was never recaptured.'

'How did he turn himself into Dinescu?' Halliwell asked.

'Identity theft. The real Grigore Dinescu was a businessman from a town further up the coast who planned to emigrate to England in 2012. He had no family in Romania apart from a brother who lost touch with him after he left. But it seems the man who flew into London as Dinescu was Stoica. They now believe the passport was a fake one showing Stoica's photo and Dinescu's name.'

'Do we need to ask what happened to the real Dinescu?' Paul Gilbert said.

'The Romanian police are investigating.'

'Any of us could tell them.'

'Thanks, Jean,' Diamond said. 'You two did a fine job.' Turning to address everyone, he said, 'Ingeborg called to update me while I was interviewing Ann Bugg and gave me this man's record. Three killings in a year in Romania. At least two here. Bugg still doesn't know how lucky she is to be left alive.'

330

Everyone fell silent, struggling to understand Stoica's mindset.

'What got him started on his killing spree here?' Gilbert eventually asked.

'To him it's as straightforward as deleting words on a computer. He got the job with Swift and Proud and learned he would be working with a fellow Romanian, Dave Tudor, who could well have known about the serial killings in Mangalia. It was a risk he couldn't take, so he killed him within days.'

'We don't know that for certain,' Leaman, the team's stickler for facts, said.

'Get real, John,' Ingeborg said. 'Tudor went missing shortly after Deans got the job as production assistant. He had to be eliminated.'

'It's still supposition. The body was never found. All we know for sure is that he failed to turn up for work and when someone eventually went to his lodgings to enquire, it was clear he hadn't been there for a couple of days. The same goes for Jake Nicol.'

'Not the same at all,' she said. 'Nicol's flat had been emptied as if he'd moved out. And there was blood on the floor.'

'A few drops,' Leaman said.

Paul Gilbert spoke up. 'May I?'

'Of course you may,' Diamond said. 'As investigating officer, you know better than anyone about this. You were the one who found the blood.'

Gilbert blushed. 'Well, it seemed important at the time because we assumed it was Nicol's. But there was a lot of difficulty getting a DNA reading and when the lab finally came up with something it turns out the blood was Dean's. In his hurry to clear Nicol's things out he must have nicked his hand.'

Leaman was frowning. 'No one told me this.'

Ingeborg said, 'Because we didn't know. We only just found out. We didn't have Deans's DNA profile until now.'

Diamond interrupted before the spat turned ugly. 'Deans had already had a busy night. That's why he was in the flat so late, after midnight. Let's go over it. He knifed Nicol to death at the airfield after everyone from the film unit had left. He used the last TV truck to move the body to the pottery.'

Gilbert said, 'Will Legat saw the lights of the truck being driven off. That was Deans.'

'Right,' Diamond said. 'After unloading the body at Combe Hay, he drove out to Cold Ashton and returned the truck to the Gripmasters depot.'

Gilbert raised a thumb in confirmation. 'Yes, the manager told me it was returned there as usual.'

'Nicol had his scooter parked there,' Diamond went on.

'Do we know that?' Leaman said.

Gilbert said, 'You've got it on file. It's in the report I gave you of my interview with Able Mabel. He used a blue Vespa and she showed me where it would have been parked.'

Diamond picked up the thread again. 'And Deans, well organised as always, had brought Jake's keys with him and rode the scooter back to the airfield to collect his Range Rover. He then drove home with the Vespa in the back. We already found it in one of the barns at the pottery. After all that, he still needed to make sure there was nothing to connect his victim to Romania, so he drove to Fairfield Park, let himself in with Jake's door key, stuffed everything into a bag to give the impression Jake had packed his own things, and took off.'

Everything seemed to be explained except the most

obvious – and Leaman was quick to seize on it. 'So where's the body?'

'I may have news of that. I'm expecting a call. In fact, I'd better check.' He took out his phone and looked at it.

Ingeborg said, 'You're not switched on.'

Looks were exchanged among the team. Their technophobic boss would never learn.

While the phone powered up, Gilbert said, 'We know Jake Nicol was knifed because we found his bloodstained belt.'

'But not the body,' Leaman continued to insist.

Diamond flapped his hand for silence. 'It's a bad line.' He said into the phone, 'Can I call you back? . . . Really? All right, then.' He looked up. 'He's in the building. He's on his way up.'

'Who is?' Halliwell asked.

'Didn't I say? Wolfgang, the crime scene investigator.'

Even this bumptious little man might have been surprised to open the door and find the entire murder squad staring at him, ready for his news, but he didn't let it show. 'Have I interrupted something?'

'We're waiting to hear from you,' Diamond said.

'All of you?'

'Only if you have something for us.'

'I do.' He lifted high the holdall that went everywhere with him. 'In here are the remains of at least one individual, presumably the rigger who went missing recently.'

'May we see?'

'There's not much left of him.' He unzipped the holdall and took out an evidence bag that he displayed to his audience like a market salesman. 'To you, it will look like a piece of broken china. To an experienced eye, this is a large chip of human tooth. I also found sixteen other fragments of bone.'

'Where was it?' Diamond asked him.

'At the pottery, where you asked me to go. I had my doubts about this trip after the fiasco at the marina, but this time you got it right. I explained to the lady of the house that I was sent by you and she told me to go right ahead. She said she doesn't load the kiln herself. She can't, being disabled. I gather there's a man who does the heavy work for her. The kiln is housed in one of the barns. It's an industrial-sized thing, gas-fired, which means it can heat to very high temperatures. Why a potter needs a kiln as big as a bank safe I have no idea.'

'Natalie creates large ceramic artworks that sell for high prices,' Diamond told him.

'Well, this one is large enough to take a corpse and evidently that's what has happened at some time recently. I'm glad to say the kiln was cool by the time I examined it.'

'She didn't mind you poking around?'

'Please, superintendent. I don't poke. I'm a trained expert.'

'And where did you find the remains?'

'Most weren't inside the kiln. Some were underneath on the floor and others were lodged inside a machine I first assumed was a pugmill for preparing clay, but turned out to be a pulveriser. You see, the firing process at extremely high temperatures is a good destroyer of organic tissue, but is not all-consuming. Small pieces of bone remain. Your killer's method was to remove them from the kiln with the ash and put everything through the pulveriser. He was organised, but so am I. I took the machine apart. He didn't allow for small bits in the mechanism.'

'Or for a dogged crime scene man like you,' Diamond said. 'We're in awe of you, Wolfgang.'

'Have you arrested anyone yet?'
'That's the final challenge.'
Wolfgang was unimpressed.

28

Diamond read the headline upside down: BATH TEC FOILS MURDER SCAM. The paper was lying across Georgina's desk. Her coffee mug was resting on it, hiding his picture.

'Congratulations are due,' she told him.

'No need, ma'am,' he said, 'unless you'd like to speak to the whole team. This wasn't a one-man show.'

'The newspaper seems to think it was.'

'I've been around too long to care what they print. One day I'm a disgrace, the next all is forgiven. Thank the Lord I know how I stand with you, ma'am.'

She shifted her gaze higher and avoided eye contact.

'Tomorrow's papers will have a different slant,' he went on, regardless. 'I'm expecting the Met to get the glory.'

'For finding the killer?'

'Yes, once we told them what Deans had done and what he's capable of, every bobby in London was given his picture and description. CCTV footage at Paddington station told us he was there. I suggested they concentrated the search in the West End, theatreland, because that's where a man of his background would feel at home, mingling with the luvvies after the show in some Shaftesbury Avenue bar.'

'Is that where he was found?'

'No. I got that wrong. He was caught shoplifting in a

Wembley supermarket. He'd run out of cash. He knew he'd be traced if he used his cards. When they searched him, they found the knife in one pocket and the Dinescu passport in another.'

'Simple as that?' She sounded disappointed, as if it was a pity Deans hadn't gone berserk with the knife and charged up and down the aisles stabbing the terrified customers.

'Arrests of major criminals often are, ma'am. He's locked up now, and that's the main thing.'

'We can agree on that. Does he have anything to say for himself?'

'He's in "no comment" mode. But there's enough DNA evidence to hold him and when the Met get serious and talk about extraditing him to Romania, he'll sing. He's had experience of their prison system.'

'They may ask our government to send him back, to serve the rest of his sentence in their country.'

'I expect they will.'

'You don't really care, do you? I can't blame you.'

'First, I want him put on trial for the murders he committed here. He's the most callous and cold-blooded killer I've met. Intelligent, efficient and completely ruthless.'

'He'd better not ask you for a character reference.' Georgina cleared her throat before coming to the real reason why she'd called him to her office. 'Peter, the Police and Crime Commissioner has asked to meet you. This headline seems to have pleased him. He'll be here about three.'

'How nice. I'll invite him to meet the team.'

'He didn't mention that.'

'But I will. They deserve a collective pat on the back. Is that all, ma'am?'

'Not quite,' she said. 'Early on, I believe I mentioned something about, erm, your retirement.'

'You did,' he said. 'Knocked me for six. You told me to drop the jinx investigation, think about retirement and send all my people on courses.'

'Is that what I said?'

'Almost verbatim. It sounded as if you wanted to close us down.'

'I didn't go that far, I'm certain.'

'I seriously wondered if the damned jinx existed and had struck again – at us.'

'Oh no.'

'You changed your mind later when the *Post* ran the story that we were hot on the trail.'

Georgina seized on that. 'So I came to my senses – and what a good outcome you achieved. I must have been at a very low ebb.'

'I can't speak for you, ma'am, but I was.' By now, he knew exactly where this was going and he was starting to enjoy himself. 'Are you telling me your remarks weren't intended?'

'I couldn't have been thinking straight.' She paused. 'Forget that I ever said such things, would you?'

'Erase them from my memory?'

'Utterly.'

'A clean slate?'

'Totally. And if by some chance the PCC should ask you whether you can always rely on support from the top . . .'

'I know exactly what to say, ma'am.'

He came out smiling. Free to continue in the job he constantly complained about and truly loved. Quite unexpectedly, he felt tears on his cheek. They were tears of relief.